Return of the
SNOW VILLAIN

Michael P Blattenberger

Dedication

To my wife, Catherine, who has brought me not only love and happiness but a partner who brings joy and harmony every day for over 23 years for which I am eternally grateful. Love you, Beautiful.

Table of Contents

PART ONE...1

PART TWO...38

PART THREE 70

PART FOUR...112

PART FIVE 140

PART SIX 173

PART SEVEN 215

PART EIGHT 251

EPILOGUE..287

ABOUT THE AUTHOR 294

PART ONE

A Police Detective named Perry Kline lived in Buffalo, New York. He had come up in the ranks in the Buffalo Police Department from Patrolman to Detective in a short span of time. He had helped solve a huge case the previous year solving the case of the person who murdered the local mayor, Johnny Galway, and three others. The FBI was also secretly involved in the investigation which helped bring down this significant figure and others in an East Coast drug syndicate. They were running drugs from their headquarters in Venezuela to Key West and points north and they murdered prominent citizens who got in their way.

Perry was promoted. Unfortunately, it was not with the Buffalo Police. He was offered a position with the Federal Bureau of Investigation to work under his associate in the Snow Villain murder, Micah Blair. Micah Blair, who posed as a photographer and consultant to the police, was working for the FBI in an undercover capacity in that investigation and only Perry Kline was aware of that fact. The Chief of Detectives in Buffalo's Police Department, Parker Clark, was the "kingpin" of the drug syndicate, and after he was sent to jail, his position was offered, not to Perry Kline but to a Chief of Detectives from Denver, Colorado. His name was Randy Weeks. He lasted only two months, then resigned. His old Army injury precluded him from continuing in this career. He then went to China. He married a young schoolmate there, Belinda Zee. Eight months later, they moved back to Denver together where they both are now working in the Information Technology field.

After Mr. Weeks left Buffalo, the Chief of Detectives position was given to Perry's former car partner, Paul Gorci. Perry now worked for Micah Blair who was the Assistant Director of the FBI Buffalo Regional Office. Micah was being transferred temporarily to Denver, Colorado. Micah knew Perry was disenchanted with the Buffalo Police for not giving him the Chief of Detective's position after helping solve the Snow Villain murders so he asked Perry to come to Denver and work for the FBI there. Micah knew the Mexican drug cartel was very powerful and used Denver as a stronghold when El Plato took over from the former czar who was now imprisoned again.

The woman in Perry Kline's life in Buffalo was Christie Mahern. She was a partner in the law firm of Mahern, Miller & Associates. She ironically went to the same school as Perry in Long Island, but both had migrated to Buffalo New York where they met again at a Policeman's Ball. He was immediately attracted to her and she to him. They left the Ball early that night and met at a local motel bar where they then got a room and explored each other's obvious physical delights. They have been an item ever since. Both had been married before; however, Perry initially wanted to go slow and used the rebound excuse for not moving to a more permanent status like marriage.

Now that Perry was transferred to Denver by the FBI, he proposed to Christie the night before he left and she was ecstatic saying, "Oh, Oh, My Gosh. Yes! Yes! YES! They professed their love for one another, and he left for Denver, Colorado that night. Each wondered, 'Where would things go from here?'

Meanwhile, Christie began thinking about beginning the process of dissolving her partnership in the law firm. She had made a great deal of money in the last two years with three major cases which resulted in large settlements for her and the firm. She wondered if being on the prosecutor's side of the courtroom would be more satisfying, though not as lucrative, than the defense table. Maybe.

Michael Donlevy had worked in the past eighteen months to arrest and imprison six of the Mexican drug cartel's lieutenants. Donlevy was on loan from the Buffalo Region FBI to work in the Denver Region. Michael called Micah Blair who was his assistant Director in Buffalo, "Micah, this is Michael Donlevy in Denver. I am looking for a Regional Director out here to take my place when I leave; and I am offering you the position. Think about it overnight and we can speak tomorrow around 2 pm your time. Any questions?" Micah knew he would be well served to get out of Buffalo as his cover was blown and there were many ghosts in the area that would hinder his continued effectiveness in the FBI there. He would call Catie Fuda, his lady, to see what her take would be on the decision. Micah said, "I will give it serious thought tonight and speak with you in the morning. Thank you." Micah returned to his office to think about the ramifications of taking the position and making the move and most importantly how it would affect the relationship he had with Catie Fuda.

Perry was very disappointed that he was overlooked for the Chief of Detectives position in the Buffalo Police Department and now vowed to become the best FBI agent he could, proving all of them wrong. Perry had gone to school in Long Island but moved to Western New York, his senior year then went to college and joined the police force. He made it to the level of Detective and partnered with Paul Gorci, an academy classmate. He met Christie Mahern at a Policeman's Ball and found they went to school together on Long Island. She was a successful lawyer in Buffalo and co-owned her own law firm when they began dating in Buffalo, New York.

Micah knew that Perry had these angry feelings about the Buffalo PD that may affect his decision-making if the Buffalo Police were involved in a case. So, he thought transferring him would be best. He knew the drug cartel in Mexico had strong ties in Denver, Colorado so that might be a good place for his talents.

Micah called Perry into his office, "Perry, I have an assignment I would like you to consider. We have been following the Cartel once led by El Jefe in Mexico. El Plato has taken leadership but is aging and it is thought that the four lieutenants of the El Verdugo Cartel will wage an all-out war for the ultimate leadership and control of this multi-trillion-dollar operation. I would like you to consider moving to Denver." Perry thought a minute and said, "Can

I think about this until tomorrow, Micah?" Micah replied, "Let's meet at four o'clock tomorrow so I can answer questions if you have any before you make this decision." Perry just said, "Thanks, Micah."

Micah had his own decision to make. His supervisor, Michael Donlevy, was already in Denver and asked Micah to join him. Both the Director and the Assistant Director positions in Denver would need filling, and Micah would need help with Immigration and the mass illegal migrant infiltration as well as the drug cartel using Denver as a central distribution point. Micah would ask Perry to come to Denver, train him, and then have him hired as an Assistant Director. That would give them a solid base to grow the Bureau within the region and keep a handle on all the issues presented there. He would need one or two more key players for this plan.

Christie Mahern was in her office at the Chase Bank Building at West Mohawk and Delaware in Buffalo, New York. She thought of the night she met Perry Kline. They had sat together at the Policeman's Ball then left to meet for a drink at a local motel bar. They had a wild night of passion and have been together ever since. She was in love with him, but he never mentioned love since they'd been together. She wondered if they would ever get to the next level in their relationship.

She called in her Assistant, Wendy McKellar. Wendy brought in a fresh cup of coffee for her boss, "Yes, Ma'am. How can I help?" Christie took the coffee from her, "Sit a minute, Wendy. I need to run a few things by you and get your feedback. Let's look at the cases we have on the docket. First is the Private Sector Providers case. A group of agencies that serves the mentally and physically challenged populations. We can put that one to bed as we should be getting the final awards from the State of New York on Friday. Our share of the $25.6 million award is $2,560,000. After taxes, we will make almost two million for the five years we have worked on the case. I have spoken to Wilson. We've agreed to award a $25,000 bonus to all the employees who worked on the case.

My personal award on top of that to you will be an additional $50,000. You, of course, will sign an NDA for our records but it is just a formality as I trust you would never let anyone known what amount you received. I just wanted you to know how all your efforts helped me during the last five years."

Wendy was crying, "Christie, that is the best news I ever received. Wow. Thank you. I really love working with you. This means a lot to me that you would give me an additional bonus for all the work we did on the case."

Christie continued, "Next is the VASCO vs The City of Buffalo case. With Victor A. Sinclair dead and his wife, Charmaine Sinclair, in prison, it doesn't look like we'll be doing anything but collecting a fee for service from his company. I spoke with their comptroller, and they are dissolving all their assets and paying the debts very expediently. Our fee to them was $750,000 for 2500 billable hours over a year and a half.

Our award will be divided into thirds. Mr. Millers, mine, and then the last third by 20 employees which will give each of them $12,500. Sadly, VASCO would have won if the case continued, and we would still have them as clients.

Finally, the Sorrento Cheese Co. take-over by Perrier was finalized last night. They received $222 million for their company. Our fee after taxes is $19,980.0000. That is over 20 million in revenue from those three cases alone. It has been a very lucrative couple of years." We decided to take this last award and again split it into four equal parts. The firm, Mr. Miller, and I each get a quarter. The 20 employees share the last quarter and will each receive 1/20th of $4,662,000 or $249,750. Wendy just whistled. Wendy thought to herself, 'I can pay off some things, get some furniture, help get the kids started, and buy myself something nice. Maybe something like a nice, new house'.

"Now", said Christie, "I have to make a major decision in the next week." Wendy feared something dark was heading into the conversation, "Oh. Nothing health-wise I hope?" Christie laughed, "Well, it could be a positive health outcome in a manner of speaking. I have been offered a position in Denver, Colorado." It was like a small bomb exploded in the office.

Wendy was in shock. Christie watched her reaction. She continued, "Well, it will take three to four months or so before I am scheduled to be there but in the interim, I am being asked to take a position here in Buffalo as Assistant U.S. Attorney working under Trini Ross. They want to get me familiar with the prosecutorial side of the court; then if all goes well, they may transfer me to Denver as they are anticipating a major influx of cases surrounding the Planned Parenthood facilities that will be inundated from their surrounding states there because of their already established liberal stance on the new Supreme Court decision on Roe v. Wade."

Wendy thought a minute then said, "Are you going to ask me to join you in Denver?" They both laughed uncontrollably. Christie said after gathering herself again, "Gee whiz, Wendy. I don't think I will ever get used to you reading my mind. Yes, would you like to move to Denver?" Laughter ensued again. Wendy exclaimed, "I don't know what I would have done if you had up and left and didn't ask me to tag along. My children are grown. I am seeing someone, but he has lots of kids and I don't know if we will end up together. I hope but I am not confident he'll stay. Maybe this will help him decide."

Wendy continued, "Christie, I don't know if I can find another boss to work for whose mind I can read, so yes, I would love to move to Denver. I will, of course, need money for the move, an assistant, and some new skis."

They both got up and went to the side of Christie's desk and hugged. Christie said, "Thank you. I was hoping not to have to train another clairvoyant." There was much preparation for them in the office prior to her taking the U.S. Attorney position. They had to finalize all the cases that were unresolved. Christie would have to meet with Wilson Miller, her partner, to dissolve their partnership. They laid out a plan and assigned duties. Christie and Wendy both felt better now.

It was November in Denver, Colorado. The fall as usual had been spectacular. The aspens were brilliant in yellow, and the maples were showing red as far as the eye could see. It had begun snowing early and the ground was covered after a recent storm. Michael Donlevy had been working out of the Denver office for eight months since March and was very busy with the illegals gaining ground after the last election. The current administration had freed the border restrictions so much so, that the towns from the border through Sante Fe, New Mexico to Denver were beginning to grow in multiples of 1000 each month. This was terrible; however, the real problem was that because of their illegal status, the only hope for employment was entering into a job with the drug organizations who recruited them as runners daily to bring their shipments north or with some other company whose main interest was an illegal activity of some kind. This created not only an increase in the criminal element in the region but also a more dependent non-English speaking population of multiple countries of origin seeking health care and welfare.

Another issue that now began to raise its ugly head was that the influx of illegal aliens was so overwhelming to many border cities that some mayors began sending truckloads of them to cities up north whose liberal mayors had identified themselves as sanctuary cities. This became quite the political struggle for control as even high-ranking Washington officials had busloads of immigrants bussed to their front doors.

There was a major chasm between the liberals and conservatives on this issue. The liberal politicians, as always, thought America was the land of opportunity and should harbor all the poor souls who found themselves in a country that abused their citizens or was unwilling to grant their citizens their rights.

Many of the southern states were now being inundated with migrants from Mexico and all points south into Central and South America. The conservatives wanted to protect the sanctity of the freedom of newcomers to America by applying for citizenship as all our forefathers had. They asked the liberals who would be paying for the care and housing of these migrants who were now freely allowed into the country without a screening process in place. They got no satisfactory answer. The southern states now were forced to accept a poor, non-English speaking, untrained and vulnerable population, dependent upon the country to provide for them.

To keep Michael Donlevy even further distracted from his many challenges on top of all that, he was now looking for a dentist in Denver as he felt the beginnings of an issue one morning while brushing and flossing his teeth. As luck would have it, the house he was renting got a bunch of flyers in the mail every other day. Yesterday was no different.

He looked through the mail of most advertisements and saw the largest ad was a shiny depiction of two female dentists in pristine white lab coats. He saw them both but only really saw one. That was Dr. Jennifer Steinberg. Wow, he thought, going to the dentist would be easier if she was there to look at each visit. He called and made an appointment. He hoped she was good and then laughed at himself and wondered if she was single. She's quite 'the looker'.

Agent Donlevy hung up the phone after talking with the nice young girl who had scheduled him an appointment that Thursday to get him in as quickly as they could. Into his office walked his secretary, Megan Rolling. As she put down a steaming cup of coffee for him, she said, "Morning Michael, I overheard your call. Toothache?" Michael smiled, "Thanks for the coffee, Meg, yeah, I felt a slight twinge this morning during the brushing, and I know better than to wait for it to get any worse because it never turns out well."

She answered, "Michael, you have three appointments for interviews today and court at one o'clock this afternoon. Here are the resumes for the interviews and in this pile is what we prepared for the two cases in court. Let me know if I can get anything for you. Are you ready for interview 1?" Michael replied, "What would I do without you Meg? Thanks. Yes, send in the first person." Megan turned and returned to her office and motioned for the first candidate, Scott Cimmons, to follow her.

On Thursday, Michael left the office feeling good about all he had accomplished. The four lieutenants from the cartels were awaiting trial that would put them behind bars for the next decade or two if all went well. He had begun to build his team out in the west with Micah Blair and Perry Kline possibly on the way soon. He was feeling good about his short-term progress.

He walked into the Dentist's office five minutes early. He thought about the drug lords going to prison sitting in the waiting room and it pleased him because his new region had worked hard on this case. He filled out the usual forms, got the x-rays from the attractive young dental assistant, Rebecca Weigh, and was ready to see Dr. Jennifer Steinberg, who looked six-foot tall if she was an inch. She wore high heels that made a click-click-click sound when she approached the treatment room. She was very personable and spent a few minutes getting to know Michael before addressing the start of a small cavity they had found. Her pictures did not do her justice. She was breathtakingly beautiful. After the shot of Novocain numbed Michael's jaw, Dr. Jen did quick work of taking care of the filling needed. Michael thought to himself, 'Boy oh Boy, what a beauty. That was really a painless and fun experience.'

Perry Kline walked into the Ace of Clubs after work. He had some huge decisions to make about his future. The girl he was living with, Christie Mahern, was a lawyer in town. They had two homes, his in Buffalo across from Kleinhan's Music Hall on Symphony Circle at Richmond and North. Her home was nestled in a quiet little town of East Aurora, New York about 30 minutes southeast of the city. They were supposed to decide this week which house they would want to live in and which they would sell. He was thinking of asking her to marry him and he was looking at wedding rings. He just saw Tom Lafleur, his jeweler last week. Tom was known to many as the best diamond setter in Buffalo. They talked about some designs and prices. Perry put in a rush order. Now he was being asked to decide whether he would move to a whole new state. He needed a drink. He sat at the Ace of Clubs bar and Melanie Barstow was not waitressing but behind the bar.

She smiled as he sat down. She walked over and set his drink in front of him, "You look like you could use one of these, Mate!" Perry replied, "Girl, you have no idea. It has been one crazy day. Thanks."

Perry picked up his grey goose on the rocks with a splash of soda and a twist of lime. He drained half of it. Mel said, "I'll be right back." She went to the service bar to fill a waitress's order and returned in two minutes with a second drink for Perry as he was downing the first. "Holy smokes, lady, are you trying to get me drunk?" said Perry laughing. Mel looked at him almost maternally saying, "I have seen that look on your face several times in the past couple of months and this isn't my first rodeo, Mr. Kline!" Perry was happy it was Mel behind the bar.

Perry felt he could talk to her and get a woman's opinion on things. He wasn't certain that he had thought it all out yet but maybe

Mel could give some guidance. Maybe she would shed some light on these issues he was facing. He knew she became a close friend of Christie's since her best buddy, Joni Wilsco, was imprisoned for money laundering. He said, "Mel, Thank you. You've been a good friend over the years. Can I run a few things by you?" Melanie only had one other customer at the other end of the bar, and they were probably leaving. She had just filled the orders for the two occupied tables, so she said, "I am all ears, Perry." He laughed and said, "Well, no, not exactly but I'll behave. I am faced with some real decisions that, of course, must be kept under your hat. You know Christie and I are living together. We have two houses and need to pick one to live in. I just saw Lafleur yesterday to pick out a ring for her. Now I just found out my job may be moving out west. I really need to decide everything by tomorrow. Got any ideas?"

Melanie had known Perry for years. She wondered if he knew how much Christie was in love with him. They had talked often as ladies will do. She held one finger up and turned to walk to the service bar to fill a waitress' new order. When she returned. she had a drink for Perry and one for her. She said, "You know, Perry, since all those murders happened months and months ago, Christie and I have become close friends. I think I replaced Joni Wilsco in her life now that Joni is in prison. I am happy to hear you are thinking of proposing." They were interrupted as Paul Gorci appeared through the door and walked up to the bar.

Michael Donlevy spoke to three candidates, on that morning. He knew any of them could be a replacement for Assistant Director in Denver. He called their references of his first choice, Ryan Coleman. It took him only thirty minutes to check his references and his performance evaluations. Ryan was his man.

Michael would call Ryan in the morning and offer him the job. Michael would groom Ryan and Micah so he could return to the East Coast. As Michael Donlevy was in court in the afternoon, he thought to himself, 'Our secretary, Megan, knows almost as much as I do about all the players in this criminal investigation of the cartels. They had arrested four underbosses in the organization. Each was being arraigned today. Megan would be an asset in training the new Directors.'

In court, he had planned to ask for jail time for each of the underbosses as deporting them meant they would just slowly filter back into the States illegally and continue their criminal behavior. Maybe a stint of 5 to 8 years in prison would put a dent in the organization. He was frustrated because deep in his heart, he knew they would replace them as quickly as he had just replaced the Assistant Director here in Denver. The arraignments went well. All four had been charged and at trial, they would face 5-8 years as he had planned. He was elated. He called Ryan Coleman and offered him the job in Denver. He knew Megan could help bring Ryan up to speed when he arrived.

Ryan was gracious in his acceptance and promised to make Michael proud with his performance. They spoke for a few minutes detailing when he would start and what some of his responsibilities would be. Ryan had many questions about the new position but would be excited for this new challenge. He said, "Mr. Donlevy, again, thank you for this opportunity. I can't wait to get started. I will give my department my two-week notice. I have some vacation time stored so I might be able to begin as early as you need me."

Into the Ace of Clubs restaurant on Delaware Avenue in Buffalo walked Paul Gorci. His appearance is what interrupted Perry and Melanie's conversation. He was now the Chief of Detectives in the Buffalo Police Department. He was Perry's former partner and best friend. They tried to replace Parker Clark with a Detective from Denver, Colorado; however, he resigned and went elsewhere.

As Paul sat, Mel Barstow placed a drink in front of him before he even spoke, "Thanks, Mel. I'll never get used to having someone know what I am drinking as I walk into a bar." She walked away tending to another customer. Paul held up his glass of Bourbon and said to Perry, "Here is to Michael Donlevy. May he rest in peace!"

Perry almost spit his entire drink out. As he choked, he yelled, "What the hell did you just say?" Paul looked stunned, "I am sorry Partner, I thought you heard. Michael was shot to death coming out of a dentist's office in Denver at about noon their time this morning.

Perry stepped away from the bar and went outside. He telephoned Micah Blair, "Micah, I just heard about Mr. Donlevy. I am so sorry."

Micah replied, "Thank you, Perry. I just spoke with Michael's boss. He is the Director of the FBI, Lewis Greeley. He recently worked on the "Pizza Connection" case that put a dozen and a half Sicilian drug traffickers in prison. When I called, Mr. Greeley answered the phone from his airplane, "We have lost a good friend today. I know he was recruiting you for Denver. I need you to meet me there as soon as you can to take over the Director's position. I can bring you up to speed very quickly on what Michael was working on. Do you have any questions?" Micah replied, "No sir. I will be on a plane as soon as I can."

Micah dialed his cellphone to call Catie Fuda. She answered, "Hi, Mr. Blair, how can I help you?" Micah said, "Where are you? I need to talk to you in the next thirty minutes." Catie got nervous. She knew something bad had happened as she knew Micah well enough to sense his seriousness was alarming. He was generally very upbeat and comical when they spoke on the telephone. This was not Micah.

Catie said, "I am at the restaurant now. Will you come here, or can I meet you somewhere?" He replied, "I'll be there in ten minutes." The phone went dead.

14

Catie waited in the office of her restaurant and drank a cup of freshly poured coffee. She had poured one for Micah as well. Only 8 minutes had passed, when he walked into the restaurant and knocked on her door. She said, "Come in." He entered and grabbed the coffee and took a swig. He walked around the desk and kissed her before he sat down.

Micah began, "Catie. I love you. Please know that first and foremost. My former boss here in Buffalo, Michael Donlevy was shot and killed this morning in Denver, Colorado. I spoke with him last night and he wanted me to join him in working a case out there as his Assistant Director. I was going to present the idea to you and get your take on whether I should leave here and move two thousand miles away alone or maybe you might consider joining me in Denver."

He continued, "When I heard the news, all I could immediately think to do was to call The FBI Director in Washington who was, at the time, on a plane to Denver." Lewis Greeley answered the phone on the Air Force jet used by the FBI. He said, 'Micah, I will need you in Denver A.S.A.P. I want you to take over Michael's position as Director of the Denver office.' He said he would spend a few weeks training me on what Michael was working on. They sat in silence for a moment. Catie was going to ask a question, but Micah continued.

"I was going to take you to dinner tonight to talk to you about me moving there. I guess I am here to say I am taking the position to avenge Michael Donlevy's death. Do you want to come with me?" Catie was shocked, "Micah, I love you, too. Let me give you my proposed plans."

Catie began, "I have just gotten this restaurant to a level of service where I am comfortable with leaving it to the manager and the three cooks. I was looking for a new venue. Maybe Denver has some opportunities. When are you going?" Micah jumped up and hugged her. He was thrilled she was considering moving to Denver even to look at the possibilities for residence and a new restaurant venue. He knew he did not have much time, so he went for broke.

Perry held Christie at arm's length and said, "I am leaving on the next flight tonight. It will take a week to get settled in. I will look for a rental so you can come out, find us a place, and then look for restaurant opportunities. I love you, Catie. I will call you before I leave. Once I get there and see what is happening, I will call and give you the specifics of what we'll need and when. I figure about a week or two. Sound like a plan?" "Yes, Baby", she replied, "Talk to you later." He hugged her and then knelt on one knee. He held out the box with the ring inside and said, "I love you madly. Will you marry me?" Catie screamed, "YES! YES! YES! Oh, Micah, I love you." They hugged. Then he was gone.

Catie had a hundred things to do suddenly. She would pack a bag to be ready when Micah called. She would meet with the staff in the morning and maybe hire an assistant manager. She made an agenda for the meeting. She knew her staff was very capable of not only running the place but also would be energized by the challenge and opportunity to shine. She called her assistant, Sue Crull, to set up a morning meeting to orchestrate her personal move and packing help. 'What fun", she thought.

Perry was driving home from the Ace of Clubs after leaving Paul. He called Christie on her cell phone. She answered, "Hello, is this, a sales call?" Perry didn't laugh as he usually did. He said, "Christie, where are you? I need to talk to you as soon as possible." Christie said, "I am just leaving the office. Are you home?" "Yes, in five minutes", said Perry. "I am on my way Perry", was her reply. The call ended.

Michael Donlevy had walked out of the dentist office in Denver on that Thursday morning. It had snowed all night, and it was cold, but the sun had just come out. In Denver, he noted that it would snow overnight resulting in 5-6 inches. The sun would come out at noon and the snow would melt on the roads by evening rush hour that day. He really liked his new dentist and was saddened to find out she was engaged to be married. 'Too late', he thought, 'another lost opportunity.'

As he walked to his car across the parking lot, he heard a horn beep behind him. He turned to look in the direction of the noise but was blinded by the sun. He heard two shots and then there was blackness. Michael Donlevy was dead.

He had been shot by a person in a passing automobile. No one saw what happened or the car. A man on his way out of the dentist's office heard the shots but did not put it together until he walked outside and saw a man lying by his car with the door opened. He saw the blood. He turned back into the office and yelled at the lady on the reception desk, Robin Moyers, "Call 9-1-1 immediately." Dr. Steinberg was just coming to the front desk and heard the 9-1-1 request. She yelled, "What happened?" The man at the door said to her and the receptionist, "A man has been shot in the parking lot and is bleeding. Have them send the police and an ambulance. I will try to give him first aid."

Then, he was out the door. Jennifer Steinberg screamed, "Oh my God, that is Mr. Donlevy, who was just here!"

All the staff in the dental office watched in horror as the police arrived in minutes, followed by the ambulance. The paramedics relieved the man from the dentist's office who was doing CPR. They used their paddles to shock him, but they quickly loaded him for transport.

There were now police cars everywhere. The first officers came across the parking lot to their door to begin their investigation. Michael Donlevy had his last dentist appointment. Michael had been shot dead.

Ryan Coleman had received a call that Thursday morning from Michael Donlevy offering him the job. Ryan thought he had done well in the interview but was surprised to hear from him so soon. He wanted him on board in a week. Ryan gave his notice to the Denver Police that day. Ryan had never really meshed with the new Chief when he came on to the force, three years ago. There was something about him that rubbed Ryan the wrong way, but he couldn't put his finger on it.

Megan Rolling was now in Michael Donlevy's car with his driver, Chris Therston, as they arrived at Centennial Airport located southeast of Denver. As they waited for Lewis Greeley to arrive, Megan thought about how she had come to this place in her life. She was married, had two children but is now divorced after five years. She was an attractive brunette but now attracted some unsavory characters which she avoided like the plague. She had worked in Insurance but applied for an administrative position with the FBI.

Megan had now worked for the FBI for over eight years. Just five minutes after they arrived, the Director's plane landed. It came to a stop at the black hangar at the end of the parking area off the main runway. Chris, the driver, pulled out onto the tarmac and approached the plane as the gangway was lowered and out stepped, Lewis Greeley. He was a tall man who was about six foot five inches tall. He had on a very expensive suit and Megan noted it looked like silk. His shoes were black and shone like glass. His briefcase looked like it was designed by Michael Kors. He walked straight to the black limousine.

Chris was out of the vehicle holding the rear door open for him. One of the pilots brought his luggage, a small suitcase, and placed it in the open trunk. Mr. Greeley sat in the back and held his hand out to Megan, "Hello, Miss Rolling. Thank you for meeting me. I'm sorry about Michael. He said you and he were close."

Megan began to tear up a little but held it together. She looked over at Mr. Lewis Greeley and noted how well he was dressed and what great shape he was in. He had no wedding ring on and remembered she had heard he had lost his wife not long ago. Megan seemed to be in a trance but gathered herself.

Megan finally spoke, "Thank you, Director Greeley. It was a tragic loss. He will surely be missed by all of us. Now please let me know how I can help with anything. I have the files Michael and the team were working on. I have developed a briefing module for the new Assistant Director he was looking to hire so I can pass all that on to you."

Lewis Greeley took out his ringing phone and pushed a button and it went silent, not wanting to take the call at that moment. He looked at Megan and could see she was upset about losing her boss. Lewis had lost his wife a few years ago and understood and could recognize the look of overwhelming loss. She began to say something, but he held up his hand, stopping her.

"Miss Rolling." He said, "I will need you to help me train the new Director, Micah Blair who is coming out from Buffalo, New York sometime today. You and I can discuss Michael's final arrangements as well. How are you holding up?"

Megan was emotional knowing this man was so kind to her as he must be suffering the loss as well. They rode silently to the office. The driver pulled into the garage and stopped at the elevator. Chris opened the door and said, "If you would like Mr. Greeley, I can bring your suitcase to your room while Megan takes you to the office area." Mr. Greeley said, "Thank you, Chris, that's fine and thanks for the ride." Lewis and Megan walked into the elevator.

Megan led Mr. Greeley into Michael's office. She would have to stop calling it that. She brought him a cup of tea with one sugar. She had called his admin in Washington to find out his likes and idiosyncrasies. She told Lewis, "I am here to get you settled. Let me know what you may need or how I can help. I can order lunch in if you would like. Just let me know what you are in the mood to eat." The Director replied, "Thanks, Miss Rolling. Order something you would like. I am not fussy. Also, if you can reach Micah Blair, I would like to talk to him and see how soon he will be here."

With that, Megan returned to her desk. She called Chris downstairs at his office and asked him to send someone to get sandwiches for the office from the Blake Street Tavern, it was a couple blocks away and the food was outrageous and well-known in the area. She called the Buffalo Bureau's office, and her caller I.D. identified her. Deborah Thomas answered the phone, "FBI. How may I direct your call, Ms. Rolling?"

Megan answered, "Ms. Thomas, I need Micah Blairs' cellphone number, please. He is on his way here and Director Greeley would like to speak with him." "Hold one moment, Ms. Rolling," Deborah said as she searched her directory, His number is "7-1-6-9-9-5-0-1-1-0 Ms. Rolling. Can I help with anything else?"

Megan wrote the number and said, "Thank you Ms. Thomas. That is all I needed. We will try to take diligent care of him here in Denver. You have a wonderful day." They ended the call.

Megan called the 7-1-6 number. Micah answered the phone on the first ring, "Hello, Micah Blair." Megan said, "Micah this is Meg Rolling from the Denver office. When are you arriving here? Let me know so I can have the driver at the Centennial Airport to pick you up." Micah said, "I am about to land in ten to twelve minutes and should be at the terminal in five minutes after that. You said you'll send a car to get me, where do you want me to meet the driver?"

Megan said, "There is a coffee shop on the lower level of the airport there. Our driver is on his way and will have a white sign with your name on it. He should be there in 15 to 20 minutes. Do you have a minute to speak with Mr. Greeley?" Micah said, "Absolutely. Thanks." Megan put him on hold and stepped into the Director's office. He was on his cellphone, so she waited as he hung up, "Mr. Blair is on line two for you." She closed the door.

Lewis Greeley picked up the in-house phone, "Micah, Lewis Greeley here. Welcome to Denver. Thanks for getting here so soon. The driver should be there soon to get you and bring you back to the office. We will meet, have something to eat and I will get you settled into the hotel across the building. We will put you up there until you can find a permanent place to live. Here is a real estate agent you can work with; Her name is Diane Sorenstone. I will see you when you arrive. Thanks again, Micah. I look forward to collaborating with you. Goodbye."

Micah laughed out loud. He never even said Hello to the Director. He laughed again. He said to himself, 'I hope I can get a word in when I meet him in person. I will have to remind him of this call after I have been there a week or so.' Micah walked into the airport with his briefcase and one rolling suitcase. He stopped at the restroom then went to the coffee shop and ordered a black coffee from a lady whose name tag said, Robin Zander.

Robin set his coffee in front of him at the counter. She had it in a to-go cup as he requested. He thanked her and opened the spout. He noticed the steam rising so he set it back down to let it cool a bit. He turned toward the door to his left as he heard it open.

Walking in was a gentleman in a black suit with a driver's cap on, carrying a sign with BLAIR written on it. He raised his hand to wave and the driver walked straight to him, "Good morning, Mr. Blair. Welcome to Denver. My name is Chris. Let me take your suitcase. We are right outside." Micah said, "Thanks, Chris. I appreciate the welcome and the ride." He followed with his coffee and briefcase and as Chris opened the back door, Micah threw his briefcase in and got in the car being careful not to spill the hot coffee on himself. With the suitcase loaded in the trunk, they sped off to downtown Denver.

As they approached the I25 entrance on Arapahoe Road, Micah asked, "Chris, does it always snow this much in Denver?" Chris laughed, "Micah, this is a common misconception about our fine city. By four o'clock this afternoon all or much of the snow will have melted. The streets are generally bone dry. There may be residual snow on the grass but anything under four or five inches will have melted."

Micah said, "Coming from Buffalo will be an adjustment. We do not generally get a lot of sunshine from Halloween to Saint Patrick's Day and the temperature stays cold that long as well." Chris took the 2-2-5 exit off the I-25 toward Aurora. Five minutes later he was exiting at Colfax where they headed West to Quebec Street. They went North to 35th Street and took a right into the parking garage. Chris said, "Do you need your suitcase, or shall I take it to the hotel for you?" Micah said, "Where is the hotel?" Chris laughed, "It is not widely known but we have about forty rooms right at the end of the Federal Building. It is about a three-minute walk from your office. Megan Rolling, your Lead Admin. Will show you after you meet with Mr. Greeley." Micah said, "Okay then. Thanks for the ride." He grabbed his briefcase and walked the seven steps onto the elevator. He pressed four and waited.

Perry drove into his driveway just off Symphony Circle at the foot of Richmond Avenue. He noticed that Christie Mahern had not arrived yet. He pulled into the garage and went into the house. He wanted a stiff drink but instead, he made a pot of tea. Just as he took off his coat and sat down at the kitchen table, he heard Christie's red Mustang pull into the drive.

She parked in front of the garage and was soon in the door stomping her feet to clear off the snow. She walked into the kitchen and said, "Geez, I was out of the car for two minutes and I am chilled to the bone. Oh, you made tea for me. You are very thoughtful Mr. Kline." She threw off her boots and dropped her briefcase and purse on the chair then gave Perry a very warm kiss hello.

Perry said, "Please have a seat, I will get the cups." He rose and grabbed the cups and teapot off the sink. He placed them on the table. Perry took the kettle off the stove and poured water into the teapot. "It will be ready in three minutes. Now, thanks for coming over so quickly. I have a lot to tell you." Christie had her hands around the teapot warming her hands as she listened. The tone of voice he used, and his body language alarmed her, but she would wait to hear what he had to say before mentioning it. Christie just said, "Okay, Perry, I am all ears."

Perry said, repeating a line he just used earlier, "I disagree but that conversation can wait. Christie, I got a call yesterday from Micah to meet in his office. When we met, he told me he wanted me to move to Denver. They are working on a case focusing on a Mexican drug cartel that is using immigrants coming into the country to work as drug runners. I was going to take you to dinner and discuss this but when I stopped at the Ace of Clubs, I was having a drink and talking to Melanie when Paul Gorci walked in. As he took his first sip of his bourbon, he raised his glass and said, 'Here's to Michael Donlevy, may he rest in peace.' I choked on the gulp of drink I had just taken. Then he explained that Donlevy was shot and killed this morning in Denver coming out of the dentist's office of all things. I called Micah right away and offered my condolences. I knew him as Micah's boss and had been in five or six meetings with him during the Snow Villain case. He seemed like a decent guy. Anyway, I wanted to get your feelings about me moving to Denver."

Christie had this look of horror on her face when she heard the news. She flashed back to all the murders in Buffalo that had touched her and almost killed her a brief time ago. She thought for a minute knowing someday, this same thing may happen to Perry, the man she loved. It made her shiver. She said, "Well Mr. Kline, I am so sorry about Michael Donlevy. When are you scheduled to leave for Denver? Are they giving you any lead time?"

She added, "Oh, by the way, I am dissolving my partnership in the law firm and have been asked by Trini Ross to work as an Assistant United States Attorney, here in Buffalo in two weeks. If after three or four months on the job, I show them that I can be just as effective on the prosecutorial side of the courtroom as I was for the defense, they are looking to transfer me to Denver, Colorado." Perry's head snapped around to look at her and she did not seem to be kidding. He said, "Are you kidding or are you really going to work as a U.S. Attorney?" She smiled and nodded.

Perry continued, "That I'd say would be very fortuitous for both of us." Perry stepped to the table and hugged her, "Christie, this is great news and a real weight off my mind. I was really struggling with this decision because when I thought about it, the only reason I would even hesitate was that you are here. I don't want to be away from you." Christie leaned back and looked into his eyes, "So, what are you saying Mr. Kline?" Perry laughed, "That means I love you Christie Mahern and I want you to live with me in Denver. Can you confirm?" Christie hugged him again, "Perry, I love you too. I would love to live with you in Denver." "Great," said Perry, "I will put my house on the market immediately. I am due to leave for Denver in the late morning tomorrow. I will meet with Micah in the morning and tell him I accept his offer. Can we have dinner tonight?" Perry was taking off his shirt. "Maybe later for dinner. I have an investigation to continue right at this moment."

After they made love, Perry cooked her a delicious meal of chicken on the grill and tossed salad. It took him 20 minutes to clean the snow off the grill, but Christie said it certainly was worth it. Dinner was delicious. Perry was due to fly out in the morning so he would take an Uber and Christie would go directly back to her office.

24

She was glad because their goodbyes were tough. She loved the fact that she had five changes of clothes in the spare room closet at Perry's for almost any occasion, so driving all the way back to East Aurora in the morning before work was not an issue. She wondered why she hadn't thought of it sooner as it was often treacherous negotiating Route 400 back and forth at rush hour in the morning especially considering Buffalo's notoriously unpredictable weather.

She had offered Perry a ride to the airport. He said it would be too long a drive going there then home and back to the office. They hugged goodbye and kissed at the door when the Uber arrived. As she watched him drive away, she straightened up the house, showered, dressed, and drove into the office. It was early so Christie stopped at Tim Horton's and got two coffees and Danishes for her and Wendy.

Perry had received the message on his cell that Micah was flying to Denver that morning and that he was replacing the recently slain Director. He called Micah on the way to the airport. He forgot the two-hour time difference. It was 5:30 a.m. in Denver.

Micah answered the phone sounding groggy, "Hello Mr. Kline. Are you calling to see what time our meeting is today?" Perry groaned when he realized that it was so early there, "I am so sorry Micah. I totally forgot about the time change. I wanted to tell you I accept the offer and I am on my way to the airport. My flight leaves at 9:45 and should arrive at DIA at 1:55 p.m., your time. I can take an Uber to the office. Sorry to have awakened you so early. My most humble and sincere apologies."

Micah was sitting up now, feet on the floor ready for his workout, "Perry, do not worry about the wake-up. It will get me to the gym and the office early so I can be ready when you arrive. I want to thank you for taking the position in Denver?" They both laughed. Micah continued, "I will have our driver, Chris, be at the airport with a KLINE sign in hand. What airline are you on?" Perry replied,

"American flight 554 out of Minneapolis/St. Paul." Micah said, "OK Perry, he will be there waiting. Have a smooth flight and I will see you when you get to the office. Goodbye." They hung up and Perry was kicking himself for not remembering that Micah flew out yesterday and my goodness it was 5:30 am there.

He got to Buffalo International Airport and went through check-in and security in twenty minutes. He had a small carry-on and a briefcase so he would not have to go to baggage claim in Denver. He had a stop in Minneapolis/St. Paul and should have an easy time getting to Denver before 4 o'clock Mountain Daylight Time.

Christie had showered and drove to the office after stopping at Horton's for coffee and Danish. She walked into the elevator at her building and noticed the parking spot she used to use when she was shot by the woman working with the Snow Villain. She shuddered to think where she would be if she had not dropped her keys and avoided the initial bullet that may have killed her. The doors closed and the elevator went to the second floor.

She stepped off the elevator and set her briefcase coffees down so she could open the door. She looked behind her nervously as her hand shook, getting the key in the lock. She swung open the door and grabbed all her stuff, stepped inside, and quickly relocked the door from the inside. She realized she was breathing very heavily and was a bit dizzy.

Wow, she thought, what brought that on? She did not even turn the lights on as it was still early. She set Wendy's coffee and Danish on her desk. She went into the copy room, turned on the printer, and made a fresh pot of coffee for the day. She went into her office, doffed her coat and sat at her desk as she opened her computer. She took a long swig of the coffee and looked out the window facing west toward Elmwood Avenue. She could look out and see the lake from her desk and marveled at how something so beautiful in the spring and summer could now be so cold and desolate in mid-winter. She then heard Wendy open the door. She yelled, "Wendy, I am back here."

At the Bureau, Megan heard Mr. Greeley call on the intercom. She was just walking to his office with a fresh cup of tea. She said as she passed her desk, "Yes Sir, can I help you?" Lewis Greeley said, "Ms. Rolling can you come in here a minute?" Megan knocked lightly on his door, which was ajar, and walked in. "Yes, Mr. Greeley. I brought you fresh tea." Lewis said, "Sit down a minute Ms. Rolling so we can chat." She set his tea down on his desk and took a seat in the large leather chair in front of the desk.

Megan felt saddened as she and Michael Donlevy had gone shopping together at Furniture Row to buy office furniture when he arrived in Denver. Lewis began again, "Ms. Rolling." Megan interrupted him, "Mr. Greeley, please call me Megan. My ex-mother-in-law is Ms. Rolling, and I was hoping that you and I could be a little less formal." She waited a few seconds wondering if she had been too forward so early on with her new supervisor as she really did not know him at all.

Lewis began again, "Okay, Megan. Call me Lewis. I want to talk with you about the training for Micah Blair. Do you have anything in place for training a Regional Director? Megan said, "Thank you. Lewis. We do, indeed, have a full packet of training that Mr. Donlevy and I put together when he first arrived. I just wanted you to know that I am familiar with all the current cases worked on by the agents in our region and would be more than happy to bring you and Micah up to speed rather than you having to go through the files." Lewis said, "Well Megan that sounds fantastic. Let us get Micah in here and you can begin filling us in on all the cases we have pending."

Perry stepped off the plane in Denver at 3:15 pm. He called the FBI Denver office and Megan answered the phone, "Good afternoon, FBI Denver. How can I help you?" Perry replied, "Yes. This is Perry Kline. I am scheduled to be in your office today." Megan said, "Perry, this is Megan. Your ride will meet you at the customer pick-up on level 2. Go to door, 210 and our driver Chris should be waiting in a black limousine just outside. If you cannot find him, call me back. I will call him and give him your cell number. Did you check a bag?" Perry said, "No Megan. I have a briefcase and one carry-on. I just got on the train to the main terminal." Megan said, "when you get to the Main Terminal, take the escalators up two floors, turn left passed the luggage carousels to the elevators and go down to level two and you should be able to go outside door, 210, and see the driver. It should take you about 15 minutes." Perry said, Thanks, Megan. We will see you soon."

Christie was extremely excited as she had an awful lot of work to get done. She said to Wendy as Wendy sat in front of her with her notepad at the ready, "Well, Wendy. We have a ton of things to do. I hope this is the right move. I have always been a defense lawyer and from my education and schooling, I developed a real liberal view of the law and was appalled at the injustices to innocent people." Christie continued, "Now that I have grown and been the victim of a crime and seen the underbelly of this world, I was able to see the prosecutorial side of each case I worked in the last year much easier than I could the defense side of things." Christie sat while Wendy named cases from the work log. Christie would then decide whether to pursue the action in the next three weeks or give it to her partner, Wilson Miller.

After three hours, they had decided to take four cases for Christie and seven they would give to Wilson. The four cases she kept were either personal friends or easily completed within a week or two. Christie said, "Wendy, thank you so much for being this organized. Set up a meeting with Mr. Miller and me so, he and I can draw up the dissolution of the partnership, schedule case turnover meetings and let him know you are coming with me if I go to Denver."

Wendy replied, "I have begun to draft a partnership dissolution agreement for you to fill in for him to review. I will get a meeting with him for the first of next week and then draw up a draft agenda for you to look at before I send it to him."

Christie's cellphone rang, it was Perry. She answered with, "Is this another damn sales call?" Perry laughed. He thought how nice it was to hear her back to her old jovial self. He answered, "Would you be interested in renting a tall, graying bodyguard for a trip to Denver's ski area for the week at the end of the next month?" They both laughed, she said, "Hello Mr. Kline, how are you?" Perry said, "I am well Ms. Mahern, I just called to tell you that I am riding in the company limousine heading to the Denver office. I thought I would call before my meeting with the Director and begin to get into the thick of things. I miss you already."

Christie, getting almost teary said, "Perry, I miss you too. Thanks so much for thinking of me. I am trying to keep busy with packing your stuff for storage and forwarding to you the things that you requested. Then I need to get ready to dissolve my partnership with Wilson. Wendy and I worked all morning on the opened cases; seven of which will be given to Wilson for his caseload or closed. I know you will be busy, so you call whenever you get a free minute. I love you, Perry." Perry said, "I feel the same doll. I must run, so have a wonderful day. Talk to you soon. Bye for now." They ended the call without him getting mushy in the car with a strange man driving.

Chris pulled the limousine into the garage at the FBI Regional Office in Denver. He parked at the door to the elevator. He said, "Mr. Kline, We have a suite ready for you in the East Wing. If you want, I can run your luggage up there while you meet with the Director.

Miss Megan will give you the keys and directions when you see her. She will be at the reception desk waiting for you on the fourth floor." Perry said, "Thanks, Chris. Yes, please take care of the luggage. Is it appropriate to tip you?" Chris laughed, "No thank you, Mr. Kline. We are all working together but you should know that you are the very first person to ask me that or offer a tip in the thirteen years I have been here. Thanks. You just made my day." Perry felt his face get a little warm from the blushing he must be exhibiting. He said, "Next time we're out, I'll buy you lunch." They both laughed as Perry walked into the elevator and pushed 4.

Megan was standing at the front desk with Robin Phillips, the receptionist. The elevator doors opened and out walked Perry Kline. She said with her hand extended for a handshake, "Welcome to Denver, Perry. I am Megan, I look forward to collaborating with you. This is Robin Phillips, she can get anything you need as far as lunch, paperwork, case files, etc. Just press number ten to reach her." Perry said, "Thank you, Megan. It is nice to meet both of you." Megan continued, "I will take you to your office and then Mr. Greeley wanted to meet you as soon as you were here. Follow me."

Perry followed Megan down the hallway and tried to get a lay of the land. He felt like a fish out of water, but he was excited to begin this new chapter in his career and his life. They walked into an office at the end of the hall. The door had a sign marked, PERRY KLINE-AGENT.

There was a desk and a very well-padded office chair behind it. He saw seven or eight plants on the large windowsill to his right. Three four-drawer file cabinets on the wall to his left. Behind the desk was a breathtaking view. This wall gave him a panoramic view of the Rocky Mountains. He almost knocked Megan over while looking at the view as he had not seen her stop and turn around. "Oh, I am so sorry," said Perry. "That is some kind of view. Are you all right?" Megan laughed, "I did the same thing to the lady who brought me into my office about fifteen years ago. Not to worry."

Megan continued,   "My office is right next door so if you need anything, do not hesitate to holler. Here is the phone. The

Director is #1. Micah is #2. I am #3. The rest of the phones are on a tray below for quick reference." "Here is a set of keys. One is for the elevator. One is for the front office, and this is your office key. I will go through the rest of your welcome when you are finished with the Director and Micah. I will come into that meeting later when they are ready to go over cases. Then I will familiarize you with the office. Come with me and I will take you to meet Mr. Greeley and Micah. Here are the bathrooms halfway to their offices."

Megan stopped at the door to the Director's office and tapped twice knowing they expected her. "Come in," Lewis bellowed. She opened the door to find Mr. Greeley and Micah seated at a small eight-person conference room table. They both rose as Megan and Perry entered. Lewis Greeley held out his hand to Perry saying, "Welcome Perry. Micah here has been telling me some remarkable stories about your excellent work in Buffalo with the BPD. I hope you will be as successful here in Denver for the Bureau." Micah stepped around the table and shook Perry's offered hand. He said, "Great you could make it so quickly. Thanks. Have a seat." Then to Megan he said, "Megan, would you please grab those sandwiches and a fresh pot of coffee for us? Then give us about 30 minutes to update Perry and then if you can, return to bring us all up to speed on the current caseload." Megan turned and said over her shoulder, "I'll be back when you are ready for me."

After they were seated, Lewis began, "Perry, we have three major areas we want to address here in the West. Drugs, Illegal Immigration, and the trafficking of young women for the illicit sex industry. The first two are a double priority as one affects the other. The third, trafficking young women began as a separate industry but has morphed into the other two and is the most problematic. The young girls are used as couriers and when arrested, are underage or certainly hooked on some substance and require more care to wean them off that substance. They provide little help to us in finding the lieutenants or even their soldiers." Megan stepped into the office with the sandwiches and sodas then left them alone.

Lewis continued, "We have two cartels working. One out of Venezuela and the other out of Mexico. The Venezuelan group works out of Key West Florida and you all in Buffalo put quite a dent in that one six or seven months back. Great Job to both of you. Perry, we will want you to be a presence in Sante Fe, New Mexico. Our main two operatives there are Eric Slay and Christopher Wiser." Lewis continued after walking to the window, he turned and said, "These guys do an excellent job keeping on top of what the cartels are up to working their games. They have intercepted thirteen shipments of drugs this year at great cost financially to the cartels."

Megan received a text from FBI-Florida. It read: **To All Agents: Parker Clark has died in Florida's Federal Prison. Services will be held this Friday.**

Lewis then said to Micah, "As we have discussed, you will lead the Region." "Micah, you will be my direct contact and we will meet soon to strategize our plans when Megan gives us her briefing. I have also hired Ryan Coleman as your assistant. He will be here next week. Megan can give you these men all the info and addresses they'll need. Do either of you have any questions?"

Perry asked, "Do we have vehicles, or do we need to purchase them? Micah replied, "I can manage this one Lewis, Perry, each of you will be assigned a vehicle. You will use it 24/7. We ask that you track your fuel with the card you will have and schedule a monthly stop into the motor pool for oil changes, etc." Lewis continued, "Megan, will you now bring us up to date on where Mr. Donlevy's efforts were focused?" She had just stepped back into the office.

Megan said, "FYI. I just received a text from Florida that Parker Clark died today in prison. There was no cause of death, but I will follow up with the prison in Florida." Opening a folder, she handed copies of a report to each of the gentlemen in the room. She began, "Here is a quick reference guide to the cases that Mr. Donlevy was working on. Cartel 1 is called El Verdugo. The leader is Andres Semanas. His main office is in the Hotel San Carlos located on the south side of Puerta Palorma. He is originally from Mexico City and is around 38 years old. El Verdugo is predominantly a drug cartel but they also traffic illegals to be their sacrificial drug runners. They run them north with the drugs up Rt. 11 to Deming then east on Rt 10 to Las Cruces. All the products travel up Hwy 25 to Sante Fe." Megan continued "These drugs are sent to points north to Denver and beyond. El Verdugo is estimated to traffic over $100 million dollars of product annually. With the growth over the past five years, those numbers could be in the billions.

Cartel 2 is, Chica Fuerte. Its leader is by Petirrojo Cantante, a beautiful woman they say is as ruthless as any three men and more powerful than any leader we have seen in the past twenty years. They have been quiet in the drug market until the last year and a half as they started dealing with fentanyl. This new drug is said to be fifty times stronger than heroin and one hundred times stronger than morphine. They have a strong history of illegal trafficking of humans of all ages into our country. These individuals are comprised of a large percentage of criminals from Central and South America." "The cartels have been rumored to now be bringing pregnant women across the border to ensure citizenship for their children.

As Perry looked through the information, he knew the second cartel would be his primary focus. The fact that a strong woman ran it was very intriguing to him. He asked Megan, "Do we have any photos of these leaders? Is there an organizational chart of any kind?" Megan laughed and replied, "With all due respect Agent Kline, it will be your challenge to develop both of those for Chica Fuerte."

Perry replied, "Thanks. Would it be poor form to jump up and down on hearing Parker Clark is dead?"

The telephone began to ring. Megan excused herself and returned to her desk, "Hello, FBI-Denver , how may I help you?" It was Ryan Coleman calling, "Hello, is this Megan? This is Ryan Coleman calling for Mr. Greeley. Is he available?" Megan said, "Let me ring his office and see, please hold." She pushed the hold button and hit #1 on the dial. Lewis Greeley answered, "Yes, Megan." Megan said, "Mr. Greeley, I have Ryan Coleman on line 2 for you." He said, OK Megan, thanks." He pushed two, "Hello Ryan. How are you?" Ryan was surprised to get through so quickly, "Hello Mr. Greeley, I was calling to tell you that my office here in Denver has given me a nice separation package and after two days off, I find myself chomping at the bit to start in your organization. Any chance I can meet with you today or tomorrow to begin my indoctrination?"

Lewis responded, "Ryan, thanks for calling. This is an opportune time for you to come in. Can you be here at 8:30 am tomorrow? We are having a general meeting of all the staff. It will be a perfect time for me to introduce you and explain the strategy going forward for the region."

Ryan was ecstatic, "I can certainly be there. Thank you again for the opportunity. See you at 8:30 then. Goodbye." Lewis hung up the phone and buzzed Megan, "Meg can you put a quick meeting together for tomorrow morning? I will be introducing Perry and Ryan, as well as giving a state of the state address with my plans for the region going forward. I would like all the agents to attend as well as our support teams."

Megan was already typing the email to all the staff, "Yes sir. I have already started the memo and will send the draft to you for your approval." Lewis replied, "Not necessary, Meg. Just run it. I trust you will convey my thoughts perfectly. Thanks." Megan beamed,

"Okay, I will send it. Anything else?" "Yes," said Lewis, "Set up an office for Ryan for tomorrow as well if you have not already. Thanks."

Megan was jotting down notes of the things she needed to do that the Director requested. She began with calls to Ryan regarding the expectations for his presentation. As he will not begin with the Bureau officially until tomorrow at 8:30 a.m., Megan suggested he come in early around 7:30 a.m. if he could so she could give him a quick overview of what the plan was for the Bureau and what part he and his team would play.

Ryan replied affirmatively that he would be chomping at the bit to start his work at the Bureau, and he would see her there at 7:30 a.m. sharp. Megan then sent an emergency notice to all agents requiring them to be in attendance tomorrow at 8:30 a.m. She included a brief agenda of the points that the leadership would cover to pique the interest of new and experienced agents. She quickly received 100% positive replies.

Megan then reminded Lewis that he might begin the meeting with the introductions of all the agents. Maybe play any video of the two cartels, to be able to present to the group of agents in attendance as it would give them a visual as well as Greeley's narratives to expand the descriptions.

She also suggested that they go over strategies for all three prongs of the attacks on the issues the Bureau faced. The first concern was drug smuggling. The cartels have increased their shipment attempting to cross the border to minimally once a day. The Bureau's teams have isolated the attempted crossing for mass shipments to the I-25 corridor. There were lesser shipments crossing at three other locations that local police were not monitoring with a presence. The second concern was the undocumented immigrants infiltrating the borders now that restrictions had been lifted by the current administration in Washington.

The last issue was the predictable backlash from the Supreme Court overturning Roe v. Wade. They should all be ready for explosive activities at the Planned Parenthood Centers around the region. She had put together a list to hand out color-coded for each region. Lewis or Micah could speak to their strategies for dealing with any disturbances.

Lewis asked Megan if she had contacted all the agents. She gave him a thumbs up. He then said, "Can you speak to Micah and Ryan I want them to be prepared to speak about the strategies we have outlined and how it relates to their individual regions? I do not think we will include the far west group in San Francisco, at this meeting as I have other plans for them."

Megan replied, "I will make sure they are prepared for the meeting, Lewis. I have ordered the food and beverages as usual for the meeting. I will have copies of the Regional strategy for each agent for the Directors to distribute and will wait for any further directives. Do you want me to return to your office and continue the discussion we began earlier?"

Lewis said, "Of course, Megan, return when you can. We are just discussing what you have brought up so far. We need to complete that and set up who will discuss what tomorrow morning. Thanks." They ended the call.

Megan returned to Lewis' office after ten minutes. She took thirty minutes to describe the four-pronged approach that Michael Donlevy had set up when he first came to Denver. The first was the problem they had with an influx of illegals. These undocumented immigrants are being used by the cartels to advance their illegal operations.

They used these illegals as runners for the drugs being smuggled into the U.S. The number of drugs, smuggled into the country, was becoming overwhelming to not only the Border Patrol agents but also the cities in America that were fighting the abuse of these drugs. The cartels used illegals for scheduled attacks on the Planned Parenthood sites. There were one or two comments around the room about the meeting scheduled for the morning. Once the particulars were decided on, Lewis said, "I am pleased with how well the Denver team has developed and is beginning to be prepared for the upcoming cartel movements and strategies. We will discuss our strategies at length in the morning. Thank you all for your efforts. See you in the morning. Everyone rose and exited Lewis' office. Meeting over.

After clearing out the meeting, Lewis prepared notes for the next meeting. He sat and developed strategies for each area of the Mountain Region that he could pass on to Micah and Perry for them to deliver at the morning meeting. He spoke with both Perry and Ryan on the phone before the end of the day, so they were not blindsided by this responsibility.

Ryan asked some interesting questions about the lack of agents in the Sante Fe Region which Lewis addressed quickly by saying they had a group of 25 agents to start training and an open search for more applications. Lewis promised that he had a surplus of agents back east that would be willing to transfer out west to the Mountain Region to not only get away from the harsh winters but also get renewed energy from beginning over in a new Region.

Perry spoke about his need for a better understanding of the cartels, their leadership, and their workforce. Lewis said to Perry, "You can set a meeting with Megan after our morning get-together tomorrow because she is more or less the expert on the Regions oppositions and the cartel idiosyncrasies."

Perry appreciated the input and after concluding his call to Lewis, called Megan so he could work out a time for them all to meet.

PART TWO

After cleaning up her case load with Mahern, Miller and Associates, Christie Mahern was ready to leave her partnership with Warren Miller. It was Monday morning, and she was reporting to her new position as an Assistant U.S. Attorney in the Buffalo Region. She was hired by Trini Ross, the new Director of the Buffalo Region. They had established in the interview that if Christie became as proficient a prosecutor for the government as she had been a defense attorney in her own practice, she would be moved quickly to the Denver Region to begin work there and subsequently take over the Directorship.

Christie was excited when she walked into the offices at 138 Delaware Avenue, Buffalo New York that Monday morning. It was at the corner of Delaware and West Mohawk Street. She was directed to the sixth-floor office and met with Trini Ross for almost an hour and a half. Ms. Ross laid out the strategy that Christie would follow in the next two months. She would handle two cases and two at a time after that and be evaluated at the end of each of the first two months. At that time, they would both decide whether she was ready for the challenge ahead as a prosecutor.

Christie was given an office on the third floor. She had two secretaries and four law clerks. She was allowed to bring along her former secretary, Wendy McKeller, who had become her right hand while working for her at Mahern, Miller and Associates. Wendy was already sitting at her new desk as Christie and Trini walked into the office. Trini would hand Christie off to her other secretary, Karin Kaiser, who had gone to high school with Micah Blair and had been there eight years. She was standing at Wendy's desk when the ladies entered the office. Introductions were made and Trini returned to her office.

Karin said, "Christie, welcome aboard. We look forward to your expertise here in the Attorney's Office. Wendy, if you'll excuse us, I will give Christie the same tour I gave you earlier and show her the office she'll be assigned." As they walked down the hall, Wendy said, "Thanks for all your help this morning Karin."

The tour was rather quick. but Karin introduced Christie to her four law clerks and showed her the rest room, and the break room. They then entered her office. It was larger than her office at her partnership but faced the same direction. She could see the harbor marina where she jogged so often. There was a large desk in the corner set up diagonally in front of a large credenza behind it. There were four large high-back leather chairs in front of the desk to her right, so she could look out at an enormous bank of windows facing west. In the adjacent corner was a couch, coffee table, and three smaller chairs matching those at her desk. The wall opposite the windows housed a row of four-drawer file cabinets.

There were plants hanging around the office and her mahogany-colored leather swivel chair was the largest in the room. Karin quickly went through the telephone system, and handed her a box of printed business cards that said:

Christie A. Mahern

Assistant United States Attorney

U.S. Court House 138 Delaware Avenue Room 316

Buffalo, New York 14201   Ph. 716-843-5700- ext. 3161

Karin then showed her the files that Ms. Ross had assigned her to work on. Karin said, "Christie, I will give you a chance to get settled in, read over the case files and maybe before lunch if you'd like, I can come back to review what I know about the cases and how we can strategize to move forward. Then Ms. Ross would like you to join her for lunch upstairs in her private dining area. If you need anything, I will be right next door and my intercom is 62. You are 61 and Wendy is 63. Any questions so far?" Christie replied, "No questions yet, thanks for the tour and info and I look forward to meeting with you. I will buzz you when I am ready." Karin said, "OK. I will see you later, again, welcome aboard."

As Karin left Christie's office, Christie looked out the window and smiled. This was a big step and she hoped she would be a good addition.

Christie looked at her door and noticed her name was on the sliding sign holder. Printed very boldly: Christie Mahern-Asst. US Attorney. She sat back in her chair and spun around looking at her office. She felt very proud. She would be excited to call Perry later, but she would wait until it was after five pm in Denver.

She began looking at the two case files left for her. The first was a Niagara Falls case, Blaze Richards who was charged with trafficking cocaine. The second case was surprisingly enough an old friend of hers from Syracuse, New York, Robert Pinkerton, who worked at MONY (Mutual of New York).

The phone rang in her office, her first call, "Hello, this is Christie Mahern." The voice said, "Good Morning, Ms. Mahern, would you like to buy a set of encyclopedias?" Christie let out a screech. It was Perry Kline, her favorite agent from the FBI. "Well Sir, could you come over this evening and give me a demonstration?" They both laughed, hysterically. Perry said, "Wow, I would love nothing better. How are you, Doll?

Christie sat beaming in her chair, "I am much better now Mr. Kline. How are you getting on in those Rocky Mountains in Denver?" Perry responded, "I have not been in these many meetings since college. I am busier than a one-armed man in a rowboat. I am starting to travel so it is going to get busy. I just want to wish you good luck in your new job today as I have been thinking about you." Christie was a little teary-eyed, "That was so sweet of you to call. I love my new digs and can't wait to get started." Perry said, "I won't keep you but hope you have a great week. I'll be in Sante Fe this week, so I'll try to call. Talk to you soon, Doll. I love you." There was the" L" word again. She replied, "I love you too, Perry. Thanks again for calling, Goodbye." Their call ended.

Karin Kaiser entered the room and said, "I was just checking on you. I thought I heard you screech. Everything all right?" Christie laughed, "I am sorry. My boyfriend called from Colorado to wish me good luck in the new job. It surprised and pleased me so, that I guess I must have screamed a little. Now I'm a bit embarrassed." Karin said, "No worries. It was very sweet that he called. I thought I would pop in to see if you had made any progress on the cases so we could sit before you have lunch with Ms. Ross."

Wendy McKeller sat in her desk chair in the foyer area of the office. There was a bulletproof shield between her desk and the door. She felt safe knowing that but wondered why she needed one. She had to give access to people who entered the door to their office. She would learn everyone's face today Karin had told her, because there was a large meeting of all the Region's agents in the main conference room scheduled for 8:30 am tomorrow. Part of her new responsibilities would be to ensure there was sufficient coffee and snacks available. She had the key to the concession area and Karin had briefed her quite thoroughly on who could access what items. They had done this one together as there was a second follow-up meeting in the morning to set-up for. She had to make copies for that meeting. It was the agenda and a breakdown of the assignments for the coming months for all the agents. It looked like they were discussing one cartel one day and another the next day. All the agents were staying over in the rooms on the other side of our building tonight.

Attendees were scheduled for dinner at the Guard & Grace right around the corner on California Street; Reservations were for

6:00 p.m. At one o'clock sharp, the conference room was crowded with agents and staff. Everyone was there, had gotten a drink and a snack, and were now seated around a square table.

Megan Rolling called the room to order and took the roll. As she called their names, each agent confirmed their presence: Perry Kline, here. Troy Phillips, here. Christopher Montrose, here. Tiffany Nails, here. Ginger Moeller, here. Mitch McCormick, here. Chris Rocker, here. Eddie Riscoe, here. Rick Ramirez, here. Barry Moeller, here. Laiza Marie, here. Deyna Doll, Here. Greg Solo, here. Gray Nash, here. Jameson Martly, here, Micah Blair, here. Lewis Greeley, here.

Lewis Greely stood and thanked Megan for getting everyone here. He began by announcing the arrangements for Michael Donlevy. There was an unannounced moment of silence around the room. Everyone loved Michael Donlevy, their fallen Director. He had brought most of them on at the Denver office and now he was dead. Murdered and left in the fallen snow by some crazy villain who had snuck up on him in broad daylight and shot him from a passing vehicle. The services for Michael would be tomorrow after their morning meeting. They would have a quick lunch together and then return to their offices around the region.

Lewis said, "Any questions before we begin?" No one indicated they had one, so he continued, "Ladies and Gentlemen, thank you all for coming in today. We have a lot to discuss. We'll break for dinner at 5:30 p.m. and head over to the Guard & Grace around the corner. Our agenda for today will be to discuss Michael's unfortunate demise and finding the perpetrator. Then we will discuss our status and strategy for El Verdugo.

Tomorrow morning when we reconvene, our agenda will focus on a new cartel that has raised its ugly head here in the west called Chicas Fuerte. We will strategize and assign some folks to that case and then attend the services for Mr. Donlevy.

The meeting lasted over three hours as the task of finding Michael Donlevy's killer or killers took more time than was allotted. The discussion of El Verdugo was much more to the point and ended with a solid plan in place for those assigned. This was the cartel with the highest history of criminal activity.

Micah was taking the lead on this one as there was a strong feeling among all in attendance that it was El Verdugo's men who shot and killed Michael Donlevy. It was decided that Lewis Greeley would assist with the investigation of that killing. He assigned several agents and asked Ginger Moeller to coordinate communications on the case.

Micah called off several agent's names to join him in this case. He asked Tiffany Nails to assist as well as El Verdugo had begun bringing in many illegals from Southeast Asia. She was Vietnamese and was fluent in the many languages from that area so her assistance would be invaluable. The meeting ended at 5:45 p.m. sharp, and they all were beginning to file out on their way to freshen up in their rooms across the building in the hotel area of headquarters.

At 6:45 p.m., Micah walked into the bar at the Guard & Grace. Some of the agents were finalizing their drink orders and paying their tabs. The others had already moved into the private room that Megan had secured for them so their conversations about the cases, assignments or strategies would not be overheard by the public in the main dining room. This would break into four separate rooms when they were ready.

Lewis stood and raised his glass and made a toast, "Ladies and Gentlemen, I would like you all to raise a glass in a toast, to remember Michael Donlevy."

Lewis continued, Michael was a great leader, super-agent, and long-time friend to many of us. May he rest in peace." They all clinked glasses and toasted Michael. "OK, folks. We are off the clock so to speak so get to know your partners, leaders, and support team in a more social, relaxed manner for the rest of the evening. And last, but not least, I have asked our new Assistant Director for the Region to join us tonight as well. Let me introduce to you, Ryan Coleman. He has a long resume in the Denver Police Department, and I have recently learned he is a wizard with Computer technology. Welcome Ryan. So, without further ado, enjoy your dinner."

Perry Kline was seated next to Ryan as they had met at the bar earlier. Megan Rolling sat across from Perry and Ryan and Perry noticed Ryan was talking less to him now and more to Megan. He laughed to himself, thinking about meeting his main squeeze a few years back, Christie Mahern. He thought to himself, Ryan had the same look on his face that he had back then. He wondered if a new inter-office romance was blossoming or if was it just him who saw it. Time would tell if any romance would bloom. Perry was betting it would.

Christie Mahern had just finished her first day as a U.S. Attorney in Buffalo, New York and was meeting Wendy at the Ace of Clubs on Delaware Avenue in Buffalo. She walked out of the office. She took the elevator to the parking garage below and walked to her car. She got a chill as she remembered the day that she was shot going to her car in the garage at her old office just up the street. She looked over her shoulder more than once as it was still fresh in her mind even though it was almost three years ago now, but you always remember those things. She drove out of the building, and her red Mustang took her up the street to the Ace of Clubs. She found a spot right in front of the place. How lucky. She ran in and met Wendy at the bar and got a drink. They both had so much to say, one couldn't wait for the other to finish talking. They chatted incessantly for ten minutes until they took a breath and the other started talking. They looked at each other and laughed. They hugged and Christie finally said, "Oh my goodness, Wendy, that is the funniest thing. We both had so much to share with each other the stories of our day. I guess we can safely say, we both had a terrific day. Wendy then asked, "Have you heard from Mr. Kline?"

Christie's eyes lit up as she responded, "Oh dear, I forgot the most important thing of the day. He called around 10 o'clock which would have made it 8 am in Denver. It was so great to hear from him. He is doing well and is excited about the new challenges out there. I can't wait to visit and catch up with him. I miss him so much."

Ryan Coleman had a nice conversation over dinner with Megan Rolling, Perry Kline, and Gray Nash. Nash would be on Ryan's team being assigned to work with Ryan and Perry down in Sante Fe, New Mexico. After dinner, they all sat and chatted in the breakout rooms for a while then dispersed as they had an early meeting in the morning then were scheduled to attend Michael Donlevy's funeral services.

Tuesday morning started early for the FBI group in Denver. Most of them were there at 8:00 a.m. to begin their day. Some of the conversations from last evening at the Guild and Grace were reconvened and the chatter in the conference room escalated the noise level quite high. It took Megan Rolling almost five minutes to get the group calmed down to begin the meeting.

Megan said, "Good morning, everyone. It looks like we have some unfinished conversations from last night. I am glad everyone enjoyed the evening. If you did not get a chance to meet our new Assistant Director, let me again formally introduce, Ryan Coleman."

Ryan stood and accepted the applause. Lewis Greeley then took the podium and began the meeting, "Good morning, as I mentioned yesterday, we have a new cartel that has begun to grow exponentially coming in from Mexico."

Lewis spent the first hour discussing the make-up of Chica Fuerte, the newest cartel. They seemed to be led by a female and dealt heavily in drugs but also were into the trafficking of females that could be trained as carriers for their drug shipments. Many were Asian as they tried to stay away from too many Mexican illegals as the Federales, what the government agents were known as, were increasing their incidents of stopping Hispanics in transit on major highways. Lewis mentioned that there was another cartel raising its head but more of that would be discussed the next time they got together.

The meeting went on until 11:30 a.m. when all the assignments and strategies had been completed. Then the trip to the chapel downstairs where the private services were held for Michael Donlevy. No one from his family was in attendance as his closed casket was being flown back to Buffalo, New York this afternoon at six o'clock. The body was driven to Denver International Airport's Shipping area where all the express carriers were housed. There was a small four-person team of Buffalo agents in town to bring the body back to Buffalo.

After the services, Micah returned to his office. He was saddened by the day's events and sat quietly at his desk for some time. One of his team leaders, Tiffany Nails, knocked on his door and walked in, "Micah, you look very sad. I hope you can get over our loss soon. We miss your jocular presence in the office. There is a call for you on line one. I think it may cheer you up." She left the office and Micah, looking down at the phone, saw line one blinking. He picked it up, "Hello, Micah Blair here." The voice on the other end of the line was sweet and brought a smile to his face, Hello, Director Blair. I was wondering if you'd be free for dinner tonight?"

Micah did have a large smile on his face. It was Catie Fuda, his current lover from Buffalo. He said, "Well, hello doll. What a nice surprise to hear from you. How are things back in Buffalo?" Catie said, "I guess they are okay, but I am not sure because I am not there. I am sitting in a very beautiful room at the Westin Inn, overlooking

Denver's International Airport. I arrived by red eye last night. So, I am still wondering if you're free for dinner tonight?" Micah yelled, "What? You're here? Oh Baby, this is great news. You came all the way to Denver to see me? Catie chuckled, "Well, yes, I did. I also set up meetings with two local real estate agents today. I am discussing with each of them whether they can find a location suitable for me to open a new restaurant here in Denver because I am getting ready to move out here to be with this sexy man I've been dating. You still have not answered my question. Dinner? Tonight?

Micah cleared his throat and said, "There is nothing I would rather do this evening. Yes. So, you are staying at the Westin? Where are we having dinner? When can I see you? How long are you going to be here?"

Catie laughed, "Mr. Blair, you ask an awful lot of questions. I have my first meeting with a realtor in 10 minutes. I am free after about six. I can order dinner in the room for us at seven if you can be here. Then I will answer all your questions." She heard, "I'm there, see you then doll. Thanks."

Later that week, Lewis Greeley sat in his office and looked across the desk at Ryan Coleman and Perry Kline. He said, "Gentlemen, now that we have doled out the assignments, I am anxious to get moving on the operation in Sante Fe. We can fly you both out with your team late this afternoon so you can have dinner there tonight, meeting with Eric Slay and Christopher Wiser. You can then be operational first thing tomorrow morning. Does that sound doable?" Ryan spoke first, "I think that will work as we are all geared up to begin." Perry just said, "Absolutely fine." They both stood and went back to the other side of the building to their private quarters to begin packing for their trip to Sante Fe.

The flight down to Sante Fe took about two hours. The car that picked the two gentlemen up at the airport had a female driver named, Jennifer Redmond. She had long, red hair and was quite knowledgeable about the area. It took about 50 minutes to arrive at their casita on Galisteo Street. It was a quaint bed and breakfast called El Farolito, which translates to The Lantern. Perry and Ryan dropped off their suitcases in the room and then Jennifer drove them to the office. The office used in Sante Fe was the old Salvation Army building on East Alameda Street. Perry and Ryan were welcomed by Eric Slay and Christopher Wiser or as they were known in the Bureau as Butch and Sundance.

Eric took the lead in the welcoming conversation, "Gentlemen, we are excited you are here. Christopher and I have been laying the groundwork with the Chica Fuerte for seven months and they have recently escalated their operation, so your arriving is very timely. Christopher Wiser then added, "Now that Jennifer has set you up in quarters at the El Farolito casita, you will need vehicles. We have two available for you, but we can start with one until you are down here full-time. Your call."

Perry responded, "Thank you all for the accommodations and vehicles. Eventually, we will need two, but we will take one for this trip. I would like to take you folks to lunch at a nice quiet place so we can chat without people overhearing us or being seen together. The less we are seen together, the better it will be. Can you recommend a nice bistro?" Christopher spoke quickly and suggested, "If you like Italian food, we could go to Osteria D'Assissi over on Federal. They have great food, and it is usually quiet during the week." Perry and Ryan went out back and signed off on one of the cars they had been provided and followed Eric and Christopher to the restaurant.

At 6:05 p.m., Micah knocked on suite 706 at the Westin Hotel. Catie came to the door in a flowing satin gown that went down to the floor. She looked amazing and Micah told her as they hugged even before they shut the door. Micah said, "You look fabulous. It is so great to see you. I have so much to tell you about." They finally shut the door and Micah took off his large winter coat. It was 24 degrees today and the temperature was dropping as the sun had gone down already. It was toasty warm in the suite. They embraced again and Catie said, "Micah, I have missed you so much. It is so good to have your arms around me. How are things going?"

Micah stood back and looked at her, "You are breathtaking in that gown young lady. Do you have anything to drink? It has been a long day. I have been waiting impatiently for this moment. I need something to calm my nerves." He always knew just the right thing to say to her to make her swoon. She began, "Follow me, Sir. I think I can avail you of a bit of libation. She walked behind a small bar and opened the small fridge on the back shelf. From it, she pulled a chilled bottle of Grey Goose.

She filled a glass with ice and poured him four-fingers of his favorite elixir. "Here you go handsome. Now I need a little something as well. My day was quite busy and as I will share shortly, very productive," she parried while pouring herself a large glass of Robert Craig red wine. Micah held his glass to toast. They clinked glasses and Catie took a long swallow. Micah almost drained the glass. As she walked back out from behind the little bar, they embraced again. She said, "I will let you get yourself another and top off my glass and I will go to the kitchen. Dinner should be about ready."

She kissed him softly and moved into the kitchen. He got both bottles and refilled each of their glasses and went to find her. Catie was just pulling a stuffed chicken out of the oven. She had two plates on the small dining table in front of the large floor-to-ceiling window looking out into the night. You could see ground lights and planes taking off in one direction and landing in another. There were Christmas decorations at the entrance of the hotel below and Micah was lost in the beauty of the view. He said, "Do you need any help in there?"

Catie came out of the kitchen with a large tray containing two plates with baked potatoes and steamed asparagus on them along with a platter of stuffed chicken. "Here", she said, grab the chicken for me." Micah stood and grabbed the entire tray from her. She then took off the chicken platter. He set the tray down on the end of the table and placed the two dinner dishes next to each other on the same side of the table looking out of the large window. Catie said, "Do you want to carve the chicken? Better yet, why don't I do that as you relax and tell me all about Denver."

Micah watched as she deftly apportioned the chicken quickly onto their plates and sat down. She popped right back up and got the bread out of the oven and sat back down lifting her glass in a toast, "To us, baby!"

Eric, Christopher, Perry, and Ryan were seated at a table in front of the bay window looking out onto Federal Street. They looked over the Osteria D'Assissi menus brought by their waiter, Antonio. Christopher ordered his food and drink quickly, choosing the Ravioli Al Funghi and a glass of red wine.

Eric followed with the fish of the day which was Red Snapper, and he changed the wine order to a bottle for the table. Perry ordered crab cakes and fried calamari for the appetizers. His entre was spaghetti and meatballs. Ryan was now ready and ordered a coffee and an antipasto and small pizza.

When Antonio had left, they began to discuss their mission. Eric started, "Guys, we have been able to befriend several operatives from Chica. I wouldn't mention names at this point but there are reports for you both back at the house (their code word for Headquarters). With the solid work of our friend here, Christopher, he is very close to helping set up the route and transportation for the next shipment of Christmas presents (the code phrase for drugs)."

Christopher remarked, "We really enjoy living here in Sante Fe. The arts and crafts artists are plentiful so if you enjoy that sort of thing, it'll be fun."

Perry and Ryan both got a text on their phones. Each looked at his phone and realized it was from Eric who texted: 'Christopher has spotted a bug so we will suspend our work conversations.'

After dessert and coffee, they left the restaurant. Eric took Ryan in his car and Christopher went with Perry. The cars went in opposite directions. Christopher said to Perry, "That was interesting. I spotted the bug when Antonio, our waiter, went to serve another table and reached up to turn the volume of the music down above that table. He could have thought we were from a rival organization as the owners are an old-school Italian family from Chicago that still operates some business here in town. We try to stay clear of them as we have other fish to fry that are more dangerous. Chica Fuerte has begun to deal in fentanyl or as they say in Spanish, 'fentalilo'. They are using pregnant women to carry the supplies across the border. They usually come through Sante Fe and then go north to Denver where there is a greater market and larger ability to expand their markets outward from there. Our strategy here has been to capture as much of the product here before it even gets to Denver."

Christopher finished the conversation about the female-led cartel by saying, "Lately, the delivery of large 10-kilo shipments happen at random times during the week; then within hours, their distribution from the border to Denver and points west and north are completed so sales of the illegal substances can happen within hours of delivery. We understand and have tracked the sales on the street after a delivery can be concluded in a single day as there are waiting lists needed to be filled for street pushers. We know if we succeed with blocking the deliveries at the point of entry into our country, they will have a more difficult time processing the substance to route it elsewhere as the cartels have become so routinized, it is hard for them to go to a plan B." They arrived back at the office and joined Eric and Ryan.

After dinner, Micah started cleaning up and began washing dishes. Catie put on some soft music and the sound of Dave Koz's 'The Dance' filled the rooms. They had discussed Micah's new role, the sadness of the funeral of Michael Donlevy, and Catie's plan to open a new restaurant.

Catie said, "I found this lady in my internet search that I met with today. Her name is Diane Sorenstone. She has assured me that she has no less than 20 properties for me to look at with her. She said the locations are in Denver proper mostly but there are some places in the suburbs that may be appealing as well. She was really excited about a restaurant that was not a chain. She had researched the reviews of Magdelane's in Buffalo, so she obviously has impressed me with her initiative."

Micah said, "Well, I've only been here a week and I am tired of living in the hotel at headquarters already. I wonder if Diane can find us a home. It looks like I may be traveling from here to Sante Fe, New Mexico on a regular basis but after talking to Megan at the office, there are neighborhoods that are pricey, and those to stay away from. I have written them down for us."

Catie hugged him from behind as he finished the dishes. She said, "I will ask her tomorrow, but I am sure she does private real estate as well as commercial." As soon as I find a location I like, then we'll know the lay of the land better and choosing an area to live in that is relatively close to our jobs will be an initial 'to do'."

Micah noticed that Dave Koz was again coming through the speakers. She must have 'The Dance' on a repeating playlist. He grabbed her around the waist and began to embrace her as he led her in a waltz into the living room. He stopped. They kissed. She moaned as his embrace became more insistent. She looked up at him and said, "I haven't shown you the best part of the suite yet."

Catie led him by the hand into the bedroom. She had candles burning and he could see a night light in the ensuite bath to the right of a large king-sized bed. Micah lifted her and together they stretched out on the bed. They kissed more urgently now. Their clothes vanished and their lovemaking began in an elegant reunion of their lust. Then they slept.

Perry turned to Christopher asking, "All the information you've shared is good to get an idea of the landscape but when is the next big shipment? How close are your informants to the leader of Chica? Do you think the bug in the restaurant indicates they know where you eat or is there someone at Osteria that recognized you and put up or turned on the bug, like Antonio?"

Christopher replied, "Perry, I see from your questions that this is not your first rodeo. First, we think the next shipment is scheduled for this Friday. Our informants are mostly runners, but we have met one lady through Jennifer named Luisa Castro or Lazy as she's known. We think she is at the lieutenant level, so she gets her directives from Petirrojo Cantante. As far as the bug at Osteria goes, it looked very rudimentary and Antonio did, in fact, reach up and activate it. So, two things. We know that he is an agent, or the owners are involved, and they know what we do. Secondly, the bug didn't look sophisticated enough to have deciphered what our conversations were about, given the music and noise level."

Eric turned to Ryan and said, "So I understand you worked for Denver P.D." Ryan answered, "Yes sir. I was there eight years. I worked as an investigator on the crime syndicates as well as immigration. So is our cover blown up here in Sante Fe do you think?" Eric thought for a minute, "Well we have swiped that place clean as we are regulars. The bug is new and might not be detrimental as you might first think. The owners are nice enough folks from Italy, and we've checked them out very thoroughly.

Christopher and I left in different directions. He just texted that he was not followed and is back at HQ."

Ryan wondered if these two agents were as experienced as they portrayed. Christopher ended with, "We are clean as well so we can go back there now." Ryan thought to himself, 'I know when I've been made. That clearly didn't feel like it in the restaurant. He would keep his comments to himself and maybe share them with Micah when he returned to Denver.

Eric's phone buzzed as they drove into the back of HQ. He answered, "Hello, Carol. How are you?" He looked at Ryan and smiled while putting the car in park and exiting the vehicle. As he walked, Eric said back into the phone, "Yes, Carol. Christopher's cousin and his friend are here for a visit, and we can get together at our place later. I will text you when we get back. Goodbye."

Perry's head was filled with questions. He would wait until he and Ryan were back at El Farolito. After some further conversations about a schedule for the next day with Eric and Christopher at HQ in the old Salvation Army building. Ryan and Perry picked up their vehicle and bid their Sante Fe team a pleasant good evening and left for their cottage.

They saw the manager, Wayne, just leaving as they went to pull into the driveway at El Farolito. He waved to them as he passed. They waved back and Ryan remarked, "I am glad the gate was opened, I wanted to wait until the light of day tomorrow to figure out the gate passcode system.

Ryan said, "I was thinking about freshening up then walking to the restaurant next door for a nightcap if you have a mind to do so." Perry said, "That works for me. I want to make a call before it gets too late back east before we head out."

They freshened up after a long day. Ryan went first and Perry stepped back out on the patio out back to have some privacy to call

Christie. He called her cell phone. She answered on the first ring, "I hope this is not a sales call at this time of night!" Perry grinned, loving her sense of humor, "Well ma'am, I wouldn't call it a sales call, but I would like you to consider this a great opportunity. Would you be interested in planning a short totally paid vacation to the beautiful mountain resort at Vail, Colorado?" They both chuckled and she replied with, "That sounds tempting young man; however, I have to consider the schedule of the gentleman I am dating before I make any commitments for future vacations."

Perry got serious, "Christie, how are you?" She said, "I just got home, and I am having a glass of wine from the last bottle we shared before you left. I am great and love the new job. How are you doing, handsome?"

"Well Doll", said Perry, "Things are moving quickly. We are down in Sante Fe this week. Nice guys who run this area. It will be interesting to get to know the operation down here. I was thinking, I will probably be back and forth from Denver to here for a few weeks but after the first of the year, I was hoping you could get away for a bit of skiing. Basically, I am asking if I send you tickets in three or four weeks, would you like to come out and wrestle with me for a few days and maybe go out of the room once a day?" They laughed.

Eric pulled the car into their garage at home. He and Christopher went upstairs, doffed their coats and changed into relaxing attire. Eric poured them both a glass of wine, "What did you think of Ryan and Perry?"

As they sat in the living room, Christopher responded, "I think they will do well here. Both seem friendly and very aware of the situation. I noticed the look on Jennifer's face when she dropped them off and I could see she was smitten with one of them. I just couldn't tell which one. We'll see how that progresses. Your thoughts?"

Eric had just turned on some soft music, "I liked them both as well. Perry seems to be very street-savvy. Ryan seems like it has been a while since he was on the street but that may work to his benefit here. They reacted very calmly to your announcement about observing the waiter activating a bug. Antonio was just adjusting the volume on the music, wasn't he?"

Christopher grinned, "It was all I could do not to laugh out loud when I sent the texts. Antonio would die if I told him, the friends we were with thought he looked like an informant that was connected to the mob."

They both had a good laugh at this made-up scenario. They really didn't know the guys from Denver. Both seemed new to the organization but were experienced in law enforcement. This would bode well for the Sante Fe team as they anticipated being busy before the end of the year. It was their experience that holidays were always busier for the criminal element.

Christie continued her phone call saying, "Well, Perry. I have just started a new job and I don't work for myself anymore. I will check with my supervisor tomorrow to see what my availability will be during the holidays. I can't believe it will be so rigid that I can't sneak away for an extended weekend to visit the love of my life."

Perry getting serious again, "That sounds great, Doll. I will check back with you soon. We'll have to start planning. I will let you go for now. Love you. Talk to you soon." There it was again. Christie beamed. The "L" word. She said, "I love you too, Perry. Have a great night." The call ended.

Christie thought to herself that there was a time when she felt that Perry was ambivalent about his feelings toward her. She wondered if their relationship would ever mature past the 'I LOVE YOU' stage. She was very happy that a commitment had been made.

Perry went into the room and got Ryan, then he and Ryan walked next door for a drink. As they walked next door, Ryan's cellphone buzzed. "Hello, this is Ryan." He listened. Then he muted the phone and said to Perry, "It's Micah Blair. I will put him on speaker. Okay, Mr. Blair, we're both here."

Micah said, "I don't want you to think I am checking up on you, but I wanted to get your take on the meeting with Eric and Christopher."

Ryan said, "They seemed very competent and friendly. Should be fine working with them. Perry?"

Perry said, "Well, Micah. They're very nice. I did have a concern though. I was just about to voice this to Ryan, but while we were at the restaurant tonight, Christopher texted us that he observed a waiter activating a bug. It didn't seem to me that anyone was even giving us a second glance. I didn't see any bugs when I visited the restroom. I checked the décor closely for cameras as well which would have been my first instinct to use in that environment. I saw nothing. Maybe it's just me being me but I will keep you both posted."

Micah replied, "That's very interesting. I wonder if they were testing you. It would seem odd but keep me posted. Have a good night. Call if you need me. I'll see you in a few days." They both said at once, "Goodnight, Micah."

Ryan looked at Perry and said, "Could they have been testing us?" Perry laughed, "There is no telling what those fellas are up to. My guess is they may have been, but we will keep an eye on them for sure." Perry nodded.

Ryan continued, "They have done a lot of work down here and have maintained a very low profile as far as blending into the fabric of the community. Micah told me that Eric visits a coffee shop each morning and chats up the local retirees. Christopher has aligned himself with the local chapter of the Rotary. They are mostly older folks, but he relates to them to keep his cover." Ryan said, "I guess we will have to give them a pass on this one. We'll keep our eyes and ears open though. I heard you solved a very large case with the Buffalo PD before coming to the Bureau. I asked around and the scuttlebutt is you were overlooked for promotion at the Buffalo PD. Do you have any regrets about coming to the bureau?"

Perry said, "Yeah, it was a very complicated case, but I worked with the Bureau the whole time. My former Detective Chief was the King Pin of the operation we busted up. Micah was my undercover partner. We worked well together so I had no qualms about leaving to come to the Bureau. He gave me a nice commendation for my part in solving the Snow Villain caper."

Lewis Greeley sat in his office in Denver and answered the call that Megan told him he had through the intercom, "Hello, this is Lewis Greeley." The male voice on the phone said, "We got your boy, Donlevy, now we are coming for you, Greeley. We know where to find you so get your affairs in order." The line went dead.

"Megan", he yelled, "Trace that last call for me." Megan picked up her phone and dialed the code to trace. She got a 555 number which was scrambled. She rose and went to the boss's office, "No luck, Lewis. It was a 555 number. I will start tracing all the calls coming in and alert all the office staff to do the same. What was that call about?"

Lewis thought a minute and said, "I am not really sure, but it sounded like a threat from the people who got Michael Donlevy." Megan shook with a chill, "Chief, you better watch your back when you leave the office, and you are out and about." Lewis said, "Maybe we need to shoot out a memo to everyone that the cartels are making threats so they should keep a watch over their shoulders." Megan went back to her desk to draft one for him to review.

The memo read: *To all staff: Be advised that Mr. Sanders has been targeted by the chicken industry as a potential wrench in their mass production. All of Mr. Sanders' associates should be on the lookout for similar reprisals from those in that industry.*

This was confusing to no one in the Bureau. It basically meant that their headman, Mr. Greeley had received a threat from the cartel, and they should all watch their backs while in the field. It was sent and several eyebrows were raised among the agents.

Perry looked up at Ryan, "Did you see that email from HQ?" Ryan said, "I must have missed a briefing. Mind translating that one for me. I don't speak FBI code yet."

Perry laughed, "The reference is to Colonel Sanders from Kentucky Fried Chicken who was the leader of the organization. Looks like Mr. Greeley has received a message from the cartel or 'the industry' that he will be eliminated like Mr. Donlevy was. We should all keep an eye out for anything suspicious as the last court session in the case Donlevy worked on, was held this week and the indication is that they will likely put some of the Cartel capos in the clink for a long while and the Cartels may be ready to retaliate for their loss."

Megan called for the driver Chris Therston. He answered, "Yes, Miss Megan. What do you need?" Megan smiled as him always calling her Miss Megan, "Chris, did you see my memo?" He confirmed that he had. She continued, "I think it would be a good idea to change vehicles for a while. Mr. G's limo probably needs an overhaul anyway."

Chris said, "Roger that, Miss Megan. Consider it done. Are we bugging out?" Megan thought they would but said, "I think we might, but I will give you a heads up the minute I hear from Mr. Sanders."

Chris knew that hearing Megan talking in code and sending that memo about their leader being threatened meant the cartel was very angry with the Bureau and was planning something large and probably destructive. They had moved twice before over the years. It always was in quick response to a similar situation. Bugging out meant the entire organization would move out of HQ. The Bureau would then re-establish their location in a nearby, predetermined location. They would be much less visible, and communications would be from their secondary network of communication devices.

Chris went to the garage, changed the vehicle he was driving. He let the chief mechanic know of the impending move. The other agents would by protocol put their current vehicle in a storage location, wherever they were.

Then they would be dropped off at HQ in a cab or by a friend, grab their travel kit and a new car and move into their safe location until further notice.

Megan asked Mr. Greeley if a Bug Out would be ordered. He responded, "Absolutely, Megan. Can you send out the communication A.S.A.P?" She replied, "It is all ready to go. I just wanted your order."

The message read: 'All personnel, Colonel Potter has ordered a bug out as the Koreans have indicated their advance. Get your jeep and new tent and be ready to travel. Regards, Radar.'

Every agent from the region knew exactly what that memo referenced. It was the TV show M.AS.H. (Mobile Army Surgical Hospital) from the 1970's. In the military, Bug Out meant that being mobile, they would pull up the tents and move lock, stock, and barrel to a new safe location away from enemy attack. The Bureau leaders from the surrounding regions would also receive the message alerting them that their units may also be in jeopardy. They should at this point be on stand-by. Micah read the memo from Megan. He knew what it meant and went back into the bedroom to let Catie know he would need to leave as work called with an alert. "Nothing serious," he said, "just routine."

Eric Slay and Christopher Wiser were having a wine cocktail in the quiet of their home in Sante Fe. Eric remarked, "Did you see the memo from Colonel Sanders?" Christopher replied, "Ha. I always thought it was a silly way to code a message rather than just tell folks what has happened. We really don't know who the threat was directed at but can only guess it was Greeley. We should be careful though because the cartels are really steamed about losing so many top echelon capos to prison sentences due to the work largely of Mr. Donlevy. God rest his soul."

After a comfortable sleep and morning shower, Eric walked down the stairs to head to his morning rendezvous at the coffee shop. Downstairs, he passed Loren Walters, who just moved into the front lower flat on his way to the gym. They exchanged morning greetings and went their separate ways. About a half block from the coffee shop, as Eric walked briskly in the quiet of the morning, he thought of how happy he was in this relaxed environment. Just then, a black sedan pulled up beside him and three men jumped out.

The men were all wearing ski masks. The man from the passenger seat quickly placed a black sack over Eric's head. Another man slapped handcuffs on him. This left Eric very surprised and vulnerable. He had tossed his cell phone out of his pocket as he was being accosted and it landed in the bushes of the house two doors from the coffee shop. It happened in a flash. Eric was tossed forcibly into the rear seat of the sedan. They were gone before anyone would notice anything.

Christopher walked downstairs to check the mailbox as their mail always seemed to be delivered quite early. He would then head out for his morning jog. He found a note taped to the front of the mailbox in pale blue paper the size of a large post-it note. It read: 'YOU ARE NEXT'. Christopher felt a bit of panic retrieving the rest of the mail and went back upstairs. He called Eric immediately. It rang twice and went to voicemail. He waited for what seemed like twenty minutes but was really, just three minutes. He called again. Again, he got Eric's voicemail. He then called Micah Blair, who answered on the first ring, "Hello Christopher. What is up this fine morning?" Christopher tried to remain calm, however, he noticed his hand was shaking, "Micah, I think something has happened to Eric."

Micah sat up and spoke calmly, "What do you think might have happened?" Christopher responded, "He left for his morning coffee this morning like always. I went to get the mail and taped on my mailbox was a note, handwritten saying; 'You Are Next'. I called Eric right away and twice I got his voicemail. I traced his cellphone. It shows it is pinging at a location five houses from the coffee shop."

Micah interrupted, "Call Ryan and give him the location of the phone. Let Ryan and Perry see if they can grab the phone or find Eric. You go directly to your bug-out location and wait for me to call you back."

Micah had just stepped out of the shower at Catie's suite at the Westin Hotel in Denver when the phone call came from Christopher in Sante Fe. He sounded a bit rattled as his partner might be in danger. Micah hoped he was not missing or hurt but they would find out soon enough.

Catie handed Micah a cup of coffee still steaming. He said, "Thanks, Doll. I may have to leave soon to catch a flight to Sante Fe. We may have an agent missing." Catie cringed saying, "Oh, I hope not. The work you do is vital to the security of our country but sure can be dangerous. I look forward to the day when you can retire and work part-time as a maitre 'd in one of my restaurants or something similarly less dangerous."

Sitting at the counter in the small kitchen with Catie, Micah's phone rang. It was Ryan Coleman from Sante Fe. He said, "Good

Morning Sir. Bad news to report. Eric Slay was taken by three men in a car on his way to his coffee shop."

"It happened five doors away from the Downtown Subscription this morning. He was smart enough to throw his phone into the front bushes of a residential home five doors down from his destination. We traced the phone there and when we arrived and secured the phone, a sweet neighbor lady named Katy Best came out and told us that she had seen what happened but didn't know whether to contact the police but when she saw us, she wanted to do the right thing. Get this, Chief. Her son who is home with her, Daniel Best, even got the license number and make of the vehicle. We have an address. Do you want us to try to storm in and take him or keep the address under surveillance?"

Micah was now getting his clothes on as he knew he would have to fly there and assist in their attempt to recover Mr. Slay from what he assumed was one of the cartels. He said, "Great job, Ryan. I am at the airport now and will get our private plane to jet me down there. I will take the helicopter to the bugout office location behind The Bull Ring Restaurant on Washington Street."

The office was behind the Children's toy store next door to that restaurant. He would make connection calls for his transport when he hung up but continued with, "I should be there inside of two hours so keep the place under surveillance with as many cars as you think necessary. Tell your agents down there to be extra careful about using regular cars and attire as this could be a major entrapment plan to gather up as many agents as comes to the aid of our captured agent so they can negotiate with the Bureau to exchange them for the capos that are due for sentencing next week here in Denver. Keep me posted. I'm on my way."

Micah made a couple of calls, the first to Megan, who would get transportation ready. The next to Lewis Greeley to update him. Micah was dressed now as he gave Lewis Greeley the outline of the situation and his plan. They would use local PD personnel to do the initial raid then back them up, etc. Lewis liked that plan saying, "Keep me in the loop Micah. Good Luck."

Micah looked at Catie and sadly said, "I was really looking forward to spending some time with you. Our leader received threats which means we go into a safety shell for a while. If you want me, ring once and wait five minutes, then call again. If I don't answer on the second ring, hang up. I will call you back when I can. I am hoping to knock this operation out in less than a day or two. How long are you in town?"

Catie smiled and said, "I have no commitments to return until I find a restaurant location and a home for us whenever you're ready, so I could be here a while. Stay safe and call when you can. I love you." Catie kissed him then and began her usual worrying routine. He left, admiring the short robe she was walking around in after their shower. As he called the ground crew for the Bureau's plane, he thought to himself that he should put a tail on Catie just in case the cartel was following him as well. Better safe than sorry.

Micah boarded the plane fifteen minutes after leaving Catie. He would be in Sante Fe in an hour with the current winds. The helicopter was waiting ready to take him into the city.

Christie Mahern just returned from Buffalo Federal Court. She had prosecuted her first case all by herself and won without any serious argument from the defense. She sat at her desk and let out a sigh of relief. She had anticipated a more vigorous defense challenge from the defense team, but it never materialized.

The judge in the case, the Honorable Brayden Coleman deemed the sentencing of the defendant would be held in two weeks which indicated the sentence was already determined and based upon her history on sentencing of the drug pushers, the guy would spend many years behind bars.

As she looked out her window with her back to the door, she heard a soft knock and spun her chair around. There in front of her desk was none other than Trini Ross, her boss and Director of the FBI Regional Office in Buffalo New York. She stood as soon as she recognized Ms. Ross, "Good afternoon, Ms. Ross."

Trini Ross smiled and said, "May I sit?" Christie said wanting to slap herself for not having her wits about her, "Yes, Please, do so." Trini Ross started, "Christie, you have only been here six weeks and have been a major assist on twelve cases and handled one all by yourself today. I just received a call from Judge Heart telling me what a fine job I did finding that new U.S. Attorney who presented to her this morning. I had to tell her that because of her outstanding performances this month, I would be transferring her out west to the Denver Region. I know this is short notice, but that area really needs a leader like you and based upon what you have done this month and your impressive resume of cases and awards, you could really make a mark in their current situation based upon their initial influx of cases both in the drug arena and those centered around rights violations in the abortion area."

Trini continued, "I think you are indeed ready for the move. I am sad to lose you. You can certainly help us out there with all your experience and expertise. Thoughts?" Christie was really surprised and pleased, "Thank you so much for the opportunity, Ms. Ross." Trini interrupted her, "No need to thank me Christie, just go to Denver and be the best Regional Director the FBI has ever seen! And call me Trini."

Christie Mahern was now officially flabbergasted, "Trini, wow. That is quite a promotion. Are you sure I can be a director at this juncture?" Trini Ross replied, "I guess there is no time like the present to find out." She then laughed and standing said, "You'll do great. I have every confidence. If you ever have a question, don't hesitate to call. Here is my private number. Just be mindful of the two-hour time difference." They both laughed and shook hands. Christie watched her turn and leave. She turned back and asked, "How soon do you think you can leave?" Christie said, "Well, you know I am taking my assistant with me. I can make the arrangements by next week to fly out and start next Monday if you need me to be there that soon." Trini answered, "I will alert them you are coming. The contact is Deyna Doll. She is one of the junior attorneys though very experienced and a great asset. She will give you the details on your residence, the team they have and the need to expand. All you'll really need initially is clothes and personal things. We can have whatever furniture you want delivered and the rest stored until you request our assistance on distribution when you are ready."

Christie thanked her again and flopped back in her chair as she watched the Director leave. She picked up the phone and called Wendy. Wendy answered, "Yes, Miss Mahern." Christie said, "Start packing your bags, Girl, we are moving to Denver next Monday." Christie pulled the phone away from her ear as Wendy was yelling at the top of her lungs. She could hear her through the doorway as she was not far away down the hall. Wendy ran down to her boss's office. She was literally jumping for joy. Wendy said, "I have been waiting for this call every day. It seems like 100 years since we left Mahern, Miller & Associates. Well, a new chapter begins now. Miss Christie. I have some things in place I should tell you." Christie said, "Sit down here a minute, let's talk." Within seconds, Wendy began, "I have the number for the hotel in Denver, I'll get rooms. Then we can get settled in. I can make flight reservations and I'll have an uber take us to the Airport Saturday morning."

Christie said, "That'll be great. Leaving Saturday gives us a day to acclimate before we begin working. I will call the admin in Denver and let them know when we are coming. This is quick but very exciting."

Christie was smiling broadly but a tear formed in her eye as she watched Wendy's complete joy. She asked, "Hey Wendy. You seem extremely happy that we are moving. Any reason you're so overjoyed for lack of a better word?"

Wendy stopped and took a breath, "Christie, I have been mired in this town for my entire life. My kids are grown and gone. I am a relatively young woman. I have never lived anywhere else. I have always dreamt of moving out west and from all the research I did, Denver seems like nirvana to me. They get 300 days of sun each year and winters are mild." She added, "Compared to Buffalo's climate it's a dream. The views I have seen are so majestic. I checked the market for housing, and it seems just the right time to buy before there is a major influx of people. Bottom line, I just am really pumped as I just need a change." Christie said, "Let the exodus begin."

Christie was still sitting at her desk in the Buffalo office when her assistant, Wendy McKeller returned, "Well, Christie. When did you hear the news?" Christie replied, "Five minutes before I called you and oh, by the way, did you give anyone a heart attack after you screamed other than me?" Both women laughed and hugged at the side of Christie's long mahogany desk. Christie said, "Sit a minute and let's strategize." Christie, closing the door, said, "Trini came into this office twenty minutes ago and told me I had done a great job so far this month and after winning a great verdict on the Benson case, she wanted me in Colorado. They are promoting me to U.S. Attorney Regional Director. I will work with Judge Phillip Brimmer. I can have the week to pack and travel so how soon can you be ready?"

Wendy said, "I am already packed. I have two suitcases filled. One with work clothes and one with casual attire. I can have my kids send me whatever I need with regards to anything else when I need something. They will put all my furniture in storage until I find a place there and I spoke to Catie Fuda who told me she is moving out to Denver as well."

Christie was happy. She had worked hard here but was now getting a fresh start in Denver; no longer haunted by memories of the awful murders. She couldn't wait to call Perry Kline and hear how he felt about how soon she was coming out to Colorado.

PART THREE

Gray Nash and Eddie Riscoe were pulling out of the garage at Headquarters when they were fired upon from across the street. The agents inside the building rushed out to see about the shots fired, when two loud reports rang off the roof of the building they stood in front of and they watched a man across the street on the roof, stand as another shot rang out. That man staggered and toppled off the five-story roof to the ground.

The two agents in the car were bleeding but still alive. A medic came out of their Headquarters to attend to them as they waited for an ambulance. When one arrived, the two injured agents were whisked away within minutes. The Bureau's mechanic came out and retrieved the car.

Lewis Greeley told Megan to call Dominick Conley. He was the best sharpshooter in the bureau's region. He arrived within minutes and was given the task of working shifts on the roof. Nico, as Dominick liked to be called, entered the roof. The roof wall was five feet high with three turrets in each direction. He intended to set up lookouts in each direction but what he found were stations already set up. The station facing the front of the building had a water bottle on the small desk and after a closer look, Nico found three spent shell casings on the ground next to the edge of the roof to the right of the station. He wondered.

Gray Nash and Eddie Riscoe were released from the hospital later that day and were given two weeks to heal their superficial wounds before returning to duty.

Jameson Martly replaced Nico Conley at 4 pm and would work until midnight. A third agent, Laiza Marie, would relieve him at midnight so the building would have 24-hour coverage of anti-sniper surveillance.

Nico Conley walked up to Megan's desk and said, "Meg, May I see Mr. Greeley if he has a minute? She nodded and pressed the intercom button on her phone, Mr. Greeley. Agent Conley needs to speak with you, Sir." Lewis said, "Send him in Meg."

Nico was a bit nervous as he had not ever been alone in the office of the Director. He stammered as he began, "Cha.. Chief. I saw something on the roof that seemed a bit strange and wanted to let you know as soon as my shift ended. I went up to the roof upon your request earlier this morning after the shooting. I wanted to set up stations on each side of the roof so I could have extra rounds, a place to sit and binoculars at each station. What I found was that someone had already completed that task." Lewis's eyes widened as he listened. Nico continued, "One more thing, Mr. Greeley. The station facing the front of the building where the shooting occurred earlier today, had a bottle of water sitting on the table next to a chair and below the chair were three spent shells from what looked like an AK-47 which is what I was then holding in my hand." Lewis looked at him and said, "How do you think those spent shells got there? Nico was drawing a blank but said, "Maybe one of our agents?" I really don't know. That is why I thought it was important to let you know." Lewis said, "Thank you Agent Conley I appreciate the report. Keep up the good work. Feel free to stop in regularly to give me updates."

Lewis wondered to himself. I think I know who was on the roof, but I hope we find out soon. I will make sure to have security eyeball the badges of all agents and support personnel when they come into the building at the bug-out sight. He said to Dominick, "Thanks for the heads up, Nico. I will look into the matter. Are you all set for the move?" Nico replied, "Yes, Sir. Have a good evening. Oh, by the way, if you want someone on the roof to keep watch during the move, let me know." Lewis replied, "Thanks, I will."

Wendy continued her talk with Christie saying, "Catie gave me the name of a very reputable real estate agent there named, Diane Sorenstone. I already looked at where we'll be working and called her with the specifics I need and when I would be flying out. I made reservations at the Hilton Garden Inn on Welton Street. It is about 5 or 6 blocks from the office. What are you doing for a place to stay?"

Christie was not surprised, "You are so on top of everything. I have no immediate plans, but I guess I could get a room there as well and we can share a cab to the office or walk." Wendy laughed, "I just told them to hold the room next door because I may have my friend stay there as well. Do you want me to confirm with them? I have your credit card info, so I can."

Now it was Christie's turn to laugh, "I suppose you already made airplane reservations?" Wendy just smiled, "Well as a matter of fact I booked us on Friday night with United and we fly into Chicago and arrive in Denver at 7:10 a.m. Saturday morning." Christie stood and walked toward Wendy, and they hugged very tightly and both ladies misted up a bit and Christie said, "I don't know what I would do without you, Lady. Thank you so much. I love you. We should go to dinner tonight and celebrate, my treat." Wendy said, "We have reservations at Magdelane's for 6 o'clock. Do you want to know what you are eating?" Laughter filled the room and both ladies needed tissues to wipe the tears of joy from their faces.

Eric Slay couldn't see anything and had tried to nudge the blindfold several times before they reached their destination. He was very aware of where they were in town as they had not traveled far and driving as much as he did around Sante Fe, he had a pretty good idea where he was.

He thought to himself, 'I hope Christopher called my phone when he sees I didn't return to the apartment as usual.' He was confident that Christopher would. Knowing Christopher, he probably had the militia out tracking him already. The vehicle stopped and the engine went off. He immediately heard a bell in a tower begin to ring. It sounded like the Monastery chapel bell at Carmelite Monastery. They had traveled a little over a mile or so, he guessed 20 to 25 minutes. The men pulled him out of the vehicle without speaking and two of them had him arm in arm walking. He tripped on a stair, but they held him so tight, he never missed a beat. They must be men at least as large as he was. He heard a door creak open, and they began to walk again. He smelled the candles from the Chapel. They sat him in a very sturdy chair and placed ropes on his wrists as well as his feet. They then removed his handcuffs. His arms were stretched to the side, and he found them comfortably resting on a long bench which he assumed was a pew in the chapel. What he heard next was a woman's voice, "Well good morning, Mr. Slay. I hope your car ride was comfortable this morning. I am sorry you missed your coffee. Can I get you a cup?" Eric just nodded his head.

The woman's voice was not familiar to him, but he tried to get her to talk more so he could remember it. She asked, "You take cream but no sugar and generally have a scone. Would that be okay with you?"

Eric's mind was racing as she spoke. She knew exactly what he ordered each day. He splurged on a sweet roll as he walked there and back in the morning as he usually burned it off quickly anyway. He answered, "That would be great. Thank you very much Ma'am." He spoke as respectfully as he could. He heard a bit of Spanish lilt in her voice and knew it was important to be respectful to a woman in power in this situation. She then said, "Eric, do you know why you were apprehended this morning and brought to me?" Eric thought a minute and it struck him then. A woman of power. The Chica Fuerte Cartel leader, Petirrojo Cantante. He said, "With all due respect, Senora Cantante, I assume you know who I am and because of some of the people who are to be sentenced in Denver for illegal activities, you would like to have a bargaining chip." She laughed, "You, Mr. Slay, are a formidable opponent. I guess there is no sense in prolonging the drama. Yes, I am who you guessed. You will be taken care of while you are here as a captive as you are only good to us if you are happy, healthy, and alive. You may remove your blindfold as you have enough rope to move each hand but not together and we are all masked thanks to our recent pandemic protocols. Enjoy your coffee, we will speak further after I contact your new superior."

Eric pulled on the rope, and he could just reach his blindfold. He watched the woman walk away into the rectory area. She was, indeed, masked and wore a very wide-brimmed plain brown sombrero. She was thin yet shapely and wore five-inch heels that clicked as she sauntered along the aisle to the exit door into the office area. Her dress was black satin and clung to her like it was painted on. Eric saw his coffee and scone, his usual order next to him on the pew. He picked up his coffee and it was delicious. The scone was fresh from The Downtown Subscription. He wondered if he was ever going to be outside of the Chapel alive again. He began to perspire. He also worried about Christopher.

Christopher's phone rang as he rode with Ryan to the new office location on the north side of town. He answered, "Hello, this is Christopher." "Well, Good Morning, Mr. Christopher. Please don't be alarmed as Eric is in good hands and doing fine. We will not hurt him unless you and your supervisors fail to comply with our requests." It was Ms. Cantante calling. She continued when she heard the beep of Christopher's phone trying to trace her location, "Please Christopher, don't jeopardize Eric's health by trying to trace this call, we are not novices here.

Please tell your new Bosses, Mr. Coleman, and Mr. Blair that we want the four capos released in Denver by noon tomorrow or Mr. Eric will become another sad statistic of the wrath of the new cartel."

Christopher heard a click cutting off the call. He was unable to trace the call. He looked at Ryan Coleman who was driving the car and listening to her words. Coleman said, "I am calling Micah as we speak to let him know what the situation is." Micah picked up on the first ring. He listened intently as Ryan related the details as they knew them and the specifics of the phone call from the head of the cartel. Micah's response was, "Thanks, call you back." The line went dead. Ryan looked at Christopher and said, "Wow."

Eric heard gunshots being fired not two minutes after he took his first bite of the scone. It was a small bite to see if they had put any tranquilizer on it. The gunshots were right outside. His mask had been returned over his eyes and his restraints tightened. He felt very vulnerable. He heard some yelling in Spanish and clearly heard, 'Vamonos ahora' which, of course, meant 'Let's go now'. He heard tires squealing as engines roared out of the complex. Gunshots were then sporadic and ended abruptly. Then, it was quiet. He heard the large front door creak as it opened.

He heard footsteps but no talking. He began to perspire and thought to himself. 'I have come to the end of my time'. A strong male voice said, "You are going for a ride, Senor. I am tying your hands for your own safety." Eric detected a slight Latin inflection in the voice. It sounded familiar but he couldn't say whether he had heard it before. He felt himself being lifted and walked toward the front door. They were now outside, and he was gently placed into a vehicle.

The ride was not more than twenty minutes. The vehicle stopped and he was pulled out of the back seat. The voice said, "Do not remove the bag from over your head until you count to 50. You will be shot if you do."

With that, Eric heard the car leave quickly and turn a corner on two wheels. He counted quickly and ripped off the cloth bag. His eyes were blurry from the quick exposure to the sunlight. He was at the side door of the Downtown Subscription. He looked around, saw no one, then entered the café's side door; grabbing the phone to call Ryan.

Micah was whisked off the plane in Sante Fe 75 minutes after leaving Denver Airport. He jumped on the New Mexico State Police helicopter and within 30 minutes he was dropped off in the back of the bugout office. As he walked through the door, there sat Eric Slay on the phone. Micah's phone rang and he looked at the caller I.D. and laughed. It was Eric S.

"What the heck are you doing here", said Eric. Micah answered, "I might ask you the same thing, Mr. Slay." Eric said, "I just walked in the door. There was a shootout at the chapel where I was being held by Chica Fuerte. It didn't last long, and I heard them yell to leave out the back door. I was blindfolded when the shooting started. I thought I had met my maker."

"It was quiet for 3 or 4 minutes then a man with a deep voice came in, blindfolded me, tied my hands, put me in a car and dropped me off at the Downtown Subscription where I was abducted hours before. I called Ryan and he called one of the agents from the surveillance team. They had me back here in twenty minutes. I called Christopher first then called you." Micah said, "Well that was strange. Was it any of our guys do you think? Well, if it were, they probably wouldn't have kept you blindfolded."

Christopher walked into the bugout office and hugged Eric and patted him on the back saying, "Nice to see you in one piece partner!" Then he noticed Micah in the room, "Hey Chief when did you leave Denver?"

Micah laughed, "Well, I left about an hour and forty-two minutes ago, which now is the official airtime from Denver if one of our agents gets kidnapped. Ryan called and told me what happened. So, I jetted down here A.S.A.P. Ryan, did anyone on surveillance see who dropped off Eric at the coffee shop?"

Ryan having just walked into the main office said, "No Chief, they were distracted by a woman who asked for directions to the hotel from them as they sat out front. Eric was released on the side of the building around the corner."

Micah said, "Well, it seems folks that our cover has been blown with the agents here by the Lady Cartel, Chica Fuerte, so Eric, why don't you and Christopher go back to San Francisco for a couple weeks of Rest & Relaxation."

Micah then picked up the phone and dialed, "Hello, is this Roger Okie?" The man answered, "Yes, it is. How may I help you?" "Roger, this is Micah Blair. I was wondering if you and Carol could possibly be free for lunch today?" said Micah. Roger answered, "Just a second, Micah, let me check with Carol."

Carol picked up the phone, "Hello Micah, to what do we owe this pleasant surprise?" Micah said, "Hello Carol, can we meet for lunch today? I may have some work for you guys." Carol knew exactly what the work might be, "Yes, we would love to meet you for lunch. Where and what time?"

Micah answered, "How about Dolina's Bakery in an hour?" Carol Imrie gave Roger a thumbs up and said to Micah, "Perfect, we'll see you then."

Next Micah called Lewis in Denver. Lewis Greeley was just about ready to turn over the Denver Region to Micah and return to his Headquarters in Washington, D.C. He was confident after a short period of watching Micah in action that he could more than handle replacing Michael Donlevy, the slain former Regional Director in the Mountain Region. He was anxious to hear any news about their agent in Sante Fe, Eric Slay, who had been abducted on his way to have coffee this morning.

The call came into Lewis' private cell. The phone I.D. said, 'Blair'. Lewis said, "Hello, Micah. How are things in New Mexico?" Micah smiled as he was happy to report good news. Reporting the news this quickly to the Director would be impressive, "Lewis, our agent has been returned and I gave him and his partner a few weeks of Rest and Relaxation until it settles down a bit here. Something unusual happened though that has me puzzled."

Micah continued, "The Agent was taken to a local church chapel initially and served the coffee that he missed having at his favorite café. Then after twenty minutes or so, he was re-blindfolded and listened to what sounded like a gunfight in front of the church as his captures left hurriedly out the rear of the chapel. He was then placed by someone into a car, driven to the coffee shop he was headed to in the morning and dropped off, still blindfolded. He has no idea who it was that rescued him from what he found out was Chica Fuerte's leader, Petirrojo Cantante. I checked and it was not any of our people. Any thoughts?"

Lewis thought while Micah was talking and then said, "Well, it might have been people from El Verdugo. They hate that Chica Fuerte has moved into their territory and might be trying to disrupt anything they try to do. What are you planning next?"

Micah said, "I just got off the phone with Carol and Roger and will ask them to step in for those two men while they go under the radar for a while. I will send Laiza Marie and Jan Casanueva to swing down here to keep the agent numbers up here. I can then go back to Denver as I have a group of twelve more agents graduating from Elite Team Training. I will split them up between the two areas to bring some fresh faces to the Regions."

Lewis smiled to himself, realizing he had made a great decision in appointment Micah, Lewis said, "Great plan. Stop into my office when you get back here. We can chat further. Thanks for the update."

Micah said, "Will do, Chief. Talk to you later." The call was ended. He then called his assistant, Megan back in Denver to see how the bugout was going, "Megan, how are things in the big 'D'?"

Megan was just setting up her computer in the bugout office. The space was a little tight but functional. The bugout location was in an old radio tower building off Hampton Avenue in Lakewood, Colorado. It was set back off the street and had parking for their vehicles as well as office space that was almost as large as their office on the west side Headquarters in Wheatfield. This structure was adjacent to a facility for the Rehabilitation of Brain Injured individuals. There were plenty of vehicles going and coming and this would draw attention away from the old radio station facility that housed the bugout location for the FBI.

Megan told Micah that they would be fully functional in about an hour. This made him feel better. He said, "Thanks, Meg. Nice job getting this together. I will be back in town by day's end so I will let you get back to it. They ended their call.

Catie was meeting with Diane Sorenstone, her realtor today. She dressed casually in sweater, skirt, and tights. Diane texted Catie five minutes before their appointed meeting time of 11:00 am. Catie walked out to meet her, and they left.

In Buffalo, New York, Paul Gorci was the Chief of Detectives. He had worked on the Snow Villain case a while back that put his predecessor in jail for murder. His partner was Perry Kline who had applied for the position of Chief of Detectives but was overlooked in favor of someone out west. He left, and then Paul was chosen.

Perry was very disgruntled but remained friendly with Paul despite this being, in his words. 'a slap in the face'. Now that Perry was working for the FBI in Denver, Paul needed to talk to him as the case he was working on, reminded him that people were not always who they portrayed.

Paul Gorci called Perry Kline's cell phone. Perry answered, "Hello, Paul. To what do I owe this pleasure?" Paul said, "Hey

Partner, if you have a couple of minutes, I'd like to run a scenario by you." Perry replied, "Shoot!"

Paul said, "Great. Do you remember Neal Seagle from the Mayor's office? He had that restaurant in Key West. The bar manager he hired was Jody Petruzzi, who went to jail for smuggling drugs in The Snow Villain case. Wasn't her friend Kathy Mony down there with her?" Perry jogged his memory and said, "You know I think she was also one of the bar maids at Neal's place. Why do you ask? Paul replied, "My girl, Danielle Riches, was down in Key West for a week's rest and relaxation. I told her to stop at the Buffalo Café and say Hi to Neal. She did and she ran into Kathy. Danielle said she overheard Kathy talking about drugs."

Perry got a chill remembering the whole Snow Villain case. There were so many folks that had normal jobs and good reputations but were found to be doing some very illegal business dealings. He was shocked when it all went down but not nearly as bewildered as many of those closest to those individuals.

Those arrested were running drugs through the Café up to Buffalo and points east and west then distributed throughout their established network.

Perry said to Paul, "This may be an indication that the Venezuelan cartel was still working with someone out of Buffalo. Was there anyone still in City Hall that was there when we worked that case?" Paul said, "That's why I called. I thought maybe I could have you look through your notes or check with Micah Blair to see if you could point me in the direction of any possibilities."

Paul Gorci continued his story to Perry, "There is a new mayor in office in Buffalo, and she is very popular with both parties as well as the police, fire, and community leaders. Her name is Diane O'James. She was from Lackawanna, New York originally but moved out to Arcade, New York where she lived for twenty years; she then moved back to the house she grew up in on Cherry Street in Lackawanna. She now lives on Marilla Street in South Buffalo.

Diane is a very attractive lady, with short brown hair framing her perfect facial features. Her figure was the envy of all the ladies in her palates group as well as the men in her cabinet. Her personality was what struck people the most as she could function in any situation from dealing with the Common Council where both parties struggled for the upper hand in political decisions or in a neighborhood bar debate, talking about the local sports teams. She was a huge Buffalo Bills fan. She and her husband Peter were season ticket holders for many years. She had appointed her brother, Dennis O'James to be the police commissioner and because Dennis had such an exemplary record as a patrolman, then lieutenant and subsequently assistant Chief, there were no complaints from the politicians or the public about the appointment.

Paul had told Perry they suspected that there were drugs still being sent into the Western New York area and they also assumed from some of their intelligence that the drugs originated in Venezuela. Perry had given Paul the number of the current Buffalo Region Bureau chief who had replaced Micah when he moved out to Denver. He was sure that Karl Bradley could help.

Christopher and Eric got back to their house in Sante Fe, packed a bag for travel and had Jennifer Redmond, their downstairs neighbor, drive them to the airport. They left their car in the garage and would return in a month. They flew to San Francisco and went to their condo. Upon arriving, they checked their mail and went for dinner. They met their friends, Leticia Rico, and Rebecca Gia at the Crab House on Pier 39 in Fisherman's Wharf where they had dinner.

They had all known each other for years and always enjoyed being together. Eric ordered two orders each of Garlic Truffle fries and crab cakes for an appetizer for the table. He chose two bottles of Jordan wine, a Sonoma CA 2017 vintage. After the first bottle and grazing on the finger food, they ordered from the waiter, Ross. Leticia had a house salad with the Salmon plate.

Rebecca ordered a house salad with Fish & Chips. Christopher had a Beet & Mozzarella salad with the Cod Picatta. Eric finished with a Caesar salad and the Surf and Turf which was a NY Steak and ½ Garlic Roasted Crab. Eric opened the second bottle of wine and began the conversation, "Christopher and I are taking a month off from our jobs to go to Portugal and purchase a house there." Rebecca and Leticia both laughed. Rebecca commented, "So living in the U.S. has gotten both of you bored?"

Christopher jumped in saying, "Well, Eric really likes it in Sante Fe and has made many friends. I, on the other hand, am more partial to San Francisco, where so many of our friends are. We have been talking to lots of folks about Portugal as the language is mainly English, the cost of things is comparatively inexpensive, and the people are very friendly."

Eric added, "I think there are no less than seven couples we know that are seriously looking into buying property in or near Lisbon. Lisbon only has about 500,000 people and the architecture is breathtaking." Christopher then said, "We've made friends in Lisbon. If you guys want to visit us in Lisbon for a portion of our stay, you can then see for yourself how beautiful and peaceful the country is. Are you ladies interested in maybe checking out the area for a potential purchase for a retirement destination?" Leticia and Rebecca looked at each other and smiled. Rebecca said, "Maybe that could work for us."

Micah walked into Lewis Greeley's office at 4 pm that evening. He said, "Chief, I am back. Very strange happenings in Sante Fe." Lewis looked up from his desk and said, "Hey, Micah. Please take a seat. Coffee?" Micah said, "I'll grab one. You?" Lewis said, "I am good. I just made tea. Tell me what's going on in New Mexico."

Micah began the tale of Eric's abduction and then strange reappearance. After he finished, Lewis said, "I think we may have a friend in New Mexico who is maybe undercover. Keep your eyes and ears open for clues or messages from them. You are right, though, it sounds very mysterious. Almost like it was planned for agents to get a few weeks off."

Micah's head was spinning, "Chief, do you think Eric and Christopher set that up to get a few weeks away from their jobs?"

Lewis just smiled, "Well, you never know. Maybe it is someone they are working with who knew they needed to get out of sight for a bit. Like I said, keep your radar on and we'll see what happens."

Micah just sat and imagined how the scenario really went down. He would keep this under his hat and wait for clues like Lewis suggested.

Then Lewis changed directions, "Micah, I am very pleased with how you have handled things in the past couple of weeks. It indicates to me that you not only have the metal to take the needed action, but you are nicely interweaving yourself into the fabric of our family here in the Rocky Mountain region. That said, I want you to know that I am planning on returning to Washington next week. I have lots of other regions to attend to and it is much easier from HQ in D.C."

Micah was shocked, "Well Lewis, thank you for the vote of confidence. We have a very solid team here and with the twelve new recruits we have starting on Monday, we will be in good shape to handle the upcoming challenge. I don't know if you know but we are getting a new U.S. Attorney here in the region. It is Christie Mahern. She was instrumental in helping flush out the murderers in the Buffalo caper months ago." Lewis said, "Yes, I have heard of Ms.

Mahern and her excellent record as a litigator. Let's hope she does as well as a prosecutor."

Catie jumped into the SUV that Diane Sorenstone drove to the main entrance of the hotel at Denver Airport. They exchanged pleasantries and Catie said, "Thanks Diane. I am really looking forward to seeing what Denver has to offer. Being able to find a restaurant space as well as a home to live in would be ideal." Diane said, "I have a bunch of places for both so here we go."

Diane drove out of the airport and headed down Pena Blvd to the E470. She exited south toward Parker and exited off E. Smokey Hill Road. Then east to S. Powhatan and South to E. Phillips Place. The house was a two story 5000 square foot home with a garage on the side. It faced west toward the Mountains. It took twenty minutes to go through, but Catie was not impressed with the layout.

They jumped back into the car and headed back to the E470 highway. They traveled south to the Jordon Road exit turning north on Jordan to Otero Drive then a right on Mobile around the bend to East Phillips Place. Catie said, "Another East Phillips Place?" Diane said Laughing, "Yes, I guess Mr. Phillips' company was quite prolific as a builder twenty years ago so there are no less than 10 streets named after him. It had a small backyard facing a green space. The green space was separating the backyards of adjacent houses and those on the next street behind them. It was forty feet wide and maintained nicely by the Homeowners Association. I think you may like this one. It was a two-story, 4000-square-foot house with a very open concept. Catie carefully looked at the amenities of this house, seeing three bedrooms and a loft with two bathrooms upstairs. A small bath on the first floor with a spacious basement albeit unfinished. She made mental notes to tell Micah when the tour was done. She was not really impressed with the place but did not relay this thought to Diane.

The third house they visited was south from there into Parker. It was off Chambers Road in Meridian Village. It was on Worthington Place and was a gorgeous 5000 square foot two story with a large deck facing west with an outdoor jacuzzi and an indoor/outdoor heated pool. There were two upstairs bedroom suites and two spare bedrooms downstairs with a den on each floor. Catie looked at the price and said to Diane, "This is the one. We need look no further." Diane was ecstatic. And it was only 12:30 pm so she offered lunch. Catie said, "Let's go to that restaurant I looked at the other day."

Diane said, "The Quality Italian on Columbine Street should be just ready to take a couple of ladies for lunch. I'll call for a reservation. Is Micah in town? Maybe we can invite him if you'd like?" Catie said, "I think he was in New Mexico today, but I am not sure I want to bother him at work."

After a delicious lunch, Diane went to her office and prepared the offer for the house Catie had chosen. Catie went to her new bank in Denver, the Wells Fargo on Lincoln Street just north of E 17th Street. She spoke again to the bank President, Michelle Dale who had moved to Denver just months ago with her husband, Randall. They had lived for years in New Hampshire but when Michelle received the new offer, they made the move.

She was given the Bank President position in Denver, they jumped at the opportunity. Michelle welcomed Catie into her office which looked like it was higher than a first-floor office and had a great view of the Rocky Mountains. Catie said, "Michelle, I just found a house that my realtor, Diane is currently putting in a bid for." With the seven-figure deposit Catie had given Michelle a few days prior, she knew there would not be a problem with any purchase she would make but wanted to give her a heads-up. Catie's cellphone rang, "Hello, Diane. Do you have news?"

Catie made a fist pump listening to Diane telling her the offer had been accepted. Catie said into the phone, "I am sitting with Michelle at the bank right now. How soon can you get here with the paperwork?" Catie again made a fist pump, now jumping out of the chair in front of Michelle's desk. She said, "Can we do a two-for-one?" Michelle nodded.

She hung up the phone and said to Michelle. What does the rest of your day look like?" Michelle said, "Whatever you need, Catie." Catie said, "I am buying a house and a restaurant on the same day. How great is that?"

Michelle began getting the forms ready for the bank to process both transactions for her newest millionaire client. Catie phoned Micah. He answered on the first ring, "Hey beautiful. How are you doing today?" Catie was so excited to hear his voice, "Hey Doll. Are you in town?" Micah said, "As a matter of fact, I just got off the plane from New Mexico. What's up?" Catie said, "I am in the process of buying us a house and me a restaurant. I am at the bank and wanted to know if you are available for dinner this evening." Micah said, "I will be there with bells on. Where and when?" Catie was very excited that she would see him tonight and share the news in detail.

Catie said, "I will text you the time and an address, but I am thinking 7 pm at a downtown restaurant. As soon as I wrap things up here at the bank, I will text you the information. Talk to you soon, lover. Let me know when you're done for the day." They ended the call. Catie was brimming with excitement about all she had accomplished since coming to Denver.

At the bugout location, Megan was sitting at her desk and the phone rang. She answered, "International Botany Federation, may I help you?" The man on the line said, "I am inquiring about whether all the butterflies have flown out of their cocoons?" It was Perry. He knew the code to get access to the phone system. Megan recognized his voice laughing, "It has been a while since we used this new system Mr. K. and I chuckle each time I think about making up this code. BUGOUT-BUTTERFLIES." Perry responded, "I don't understand about the IBF?" Megan grinned remembering when she and Michael Donlevy created this backup communication protocol. She said to Perry, "FBI backwards is IBF which stands for International Botany Federation, so bugout. Head Botanist is our leader Micah and I, of course, am the queen bee." Now it was Perry's turn to laugh, "That is very creative, Megan. I am guessing you had a hand in developing that."

Megan just smiled, "Anyway, Mr. K. how can I direct your call?" Perry said, "Micah wanted Ryan and I to return to the cocoon when we had identified the main characters in our federation down here." Megan knew that this meant Ryan and Perry had identified the players on the cartel leadership team and had put together a list of cartel principles." "Hang on," said Megan. She pushed a button to transfer the call.

Micah answered, "This is the Botanist, can I help you?" Perry replied, "Yes sir, Mr. K. here. I have the information research completed. How and when should we return to your location?" Micah replied, "That's great. Have the charter meet you and return as soon as you can with your team. Thanks for the call."

Micah went into the gymnasium of their temporary location. It was time to swear in the 13 new recruits who had completed their training. Megan was at the podium calling their names as Micah walked in with their badges and certificates.

She read: Jan Casanueva, David Moltoni, Donald James, Beth O'Brian, Loren Walters, Donna Kay James, C. Randall Dale, Gayle Arthurs, Troy Phillips, Greg Solo, Levi Bailey, and Quinn Benjamin.

She read a short vow that they all affirmed, and she explained they were now Agents of the Federal Bureau of Investigation.

After they all were seated, Micah stepped to the podium and said, "Welcome and Congratulations to all our new agents. You will be given your assignments today and as you know we are in 'Bugout mode' but we will return to HQ in two weeks. I would like to thank Mr. Lewis Greeley, our National Director, for taking over for Michael Donlevy whom we unfortunately lost last month. Mr. Greeley, would you like to say a few words?"

Lewis stepped up to the microphone and said, "Thank you Micah. I cannot emphasize strongly enough how important your mission is here with the Federal Bureau of Investigation. In this region we have increasing criminality in the form of drug trafficking of fentanyl which seems to be the fastest growing concern, the continued trafficking of illegals from both South America as well as Southeast Asia through Mexico. The newest area of concern will be the influx of women visiting the Planned Parenthood centers in Colorado due to this state's current policy in response to the Supreme Court's overturning of the Roe v. Wade decision.

You all will be busy and an added relief to our current staff who have become stretched very thin. Thank you for your service and Welcome Aboard. I should tell you now that I am leaving after the weekend to return to Washington. Micah Blair will be the official 'Botanist' going forward. Thank you, Micah, for joining us here and helping Megan and me put together this new team. Good luck to all of you."

There was a loud round of applause and Micah then gave them their assignments, had them take the rest of the day off then explained they should report first thing tomorrow morning for duty. The group milled around the gymnasium for a few minutes then the room cleared out. Megan returned to her desk and, there sat, Ryan Coleman waiting in her chair. He said, "Hi, all done with the ceremony? I wanted to ask you a question." "Yes?" she said. Ryan said, "Would it be inappropriate to ask you out to dinner?"

On Monday, as planned, Lewis called Chris Therston and indicated he was ready to leave. Lewis said goodbye to all the office staff led by Micah and took the elevator down to the garage at the Denver Headquarters.

Chris was standing by the car, opened the door for Lewis, and off they went to Centennial Airport. The company jet had landed yesterday and was serviced and refueled awaiting the trip back to Washington. It took 30 minutes to get there, and Chris drove onto the tarmac to the waiting plane. There were three agents going to Washington waiting on the aircraft as they would be decorated in a ceremony at FBI Headquarters later that evening. Chris got out onto the tarmac and opened the door for Lewis. The trunk was opened as Lewis' luggage needed to be carried onto the plane. As Lewis exited the limo, he leaned back in to retrieve his briefcase and shots rang out. The ground crew hit the deck as did Lewis. He turned and saw that Chris had been shot in the chest. Security was out of the terminal and rushing to the Director's vehicle. Lewis then realized that he was also shot.

One of the ground crew on the opposite side of the plane was yelling that the shots looked like they were coming from a small twin-engine Cessna that was on the runway starting its take-off.

Security radioed the tower to order the plane to stay grounded, but the terminal indicated there was no tail number and they had not scheduled this plane to enter their airspace. They watched in horror as the plane sped down runway 1 and got airborne in minutes. The security officers fired on the Cessna but to no avail. They were gone within seconds and headed south into the blue skies over Littleton.

What was left in the aftermath was unfortunately two men shot and critically injured as they boarded the FBI jet to Washington.

Lewis Greeley, the Director of the FBI, was presumed dead. He was carried to the plane, and as the paramedics got out of the plane, it was closed and began its taxi down the airfield to take off. It was in the air going back to Washington within minutes.

The Bureau driver, Chris Therston, was also shot on that Monday morning. The ambulance had arrived with paramedics from the airfield within minutes working feverishly to revive these men, Chris being shot twice in the chest. The local Sherriff's Departments were alerted immediately. They began trying to track the plane that was believed to be carrying the person or persons who shot these two men. It would be a difficult task.

They searched for hours and had many of the police agencies within a fifty-mile radius of the Centennial Airport scanning their radar for this small Cessna. As the search began, an agent spoke to the controller in the tower.

The controller had the intuitive sense to take a picture of the plane with his high-powered camera. They looked for markings and only saw the letters, CF, on the tail.

Megan's phone at the bugout office in Denver never stopped ringing all day. The President, their ultimate boss, called to talk to Micah who at the time had little information to give him but pledged to track down the people responsible and bring them to justice. The Assistant Director of the FBI also offered his Washington team of investigators to assist the regional folks in Denver, but Micah said, "Mr. Director, with all due respect, this may be what the cartels are hoping to accomplish with this attack. Make the FBI scurry around in response to this and lose sight of things everywhere else in the country."

The Assistant Director, Elijah Lindell, responded, "Micah, you make a salient point we must consider. I agree. I will include in my message to the Regional Directors and the President that we are considering this an act of terrorism. I will let your people conduct the investigation but let me know if you need any other resources in support." Micah said, "Thank you, Mr. Lindell. I will keep you closely in the loop as we move forward.

Lewis Greeley's body was on the jet and taken back to Washington. Chris Therston was taken to the morgue here in Arapahoe County awaiting his family's notification back east. Local news media was clamoring for information from the Bureau and all Megan would give them was a statement that Micah had drafted:

On Monday morning at Centennial Airport outside of Denver Colorado, two agents were wounded in an act of terrorism from one of the Mexican drug cartels. No further information is available. The Bureau will put out statements as new information is uncovered in the investigation.

There were no follow-up details, however, the local press was asking questions as was expected. Micah Blair assigned four new agents to travel to New Mexico to bolster the team there. Jan Casanueva, Donald James, Greg Solo and Quinn Benjamin drove in an unmarked van down I25 to Sante Fe. They would arrive at the location there around 5:30 p.m.

Micah then created a Special Investigation Unit headed by Troy Phillips and his partner, Dominick Conley. They were given four of the new recruits who had police or private investigation background, Loren Walters, Beth O'Brian, C. Randall Dale, and Gayle Arthurs. They would investigate the airport shooting.

Quinn Benjamin was appointed the Region's new driver and Levi Bailey was paired with Markus Edwards to head security at Headquarters in Denver as the team would return to that location with the intensified security on the perimeter as well as atop the roof. They prepared for any situation by ensuring there were sufficient agents to handle any potential altercation.

Eric Slay and Christopher Wiser landed in Lisbon the next afternoon. They immediately heard the news of the chaos at Centennial Airport. Eric called Ryan Coleman, "Ryan, we just heard about the shootings in Denver. Is everything okay? Should we return to the States? We just arrived in Portugal an hour ago."

Ryan knew that things were crazy but under control and told Eric, "Stay where you are. Enjoy your R&R. We have everything under control and just put twelve new agents on duty so we're good. I will call if things get hairy. Thanks for calling."

Eric looked at Christopher who had been listening to the call. Christopher said, "Maybe we should take care of the business goals we established for here, enjoy some time with Leticia and Rebecca, then head back to San Francisco. We will then have a 2 ½-hour flight to Albuquerque and an hour's drive to Sante Fe." Eric agreed and they made plans to talk to their realtor in the morning to look at the new condos being built on the ocean.

Perry was exhausted. It had been a crazy week in New Mexico but then with the Director and his driver being shot, everyone was on high alert. He wondered how Christie Mahern was doing as a prosecutor in Buffalo. She had told him that she was promoted and would at some point be moving to Colorado. He thought of the last time they were together and the ravenous intimacy they shared. He was snapped out of his reverie when his cellphone rang. He answered, "Hello, Kline here." The voice on the line said, "Yes, Mr. Kline. Your name was given to me as an excellent guide to the restaurants in Denver for taking a new girl in town out for a meal. Can you assist?" Perry laughed hearing Christie's voice. He smiled as he replied, "I was just thinking about you Beautiful. How are you? Wait did you say, restaurants in Denver???"

Christie laughed out loud, loving that she had gotten him at his own game, "Yes, Perry. Wendy and I flew to Denver last night. We had a late dinner and crashed. We are at the Hilton Garden on

93

Welton Street downtown. I am meeting with a realtor, Diane Sorenstone, tomorrow who has promised to show me our new home.

I will begin working in the Denver office on Monday, so I have the weekend to prepare. Maybe we could have dinner and Wendy can join us. Maybe you could bring along a partner for her to meet. She needs to make some friends here in town."

Ryan drove out to Parker past Lincoln and Jordan to pick up Megan at her home. She was ready to go when he arrived and looked stunning. She was 5 foot 5 inches with light brown hair. She had a great figure, even after having two children. She had a blue dress on which accentuated her cleavage which Ryan had difficulty not staring at. He said, "Wow. You look a whole lot different than you do in the office. Pretty spectacular if I had to put it into words. You look great Meg."

Megan beamed, "Why, thank you, Mr. Coleman. You clean up very well yourself. I hope I am appropriately dressed for where we are going?" Ryan said, "There is no one going to toss you out of any venue looking like that Ms. Rolling." "It shouldn't take us long to get there as it is off I25." Said Ryan. They left the house as she locked the door.

He held her door for her as she got into his vehicle. She noticed it was not an agency car but rather his personal vehicle. He drove a Ford 150 all decked out with the new gadgets. It was dark gray and looked very sleek. Ryan noticed her dress was one of those that had a slit up one side and when she stepped up into the truck, he got quite a gander at those shapely legs of hers. He closed her door and rounded the truck and entered the driver's side. She looked at him and said, "Maybe I will consider your vehicle's difficult entrance if we ever do this again." Ryan laughed, "If the rest of the date goes as well as the first ten minutes, there will definitely be more invitations and maybe some dress shopping in your future." They both laughed and the conversation was much easier after that.

Their drive was only 10-12 minutes as they exited E. Orchard Avenue going north on Interstate 25. They entered Del Frisco's Double Eagle Steak House and used the valet service. The young valet was beet red after letting Megan out of the truck. She just smiled at him and Ryan as he gave the keys to the young valet. They went into the restaurant and were seated immediately.

Ryan asked her what she was drinking. She said she loved red wine, so he ordered a bottle. They both ordered the Shrimp Cocktail.

Megan had the cauliflower steak. He ordered the strip steak. The sides were Chateau Mashed Potatoes and sauteed spinach. They enjoyed their meal and the conversation flowed easily. They didn't talk about work once. They skipped dessert but she asked him if he wanted an after-dinner drink at her house. Ryan said, "That sounds great." He motioned the waiter for the check, they were on their way south on I25 back to Parker. They held hands in the truck, and he had a tough time focusing on driving as her legs were distracting him, and her smile was captivating.

Perry picked Christie and Wendy up at their hotel and they exchanged hugs all around. Perry said, "Boy, it is great to see you both. It's nice to see familiar faces out here in the 'big D'." They laughed and Wendy said, "I guess I will be the third wheel for dinner tonight." Perry calmly replied, "Well not exactly Miss McKeller, one of my partners is meeting us at the restaurant. I hope you don't mind me taking this liberty to invite a friend." Wendy was kind of shocked but remained quiet.

Christie asked, "Where are we headed, Mr. Kline?" "It's right up here off 19th Street on Curtis," said Perry, "it is called Elway's." Wendy got her voice back and asked, "Who is this mystery man you are pairing me up with tonight, kind sir?" Perry smiled at Christie in the front seat, "He is new to the area. He is a private investigator who used to work for his dad back east. I think you'll like him." Perry pulled into the restaurant on Curtis Street and valeted the car. He escorted the ladies to the bar. It was busy and they found an open seat near the end. As they walked up to the end of the bar, the gentleman seated next to the empty seat got up and turned toward them. Wendy screeched and threw herself into the arms of the tall yet burly man who hugged her. They kissed passionately and drew many glances from the patrons around them. It was Markus Edwards. Her beau from 'back east" in Buffalo. Wendy spoke first, "What are you doing here?" Markus and Perry laughed.

Markus said, "Well, I guess that is the most interesting greeting I've had this week. For your information Miss McKeller, I am currently working with Mr. Kline who needed some of my expertise on the case he is working on." Wendy was flabbergasted to say the least, she began a quick-fire stream of questions, "How long have you been here? How long are you staying? Where are you living? Do you have a hotel room or a private residence? How are the kids?" Why didn't you call me to say you were here?"

Just as she was going to continue, Markus interrupted her, "Hi Wendy, it sure is great to see you. Hi, Christie. Both of you guys look beautiful. Is everybody thirsty?" They all laughed.

Perry began the bar order as he had gotten the bartender's attention, "I'll have a grey goose on the rocks, splash of soda and a twist of lime. I also need two cabernets and a Tequila on the rocks." Just then the hostess tapped Perry on the shoulder and said, "Perry, your table is ready whenever you are." Markus and Wendy were hugging again but as the drinks were handed to them. They all toasted and followed the hostess to their table which sat by the window overlooking the mountain view in the setting sun to the west.

Megan and Micah were packing up the bugout office. They determined the time was right to return to Headquarters in Denver. Megan's staff was just finishing up when the telephone rang.

Megan answered the telephone, "Hello." The caller asked for Colonel Potter. Megan yelled for Micah to pick it up. He heard, "Mr. B., This is Quinn B. calling. I am just turning the corner next to your location with a truck, are you all packed for your trip?" Quinn Benjamin was the new driver, and his partner was Jameson Martly. Micah decided that no agent would travel alone for the foreseeable future. Micah replied, "Just back up to the door and we'll start carrying things out." They left most of the furniture and fixtures as they never knew when they would be returning. Deyna Doll, Megan's right hand around the office, began carrying boxes of files to the truck. Micah and Megan soon followed and within thirty minutes, all the computers and important files were loaded on the truck. Deyna drove her car and Megan and Micah rode with her. She was excited to get back to HQ as were all the support staff as well as the Agents. It seemed more secure even though they had received an attack. Micah was determined not to let that happen again, so he was beefing up security as they drove back to HQ.

When they got back to Headquarters, they were met by Dominic Conley. He was their new security person. He helped load the elevator with the office supplies from the bugout office. They took the elevator up to the fourth floor and the equipment was unloaded to the inner lobby.

Megan told them that her office staff would reassemble the offices. She said, "Thank you for making that such a smooth transition."

As Micah left the office, he called Catie to find out a time and place for dinner. He then called in Troy Phillips and Dominick Conley into his office to get an update on their investigation into the airport incident which left Lewis Greeley and Chris Therston murdered.

Micah asked, "What have you gentlemen been able to find out about what happened?"

Troy began, "Well Micah, we tracked the plane down to Chica Fuerte. It landed at the airfield right outside Puerto Palomas Mexico almost exactly two hours after the incident. We have pictures of the plane landing and those exiting the plane." He handed Micah a large, 8 ½ by 11 inch, manilla envelope. Micah pulled out the contents and he saw the photos enclosed.

Micah identified the plane easily from the CF in red on the tail. The first picture he saw was Petirrojo Cantante in her long blonde hair with an AK-47 strapped over her shoulder.

The next picture was a group of four ladies exiting down the gangway, Luna Garcia, Filomena Fuentes, Olivia Hernandez and Sara Sanchez and the final picture was the pilot, Santos Guzman, exiting the plane, also with an AK-47 strapped over his shoulder. Micah looked at Troy and said, "Great work, Troy. I see these are time-stamped as was the picture from the airport that was taken by the controller. This will be a major coup if we can catch them with those firearms."

Dominick added, "Micah, we have a plan to propose when they next cross the border to apprehend them and put them away for good." Micah sat straighter in his office chair, turning toward Troy asking, "Are you ready to propose this plan?" Troy replied, "Micah, we are. I have an infiltrator down in Puerto Palomas who is at this moment working on the ground crew at the airport where that plane landed three days ago.

They will place a tracking device which has a range of 1000 miles so we will be able to track the planes comings and goings until we can apprehend them." Micah said, "I hope you can make it work. It would be a feather in our caps as well as decrease their growing footprint on the illegal activities we are facing these days. Go for it when the opportunity arises. Make it as safe as possible."

They left Micah's office and gathered their team and headed to Sante Fe in an alternate location so they would be in striking distance from any potential crossing of Chica Fuerte into the U.S.

Megan buzzed Micah on the intercom, "You have Ryan Coleman on line two." Micah picked up the phone and said, "Hello. Ryan. What's up?"

Ryan was checking in saying, "Micah, I think we may have found a duplicate plane that was spotted at the airport in the Greeley incident. Perry and I just ventured to Albuquerque to assist with the surveillance of El Verdugo. Our team there was on the lookout for the CF markings and observed one flying into Albuquerque, but it had a different group on it."

Micah was listening more intently now. Ryan continued, "The team there has taken some pictures. I am emailing them to you on the secure line.

It looks like Andres Semanas and a few of his lieutenants getting off the plane. I don't have the number of the plane from Centennial Airport but this one may have different numbers."

Micah pulled the file and looked at the picture of the plane from the Centennial incident. The plane numbers under the CF were 6660-989. He read them to Ryan. Ryan said, "I guess my hunch was right. The plane Semanas just exited here has the number 6660-303 under the CF. Another thing I did was research small jet builders in Venezuela and found a group called Hot Fire which in Spanish is Caliente Fuego (CF). We assumed that it was a Chica Fuerte symbol on the tail, but it seems that both cartels have planes built by Caliente Fuego in South America."

Micah was now disappointed, "Ryan, thanks so much for the info. I will forward this to Troy Phillips as he is heading up the Airport investigation. Great work." They ended the call.

Micah immediately dialed Troy's number. He answered, "Yes Sir." Micah said, "Troy, I just got off the phone with Ryan in New Mexico. His team eyeballed a plane with the CF markings in Albuquerque airport. The only problem was the leadership of El Verdugo got off the plane. The CF apparently doesn't indicate Chica Fuerte, it is a production mark of a Venezuelan company called Caliente Fuego. He and I compared the tail numbers he had with the ones from the Centennial incident, and they were different.

We need to make sure we have these numbers correct as there may be more planes with the CF logo. I rechecked the photos from the Centennial incident and the numbers on the wing are partial, so it could have been either plane."

Troy said, "Well Micah, that sure puts a crimp in our plans. I guess we'll have to keep searching for them. I just heard from the ground crew that the tracking device has been installed. I won't even tell you where it is, but it will never be noticed unless they are dismantling the plane." Micah said, "OK. Keep me posted on any new developments. Talk to you later."

Micah thought to himself, we'll be hard-pressed to nail either of the cartels for the shootings at HQ or the Centennial Airport. I should call my ace in the hole, Camryn Graystone. She was an old friend who had shown a great instinct for finding the motivation of many of the criminals Micah had her study. She was newly engaged and living in Ohio working on her doctorate in, he thought, criminal justice or mathematics. He called her, "Camryn, Micah Blair here. How are you, my dear?" Camryn was very excited to hear from Micah and her voice relayed as much with an almost uplifting lilt,

"Micah Blair. I was just talking to my fiancée Eli about you. What's up?"

Micah answered quickly, "Cam, I was wondering if you could steal away from the Buckeye state for a few days to help on a case?" She looked at her calendar and class schedule. I am writing the draft of my thesis, but I do have a break for the upcoming holidays. When will you send a plane for me?" Micah smiled to himself, "Can you be ready in three hours?" Camryn said, "Of course. The usual spot?" Micah's only response was, "Yes. Same hanger. Tail number EPP16446. See you soon." The phone went dead, and Camryn called Eli into the room to tell him.

She always had a bag partially packed and after a shower and a bite to eat that Eli whipped up, they were off to Wood County Airport which was off Route 75 about 12 minutes from their apartment near Bowling Green University. As they entered the private plane entrance, she flashed her badge and was granted immediate access. Eli knew exactly where to drop her off. She exited the car, grabbed her bag from the back seat and after kissing Eli goodbye, walked into the hangar marked IBF in bold letters.

They were just refueling the plane with 16446 on the tail. The pilot, Robert Pinkerton, walked out from under the fuselage and greeted Camryn, "Hello Miss Graystone. So nice to see you again. Christopher Montrose and I will be ready in five minutes, and we'll be ready for takeoff.

The three-hour flight into DIA (Denver International Airport) was typical. A little rocky coming in from the east with the notorious strong mountain winds coming off the mountains at this time of the afternoon.

It looked like they were ready for a winter storm that Camryn had noticed when she checked the weather report, so she knew what clothes to bring. There was a car waiting for her.

Quinn Benjamin introduced himself and asked her, "May I take your bag, Miss Camryn?" She nodded and said, "You are a new driver, Quinn. Nice to meet you." She was about to ask where Chris Therston, the driver she was used to, was but she reconsidered knowing how secretive the FBI folks were anyway. It was twenty minutes until they were pulling in the rear door of Headquarters.

Megan walked into Micah's office and announced his guest, "Miss Camryn is here, Chief." Micah stood and walked to the front of his desk and hugged his granddaughter who hugged him right back. Camryn stood back and looked at him, "Grandpa, you look good. How have you been?" Micah was so proud of all her accomplishments and said, "I am well but never as well as you, young lady. Eli must be taking good care of you as I have never seen you look better." Camryn blushed and hoped the pleasantries were over, "What is this case I can help with, Nonno?" This was her respectful nickname for him in Italian, while they worked together.

Megan again walked into the room and brought the file he had requested for Camryn to get up to speed before they could proceed. Micah said, "Look this over before we go to dinner. Your room is ready, and Megan has all you'll need. We'll go casual for dinner if that's okay?"

Camryn took the file and got up to follow Megan saying, "That would be great, Nonno. See you at around 6:00?" "Perfect," said Micah, "Thanks for coming!"

Camryn followed Megan down the hall to the elevator and then up one floor to her living quarters. The room looked like a five-star hotel. The amenities were quite lavish. There was a living area inside the hall door which included a sitting area with a couch, loveseat, and two comfortable matching chairs. Behind the couch was a dining table that sat eight people. Back in the corner was the kitchen. It had a small table with two chairs for coffee or a workspace for a computer.

Down a short hall was a room and a bathroom on the left. On the right side was the master bedroom with an attached bath/shower combination. The window in the bath was as wide as the wall above the tub at shoulder level which faced the mountains to the west.

Megan said to Camryn, "I was going to hang up your clothes and store your toiletries, but I had not thought to ask first so if you need any help, let me know." Camryn replied, "Thank you, no. I'll be fine. I just wanted to take a quick shower, and read through the case notes. Then dress in something comfortable for dinner. Did Micah mention where we are having dinner?" Megan replied, "Funny you should ask. I asked where to make reservations and he said to show you to his room at 6:00 p.m. as he is cooking for you." Camryn just laughed, "That is so Nonno!" Megan took her leave.

Back in her office, Megan's phone rang again. It was Jen Andrewson, "Hello, Megan. It's Jen Andrewson. I live with Ryan Swinson who works for you. He left for work yesterday and has not returned so much as a telephone call since. Have you heard from him? I am getting worried because it's not like him."

Megan said in as calm a voice as she could, "I am sorry, Jen. He is probably out on assignment and got involved in an apprehension or other matter that has him distracted. If you don't hear from him again tonight, please call me back. In the meantime, I will check with his supervisor to see if we can track him down and have him contact you." Jen was somewhat relieved but still wondered what had happened.

Megan telephoned Perry Kline. "Perry, Megan here. I got a call from Ryan Swinson's live in girlfriend. She hasn't heard from him since yesterday at nine a.m. Have you heard from him?" Perry recalled, "I sent him to guard the Planned Parenthood office on E. 38th Street with Eddie Riscoe. I will check it out and get back to you." Perry thought a minute and called Swinson's private cell. No answer.

He then called Eddie Riscoe's phone. He got no answer. He wondered.

Perry picked up the tab at the soon-to-be Vincenzo's, Catie's new Restaurant site. He said, "I can't wait to see how this will look in a month after Catie does her magic." They had run into Catie as she was speaking with the current owner, and they found out that she had just purchased the restaurant that day.

She told them she also bought a house saying, "Micah hadn't seen yet." This surprised no one. They waved goodbye as they left knowing they would be regulars. They heard it would be called Vincenzo's not Magdelena's 2 like they thought. Perry and Christie had both eaten at the Buffalo restaurant many times. Perry dropped the ladies off at the hotel, begging off for the night as he had an early call, first thing in the morning.

Christie really wanted him to stay, however, she knew it would have been awkward for Wendy to have Perry in their room. She was impressed as always with Mr. Kline who always made the most thoughtful choices each time a potentially uncomfortable situation arose. A trait she loved about him.

As Wendy and Christie rode up in the elevator, Christie said, "Wendy, I am really head over heels for that man. When I sit at my desk sometimes, I think about my life in Buffalo, New York over the past two years since we met. I was able to land three major cases for the firm, made a ton of money but almost got killed in the process. Saw my brother and best friend go to jail."

Wendy nodded knowingly. Christie continued, "Also two of my clients were killed during the case that Perry worked on and ultimately solved. Now we are living in Denver, Colorado and he has proposed marriage. Wow!"

Wendy said, "Christie, you forgot that you were almost killed in Buffalo, built a successful law practice, and established a reputation as a litigator that eventually prompted you to think about being a prosecutor. Then you were recruited by the State Attorney to realize that objective. You performed so well that they transferred you in less than a month to be the Director here in Denver."

Christie interrupted her and said, "Gee whiz, lady. If I didn't know better, I would think you are preparing to make a speech at my funeral or maybe repeating what my supervisor said after I was just being fired from my job."

Wendy laughed but continued, Oh no, my friend. You are a super, sexy lady and he is lucky to have you be available when he was ready to make a commitment. It is no surprise to me. One who has watched your progress with a very close lens. You deserve all the happiness you seem to be enjoying at this point in your life. You worked like a dog in getting your partnership off the ground in Buffalo."

Christie's mind remembered. Wendy continued, "You used to burn the midnight oil regularly and all that work has paid off nicely. I am sure you and Perry will live a very happy life together. I have seen the sparks fly between you two many times. I must laugh when I think about how you both look like high schoolers when you are together, like you're alone on the planet. Many people in the world strive all their lives for something like you have."

Christie sighed and said, "Well, Wendy, I don't know if I truly deserve all this happiness, but I am certainly going to work at keeping that man happy and I'll try to make our lives exciting and adventurous. I have never felt about someone like I feel about Perry Kline. He sure rings all the bells for me in a lot of departments."

They both laughed because they both knew what she was talking about. They were compatible in so many ways. In humor, sexually, the restaurants they gravitated to, the wine they drank, the movies they both loved to watch, the music on their phones and the music you play around the office is each other's music, just to name a few areas.

Wendy commented, "You do deserve the happiness. I think we all do. My man makes me feel the same way and I wish I could get him to commit and join me out in Denver. Most of his kids are raised and gone so if not now then soon. He really completes me, so I know something about what you're feeling."

Christie said, "I guess you are right Wendy. You usually are correct about things in my life both my professional, as well as in my personal life. I can't count the number of times we have been out together, and you had to steer me away from some Casanova who was just looking for a one-night stand. My heart has always looked for another long-term relationship that has both romance and stability. I never see through those flashy guys that are shallow and insincere."

Wendy said, "You always need a good wingman, girl. It is a tough world out there and sometimes you need 'eyes in the back of your head.'

Eric Slay and Christopher Wiser were on a plane back to the States from Portugal. They had purchased a property on which they would build a house. This would begin in March. They had now convinced five other couples to purchase property there. They were intent on forming their own nirvana. If not that then at least a friendly community that they could ultimately retire to in the future.

They landed in San Francisco. They took an Uber to their downtown condo. It was in the financial district. It had certainly changed over the years. It had become more of a neighborhood rather than a bunch of concrete buildings housing multi-national companies. They were quite comfortable there and had many heated discussions over whether to work for the Bureau in Santa Fe.

As they entered the third-floor condo, Eric's phone began to ring. It was from Micah, "Hello Eric. Have you guys returned stateside yet?"

Eric replied, "Just got into my home in San Francisco. What's up?" Micah said, "Is Christopher with you?" Eric said, "Yes, he just walked in with all our mail." Micah said, "Put me on speaker so I only have to have this conversation once." Christopher said, "I am here Micah, what is this all about?"

Micah said, "Well we had another incident in Sante Fe. Your home there has been bombed. We will replace as many things for you as we are able to, but I have decided that it has gotten too risky for you both here. Would you consider working out of the office in San Francisco?"

Eric and Christopher were stunned; silence filled the room. Micah said, "Are you guys still there?" Eric had muted the phone while they discussed the offer. They decided, at that moment, it would benefit them greatly to only have one home to manage here. The travel there was difficult, having to fly into Albuquerque and then ferry back and forth to Sante Fe. Eric unmuted the phone, "Sorry Micah, we muted you while we checked in with each other. We concur. San Francisco works better for us. Was anyone else hurt?"

Micah replied, "Carol and Roger were not home at the time but their place in the back of yours was shaken but repairable. Nor were the two downstairs neighbors hurt or greatly affected. I can fly to San Francisco tomorrow and introduce you to the regional folks there. I think we are going to put you both deep undercover. Keep your afternoon open for me. I will have Megan let you know when I can get there. Ok, Thanks."

Megan called Lyla Baroni in San Francisco. She was the Regional Director for the Bureau there. The first woman in decades to crack the glass ceiling in California. She was notorious as an agent. She worked for years under cover posing as an insurance professional but was so ruthless with the criminal element that she was known to them only as, Asesina Malvada, which translates to Evil Killer. She rose in the ranks very quickly and her reputation was legendary. She wore so many different disguises that not many people knew what she really looked like. She seldom brought back prisoners from an engagement with the criminal elements, only black body bags. Lyla's phone rang and she answered, "Hello Megan. How are you, my friend? What can I do for you?"

Megan replied, "Lyla, I am well, thanks. I am just giving you a heads-up as we are transferring two agents to you from our region. They live in San Francisco but have most recently been in New Mexico. They are…" Lyla interrupted her, "Don't tell me you're sending me Slay and Wiser?" They both laughed. Megan replied, "How did you know?" Lyla said, "I heard through my sources that they got bombed out of their place in New Mexico and would probably be laying low for a while. When are they coming?" Megan said, "I have sent their files through the encrypted line and Micah would like to meet with you as soon as we can set it up." Lyla said, "Anytime that Micah is available, I will clear my calendar. Put him up at the Americana Hotel right up the block from my office on 7th Avenue. Just email me when they all want to meet." Megan said, "Thanks, Lyla. Could you pencil in Friday morning at ten? I have already confirmed the room for Micah at the Americana. Great minds, you know." Lyla said, "I will have breakfast set up for them in our conference suite. How long will Micah be here?" Megan said, "Just the day. He will fly out late Friday. Thanks, Lyla." Lyla printed the files for the two new agents but really didn't need to.

Ryan Coleman called Megan Rolling. He asked her if Micah would be around on Friday. She told him he was on the road all day. Ryan asked, "Well, since I can't see him, maybe you and I can have dinner again? I really enjoyed your company on our first encounter so I would like to see you again." Megan blushed seeing herself in the mirror on her desk but replied, "Mr. Coleman, I would like nothing better than to have dinner with you. I know a great place that I have been anxious to visit, and it comes with very high reviews from several of my close friends. It is named Avelina. It is in the Fortes Private Bank Building on 17th street, downtown in LODO (The shortened label of LOwer DOwntown). Ryan said, "It's a date. I'll pick you up on Friday at 7."

Gray Nash and Eddie Riscoe were back in the office and got a call from the local PD in Aurora, Colorado. It seems they found a small panel truck sitting on the side of the road under an overpass and it seemed like it was out of gas. The officer in Aurora, Armando Ericas, said the truck smelled foul and they thought there might be a dead body inside. When they pried open the back doors, they found fifteen illegals dead or close to death inside. Gray noted the location and he and Eddie headed out for the location on Rte. I-225 near Parker Road. Eddie let Megan know where they were headed, and she alerted Micah. Micah said, "I hope this isn't going to be the start of a trend." Megan replied, "I can see where these people were being mass smuggled into the states and may not have eaten anything since crossing the border. It is a terrible way to die, being locked in a vehicle either freezing or starving to death."

Micah's phone rang in his office. He answered, "Hello, Micah Blair." He heard a woman's voice say, "Mr. Blair. This is Shayla Beth from Planned Parenthood. We have a situation that we could use your help with." Micah asked, "What is the issue you need help with Shayla?" Shayla replied, "We have just gotten our third threatening phone call today. I have a security guard on site, but he is a nice older gentleman that may or may not be effective in handling any potentially serious issue like the ones discussed on these calls." Micah asked, "What specifically were the threats?" Shayla said, "They all said they will be taking out the doctor that is performing these murderous procedures." Micah said, "I will send a couple of agents to your location as soon as possible." They ended the call.

Micah telephoned Randy Dale. He said, "Randy, it's Micah Blair. I need you to grab Kenny McShaw and go over to Planned Parenthood at 7155 E. 38th Street. See Shayla Beth the Director there. They have received a few threats regarding their doctors. Give me a heads-up as to the ability of their security guy to handle any possible situations. Thanks." Randy replied, "We are on our way, Chief. We'll advise as soon as we can."

Randy pulled his vehicle around to the back of the building and called Shayla from his cell. She answered, "Hello, Planned Parenthood." Randy said, "Miss Beth, this is the FBI, Agent Dale. We are at the rear entrance. I wanted to leave my vehicle back here while we visit." Shayla said, "OK Agent Dale, I am on my way back to get the door for you."

She pushed open the door and let them in. Randy was the lead in the car and began talking with Shayla Beth as they walked to her office. Kenny looked at the young woman who seemed to be in her mid-thirties and a very attractive blonde with several visible tattoos. Kenny also noticed she was in great shape and looked to be either a runner or an active fitness type. Randy asked her, "Does someone answer the telephone live or do you have a message machine?" Shayla replied, "I usually answered the phone as I am the one who generally coordinates the clients with the doctors' schedules of availability." Randy said, "I would like you to use a machine if you have one. This lets us do some things electronically to identify the callers. Do you have a machine?" Shayla eased up a bit and said, "Yes, indeed we do. We just use it after hours and weekends."

Kenny interrupted, "Can we look around the offices? I'd like to meet the security guy and get a rough layout of the security system in place." Shayla felt much more comfortable now that the

FBI was involved and said, "Sure, follow me." She led them to the front entrance. There was an enclosed foyer with an outside steel door and an interior door with a small window no more than one-foot square. Kenny noted that the outside door was unlocked but the inside door was electronically controlled from the sign in desk and had a camera with a monitor at the desk. Kenny asked, "Is the outside door manually locked or do you have it on an electronic opening system?" Shayla replied, "We can do both." Kenny said, "Keep it locked."

PART FOUR

In San Francisco, Micah walked into Lyla Baroni's office on Friday at ten a.m. In her office there was a large oak desk with a matching credenza behind it. There was a large wall of windows facing southeast toward the San Francisco Bay and Oakland. There was a conference table which sat 12 on one wall and the opposite wall had a couple of couches facing each other separated by an oak coffee table. Behind them was a wall of six drawer file cabinets all in Oak. It was quite a spacious office. Lyla stood to greet them at her desk, which also had five cushioned chairs that matched the rug trimmed in oak, facing her desk. In these chairs sat Eric Slay and Christopher Wiser who had already had a cup of tea and a chance to catch up with Lyla. Lyla said, "Welcome to San Francisco, Micah. Please join us. Can I get you a coffee or tea?" Micah answered, "Just black coffee, please. This is quite the office you have here Miss Baroni!" Lyla said, "I redecorated it myself, thanks. I get some great afternoon sun which is great for all my plants. The views are spectacular, giving me the ability to see the waterfront as well as Union Square. Please have a seat."

Lyla continued, "The gentlemen and I had a chance to catch up. We've known each other for some time. I am a friend of Christopher's mom. They are friends with Rebecca Gia who I went to school with down in Miami. So, Micah, why don't you take it from here.

Micah placed his coffee down and said, "Lyla thank you for meeting with us today. These two gentlemen did a yeoman's job in Sante Fe. We were lucky to have their expertise to lead the way in identifying some of the drug cartels' heaviest hitters and the routes and methods that they used coming in from Mexico. However, because of their help, the bureau's work in bringing six of the cartel's more productive capos, they were made by both groups we are working against. As you know, not only was Eric recently abducted on his way for morning coffee but also their apartment was bombed. Our investigation showed that it was ill-timed, or we would not be sitting here with them. So, we decided it best to move them away from Sante Fe altogether. They have agreed to relocate here to San Francisco where they live.

I think they will be invaluable in assisting the region in helping clean up not only the illegals but also the anticipated issues with the planned parenthood locations. We have already had some unsavory phone calls in Denver about eliminating the doctors as well as harassing the clients and staff. Thank you, gentlemen, for all your past work."

Micah's cellphone vibrated. He looked and it was Megan. He said, "This is my office in Denver, it must be important as Megan knows I am with you folks. Excuse me while I take this." He stood and walked to the windows. "Hello, Megan. What's up?" He listened to Megan's report. "Micah, there was a car bomb in the parking lot of the E. 14th Street Planned Parenthood. A lady received only minor injuries, but the staff was very shaken up. McShaw and Dale were on their way to check in with them as they had visited the site on East 38th yesterday. Did you want me to have them call you or can you advise them?"

Micah said, "Have them call me after forensics is completed and ensure their security is round the clock in both locations. Get Denver PD involved as well. Call me after lunch. Thanks."

He turned and walked back to the desk and told them what had happened in Denver. He said to Lyla, "It might be advisable to beef up security at the sites here in town. All the cities like Denver and San Francisco that have identified themselves as sanctuary cities should be alerted." He was sending a text to Megan while he said this to Lyla.

Lyla's Assistant Director Kathy Mony walked into the office having been summoned by Lyla. Lyla introduced Kathy to them indicating she was a fellow New Yorker who came from Syracuse originally. She greeted them all with a request for them to join them for brunch which has been arranged for them in the small conference room next door, "Gentlemen, it is nice to meet you. Would you join Lyla and I for some brunch next door?"

They all rose but Micah said to Lyla, "We can join them in a minute. Why don't you send a memo to the locations in San Francisco of the Planned Parenthood so they can decide to beef up their security. They can also contact the Police or contact you for additional support.

At least you can give them a heads-up that there has been an incident in Denver so they should be on the lookout for any possible threats. Lyla sat at her computer and sent several emails to the main location and asked them to forward the message. She also picked up the telephone and called the Chief of Police in San Francisco, Eric Glenn, to let him know the situation in Denver and the Planned Parenthood sites and they may call on SFPD for security support.

Denver Police was on the scene at the E. 14th Street site when Randy Dale and Kenny McShaw arrived. Randy noticed Assistant Chief of Police, Christian Alfonso standing in the parking lot. Randy went up to him and said, "Christian, how bad were the person's injuries?" Christian replied, "Hey, Randy, the first responders said there were superficial wounds to the woman's arms from glass. They could have just bandaged her and sent her home but just to be safe they took her to CPMC Davies Campus at Castro and Duboce Streets. They may keep her for a few hours or keep her overnight, whichever she prefers." Randy asked, "Any prints?"

Christian smiled, "Man, it was like a fingerprint training class. They were so clear that we got a full set both inside the car on the dash and outside on the roof of the car. We are running them through NCIC as we speak." Randy said, "Thanks, Amigo. Looks like you have everything under control here. If you need anything from us, give us a call. See ya later." Christian said, "Gracias! Buenas tardes mi amigo."

Back in the San Francisco HQ, brunch was served in the small conference room down the hall from Lyla's office. They had scrambled eggs, bacon, sausage, muffins, toast, fruit, and plenty of coffee. When each of them filled their plates, they sat around a six-foot round table. Eric spoke first, "We talked about the move last night and Christopher and I agree it will certainly benefit our situation. We appreciate all the friends we've made in Denver and Sante Fe, but this is our home. We look forward to working with you, Lyla as our paths cross again."

Lyla then said, "Gentlemen, Micah advised us that Denver's abortion clinics have been under attack and their security has been beefed up significantly. We will be doing that here in San Francisco."

Lyla continued, "I would like you to spearhead not only the security of these facilities but also work with the SF Police Department, see if you can find out where the threats and potentially violent attacks have been generated. I will assign you four agents to assist in this operation. Your offices are down the hall so don't hesitate to drop in anytime to chat or ask for support. Kathy Mony will set you both up and give you an admin person for you to work with. I have got some pressing issues so welcome aboard. It is great to have you both here."

Friday afternoon in Denver, Colorado, Shayla Beth locked up the doors and the Planned Parenthood site at 7155 E. 14th. As she walked to her car twenty feet from the door, she clicked on her automatic door opener, the car across the parking lot began to move toward her. She pulled out her small pistol and ran around behind the car. The car stopped and the driver rolled down the window and held up a badge that said FBI. She then recognized it was Special Agent Dave Moultoni. He was relatively new to the Bureau, but a very experienced officer and Shayla noticed after her fright left her that he was quite handsome.

He was tall with broad shoulders and as she described it, smoky eyes. Moultoni said, "Evening Miss Shayla, just making sure you were safely on your way this evening. You will probably see quite a bit of me, so here is my card." He leaned over to the passenger's window that he was talking through and handed her his business card. It had the office number, his name, Special Agent David Moultoni, and his cell number.

As Shayla walked to his car, Moultoni said, "You can call the cell any time day or night as I don't live far from here and will also be working a lot of double shifts." Shayla just beamed at him and said in her dreamiest voice, "Why thank you very much Agent Moultoni. I feel much better now you will be over my shoulder so to speak. Feel free to come into the building to take your breaks or use the restroom. We even have coffee available for you to take advantage of when you need a pick me up." Moultoni just smiled as he looked her up and down trying to be discreet but being rather obvious, "Call me, Dave, Miss Shayla. Have a good night." She answered with, "Goodnight, David."

Christie pulled up to the FBI facility on Saturday morning. She immediately saw Agent Kline, talking to the guard at the gate. He slapped the other officer on the shoulder and walked to Christie's car. He jumped in the passenger's seat, leaned over for a kiss, and said, "I don't usually kiss the Uber driver on the first ride, but you are so doggone beautiful, I couldn't resist. How are you, Babe?" Christie just half giggled as she always did to most things her man said, "Well don't let it become a habit, Mr. Kline. The rate will go up exponentially with each additional kiss." Perry sighed, "Wow, I am going to have to get a part-time job Miss Mahern. I don't think I can keep my lips off you." Off Christie drove. They were meeting Diane Sorenstone, the local realtor, who would be showing them several homes today for Christie and Perry to consider purchasing. They were to meet at the Starbucks on Jordan Road near the E 470 overpass. Diane was waiting.

The only thing that the Bureau had was manpower and intelligence to pursue the cartels and their trafficking. The drugs were coming into the country at an alarming rate as were the illegal aliens who numbered in the thousands daily since the bans had been lifted by the current Federal administration. The governors on the border states were frustrated with the numbers and had begun bussing these folks to the Sanctuary cities that the liberals had identified for everyone in a strategy to get those who had been brought to their state should be given the right to vote. This would enhance their chances of winning elections more handily. Micah sat in his office thinking about this. He wondered whether his current number of agents was sufficient to handle that issue as well as the drug trafficking and the newest concern was the aggressive offense by the cartels to his agents and law enforcement in general. He wished he could speak with Lewis Greeley. Together they would be able to determine an appropriate number.

Ryan Coleman locked his desk in the office in Sante Fe. He was going back to Denver for a few days. He and Micah would strategize about hiring new agents and quite possibly restructure their assignments. He would also be able to see Megan again. He called the motor pool and had them gas up the helicopter.

The chopper was an Airbus H135. It was used for agent transport, supply pick-up and delivery as well as rescue missions all over the region. Ryan had been a pilot in the service and continued his proficiencies. He took Tiffany Nails with him as they had a Vietnamese national in custody in Denver. This woman was running a half-way house for illegals from Asia who were being brought into Mexico then routed into the U.S. Tiffany would be able to better interrogate this woman regardless of her language as Tiffany was fluent in most Southeast Asian dialects.

Ryan left Roger Okie in charge of things in Sante Fe while he was in Denver as Eric Slay and Christopher had been transferred to San Francisco. They landed at the pad behind headquarters after a three-and-a-half-hour flight. The weather was crisp at 11 degrees, but the sun was shining, and the winds were under 5 knots all the way back.

Quinn Benjamin came out to the pad and secured the helicopter for them and prepared to re-fuel it and do the maintenance for their return trip, whenever that would be.

Megan greeted them as they got off the elevator at Headquarters. She sent Ryan to Micah's office and led Tiffany to the fifth floor where the prisoner was being held. Dominick Conley of Security was the jailer that day and brought Tiffany into the interrogation room where the woman was sitting with Agent Gayle Arthurs.

Megan then returned to Micah's office to assist him and Ryan in their staff development strategy. As she entered Micah's office, Micah and Ryan were in a heated discussion about the staffing needs around the region. Ryan was championing not needing more agents and Micah was asserting his authority and knowledge of the history of agents in the field needing fresh troops to maximize the efforts and be able to afford agents the time off away from their intense vocation to maintain their sanity.

Later that day, Camryn Graystone knocked on the door she was told was Micah's in the head quarter's living area. Micah yelled, "Come on in. It's open."

Camryn walked into the living room area and was impressed. It was decorated very tastefully with the couches and chairs a tan leather with artwork adorning the walls in bright reds and oranges giving the room a warm tone that was comfortable. Micah walked in wiping his hands on a towel, held his arms open, and hugged his granddaughter. He took her coat and hung it in the entry closet. They adjourned to the dining room. He poured her a glass of red wine, a cabernet sauvignon and they toasted to each other. She said, "Nonno, I really like your place here." Micah said, "Thanks Camryn. It will do in a pinch, but my lady just purchased a house for us here in south Denver that we'll move into in a few weeks."

"So, how are you coming along with your studies?" Camryn said, "I am working on the Master's; but who knows what I'll end up majoring in. Maybe math or medicine of some sort. So, tell me about the cases you want help with."

Micah said, "Let's eat first then we'll chat afterward over some wine." Dinner was delicious as he made homemade sauce and spiral pasta with bread that he also baked. Camryn said after pushing away from the table, "Wow. Everything was fantastic. Why are you not a chef somewhere?" Micah just laughed, "Thanks. Maybe in another two or three years, I will retire from the bureau and open a little restaurant. Maybe I will just work in Catie's place either here or back in Buffalo." Camryn said, "You think maybe you guys will move back to Buffalo at some point?" Micah thought a minute and said, "We have started to talk about it of late and we have yet to nail down where we'll be. I would like to at least be back East to be close to home. It would be nice to be near your Dad and your younger siblings but that may be a couple of years and they might have already moved to different places in the country by then."

They moved into the living room. Micah turned on his widescreen TV and brought up on his computer some of the paperwork he had given Camryn earlier to look at. After an hour of discussion, Camryn said, "Now that I have a better understanding of what you are up against, I will sleep on this and have a plan for you in the morning. Will you be around at 11:00 am?"

Micah said, "That'll be perfect as I will just be finishing up a strategy meeting with Ryan Coleman." She put on her coat, hugged him, "It was great to see you and I enjoyed the meal immensely, thanks." Then she left to return to her room and begin her investigation for the Bureau.

Perry and Christie followed Diane north on Jordan to Otero Drive then a right on Mobile around the bend to East Phillips Place. This is the three-bedroom, two and a half baths home she showed Catie last week. They saw the large deck and green space in the back. The large bedrooms as well as the open concept on the first floor. Everything was perfect for them. There was a loft area just outside the master bedroom at the top of the stairs that would be used as their office. Diane met them in the kitchen and they both said, we like it. They said, "It is perfect for us. Enough room for us, not a lot of maintenance and it looks like a quiet neighborhood."

Perry added, "I could even make the third bedroom an office if we wanted. We'll look at whatever else you have scheduled but this might be the one." Diane said, "We can look at two more that are representative of what is out there. Let me know after those if you want to continue or put in an offer. It was about two hours later that they had looked at three other homes in Littleton, Highlands Ranch, and Lone Tree. Diane offered to buy them lunch and Perry said, "Diane, this has been great, but I must go back to work as does Christie. We have decided to put in an offer on the first house we looked at on East Phillips Place. You have both of our cellphone numbers but Christie is working the money on this one so she can do the negotiating."

With that said Perry and Christie gave her the number for their offer and drove back to FBI HQ. Perry kissed her goodbye and walked into the building. As Christie got to her office, her cell rang.

It was Diane Sorenstone, "Hello, Christie. It's Diane. The people accepted your offer as they are really looking to move back to the East Coast as soon as possible. Give me your fax number and I will send the forms for you to sign. I am having my associate do the house inspection as we speak. I have noted that they will be responsible for tearing down and removing the deck from the backyard and we should be able to close by the end of the week."

Christie said, Nice work Diane, Thank you." Diane continued, "I have already called my friend at the bank, Michelle Dale, who has begun those papers as well. Congratulations. You and Perry are now homeowners in Colorado."

Christie was ecstatic, "Again, thank you so much, Diane. You have been so great to work with. We really appreciate it. We'll talk soon." She then texted Perry as she knew he was probably busy. She kept it short: 'House is ours. Offer accepted. Sign papers when you get home. Love You C.'

Camryn Graystone sat in her room at FBI Headquarters. Reviewing the cases that she and Micah had discussed. The first was the raid on HQ the second was the shooting at the Centennial Airport which was a busy yet much smaller venue south of the Denver International Airport. She looked at the notes that Micah and his team had put together.

The notes were very comprehensive. They expanded on how the operations of El Verdugo and Chica Fuerte were seriously impacted by the arrests and pending imprisonment of four of the highest-ranking capos or lieutenants. Two from each cartel. Camryn thought, 'This'll be a snap.'

Camryn's phone buzzed. It was a text from Eli Thomas, her boyfriend. It said: 'Hey Girl, did you get there okay? Just waiting to hear.' Camryn picked up her phone and dialed Eli, "Oh My Good Grief, Eli. I am so sorry. I got caught up with my granddad and just sat down in the room he set up for me. I feel like such a jerk for not at least texting you when I landed. Please forgive me." Eli replied, "I am sorry. You must have the wrong number." Camryn laughed. He had such a great sense of humor and a gentle heart. He always made even the most untenable situations easier.

She said, "You're a nut. Really, I am sorry." Eli said, "Cam, I just wanted to hear your voice. I knew you would be caught up in the cases Micah wanted your help on, but I wanted you to know I was thinking of you. No worries." Camryn just beamed, "This is why I fell in love with you Eli Thomas, you are just the perfect Ying to my Yang, or however that expression goes. Thanks so much for rattling my cage. I was caught up but it's great to hear your voice as well. Thanks for being you." They said good night to each other and hung up their phones.

Camryn refocused on the cases in front of her. As she read, she realized that the cartels were described quite differently. Chica Fuerte was led by a woman. Their suspected primary objective was to compete for leadership in drug smuggling and distribution in the U.S. The other cartel, El Verdugo, was clearly upset with the Bureau's ability to infiltrate them and take down several of their most important lieutenants. Their primary objective seemed to be supremacy in drugs but also the demise of their 'sister' cartel. Camryn read for about an hour when she saw something that made her stand up and yell out. "Holy Crap!!"

She had to contact Micah to tell him of her findings. She knew it was getting late, but she realized that the information was vital and could potentially save many, many lives of not only agents but also the citizens who came unknowingly into the paths of these ruthless cartels.

It was the third time they had been out on a date. Ryan and Megan were sitting at a table in the Funguyz Bar in Parker. It was quiet so far for a Thursday night. There were maybe a dozen people in the place as it was early. They ordered some wings and a couple of beers. They began to share their life stories with one another. Both had been married before. They each had children. Megan had two and Ryan had three children. They were both looking for a long-term relationship with someone who was family-oriented, financially sound and had no hang-ups about their ex-spouse. They both decided that they had little baggage and were headed down the same highway in life. They were both a bit tentative about making another lifelong commitment, but they had great chemistry,

Megan said, "You know Ryan, we should really keep our relationship on the down-low until we decide whether or not we are going to be long-term." Ryan replied, "I don't know what the company policy is about office relationships but most often, they are frowned upon."

They decided to see each other on Saturday as neither had kids. He would cook for her at his place and maybe if that went well, they would introduce the kids at an outing in the future. He dropped her off at her house and she asked him to come in for coffee. He said, "Megan, are you wanting me to drink coffee with you or are you going to seduce me?"

Megan laughed, "Mr. Coleman, if you don't want to come in and extend this date a while, just let me know. I don't want you to feel obligated." Ryan laughed and said, "Well Miss Rolling, I would love to come in and extend our date until morning if you want to know what is really on my mind." She blushed, as she led him into the house and she started to make coffee, but Ryan walked up behind her and spun her around to face him. They kissed. It was electric and they both moaned in pleasure. She took him by the hand and led him down the hall to her master bedroom and closed the door. This was by habit as they were alone in the house. Within minutes they were divested of their clothing and laying naked on the bed. It was magical, she remembered thinking. Ryan was thrilled with her passion and her ability to light all the fires that had been left dormant for months. Their lovemaking was intense and satisfying. They slept.

Camryn walked down the hall to Micah's room. She knocked on the door and he opened it to find her in a long-sleeved pajama set of silk with a pair of slippers on her feet. He said, "Come in. What's up?" Camryn had the files under her arm and sat at the kitchen table, "Well, I think I have some findings and I didn't want to wait another minute before letting you know. Sorry for barging in like this but it might be important." Micah said, "I am all ears, Cam. Fire away."

Camryn showed him two pieces of paper which clearly indicated that the leaders of Chica Fuerte and El Verdugo were, in fact, brother and sister. The second piece of paper showed that both of their spouses were related as well. Micah was flabbergasted, to say the least. He was really interested to hear more about how this impacted their future strategy.

Camryn said, "I made some calls to the folks back in Buffalo who worked on the Snow Villain case and found that the father of both cartel leaders was the leader of the Venezuelan cartel that had been running drugs into Key West, Florida. He is Carlos Secondas. They had gotten close to charging him with drug smuggling and international law violations, but he went deep into the countryside and could not be located."

Micah was astounded by Camryn's findings but very impressed with her insight. This wasn't really her area of expertise. He said, "Wow, that tells us a lot. What else have you uncovered?"

Camryn lowered her voice and said, "Is your apartment clean?" Micah looked at her quizzically, "What?" Camryn took out a scrap piece of paper and wrote, 'When was the last time your rooms were swept to remove bugs?'

Micah started to laugh then thought, 'probably never' but wrote on the paper; 'If this isn't clean, I will certainly have the guys up here first thing in the morning. Why?" Camryn wrote again, 'I think you may have a mole in your operation. I think it may be the daughter-in-law of Andres Semanas.'

Micah walked into the hall motioning for Camryn to follow as he made a call with his cell. Micah called security. Loren Walters answered the phone, "Security. How can I help you Mr. Blair?" Micah replied, "Loren, is there anyone in the building that can do a quick sweep in my apartment for bugs?" Loren said, "I will send a crew right up, Mr. Blair." Micah said, "Thank you." So, now they could talk freely while they waited for security to arrive.

He called Megan Rolling on her cell. She was still in the building, "Hello, Micah, what do you need?" Micah said, "Could you call Buffalo Police and find out the name of the guy who took over as Chief of Detectives after Parker Clark went to jail? I also need the name of his wife. They are supposedly living in Denver." Megan said, "I am on it. Where are you?" Micah said, "I am in my apartment with Miss Graystone. Call me if you hear anything." He hung up.

Loren Walters and his three-man crew arrived in minutes from them exiting the apartment. Loren exited the apartment after five maybe six minutes, "Chief, my ace found three bugs. Doug Paver is an electrician and free lances with us. Everything is clear now. Do you want a complete sweep?" Micah said, "Thanks Loren. Yes. You, I and Megan are the only ones to know. Camryn, you're in 433, right?" Camryn replied, "Yes, sir." Micah said to Loren, "Start with her suite then Megan's and work from there." Loren said, "We're on it, Chief. I will let Megan know when we have completed the sweep. Usual protocols will apply until you hear from me or Megan."

The protocol meant he would be to sweep rooms on a weekly basis until no bugs were found. The all clear would be reported to

Micah and he would then decide whether to continue or discontinue the sweeps.

Micah escorted Camryn back into his suite. Micah asked her, "Why did you ask about debugging?" Camryn just smiled and said, "Well, Nonno. I listened to you for many years talk about security. The new person in a facility was always most vulnerable to a bug as folks wanted to know why that person was called into service. The bad guys have ways of getting their people into even the most secure facilities as servicemen of some sort. You should suggest to Megan that it might be time to go through a clearance sweep of all her vendors. TV guys, electronics, plumbers, etc." Micah was impressed, "You are special Miss Camryn. Thank you. Now, tell me more about your findings."

They spoke for maybe 20 more minutes and Camryn closed her files and sauntered off to her room hoping it would be cleared of bugs as she wanted to rest as it had been a long day. They hugged goodnight and she left.

Camryn got to her suite as Loren and his crew were leaving. Loren said, "Oh, great you are here. We found 12 bugs. You're clean now. Here is your new key. You and I are the only ones who have it as I changed the pass lock. You should not have any more visitors on this visit. Goodnight." Camryn felt relieved, "Thank you, Mr. Walters. Good night."

Micah called Megan Rolling on the office phone. The call went to voice mail, so she was gone. He would talk to her in the morning about what he had learned from his meeting with Camryn. He was a bit shocked that they could be infiltrated so easily. Maybe he would go down to the office and snoop around a bit and see if he could do some bugging of his own. He had an uneasy feeling about the people who surrounded him each day here at Head Quarters.

Megan went into her apartment after getting some paperwork done. She needed a shower and then she would send one of the drivers out to get a restaurant to go order. She unlocked the door and flipped on the light, but it remained dark in her suite. That was odd she thought. As she closed the door, she was grabbed from behind, a gag placed in her mouth, and a cloth bag over her head. The person was strong holding her close.

A soft voice said, "Don't make a sound. I am a friend and won't hurt you. I need your help. I am going to sit you down on the sofa and then I will turn the lights on. Then I will take off the headcover. OK?" Megan trembled but nodded her head. She was led to the sofa, and she sat. The intruder had taken her purse, so she just stayed still. She felt them return and then she could see when her head covering was lifted off her head, however, the gag was not removed.

As her eyes got acclimated to the soft light, she turned and screamed. The gag muffled her scream. She began to cry. There behind her stood Michael Donlevy. As he removed her gag he said, "Don't make a sound." She stood and they embraced. Michael said, "The security team just left five minutes ago. They found three bugs, so you are clean. They will be looking for you to give you access with a new key. You should have a message on your phone. "

He added, "Call security back and wait outside to get your key then we'll talk." He led her by the arm to the door. He gave her the bag she had been carrying. She felt like she was in a cloud and saw nothing else but the serious look on Michael Donlevy's face. She thought, 'IS HE ALIVE? MAYBE I'M DREAMING?'

She stepped out of the suite. She grabbed her phone and responded to the message. It was Loren Walters who answered, "Yes Miss Megan. Your residential suite has been swept and we have a new key for you. Where are you now?" Megan began to talk but nothing came out. She had to clear her throat, "Uh hmm. Hello

Loren, I am standing at the door of my suite unable to open it." Loren replied, "I am sorry for the inconvenience, I changed the lock code. I will run upstairs immediately with your new key. No one will have the key but you and me. See you in a minute. I am just on the floor below." He hung up.

She stood in front of the door and as she put her phone back in her bag, the hall door opened, and in walked Loren with the key in hand. Megan said, "Did you run up the stairs?" Loren handed her key to her, and she could see he was breathing hard from running up two flights of stairs. He said, "Yes Miss Megan. We must have just missed you as we left not ten minutes ago. Sorry for the inconvenience but we found three bugs, so I changed the lock." Megan said, "Take a breath!" Loren sighed and said, "You are clean now. I am working to get the rest of the folks completed. We only have one more floor to complete. We should be done by 10 p.m. I will send you and Micah an email when we are finished. Goodnight." Megan said, Goodnight Loren. Thanks."

She entered the suite with the new key and Michael was standing there waiting. They embraced again. She was crying, "Why haven't you contacted me before this?" He said, "It is a long story. Sit. I'll pour us both a glass of wine."

Megan was shaking when she sat. She couldn't stop crying. Michael returned to the sofa and handed her a large goblet of red wine. She took a long draw from the glass and set it down on the coffee table. She said, "Well?" Michael Laughed, "Well first, I want to apologize to you for not including you in the ruse. I had received word that the cartels were heading this way to get me. I just put their boys behind bars. I knew I had to go way undercover, to get them off my back. Micah is the only one that knew. We used a bunch of actors from a local theater group in Boulder. It is the Boulder Ensemble Theatre Company. They were held to secrecy when we told them it was a training project for the Bureau. Most importantly, it was a life and death matter to keep it under wraps. They were great. Everyone did their part and news of my demise swept into the Mexican cartels within the hour. My contacts in Mexico indicated that there was actual cheering when the news arrived about my death. I contacted Lewis to advise him. He said to let Micah know but no one else. It was difficult to just leave without contact but to throw off the cartels, it made sense to do it this way."

Megan had many questions to ask but she waited and let him talk. He resumed, "Each cartel thought the other was responsible for the action on me. So, I have been in disguise in Sante Fe since and I spent a couple of weeks at El Verdugo's neighbor's house. It just happened to be my old friend, Robert Acrum, who I worked with after college. He is a painter and amateur wine maker. He gives the cartel a few cases of wine each year and they leave him alone and provide him with air-tight protection. I was introduced as his sister's ex-husband, Sam Barfield. I was working in Sante Fe when Eric Slay was kidnapped by Chica Fuerte. My crew and I shot up the church where they held him. We were lucky enough that they ran like rats and left him."

He stopped and said, "Here drink some more wine." She took a large gulp and held onto her glass. He continued, "I was the one who gave him a ride back to the Downtown Subscription and just dropped him off. I drove past the surveillance team just as they were being harassed by one of my neighbors down there asking them a bunch of questions to distract them while I dropped Eric off at the side of the building. Okay, a couple of more things, Lewis Greeley is not dead." He let that fact sink in as he knew he was overwhelming poor Megan. She sat there and stared at her former boss thinking, 'I don't even really know this guy.'

Michael Donlevy continued, "Greeley had a superficial wound and left on the plane after the paramedics patched him up.

Chris Therston was hit twice but recovered and was flown to Scottsdale, Arizona where he has been doing some physical therapy and catching up on his suntan. He wants to come back to work and may join us when we begin our next operation. Any questions?"

Megan had composed herself by this time and said, "I am so blown away Mr. Donlevy. I spent a good number of days pining over your loss. I am glad everyone is fine. What's next?" Michael said, "Hungry? Why don't you call down to the kitchen and have a pizza sent up."

Megan did just that, Michael continued, "I am a bit hungry and after we talk, I need to lay down for an hour or two so I can slip out of here before morning. I will sleep on the couch."

Megan had called down to the kitchen and asked them to send up three calzones. She knew Michael preferred them. She hung up and asked him, "I have questions. What did you plan to accomplish with this whole ruse?"

Michael replied while pouring more wine, "I knew if I was dead, the cartels would lighten their scrutiny for a while, as they know I am a bulldog. With me dead, they could relax somewhat and concentrate on their illegal operations."

Megan said, "I can't believe you went to such lengths to ease the pressure from the cartels. You know there are a lot of people who were very broken up emotionally when you got shot."

Michael said, "Again Megan, I am truly sorry. If the cartels were going to buy into this, it would have to be believable to all. It also brought about an added benefit. I was able to go undercover instantly. I spent some time in Mexico and even had a drink with Semanas at the local bar in Puerto Palomas, Mexico. It was a little dangerous but very informative as I was able to befriend one of the capos that we didn't arrest. He gave me some good ideas about their vulnerabilities and manpower or lack thereof, I should say."

131

The food arrived and they ate the calzones with a bottle of Michael's favorite wine. When Megan opened the bottle and poured them each a glass, Michael said, "Did you know I was coming back or were you saving this for someone special?" Megan laughed, "Well to be perfectly honest, I have met someone, but the wine was purchased when you were still my boss, in case, we ever had the opportunity to share a glass socially." She thought to herself, 'It was purchased in hopes of my fantasy being fulfilled as I had a huge crush on my boss.' She would never let on now.

Michael said, "I am glad you and Ryan found each other. He seems like a perfect fit for you. I hope it works out for you and your secret is safe with me", he laughed, "I am dead as you well know." Megan joined him in a laugh and was surprised she knew who she was involved with, but sensed he was disappointed that she was not available now. Maybe it was wishful thinking.

Perry and Christie were moving into their home in Englewood on East Phillips Place. They met the neighbors on either side of them. Joanne Washington was a beautiful, white-haired lady who was very friendly but said she kept to herself and had a granddaughter doing her yard work for her. Josh and Tara were on the other side and were a newly married young couple with no children but one on the way. Perry and Christie worked all day unpacking boxes and had their bedroom set up and much of their kitchen and dining room put together. Their living room furniture was scheduled to arrive from Furniture Row the next day. They worked until four o'clock then showered and got ready to go to dinner.

Perry said, "I worked harder today than I have in years. I better make it an early night so I can give my body some recovery time. Where shall we eat?"

Christie walked out of the closet with just her bra and panties on and said, "Should I go like this or put a dress on?" Perry laughed, "You better put a dress on, or we may never leave the house and end up ordering takeout." They both dressed and went to dinner at the Perfect Landing Restaurant. This was a quaint little place at Centennial Airport not far from their house. Jimmy, the owner, met them at the door. He welcomed them and sat them at the bar per their request.

The barmaid was quick to serve them a glass of Sauvignon Blanc for Christie and a Grey Goose on the rocks with a splash of soda, and a twist of lime for Perry. They sat there for almost an hour chatting with Crissy, a tall brunette who was an amazing bartender as she worked the 22 seats at the three-sided bar as well as the service bar on the fourth side. Jimmy the owner came over and told them their table was ready. Perry asked him about opening a bar when he retired from his current job.

Jimmy said, "It's too late for you to start now, Perry. It has taken me 25 years to know what to stock, what to have on the menu and how to staff my restaurant so that I can manage it and enjoy my life. The last two and a half decades were spent in my restaurant twelve to fifteen hours a day, six or seven days a week. Now I can pick my times and delegate some of the responsibilities. Now, I work two or three days a week and have time to travel, play and do the things with loved ones I missed over the years."

Perry and Christie were waited on by Gayle Arthurs. She was a friend who had moved from Maryland, but her dad was originally from the Buffalo New York area. She was an agent for the Bureau. This was her 'second front'. Many of the agents had a part-time job to not only make some extra cash but be seen by their friends in town as regular citizens. It kept a bit of anonymity for them. They ordered the chicken scampi which was a crowd favorite and always a special on the menu. They both had another drink as well.

Christie said, "I am really excited about the house. I can't wait to plant shrubs and do something about the back lawn. Maybe we'll get a landscaper to come in and put in a new lawn." Perry said, "I noticed that Tara and Josh next door had installed an artificial turf lawn in their backyard. It is south-facing and gets the unmerciful sun almost year-round. Denver was notorious for 300 days of sun annually and being a mile closer to the sun, it was not great for growing flowers or lawns back there. We need to build a deck. We also should get an umbrella or canopy so we can sit on the deck and have drinks and hang out."

Christie laughed, "I know. Even sitting out there this weekend, it was tough to take a break from unpacking boxes and cleaning. I spoke about it to Diane Sorenstone, and we talked about one of those canopies that crank out remotely, but her concern was the frequency of the high winds they have here quite all year round."

Perry looked toward the door and realized it was his boss coming in. Micah and Catie were standing at the entrance waiting to be seated. Perry said, "Hey, Christie, there's my boss, Micah Blair, and his girl Catie. I think her last name is Fuda if I remember correctly. Should I ask them to join us?" Christie said, "Why don't you go over and find out? If they are going to have dinner maybe, we could ask Gayle to put their order in right away so we could eat together or meet them at the bar for a drink afterward." Perry got up and said, "Great idea."

Perry got to them as Jimmy was about to seat them, "Hey Jimmy, this is a good friend of mine. Hang on a second. Micah, Christie, and I just ordered, do you want to sit with us at the window or can we buy you a drink at the bar after dinner?" Micah looked at Catie and she nodded.

Micah said, "Catie says we'll join you. This will guarantee there will be a dinner conversation that is not work-related. I agree with her. We'd love to join you guys." Jimmy loved this as he doubled the orders from that table, and he could then seat another couple waiting for a table. He escorted them back to Perry and Christie's table at the window.

They began talking all at once when Micah and Catie were seated. Then they all laughed, and the waitress arrived to take their drink order.

The waitress suggested they have their dinner order ready when he returned as Perry and Christie had already ordered. Catie and Christie were talking about their new houses and made plans for a get together in two weeks to show off Christie and Perry's place first. They would meet on the following weekend to party at Catie and Micah's new place. Dinner went well.

Dave Moultoni was sitting in his vehicle at the back of the parking lot of the Planned Parenthood office on E. 14th Street in Denver. It was almost 5 o'clock which was the normal quitting time for their staff. It was also his time to change the guard with Barry Moeller who was scheduled today. Dave could see Barry drive into the parking lot as one of the Doctors was exiting the building. Dave looked to his right and saw movement on the roof of the adjacent building. Two men about 12 feet apart with long rifles were poised at the edge of the roof.

Dave got out of his car and yelled to the doctor, Helen Mantila, "Doctor, get down behind a car, QUICK!" He was running toward her as she ran toward her car. Dave yelled to Barry as he exited his vehicle, "Shooters on the roof NEXT DOOR!"

Then shots rang out from the long guns. Dave stopped behind a car and yelled into his radio on his shirt, "HQ-Moultoni at Planned Parenthood on 14th. LIVE SHOOTERS. SEND BACKUP!!" Bullets careened off the car he was at, so he began firing his weapon at the men of the roof. He looked toward Dr. Mantila and realized she was face-down behind a car. He saw she was bleeding. Barry Moeller yelled to him, "Dave, I hit one, but the other guy is reloading!" Dave got up and ran toward the doctor. He felt his legs go numb and he fell to the ground. He could hear sirens then he blacked out.

Backup arrived. There were three units in the parking lot. They found all three people in the parking lot had been hit. They called for ambulances immediately. The doctor was hit once in the leg but was alive. Dave Moultoni was hit twice and passed out. Barry Moeller was unlucky. The sniper who had reloaded got him with their first shot. He was dead.

Next door to Planned Parenthood, two units had responded for backup and were able to detain the perpetrators who were exiting the building to their vehicle with their rifles slung, one carrying the other who had been wounded. There was no further action as those two were immediately transported to Denver Police for questioning. The arresting agent was Randy Dale who was assisted by Levi Bailey. The two gunmen were members of the El Verdugo cartel. The first, Louis Castro, was injured in the gunfire exchange. The second, Jose Ortega was yelling in Spanish but when Levi Bailey answered in perfect Spanish, he calmed and became silent.

Michael Donlevy went back undercover after leaving Megan's room at the Bureau's HQ very early, the next morning from the facility in Denver. The only ones who knew were Micah, Megan, and Lewis Greeley, who Megan found out was still alive in Washington. She was sworn to secrecy. At her office, Loren Walters sat at her desk waiting for her arrival. She was shocked to see him this early.

She said, "Well Mr. Loren. Did you get the worm this morning?" Loren said, "Haven't been to bed yet Miss Megan. I did see the early bird, so yes. I wanted to report in before I crashed for a while. You can read the report but in the 100 rooms we swept, we found all but one had bugs. I am happy to say that Micah's office was the sole clean room found. They have all been swept. I will have my gang do this again randomly in the coming weeks. We should maybe have all our service companies send a particular tech when we request work done. If an unfamiliar service man comes in, we may want to send him away lest we open the vulnerability of our security. This will help control the number of outside vendors that we allow into the facility. Do you have any thoughts?"

Megan had her coat off now and the coffee pot was just about perked, "Thank you, Loren. Great job as always. I will have my staff log in the visitors going forward to include guests. I will have the security schedule more random walk throughs of the floors. We will designate a serviceman for each vendor we use, and we'll see where we are in two weeks. We have a bunch of new agents so maybe I'll put our office team on background checks again. I will not send a memo, but each team leader will be notified that we are watching all the people who enter the building." He was making notes as she spoke.

Megan continues, "Maybe you could set up more cameras in the halls so that only you and one other person know they have been implemented so we can keep our eyes open even when we are supposed to be sleeping. Then we will see after the first week if we have been effective."

Loren got up to leave and said, "I am going to catch a few winks then install cameras tonight as I have a skeleton crew on." He left and crossed paths with Micah who had just entered the office. Megan said, "I have Loren's report here. I'll grab a coffee for you and be right into your office." She handed him his black coffee and said, "Yours was the only clean room out of a hundred. We are doing random sweeps and adding a few more cameras that only Loren will know about. We'll see in a week. I also sent a memo to Loren and his staff that everyone who has access to the building will swipe their badge each time they enter the building. Guests will also be logged in so the only thing I have left to do is recheck the vendors that we use here for electric, plumbing, HVAC, and cleaning, etc. The extra cameras will help with those folks who are here when folks are away from HQ overnight to ensure the cleaning staff does not enter any unauthorized areas.

Micah said, "Well done as always Meg. You look a bit tired today, were you burning the midnight oil last night? It looks like you could use some of this coffee. I am going for another cup. Can I get you one?"

Megan replied, "No thanks. I just got a refill when I got yours. Let me ask you a question. Since Lewis Greeley was killed, do you know who has taken over his duties in Washington? Who are you reporting to now? I have asked around and no one seems to know."

Eric Slay awoke at his regular time. Early in the morning, he dressed and readied to walk to his local coffee shop. In San Francisco, he went to Philz Coffee on the corner of Folsom and Beale Streets. It was about a block away and he knew the people there as he was a regular visitor. As he walked down the street, he thought about the last time he walked in the morning to his favorite coffee shop in Sante Fe, New Mexico.

That was the time he had been abducted that morning, so he was more aware of his surroundings today than he normally was. Christopher would be leaving for his morning run about now so by the time Eric visited with the folks at Philz's, Christopher would be back at the condo. Eric stayed longer at Philz than usual this morning as he ran into an old friend, Bruce who had partied with them down in Mexico City. It was almost an hour since he left the condo when he returned. He called out to Christopher, "I am back. I ran into Bruce, and we caught up. How was your run?" He received no answer. He quickly checked to see if he was in the shower but found it empty and dry. He thought that was unusual. He got a bad feeling. He called Christopher's phone and heard it ring from atop the desk he used in the living room. Now, he was very worried.

He called Lyla Baroni and the Bureau HQ in San Francisco, "May I speak to Lyla, please. This is Agent Slay." He waited only seconds before she picked up, "Hello Eric. What's up?" Eric tried to be calm but inside he was very upset and nervous, hopefully for no reason, "Lyla, I may be a bit paranoid, but Christopher has not returned from his morning run. I was an hour late coming back home from getting my coffee and he was not back from his run. I wanted to warn you. As you remember, I was abducted in Sante Fe. They left a note for Christopher saying he was next. Could they possibly have traced us back here?"

Lyla said, "OK, Eric. Do you know what his route is for his run or is it different each time? What was he wearing? When would he have left?" Eric said, "He varies his route daily but generally goes in the immediate area of the financial district and runs three or three and a half miles. He probably had a sweatshirt and shorts. He leaves at 6:30 am and is back in 45 minutes. I tried to call his cellphone, but he left it home." Lyla said, "I'll call the SFPD chief and give him the particulars to spread the word."

PART FIVE

Christian Alfonso was sitting in his patrol car in the rear of the parking lot at Planned Parenthood on E. 14th Street in Denver. He was remembering the shooting from a week ago and hoped that it would be a quiet shift. It was early morning around 8:30 a.m. and he saw a car pull in with four men inside. He took his hat off and slid down in the seat.

Christian could see just above the dashboard. The car was pulled around the to the back of the building. Christian knew it was not a delivery. So, He radioed HQ for back up. Then he grabbed his long rifle and donned his riot helmet. He got out and sprinted toward the front door. He got into the outside door and buzzed the door to enter.

The girl on the desk buzzed him in. He said, "Are the back doors and windows locked?" She shook her head yes. He said, "Call 911, now!" He was off down the hall. Just as he turned the corner to the side entrance hallway, he saw a nurse going to open the door. He yelled, "STOP! Don't open the door." She jumped back against the wall. He said, "Check all the windows and make sure they are locked." He saw a room at the end of the hall to his left. He looked in and it was empty but a man with a long rifle was attempting to climb into the window. It was a door-sized window that he reached into the open window to its left and unlatched it.

Christian waited until he was almost ready to jump in and yelled, "Halt! Police. The man had a mask on and got stuck in the window. He tried to raise his long rifle to aim at Christian, but he was too slow. Christian shot at him and the man was disabled. He lay, slumped over and the rifle fell to the floor. Christian heard yelling in Spanish from behind the rear door down the hall. He heard a small explosion. The rear door blew into the hall. The reverberation from the blast sent Christian on his back. He braced himself for the others outside to rush into the hall. He heard a Spanish order then Spanish in answer.

In English, he heard Levi Bailey out back yelling at the intruders, "Lay down your weapons and get on the ground." Then he heard gunfire. Then it was quiet. The swat team led by Levi Bailey yelled, "All clear."

Christian checked on the intruder he had shot, and he was still slumped over motionless, tangled in the window. Christian yelled to the swat team, "Bailey, Alfonso inside. All clear."

Christian walked slowly up front and saw the staff huddled in the front foyer behind the reception desk. He said, "Everybody ok?" Shayla Beth rose and said, "Shaken; not stirred!"

Dennis O'James was the COD, Commander of the Day. He arrived on the scene as Christian was just headed outside to check the perimeter. He waved Christian over to his vehicle, "Is there anything you need? How many of those inside were hurt? Do we know who the attackers are?"

Greg Solo from the Bureau's second unit walked up to O'James and Alfonso saying, "Captain O'James, we have four intruders. Two were killed in the gunfire exchange they initiated. Alejandro Martino and Juan Flores. The other two intruders are in custody and handcuffed ready for transport by your officers. One is Diego Vazquez, and the other is Tomas Luciano. They have indicated they should be released as they are members of the El Verdugo cartel. They said it would be in our best interest to do so and not invoke the ire of their cartel leaders again." Captain O'James replied, "I am not surprised hearing the threats, but I am certainly not thrilled that we have international drug smugglers trying to cause havoc at our Planned Parenthood centers to exact revenge for their capos being sent to be imprisoned. We'll just send a communication to Senor Semanas letting him know where he can pick up his slain soldiers."

The telephone at Bureau HQ rang and was answered by secretary, Leticia Rica, "Hello, FBI-Denver." The woman's voice asked for Micah Blair. Leticia said as she traced the call, Mr. Blair is not in the office right now. Can I get your name? Would you like to leave a name and number where he can return you call?" The woman said, "Tell Mr. Blair, he killed two of my best soldiers today in Denver who were looking to secure services for their sister. We will revenge their deaths tenfold." The woman hung up. Leticia was able to get a number and location. The call was from Puerto Palomas, Mexico.

Perry and Christie were sitting in the whirlpool in her hotel room. It would be her last night there as they would move into their new house on Saturday. Perry handed her a glass of red wine. He had his usual Grey Goose and soda.

Perry said, "This is very nice Miss Mahern. You certainly look cozy, but you have way too many clothes on to benefit from the therapeutic soothing capabilities of the whirlpool jets."

Christie laughed out loud as she usually did at most of the things this handsome man said, "Mr. Kline if you would have seated yourself closer when you returned with the wine, you would have noticed my bathing suit is resting comfortably on the chair behind me." Perry leaned over and shut off the jets. The lights at the bottom of the sauna reflected beautifully off her very shapely body. He stood and slid down his trunks. He was tall enough that his impressive manhood was visible above the water and reached silently toward the ceiling, almost pointing straight at Christie. She vanished underwater and the next thing he knew, she was climbing up his legs and raising her body out of the water. As many times as he had viewed her charms, he still couldn't get over how perfect she was and how stimulating it was to see her naked form. He said, "This is way more relaxing now. Thank you for taking advantage of the therapeutic value of the experience." They kissed and groped each other's form.

She looked up at him, breathless and said, "Why don't you shut this down and join me in the bedroom? I want us to relax on a soft bed for a while, so I don't look like a prune so much." Perry reached over and shut everything down, including the lights, and helped her out of the tub. He watched her sway back into the bedroom which was lit with three or four candles creating an even sexier setting. The lovemaking began sweetly then got very heated and as they rested, the alarm clock said 12:15 a.m. They had been there almost two hours. They slept.

Perry awoke to the sound of his cellphone. He was irritated as the warm body next to him just snuggled closer. "Hello. Kline." He said as he tried to focus his eyes on the clock on her nightstand.

The voice said, "Perry, it's Ryan. I hate to bother you so early, but I was in Denver last night and I just got word that an agent here in Denver is missing this morning. His name is Gray Nash who was last heard from since yesterday when he left at quitting time." Perry's eyes just focused on the clock. It read: 8:05 a.m.

As he felt Christie roll over away from him, Perry swung his feet to the floor and said, "Who is missing and why are you calling." Ryan answered, "It is Gray Nash. I know he is a friend of yours. His wife, Jodee, called to say he did not come home from work yesterday and was not answering his cellphone. She said they were due to go on vacation with their daughter and her friend this morning and now she is a bit panicked." Perry said, "Are you at HQ?" Ryan replied, "Yes, I was just here for a few meetings yesterday and I am headed back to Sante Fe today. I have nothing pressing, if you want me to hang around for a few days, I can."

Perry was half dressed already, "I am on my way into the office, and I'll see you in twenty minutes. Let's check a few things first and see if we can trace his whereabouts in the last 48 hours and see if anyone else knows where he is." He hung up the phone and looked down and wished he could stay and snuggle as Christie was

144

certainly a delightful vision lying there half clothed. He gave her a kiss on the cheek and left for the office. On the way across town, he called Jodee Nash. She answered on the first ring, "Hello." Perry asked, "Ms. Nash, this is Perry Kline from the bureau, is Gray available?" Jodee replied, "Perry, I was just about to call the bureau as I haven't heard from Gray in a day and a half. He is not answering his phone and I have begun to worry because even if he misses my call, he always calls back making sure nothing has happened to our daughter, Minnie." Perry said, "Did he tell you what he was working on the last time you spoke with him? Judi thought a minute and replied, "Not really. I used to be a jealous type but with the job he is in, I have learned that there is some secrecy he can't share so I don't ask anymore. To answer your question, no he did not share anything about what he was working on."

Perry said, "Jodee, don't fret too much as I was just checking off all the boxes starting with you. If you hear from him or I hear anything, let's call each other. Here is my number." Jodee wrote down the number and found she had to rewrite it as her hand was shaking so much. She replied, OK. Mr. Kline, I certainly will. Thank you."

Perry arrived at the Bureau and got to his office. Megan came in and asked if he'd heard from Gray. He shook his head no. He made a call to Ryan and shared the call with Gray's wife. They began to backtrack.

Lyla Baroni answered her cell. It was Christopher Wiser, "Lyla, I just escaped my capture, and I am running toward the Ferry Building on the Embarcadero at Market Street. I don't think they followed me but hurry." He hung up. She called the dispatcher and ordered two cars to the Ferry Building. Then she called Eric Slay. He picked up on the first ring, "Yes, Lyla." She said, "Christopher just called. He escaped capture and is running toward the Ferry Building. I have two cars headed there now." Eric said, "Thanks Lyla, I was just driving there, and know where he'll be." He hung up the phone. He was at Beale and Mission. This was three blocks from the Ferry Building. He was there in three minutes. He parked in the manager's spot in the side lot and walked in as calmly as he could.

Eric was halfway down the hall when SFPD arrived. They spotted him and Eric beckoned them toward where he was walking. He was just reaching the main entrance hallway intersection. There was the Daily Driver in the right-hand corner. It was the only organic bagel place in the city. He and Christopher knew the manager, Bruce, who would certainly help Christopher hide until Eric arrived. Eric said to the officers, "Wait here at the crossroads (the intersection of the two main hallways). I know where he is. He walked down the side hall of Daily Driver and tapped on the employee door. Three knocks then two knocks. The door opened and there stood Christopher, still breathing like he had just finished one of his marathons. Eric hugged his partner and things were alright. They walked into the side hall and told the officers to escort them to their car at the end of the building.

They were then followed to their home on Beale Street. Christopher was back on the phone with Lyla. She listened to his report and found that possibly it could have been members of Chica Fuerte that had abducted him. He was taken, as far as he could tell, to the 16th Street Mission on Mission and 16th Street.

Maybe two hours after he got there, a man came into the room and whispered in his ear, 'I am going to let you go. I will let you out of the side door. Run left up the alley and turn right onto Mission Street. Here is your phone."

He took Christopher's blindfold off and pushed him out the door. Christopher just ran. He called Lyla after he ran eight blocks. He was telling her he had escaped. He said, "I recognized the voice but didn't see the face of the man who released me. It was strange."

146

Christopher was breathing hard when he got to the Embarcadero. The Ferry Building was across the street. He waited for traffic and with a quick glance behind him, he scurried into the Ferry Building and headed down the hall to the Daily Driver and was let into the employee door.

Dr. Jen Steinberg had just returned from a week-long vacation in Belize and sat at her desk finishing a murder mystery she had started on the beach. As she closed the book and grinned her appreciation of a book well written, her bursar, Robin Moyers, knocked at the door and entered, "Dr. Steinberg, there is a gentleman asking to speak to you but has only given his first name, Michael. He said it is urgent." Jen Steinberg rose out of her chair and walked into the office area. She saw a man dressed very well in a beautiful blue business suit, pale blue shirt, and red striped tie. He looked familiar but she couldn't place him. She asked, "How can I help you, Michael?" The man said, "Well, Doc, the filling you put in about six weeks ago got dislodged and I need you to refill it. I know this is a bit unorthodox but if I could speak with you in private for three minutes, I can explain everything." Jen Steinberg thought a minute and it dawned on her who he was. She said, "Michael, let me see if I can get a tech to set up an open room and we'll get you right in. It will just be a minute." Jen now spoke into a wireless microphone headset that let her talk to all her staff.

She said, "Rebecca, can you talk? OK, can you have Melissa set up Room 12 right away, please? There is a gentleman up front that needs a filling replaced. Thanks." She said to Michael, "Have a seat the girls will be up to get you in a couple of minutes." Michael turned and sat with his back to the inside wall so he could observe the entry.

She returned to her office sat back in her chair and let out a huge sigh. Robin was seconds behind her, "That guy looks so familiar. Did you remember him?" Dr. Steinberg said, "Oh yeah. I certainly

147

did. That is Michael Donlevy. The man from the FBI who was murdered outside our office in the parking lot six weeks ago." They both had chills running up and down their spines.

Minutes later, Michael sat in the Dental chair as Dr. Steinberg entered the treatment room. He said, "Okay. Ladies. I owe you an explanation. The Bureau and I especially, were targets of the Mexican drug cartels and they seemed to be getting closer as we had imprisoned a few of their leaders. I staged the shooting so I could go deep undercover. This is the first chance I had to be back in Denver. I do need a filling, but I wanted you to know you are not in any danger." Jen said, "Michael, we are glad you're alive. Should we keep this very secret?" "Yes, you are the only two who should know", Michael replied, "Once we are able to neutralize the cartels, I will reappear, but I will probably be back in Washington by then." The filling was done, then he was gone.

Wendy McKeller sat in Diane Sorenstone's office reviewing the five properties she was shown. She said, "Diane, when can we look at these properties?" Diane answered, "Well, I am free today if you want." Wendy smiled and said, "That would be great." So, they grabbed their coats and were out the door on the way to the first of the viewings.

They looked at the first three and stopped there. Wendy said, "This one is perfect. Let's put in an offer now." The house was on Zuni Street near 37th. It was a nice cape with three bedrooms and a nice fenced-in yard. The price was right. They had even talked to the neighbors. It was a nice young couple with a young son and a baby on the way. Greg and Allie were very friendly. Wendy felt that she and Allie would be fast friends. She was originally from Buffalo, New York and knew some of the same people.

Diane called the realtor and put in an offer. They heard back before they got back to the office. Diane called Michelle Dale at the bank. She said they could swing by and pick up the paperwork. The owners had been waiting for an offer as they were already out of state for their new jobs. They could get an inspection tomorrow and close on Friday.

Wendy was ecstatic. She thanked Diane and drove to the office and called the storage company to schedule movers to set up her new home. She then called her man in Buffalo. She had not spoken to him in a week or so as they both were extremely busy. Markus answered on the first ring, "Hello Beautiful. How are you? I was just thinking of calling you."

Wendy swooned when she heard his voice, I have some news that I wanted to share. I bought a house today. It is perfect and very affordable. The realtor, Diane Sorenstone, hooked me up and Michelle Dale at my bank had the paperwork ready right after the house inspection was completed." Markus said, "That's great, Doll. I have news as well. I just got a promotion, and the company liked my proposal to expand their business so, they are sending me to their new headquarters to open the company's new location in of all places, Denver, Colorado." Wendy screamed into the phone, "What!! Markus, are you serious? I will close on the house next week so you could move right in when you come." Markus said, "That is great news. This worked out perfectly. See you in two weeks, Lover."

Wendy hung up the phone and ran into Christie's office. Christie had her back to the door and spun around to see Wendy running in the door. She was crying and smiling. Christie said, "What?" Wendy came around the desk and Christie stood, and they hugged. Wendy stepped back and said, "I just talked to Markus. He just got transferred to Denver. Can you believe it? I am so excited. He will be working for the FBI as an agent. Oh, by the way, I just bought a house. I can't wait to show it to Markus when he gets here."

Christie was very happy for Wendy. They had been together for a lot of years, and she wanted her to be as happy as she was with Perry. She said to Wendy, "Let's celebrate tonight with a nice dinner.

We'll go to Catie's new place, Vincenzo's. Now, go take a few minutes to collect yourself and come back with a notepad as I have a bunch of items, we need to strategize for these cases coming up."

Camryn Graystone walked into Micah's office that morning and she was ushered into his office by Megan who then brought each of them coffee. Camryn said, "Grandpa, Here is my report on the cartels."   Micah grabbed the papers Camryn handed him. She said, "I have made some suggestions for how best to deal with their leaders and you may want to take a minute to review them on page 27 so I can answer any questions you might have. There are some glaring vulnerabilities that you might want to exploit. Some of the Mexican cartels are being controlled by folks you dealt with before."

Micah turned to page 27 and quickly read the suggestions on the page. He looked up at Camryn and grinned, "You sure are one smart young woman, Ms. Graystone. Thank you. These are very aggressive in total but the more I think about it, it makes perfect sense. I guess your mathematical mind helps you put these kinds of things into logical order. Great job!" Micah made some notes in the margins of his pad he was writing on. He could not believe what Camryn had written and described the pieces of the puzzle that was the cartel strategy, history, and motivation. All of this was outlined in the document she had shared with him.

Camryn said, "Any time, Mr. Blair. By the way, speaking of Mathematics, I just got a call from North Carolina State University before I came to your office, they are giving me a full scholarship to complete my doctorate in Mathematics with free housing until I complete it and a teaching job at the university which will provide some spending money. Eli and I will marry this fall and as he can work remotely, he'll be able to be with me in North Carolina and still work."

Micah was thrilled, "Camryn, that is impressive. I am so happy for you and Eli. What great news. So, when will you be leaving for Carolina?"

Camryn looked at her watch and said, "Based upon whether you need my assistance any further or not, I thought, if at all possible, I could leave sometime today, that would be incredible." Micah said, How soon can you be ready to go?" She said, "I am packed and can leave whenever you are finished with me." They laughed. Micah said, "Camryn, this is perfect timing. I am just on my way to Washington today so I can drop you off on the way."

Micah picked up the phone and called Megan, "Megan, can you set up a driver and have them get the plane ready? I am going to Washington to meet with the Director, and I will drop Camryn off in Ohio on my way. This will save us a trip. If we could leave by noon, that would be helpful. Thanks." He hung up and looked at Camryn, "I am packed as well. I anticipated your leaving so this works out perfectly."

They both got up and Micah said, "Should we grab something to eat before we leave?" Camryn said, "Super, I am starving. Thanks for the lift home. It was great seeing you. I will go freshen up and grab my bag. I'll call Eli and tell him when to expect me home so he can drive over to the airfield and get me. See you in a few."

Megan called Levi Bailey and gave him directions for bringing the Director and his guest to the airport. She made flight plans and buzzed Micah saying they were all set for their departure. They left within the hour. Micah dropped off his granddaughter, Camryn, at the airport in Bowling Green, Ohio. The plane refueled and then began its flight to Ronald Reagan Airport in the nation's capital.

There was a car waiting for Micah when he exited the plane. The driver took his luggage and helped him into the car. Off they drove to FBI Headquarters in Washington at 935 Pennsylvania

Avenue NW. As Micah went through security at the Bureau, he saw an old friend from Buffalo. Her name was Beth O'Brian. She now worked for the Bureau as the Assistant Chief of Security. As he walked through the metal detectors, he stopped and hugged her, "Well, Cousin. What a pleasant surprise. How long have you been with the Bureau?"

Beth O'Brian said to Micah, "Mr. Blair, I am looking for a job out west in Denver in the Security Department if you have any openings. It is time for me to get out of Washington." Micah said, "I will make a note of it when I get inside and make sure to send you an invitation. How soon can you leave?" Beth replied, "Can I fly back to Denver with you when you leave?" They both laughed and he waved to her as he entered the building on his way to see Lewis Greeley.

Mr. Greeley sat in his enormous corner office at the FBI looking out the window overlooking the capital. His intercom buzzed and his secretary, Sue Curell, said, "Mr. Greeley, Micah Blair is here to see you. Shall I send him in or where would you like to meet with him?" Lewis said, "Oh, thanks Sue. Send him in please." Micah walked in and shook the Director's hand across the desk. He then sat in a large wing-backed chair in front of the desk at Lewis' urging.

Lewis began, "Micah, we have just gotten approval from the President to hire another one hundred and fifty agents in the Mountain Region. I think you could have an Assistant Director each in Denver, Colorado; Sante Fe, New Mexico; Las Vegas, Nevada; Cheyenne, Wyoming; and even Salt Lake City, Utah. May I make a few suggestions in this regard?"

Lewis waited and as Micah nodded, he continued, "Then you will be able to oversee all five sub-regions and groom your Directors and lead Agents for upward mobility in the organization. I have a list of people who would make excellent leaders for you, but these are just suggestions. I would not want to place any demands on who you hire or promote, that is completely your purview."

Micah thought of the great opportunity for himself and for many of the Agents that he worked with. He also wondered if he could ever get a handle on the drug trade, the illegal alien issue, and the impending issues at the Planned Parenthood locations around the region with their states passing laws as harboring states which included liberal views on abortion which drew violent criticism from religious zealots as well as ultra-conservatives. He then wondered if he should use this time to outline what Camryn had uncovered about the cartels to Mr. Greeley. He decided he would not.

Micah flew back from Washington. He now had the task of hiring 150 new agents, training them, and then developing specific training for these new recruits. He would call the Chiefs of Police in some of the towns in the Bureau's region and find out if their shining stars could be stolen. He'd also contact the two wardens of the Federal prisons in the region. Megan would be charged with arranging the training recruiting program and screening new recruits.

She reported to Micah that 140 new recruits were scheduled for training.

Megan advised Micah, "We are going to use the facilities at the Air Force property in Colorado Springs. They have an old wing of one of their educational buildings set up that fits our needs perfectly. I have a list of candidates on a zip-drive on your desk, for your review should you need to check them out." Micah replied, "Megan, I trust you have the Bureau's best interest at heart so thank you. When will the training start?" Megan answered, "Next Monday and it will conclude in eight weeks. I have a proposal for distribution of these graduates, but we'll wait until they pass muster." They ended their call.

Megan's phone rang, "Hello, FBI." The voice said, "We have another two agents on ice. Maybe we can make a deal. Have Micah contact us." The call ended. Megan called Micah, "Micah, I just got a call from a phone in Sante Fe. Looks like it is a pay phone near the downtown area. The man said they have two of our agents. I have a call into Ryan asking about a headcount." Micah said, "Let me know when Ryan calls back. Have we ever heard from Agent Swinson?" Megan said, "I called his girlfriend, Jen Andrewson, and she has not heard from him in over a week. I will follow up with Ryan to see if he has a current agent count. I also will ask if he has contacted either of them in the last two days."

Micah said, "That's great Meg. Call me when you have some more info." When they hung up, Micah's phone rang, "Hello, Blair here." It was Ryan Coleman, "Micah, we just found Ryan Swinson's vehicle at a rest stop at El Moro on I25 South near milepost 17.72 close to Trinidad, CO. He was working with Jim Tatko that day and neither has been heard from since last week." Micah asked, "Have they checked for prints, etc.?" Ryan said, "The forensics team is there now. I will keep you posted." Micah said, "We got a call from one of the cartels in Sante Fe saying they have two of our agents. They want me to call them but left no number to call."

Megan's in-house phone rang. She answered and the voice said, "We have not heard from Micah yet." Megan buzzed Micah twice indicating he needed to listen in then she put the phone on speaker and said, "You failed to leave a number to call back." Micah listened.

The caller said, "We have your agents and if our capos are not released by 5:00 p.m., they will be killed, and we'll take two more agents each day until our capos are released. Don't you realize who you are playing with. If you don't take immediate action, many more lives will be lost. Please call me 505-230-2233. I will be at this number until 5 p.m. I suggest you should give me the news I want to hear!" The call ended abruptly.

Their phone went silent. Micah said to Megan and said, "What the hell was that all about?" Megan replied, "It looks like we now know where our missing agents might be." Micah replied, "Yeah, in danger."

Lewis Greeley sat in his office in Washington. He was talking to Micah Blair who had flown in from Denver to discuss the status of the Mountain Region for the Bureau. Micah was detailing the cartel's situation and the information he had gleaned from his granddaughter, Camryn's report. Lewis said, "Micah, your granddaughter certainly has a future in the Bureau as an analyst if she so chooses, however, given the relationship with the Venezuelan leader and their history of drug production throughout the globe, we are acutely aware that we must cut the lines of distribution coming out of Venezuela as their government not only condones the practice but most certainly benefits from it financially. It is an interesting fact that everyone we are challenged with is related, however, we would face the same challenges if they were strangers. We will table the discussion of this temporarily until we complete our talks about manpower."

Micah was happy to hear this as he had several strategies on why the relationship of the Venezuelan leader to the cartels could be useful in halting their operations. He let Lewis continue. "Micah, the President's approval of the hiring of 150 men in your region has begun, I assume. We have discussed the strategy for hiring but again, I will defer to whatever you see benefits the Bureau best. Now, I have something very important to tell you. Michael Donlevy is still alive."

Lewis let that last sentence sink in before he continued, "He staged the attack himself and knew that if the cartels heard he was killed, they would each think it was the other who masterminded the assault. It would lessen the focus of both cartels on revenge, and it would change their focus on improving their drug distribution and taking more risks as their nemesis was now out of the picture. The only way he could ensure that they would buy it was to stage it so even the FBI was not aware of the rouse."

Lewis saw Micah was not surprised, then continued. "I was the only one to know so I staged my own demise at Centennial Airport. My driver was also not killed and is currently convalescing down in Scottsdale, Arizona. Chris Thurston will return to duty at the beginning of next week."

Micah's mouth was still hanging open when Lewis paused. Lewis asked, "Are you okay?" Micah nodded, "That was quite the secret you just unloaded. Wow!" Lewis laughed, "I guess you're right. I just spoke to Michael Donlevy yesterday and he has just returned from working in Mexico and recently had drinks with Andres Semanas in Puerto Palomas."

Lewis went on, "Michael has been able to befriend a capo, Luis Castro, who is second in command now for El Verdugo. Michael said he was almost found out by security in your Denver office when you returned from the bugout. He snuck into Megan Rolling's room and spent a few hours there while the security team swept the rooms to eliminate the bugs that had been placed in almost every room when you were at the location on West Hampden Avenue in Lakewood, CO. She is now the only one other than you and I that know Michael is alive. You should not even talk to Megan about this. We need to find out who bugged the HQ location. My hunch is it's a member of El Verdugo or one of our people who is a cartel sympathizer who may be into the drugs, the money, or is disgruntled about their station in the Bureau. I have hired an old friend, John

Frazyak, who is a physical trainer and IT specialist. He will get the agents in shape and be able to find out who the rat is in HQ by not being in a position of authority."

Micah took a deep breath and said, "Lewis, it was a shock to hear that you weren't killed at the Centennial airport but hearing Michael is also alive is quite a shock. I agree the bugs in the rooms were an inside job and my suspicions are my security chief, Loren Walters. I will let Mr. Frazyak do his job and keep his identity safe. This was quite an eye-opening revelation, to say the least. Do you have anything more for me?"

Lewis said, "Oh, one more thing. We just confirmed that Lyla Baroni was married and still may be romantically linked to Romero Ramos who is a capo in the El Verdugo cartel. I don't know where we will go with her employment, but she is under surveillance 24/7, so don't discuss any high-security info with her. Oh, one last thing, Michael Donlevy was responsible for both Eric Slay and Christopher Wiser's release from capture by the Chica Fuerte cartel. Do you have anything more for me?"

Micah stood and stretched his legs, "I think we have covered all that I needed to discuss, and thank you for including me in the information that you shared. We have a couple of agents missing in Denver so I will focus on that upon my return." Micah left and jumped back on his plane headed for Denver, enlightened and reenergized.

The switchboard seemed to be busier than normal at the Bureau HQ in Denver. Lots of people calling in with questions about the Mexican cartel drug lords that were being sentenced in federal Court and how they should prepare for any backlash. Micah returned to HQ at 4:30 p.m. He was tired.

Megan just sat down from her break and the phone rang again. The male on the line said with a Hispanic accent, "We have two more of you men, if you want to call them that. You and your leaders have until 4:00 p.m. to release the four members of the Mexican cartel that you arrested and charged with those trumped-up charges. If you don't, we will begin killing these men." The call was ended. Megan tried to trace it, but the call was scrambled. She ran into Micah's office, "Micah, we got another call about releasing the capos in prison as they have captured two more of our men."

Micah picked up his phone and called Perry Kline. "Perry, Micah here. We received a call that another two men had been captured by the cartel. Do a voice check of all you men as quickly as you can and get back to me."

He then called Ryan with the same message. Then he waited. His phone rang and startled him as he sat there wondering whether to release the capos. He answered, "Blair!" The voice was a woman's who said in very hush tones, "Is this the man in charge of the FBI here in Denver?" Micah said, "Yes, ma'am. How can I help you?" She said, "My name is Abby Montrose. I work at a ski store in Glenwood Springs called REI. We sell skis. I opened one of the boxes shipped to us from Denver and found a body in it. He had an FBI badge on it, so I locked it back up and called you ASAP."

Micah's heart sank, "Abby, don't say anything yet. I will be there within an hour. We will come in under the guise of the Inspector General. Are you at the S. Glen St store? He had the store website up on his computer screen. Abby said, "You are correct. I will be here waiting."

Micah called Megan on the intercom, "Meg, get our helicopter ready. I am taking whoever you can get in the building with me to Glenwood Springs." Megan replied, "I just saw about 8 agents in the coffee shop two minutes ago." Micah said, "Have them grab their swat gear and be ready in ten minutes. Thanks."

The helicopter was fueled and ready. Micah and seven agents boarded within minutes of the call. They were on their way to Glenwood. Micah briefed them on the flight.

The helicopter landed in Glenwood Springs after the one hour and five minute flight. The chopper landed in the cemetery on S. Glen Avenue, which was right across the street from the REI Ski Shop. There were two vans waiting with a driver in one and keys for the other. The vans exited the cemetery and drove across the street to REI. One van in the front and the second around the back. Micah walked in with one agent as the other four stayed in the van. Abby Montrose was at the counter when they walked in. She knew immediately they were from the FBI. Micah said, "Abby? Micah." She nodded and walked to the back storage room. They followed.

Abby pointed to the box marked skis. Micah opened the box and saw lying in a blanket of dry ice, Ryan Swinson. His badge around his neck and a bullet through his forehead. Micah cringed and closed the box. He spoke into his radio, "I need four of you in here." Within seconds two entered the front door and two came in from the back. They were instructed to dust the box for prints, then carry it into their van at the store's back entrance. He sat with Abby Montrose in the office after locking the front door. Micah began, "Abby, I will need to know who owns the REI and where this box was shipped from. Then I want you to lock up the store and return to your home, lock the door, and call your owner and tell him you quit. I will have the bureau subsidize your salary until such time as you move or find alternative employment. Is that acceptable to you? Abby said, "Yes, Mr. Blair. Thank you very much. My husband, Christopher, wants me to move back to Denver so I will pack my bags, send the owner the keys, and leave as soon as possible. Thank you for coming so quickly."

Micah opened all the boxes of skis that were in the storeroom at REI. They found another body. The last box they opened held the body of Jim Tatko. He was working with Ryan the day they were found missing. He would now have several phone calls to make to the next of kin. He was very sad as they loaded the bodies onto the helicopter. They were there for forty-five minutes before the helicopter left to return them to Denver.

Eric Slay and Christopher Wiser landed at Denver Airport around 2 p.m. coming from Portugal. They had a wonderful time and were ready to get back to working their jobs. They were headed to Sante Fe, New Mexico so they could assess the damage they had incurred from the bombing and how the restoration was coming. Leticia and Rebecca were walking in the opposite direction to head back to San Francisco. They all had a great time in Portugal and the ladies even purchased a small condo in Lisbon, a block away from Christopher and Eric.

Eric and Christopher reached Albuquerque at 4 p.m. and were met by Jennifer, their downstairs neighbor. They all chatted on the entire trip back to Sante Fe. She pulled into the driveway and the workmen were just leaving for the day. They had changed the locks in both condos.

The locksmith said, "It was fortuitous that you arrived when you did. The foreman of the crew was just about to leave the keys with Carol, the neighbor in the back. I am now able to hand all three of you, new keys.

They agreed to meet upstairs in an hour for drinks. Eric and Christopher both showered and were ready with wine and cheese when Jennifer tapped on the door. It was a mild day in town but still not warm enough to use the patio. They talked about what was happening in both places they were living and told Jennifer they were considering selling their place in Sante Fe as they figured they would no longer be working down here, and the sale would give them plenty of cash profit to do some renovations in San Francisco. Jennifer said, "I may have a buyer if you are serious. Her name is Bella

Coleman. She is a dancer and artist who would fit into the scene very well here. She and I went to dance school years ago. I was doing a refresher and she was just coming up.

Chris Montrose and Chris Rocker have been a team since they both joined the Bureau six years ago. They went everywhere together. They were known as Rocker-Montrose but to their close friends, Montrose was known as Chef because of his love of preparing meals and grilling. The Rocker was known as Stoner because he historically could sniff out a packaged drug from 40 paces.

They were assigned to the Planned Parenthood Office on E. 38th Street. They worked the 8 am to 4 pm shift. One agent would sit in the car outside and the other would be inside checking doors and windows for potential invaders. It was a Tuesday and The Chef was outside in the car. Stoner was in the office with the receptionist. Today it was the Manager Shayla Beth as one of his staff had called out sick. Because of the shortness of their staffing, Shayla said she would go to pick up lunch. She said to Stoner, "Could you watch the phones for twenty minutes so I can pick up lunch?" Stoner said, "No way. Why don't the Chef and I run over and get lunch?" Shayla said, "That would be great. I have three appointments coming in within the next half hour. Thanks."

Stoner walked out and went over to the car where Montrose had parked in the sun. He jumped in and said, "We're going over to Famous Dave's Bar-B-Que on the corner of N. Syracuse and E. 36th Street to pick up lunch. Shayla ordered for us as well." It was maybe six blocks away and they would be back in 20 minutes tops.

Shayla checked in the three appointments and took four telephone calls, then she watched all three of the appointments leave the office. She looked up at the clock and it said one fifteen p.m. She got another call asking for an appointment and when she hung up the phone, the clock said:1:35. She knew the Agents had left about five before noon and knowing how close Dave's BBQ was, she began to worry. Just to be on the safe side, she called the Bureau. Megan Rolling answered, Hello, you've reached the FBI. How can I help you?" Shaya said, "Megan, this is Shay from 38th Street. I was wondering if you could check on Stoner and Chef. They drove over to Dave's BBQ to get lunch for us just before noon because we were short staffed. They are not back yet, and I am worried."

Megan said, "I will check with them and call you back." She hung up and immediately radioed Montrose and Rocker. She received no answer on their radio. She called Montrose on his cell phone. It went to voicemail after four rings. She tried Rocker on his cellphone beginning to worry herself. No response. She buzzed Micah on the intercom, "Chief, do you have a minute?" Micah said, "On my way."

Micah walked up to Megan's desk when her phone rang. She put it on speaker, "Hello, How may I direct your call?" She switched on the tracer. The voice said, "Well Miss Megan, as you might have guessed by now, we have two more of your agents. We are very serious about getting our capos released from prison. Tell Mr. Blair he has 10 minutes to confirm their release today or we will dispose of his agents. You've traced the number, so you know where to call." They both heard the phone click to end the call.

Micah said, "Get Lewis Greeley on the phone, please." He went back to his office. He knew he had to put a plan in place quickly.

He knew from his investigation after picking up the dead bodies of Swinson and Tatko in the ski cartons at the REI shop in Denver, the place where they were holding agents. Micah had just enough time to get there in time to save his agents.

Megan buzzed Micah on the intercom, "Lewis on line 1." Micah picked up the phone, "Lewis, we have gotten another two agents kidnapped by El Verdugo. In our investigation, we know where El Verdugo has their operations. I am just letting you know we are going in with guns blazing in an all-out effort to recapture those agents but also take as many of the cartel members down; dead or alive. I will call the Chief of Police the minute we go start, so he is aware." Lewis replied, "OK. Be careful Micah but give 'em hell."

Within minutes, the Denver team was ready to deploy to the site of El Verdugo's Headquarters in downtown Denver. There were 12 cars staged in various locations close to the target location awaiting final word from Micah to proceed. They had planned this attack drill many times. They each knew their job and had an overwhelming number to carry out the attack.

Micah said, "GO TEAM!!!" It was on.

Perry and his now partner, Jameson Martly were the lead team to enter. They were across the street in a van with two other teams awaiting the signal. When they heard the radio call from Micah, the driver turned into the driveway and stopped at the back door. This was an old Loew's store that had been vacated. It was on East Peakview Street at South Boston Street. The REI store was across the parking lot. They were placed here as the exit to the I25 highway was two minutes away for easy access.

The Bureau also had a team at the EVO Ski store at Broadway and E 9th. Street in Denver just in case their intel was incorrect. The advance team entered through the customer door next to the overhead bay doors for delivery. There was one man at the shipping desk. He was apprehended before he knew what was happening and said the building was empty. A text beep was sent to their leader, Perry. who motioned for the other teams of four to move out. The front of the building had been changed into an office area where two men were detained.

They also indicated no one else was in the building but Perry knew better by the number of cars in the parking lot. They completed a sweep of the location and found two men sleeping and another three in the shower area of what looked like a small boarding house set up. No shots fired.

There were boxes all over that looked like the ones found in the Glenwood location. Perry shuttered to think what he might find. The next sound heard was the elevator from the second floor. Two agents were on either side of the door when it opened. There were three men with AK-47s strapped over their shoulders and in handcuffs were Chris Rocker and Christopher Montrose.

They immediately fell to the floor and the Agents were able to take the three men off the elevator, disarm them and handcuff them. Perry recognized the leader as Tomas Luciano. He was a familiar face as he had worked with Andres Semanas for years and was considered his right-hand man. He began to yell in Spanish but was quickly silenced by Jameson Martly who was fluent in Spanish. Jameson asked, "Senor Luciano, ¿Hay más de ustedes hombres en el edificio?" (Are there any more of your men in the building?) Tomas replied, "¿Crees que te lo diría si lo hubiera? (Do you think I would tell you if there were?)

Perry said, "Keep them secured in the office while Jameson and I clear the second floor." Two more agents joined them on the elevator. Outside just arriving were four vans loaded with agents that had been summoned by Chris Therstone who was back on the job doing the driving of Perry's van.

Perry said quietly, "When we get upstairs, I'll stop the elevator. Keep yourselves low. You two, he pointed to Blaze Falls and Fred Snider, do a quick visual then enter and provide cover as Jameson and I come out. Good luck." The doorbell sounded and the door opened. Perry pushed the stop button and Blaze and Fred exited. As soon as Perry and Jameson exited, shots rang out and

Perry saw the man to his left. He and Jameson took cover behind some file cabinets as Blaze raced toward the back of the area.

One shot rang out and Blaze said, "Got 'em, Captain." Perry said, "Alright, do a complete sweep. Fred is on his way with Jameson, and I will meet you from this side. They reached the shooter who was dead. No other members of the cartel were found on the floor.

Perry said, "Nice work, Blaze. You and Fred take him down on that rolling cart. I will check downstairs."

Once they were all back downstairs, Perry assigned two teams of four to search all the boxes to look for additional bodies and other contraband. Perry then called the Sheriff in Arapahoe County, Dave Welch, to let him know what had transpired, "Sheriff, this is Perry Kline with the FBI. We have apprehended some members of the El Verdugo cartel. One is dead, five have been detained. We are searching for drugs or other contraband. Can you join us. We will use your facility on the County Jail to house these men if you have room." Sheriff Welch replied, "I am on my way. I will bring the cavalry with me. We will bring a paddy wagon to transport the detainees." They ended the call.

Jameson was twenty feet from Perry as he yelled, "Agent Kline, you are gonna want to see this." Perry walked quickly to the center aisle to join Jameson. Jameson was smiling broadly as Perry arrived, "Looks like we hit the motherload, sir!" There in four open crates marked skis were dozens of wrapped drugs. Perry asked, "Fentanyl?" Jameson replied, "OH YEAH!"

Sheriff Welch and his men numbered about thirty. Perry greeted him saying, "Sheriff, we found large amounts of Fentanyl in some of the boxes. I will leave half my guys here until the end of the day to complete our search of the rest of the boxes in the building. We also recovered two of our agents that had been captured by these men. Do any of your men speak Spanish?"

Sheriff Welch said, "Yes, I do as well as two others with me. Which one is the leader? My guess is the older gentleman with the grey mustache."

Perry laughed, "Not bad, Sheriff. His name is Tomas Luciano. He has been identified in our investigations as Andres Semanas' second in command in the El Verdugo Cartel. Not a bad result for the day, I'd say. We will try to move these guys to a secret Federal location within a day or two at most. My guess is that Senor Semanas will be very upset with us."

Sheriff Welch said, "Nice work Agent Kline. Thanks for cleaning up some of our trash. Here is my card with numbers for the jail and my cell to reach me if you need additional assistance.

Perry said, "OK. Sheriff. I will be in touch." As Perry left the building to go out and speak with those other agents who had arrived, he called Micah Blair who picked up on the first ring, "Well Chief, a very good day to report. The raid on the storage building found our two agents alive, one cartel member shot and killed with the only bullet fired, and additionally, we found several crates of packaged fentanyl ready for distribution. I will have the total amounts later tonight. You may want to alert the rest of the regions that El Verdugo may be extremely upset with us and may lash out in retaliation. I will alert the rest of our teams." Micah said, "Great work Perry. Thanks for taking the lead on this one. I will wait for the final tally, but I will give Mr. Greeley a heads-up when we hang up. Thanks for a great job."

Micah closed the door in his office and waited 5 minutes then called Lewis Greeley, "Hello, Mr. Greeley. Got a minute?" Are you sitting down?

Perry and his team left the facility they had raided leaving the Arapahoe Sheriffs teams there to clean up and wait for any stragglers from the cartel that would return to pick up drugs or just return to their home base.

Christie was in her office and buzzed Wendy, "Could you come in with a note pad please?" Wendy appeared within seconds. She sat in the chair in front of Christie's desk and said, "I am ready." Christie said, "We are closing up the office for a week. We both need a vacation. I propose a choice of two. We can go to the Mexican Riviera to an all-inclusive resort, or we can go to the place we stayed in Key West, Florida. Thoughts?"

Wendy perked up like she was shot with an energy drink, "Wow. A vacation? That sounds wonderful. Are we inviting the guys? Do you think they can get away? I have lots of questions. Isn't that a surprise."

Christie laughed, "Well, I was thinking a girl's trip. Our guys are so tied into the Bureau that they may not be able to join us for a full week. If we each have our own rooms, they may be able to come for the weekend."

Wendy thought for a minute before saying, "I vote for Key West. There is no water in Sante Fe, New Mexico. It may not be the best place for us with the cartels so upset about all their operations being found out and destroyed so those are my thoughts." Christie replied, "You're right. I was talking to Perry the other day and he said they had made a huge raid and were able to detain several key members of the cartel and a significant amount of their drug cache. I think I would like to return to Key West as there were some great places there and the people were wonderful. I will check with Perry to see if he thinks it would be advisable to return there."

Wendy then concluded the conversation by saying, "I will talk to Markus and see if he can get the time as well. Talk to you later."

Lyla Baroni sat in her office at the Bureau in San Francisco looking out the window across town to the Embarcadero. Her phone rang, "Hello, this is Lyla Baroni." The voice said, "Chica, this is Romero. I know I shouldn't be calling but I need a favor. Can we meet for a drink tonight after you leave work? I may also be able to help you solve some issues that you face."

Lyla said, "Amante'. You should not be seen in public, and I especially should not be seen with you. Meet me at my cottage. This was their code word for her house on Cottage Row off Sutter Street across from the Issei Garden. I will be there at 5:30 sharp. Wait for me to park in the drive then park behind me so you can leave first." The voice said, "See you at 5:30. Thanks."

Eric Slay and Christopher Wiser pulled up to their flat in Sante Fe, New Mexico. Jennifer, their downstairs neighbor had picked them up from the airport. She said, "Next trip, I am coming to Portugal and scout out a retirement home. See you later for drinks." Eric spoke first saying, "Thanks for the ride, Jen. We should have the place in Portugal finished by Spring, so we'll have a room ready for you when you want to come." Christopher added, "I can't wait to take you to the wineries there. It'll be a blast."

Eric opened the door upstairs and they entered. Christopher said, "It looks like they have all the work completed. Now we can put this place up for sale." Eric said, "I am going to inventory the things we want to take from upstairs. Why don't you work on the first floor, then we will compare lists for storage and/or shipping to San Francisco."

Eric's phone rang. It was Carol from the apartment behind them, "Are you gentlemen home? I heard voices when I went into my bedroom closet." Eric replied, "Yes, Carol. We are taking stock of what we'll store and what we'll ship. Do you want to meet for a drink? We are meeting at the Matador in 45 minutes." Carol said, "Roger and I are on our way there now. See you in a bit."

Christie made all her calls back to Buffalo, New York. She had everyone excited about a trip to Key West again. Some new friends. Some old friends. She, Linda Carnello, and Catie Fuda had been on the first trip. The new ladies were Tina Oliver, Ronnie Olsen, Sue Crull, Jen Steinberg, and Wendy McKeller. They would stay at the Santa Marie Suites again and get four rooms. Christie would room with Wendy. Linda would room with Catie. Ronnie and Tina would share a room. Jen and Sue would take the fourth room. They were all facing the pool and their balconies adjoined. They would leave in a week.

Micah sat in the office in the Denver Bureau and looked across the table at his Region's Assistant Directors, Perry Kline, Ryan Coleman, Jan Casanueva, Donald James, Beth O'Brian, and Randall Dale.

Micah began speaking as Megan recorded for the record, "Ladies and Gentlemen, we are expanding the Region's footprint, as well as our man power is to increase within the next month by 150 agents. Each of you will hire and train 25 new agents. I suggest you draw from current law enforcement as they will have background checks, weapon training, etc. There are some things you should know now that you are considered members of the management team. The things I am about to tell you are top secret within the organization. It is critical that you don't speak of this to anyone, even yourselves, outside this room."

All the Assistant Directors looked up from their notes and were acutely focused on Micah. He continued, "First, Lewis Greeley has resumed his role as leader of the Bureau. His injuries were superficial but we announced his alleged murder so the cartels would ease off on the strategy to dismantle the Bureau which had put increased pressure on them making it extremely difficult to run their operations. Anyone below your level in our organization need not know this information. Second, Michael Donlevy is also alive and well."

There was an audible gasp from those in the room, so Micah paused a moment to let this sink in. He smiled and continued, "He staged his own death with friends outside our organization. The only one who knew was Lewis Greeley. It accomplished several goals for us by again lightening the pressure from the cartels and giving us a view of those in our midst who may be other than devastated by his demise. This fact is especially secret as he has gone deep undercover, and it would certainly be dangerous for him if news got out. He has been able to disguise himself to be unrecognizable to those in the cartels. He has even spoken to the leaders of both organizations over coffee. I wanted you all to know this but keep this one under your hat. Does anyone have any questions about the information that I have shared with you this morning?"

Perry raised a hand and asked, "Micah, do we have a strategy to eradicate the cartels? Also, given the attacks on the abortion clinics, can we use area police force personnel to provide security? This would lessen our daily responsibilities and we could focus more on the drug trafficking and controlling the influx of illegal immigrants who mainly act as runners for the cartels."

Micah replied, "Thank you, Perry. You have brought me to the main reason for the meeting. Each of you will be managing your teams to keep a handle on both our defensive posture as well as our aggressive attack on the cartels' illegal businesses. They are also using some of their forces to create distractions at the abortion clinics. They are even using pregnant women who are illegal to clog the centers with cases to both overwhelm them and infiltrate those operations from within. Ryan will speak to our overall strategy for this as he will headman that initiative."

Micah continued, "Next, we will look at the illegals and lack of support at the borders from the current political structure. Jan Casanueva will spearhead that operation. Our current internal security has been breached. There are agents being kidnapped and we had two agents murdered this month. Your team should always work in pairs. One Agent may back up their partner undercover, but no agent shall work alone. Finally, we have determined that many of the illegal females crossing the border are being recruited for the porn industry. The bureau was asked by requests from the states in our Region for an assist as many females are underage, are drug runners for the cartels, and states are overwhelmed by the volume of production companies. Beth O'Brian will lead this initiative for us. So, each of you will work with these three to make your region able to complete the strategies we have developed and assist your leadership in the overall operation to curtail all this illegal activity. We can only do this successfully if each one of you gives 100%. If you have any specific concerns or any questions about your reporting responsibilities, your role, or the overall objective, please contact any of these three aforementioned project leaders." Micah concluded with, "Good luck, stay safe, and remember you represent the Federal Bureau of Investigation for the United States of America.

After the meeting, Micah met with all his Regional Directors. He gave them the opportunity to ask questions and there were a few questions. Jan Casanueva asked, "Micah, how can we stop some of the shipments coming into the U. S.? If we could set up an outpost nearer to the border, we might be able to better confiscate their drugs and decrease the amount of product being exposed to the streets."

Micah said, "Excellent point, Jan. You can take a squad from your team and patrol the border crossing areas but more efficiently, we can determine from our intelligence where and when the shipments will be coming and then strike to intercept them. This would give us less of a footprint but a more accurate pinpointing of the illegal drug shipments.

PART SIX

Wendy McKeller made all the arrangements and the ladies met at DIA, Denver International Airport, late Sunday morning. They were flying into Dallas/Ft. Worth then on to Key West. Christie and Wendy took an Uber to the hotel. They were soon joined by Catie Fuda and Jen Steinberg. The ladies from Buffalo, New York were two hours ahead but would land only 20 minutes after them. They were staying at the Santa Maria Suites and were being met at the airport by Juan, the jitney driver from the hotel. Late Sunday afternoon, they all met at baggage claim, and they now sat in Juan's large 10-person van with all their bags. It usually took an hour to drive to the hotel, but Juan made it in 35 minutes. Carlos, the porter, met them at the front door with a luggage cart. He knew their room numbers but asked them to let him know which bags went where when they arrived at the rooms. The ladies checked in first. Christie went to the adjacent bar and ordered a drink for those when they filtered in. All eight ladies ordered what they were drinking, and then Christie said, "Ladies. Let us raise a glass and toast to a relaxing, enjoyable week. I have set up tentative room assignments but if you want to change, then certainly, just let me know. I have Catie and Sue in Room 217, Ronnie and Tina in Room 219, Linda and Jen in Room 221, and Wendy and I in Room 223. They are all on the poolside adjacent to one another with a view of the ocean as well. Sound, okay?" The ladies all chimed in with, "Let the games begin!"

Christie continued, "As those that were here last time know, we had one of the ladies plan all the outings. I scheduled some things but if anyone wants to go to a different event or site, that should not be an issue. I spoke to Juan, and he will be available to drive us to dinner. I picked Mangoes on Duval Street. It is an American cuisine run by a husband and wife. It's about 8 blocks north on Simonton and two blocks west on Angela Street. After dinner, we can hit Fat Tuesdays or Sloppy Joe's for drinks, or the Buffalo Cafe two blocks south from the hotel. It's owned by a friend, Neal Seagle, from Buffalo. Does that sound okay to start?" Ronnie said, "Sounds like a plan. Unpack, swim and dinner." The ladies met in the pool in 30 minutes. They decided to swim for an hour or so and then dress for dinner.

Lyla Baroni pulled into her driveway at 5:30 p.m. sharp. She was not out of the car when a car pulled in behind her. It was Romero Ramos. They both hurried into the house and took off their coats. They then embraced and kissed passionately. Then they were breathless. He began first, "Thank you, Chica for meeting me on such short notice. I have terrible news. Andres Semanas was killed yesterday in a raid on our drug warehouse in Denver. He was upstairs in the loft when the Bureau came in. They shot him dead within minutes of his arrival. He was there to inspect the shipments that had come in from Venezuela to DIA. It was mostly cocaine but also a significant amount of Fentanyl. Four of our men are in custody and they don't even know they killed the kingpin of El Verdugo. The warehouse had nearly 18 million dollars' worth of merchandise. The street value would probably have topped 90-100 million. The cartel wants me to take over the leadership, but I want to go back to Venezuela and then move to Portugal as we had planned. The loss of all that merchandise will certainly lower my take if I want out but I think we'll be able to manage on what I have been able to stash away for us. I think we have around 15 million in the Swiss accounts."

Lyla sat down. She poured two shots of Tequila and raised one for Romero. They toasted and she said, "Romi, I have questions. When are you planning on being in Portugal? How are you going to get away from the cartel? How will I be able to find you in Portugal? Does the Bureau know they have Andres on ice? Didn't he have I.D. on him?"

Romero said, "Wow, you always were an investigative type, Chica. Well, I will be in Portugal in three weeks. I am telling the Cartel that I am going back to Venezuela to talk directly to the Man to get directions from him. I will then fly to Caracas to grab a few things then I have a friend who will fly me to Freetown in Sierra Leone on the West Coast of Africa. I will then, sadly, eliminate my pilot. I will take a train to Casablanca, Morocco. I have a cousin who has a sailboat that he uses for fishing. I will sail with him to Lisbon. When I get to Lisbon, I will send a text with the name of the town. When you text me back with your anticipated dates for travel after you resign from the Bureau, I will have plane tickets for you. Pack two suitcases. You will fly to Miami. Then you will fly to London. From there you will take a train to Lisbon. Text me when you leave London and I'll be there waiting."

Dinner at Mangoes in Key West was exquisite. The waiter was Ricky Martinez who waited on the ladies. He took their drink orders. Christie, Tina, and Linda ordered Tequila; Sue, Catie and Wendy had glasses of Cabernet; Ronnie had a local beer; and Jen ordered a Jameson on the rocks. Ricky never wrote anything down but returned in five minutes with all the correct libations. The ladies were impressed. They ordered appetizers, salads, and entrees. Everyone ordered different food and Ricky wrote nothing. He just said, "Thank you ladies. I'll be right back with your appetizers for the table. He returned in ten minutes with another round of drinks and Cheesy Nachos with Chicken and Fried Calamari for the table. Christie said, "Ricky, Do you have an identic memory?" Ricky blushed as each of the ladies swooned, "Yes Miss Christie. It has been a real asset in my line of work." Jen said, "I can't wait to see how well you do on the entrees." As Ricky walked away, Tina said, "He is so adorable. Did you see him blush?" The ladies all laughed but were thinking how much more beautiful he would have been if he were fifteen years older.

The entrees arrived quite quickly after the appetizers were removed. Ricky placed a Caesar salad in front of Wendy. He gave Catie the shrimp scampi. He served Ronnie the braised short ribs. He slid an order of Jerk Chicken in front of Jennifer. He placed the Blackened Cobia in front of both Sue and Linda. He finally gave

Christie her Shrimp Scampi. The ladies applauded. Ricky bowed and asked, "Another drink or coffee?" They all ordered another drink.

Christie looked around quite often to observe the room. She had visions of being watched again as she began remembering her trip last year. She looked for familiar faces but to date, saw none. It was still giving her an eerie feeling being there. She dismissed it. Linda Carnello leaned over to her and said, "Does it feel weird to you being here again?"

Christie laughed out loud in relief, "Oh my goodness, Linda. I was just thinking about last year and I was looking around expecting to see a familiar face watching the group." Linda grinned, "Well, if you see a well- built guy with dark hair more than once, it is a friend of mine. He has been hired as my bodyguard. He is also the assistant manager of the hotel I own."

Suddenly, Ronnie and Tina were yelling at someone behind Linda and Christie. They turned around and saw Neal Seagle approaching the table. He had gone to school with all of them back in Lackawanna, New York. Neal got to the table and Linda, Ronnie, Tina, Catie, and Christie all huddled around Neal as they hugged him. You could not hear anything as everyone was talking at once. Finally, Neal held up his hands and said, "Ladies, welcome back to Key West. It is so great to see all of you. Please sit as I don't want to disturb your meal. I see the group has added some new members. My name is Neal Seagle, and I went to school with these beauties. I own the Buffalo Café which is on South Street between Simonton and Duval. Where are you guys staying? Linda's place? The ladies all looked at Linda in disbelief. Jen Steinberg said, "Linda, you own a hotel here in Key West?" Linda chuckled, "Well, ladies. I am your current landlady. I bought the Santa Maria Suites six months ago.

Christie leaned over and hugged her, "Oh my goodness Girl, why didn't you say anything?" Linda replied, "I was going to tell you but then I thought I would surprise you by not charging you guys for your stay." Ronnie said, "That is amazing but I for one would like to pay my share." Tina chimed in saying, "That's right, Linda, you can't make any money if you give rooms away for nothing. It is a nice gesture. Maybe just a nice discount as we would feel guilty staying for free." Wendy said, "I'll stay for free!!" Everyone laughed hysterically. Wendy had been the one who made all the reservations.

Linda said, "Okay, Okay. You've twisted my arm. Now I am charging double 'cause we're in season!" Neal gave her a high-five. The laughter erupted again. Just at that moment, Ricky arrived and began clearing the dinner plates and asked, "One more round of drinks, ladies?" Neal said, "Ricky, put that drink on my tab, They can repay me when they come to my Café later this week." They all cheered. Then Christie introduced the new ladies to Neal, "Neal, this is Jennifer Steinberg, a dentist from Denver. This is Wendy McKeller, my trusted assistant. Finally, this Susan Crull from Syracuse, an old friend of Catie's." Neal said, "Nice to meet all of you. Please accept my invitation to my club for drinks and or dinner when you are here. I will take my leave. Hope to see you soon. Have a great week down here. Goodnight.

Megan Rolling sat in her office at the Bureau's HQ. She had just received a call from one of the assigned agents in San Francisco. She buzzed Micah's office, "Micah can I see you for a few minutes?" He replied, "Sure, do you want me to come out?" "No", she said, "I'll be in momentarily."

She grabbed two coffees and walked into Micah's office. She handed him a coffee and sat in one of the soft cushioned chairs in front of his desk, "I just got off the phone with our operative in San Francisco. She reports that Miss Baroni entertained a gentleman last night. He has been identified as Romero Ramos. He is the number two man in the El Verdugo cartel. We also have it on good authority that the John Doe who was shot and killed at the old Loew's warehouse the cartel was using when our guys raided that location is none other than Andres Semanas, the leader of the El Verdugo cartel. So, it is now speculated that Senor Ramos will take over the operation. It is also thought that much in-fighting will occur as there has been bad blood among some of the capos for power and ultimate leadership.

Micah replied, "I just heard about Semanas but the news about Lyla Baroni is most troubling. I was just on a call with Lewis Greeley. We've decided it is time for her to be replaced. We will deal with her swiftly. I will fly to San Francisco today. I will place Eric Slay in a temporary position as Regional Director. We'll see if he wants to stay as we know he and Christopher are looking to move to Portugal. We just don't know if it will be a permanent move. Regarding the cartel situation, this may be the break we have been waiting for. With our informant inside Mexico, we will be able to isolate those seeking leadership and strike when the cartel is at its most vulnerable."

Megan said, "Are you going today to see Lyla?" Micah said, "Yes, have them prepare the plane. I want to surprise her. Have Lewis' secretary call Lyla and let her know Lewis is coming in for lunch and I will walk in and ask her for the keys. Also, call Eric Slay and have him meet me there on the Q.T. at 1:00 p.m." Megan said, "I will get that set up. Do you want to meet with the Regional Directors in the morning say 10:00 a.m. to develop a strategy to strike down the cartel?" Micah said, "You bet. Thanks,"

The fax machine started to make a weird noise as Megan was getting coffee. She was preparing for the meeting about to start in an hour. She stopped and looked at the machine and it was printing a document. They hadn't used that as a printer in years. Everything was done by email these days. She clicked on the large 30-cup coffee urn so it would be ready for the meeting then picked up the fax. She began to read it but began running into Micah's office. He was on the phone, so she just handed him the fax. Micah looked at her strangely, so he politely ended the call to one of the service providers who had called about some issue they were having. He then read the fax. His mouth was open, but he quickly collected himself and said, "Megan, put this in the safe in a lock box. I just cannot believe what it says. There is no number from where it originated." It read:

FBI-MOUNTAIN REGION: PREPARE FOR THE WORST. CARTELS HAVE JOINED TOGETHER TO ELIMINATE AS MANY FBI AGENTS AS POSSIBLE. THERE ARE NOW THREE CARTELS. THE LEADER IS THE DRUG KINGPIN FROM VENEZUELA.

THE SNOW VILLAIN HAS ESCAPED FROM PRISON. HE IS ASSUMED TO BE EITHER IN VENEZUELA OR MEXICO WORKING WITH ALL THE CARTELS.

CHICA FUERTE IS PLANNING AN ASSAULT ON ALL PLANNED PARENTHOOD SITES IN THE MOUNTAIN REGION ALONG THEIR DRUG ROUTE FROM THE MEXICO BORDER THROUGH DENVER AND POINTS WEST.

FINALLY, WE HAVE REASON TO BELIEVE THAT THEY KNOW COLONEL POTTER IS STILL ALIVE AND PLAN TO STORM HQ TO ELIMINATE HIM. M

Megan looked upset, "What does all this mean Micah?" Is the M, who I think it is? Is he in danger? Are we going to bugout again?"

Micah grinned, "Megan, you should have been an agent investigator. That is a lot of questions. Yes, the M is Michael Donlevy. Colonel Potter is Mr. Greeley. We will alert the Regions in our meeting tomorrow of the Chica Fuerte plan for the clinics. They'll be ready in conjunction with the local police departments. The Snow Villain is Parker Clark. We think he is alive and has somehow escaped from the FCI Prison in Mariana which is a medium security facility down in Florida."

Megan said, "Isn't he the guy that Perry used to report to in Buffalo who killed all those prominent people there while running his drug operation?" Micah replied, "Yes. Perry and I worked together on the case as the original murder was of the Buffalo Mayor, Johnny Galway. This Parker Clark fellow was in the business of drugs for quite some time and became very influential because of the massive amount of money he made. We could never trace where he had it stashed. Maybe he used it to either bribe his way out of prison or maybe he hired the best people available to get him out. I will call Paul Gorci the Chief of Detectives in Buffalo and let him know Clark is on the loose."

Megan said, "The plane is ready. Are you taking anyone with you?" Micah said, "No, I will make the trip alone as I should be back early this afternoon."

Perry walked into HQ and went to see Micah. He caught him as he was leaving for the helicopter upstairs to fly him to the plane. Micah said, "Perry, I am glad you are here. We have a meeting tomorrow morning, but I am going to San Francisco right now. I should be back late morning or early afternoon. Do you have anything pressing?" Perry responded, "No, nothing that can't wait. Do you want me to ride shotgun?" Micah said, "That would be great." He turned back to Megan and said, "Agent Kline is going along on my trip."

The helicopter took them to DIA where the Bureau's plane was housed. They were in the air within minutes as they had a northern runway that was designated for police and military as well as dignitaries leaving Denver. They were in San Francisco by 10:30 a.m.

Lyla was sitting in her office and had just printed a document to her printer when she looked up to see Micah Blair and Perry Kline walk into her office. She said, "Good Morning Gentlemen. Are you here to meet with Mr. Greeley also? I heard from his secretary that he would be arriving for a visit."

Micah said, "Hello, Miss Baroni. Please have a seat. Mr. Greeley will not be joining us today. He sent me as his emissary. I am here to inform you that your services are no longer needed by the Bureau."

Lyla Baroni was shocked. She did not see this coming. She asked, "Micah, why would you be letting me go? I have brought order and efficiency to the chaos that was in this Region."

Micah said, "Does the name Romero Ramos ring a bell? We have been observing your activities for six months now and have heard five telephone conversations that you've had with him and others in the cartel. We know you planted a mole in the Denver HQ to install bugs in all the rooms. So, you will be sent a letter of dismissal that states you were discharged for cause. Please leave your keys, phone and badge on your desk and you will be escorted to your car immediately."

Lyla Baroni got up, grabbed her purse and coat, and walked out of the office. Perry followed as planned and made sure she went directly to her car. When he returned to the office and said to Micah, "She never said a word all the way to her car. I asked her what was going through her mind. She just looked up at me, shrugged, and got in her car and left."

Micah said, "She had been a good influence in the region as she stated but we can't have one of our region leaders commiserating with our largest enemy. We could have prosecuted her, but we know she is on her way out of the country."

Micah hit the intercom and called Lyla's secretary into the office. Sidney McKeller walked into the office with a steno pad and said, "How can I help you, Mr. Blair?" Micah said, "Sidney, I have just let your boss go. If you have any allegiance to her, let me know now." He waited.

Sidney said, "Mr. Blair, I work for the Bureau, and I am devoted to the FBI as this job has given me not only an identity but also the ability to take care of my family. Now how can I help?"

Micah said, "There will be a gentleman arriving soon who we hope will be your new supervisor. His name is Eric Slay." Sidney smiled and said, "Mr. Slay is sitting at my desk waiting for you to ask for him. Do you want me to bring him in?" Micah said, "Yes, please. Thank you so much and thanks for your loyalty."

Eric walked into Lyla's office, or he would find out in moments her former office. Micah stood and extended his hand saying, "Welcome to your new office."

They both sat and Eric began, "What did you just say?" Micah laughed, "Eric, I just let Lyla Baroni go. Her services are no longer needed here at the Bureau. I would like to offer you the position of Regional Director. Any thoughts?"

Eric was stunned. He had always thought he could do an exemplary job as a Regional Director but never really pursued it. He thought for a minute and said, "You know, Micah, I have thought of things I would like to implement if I was in charge. Now I guess I will have an opportunity. I would be overjoyed to accept the position and am pleased that you have such confidence in me that you are offering it. I am going to ask if I can sleep on it overnight. I will give you my final decision first thing tomorrow morning."

Micah said, "I understand if you need to confer with your family or consider your options, however, I really need a decision now. Would you consider taking the position temporarily and if you don't want it, I will have some time to pick another candidate, but I sincerely feel you would be perfect for the position. I am flying back to Denver in an hour so please call by 8 a.m. tomorrow. You can call earlier if you decide to accept the post permanently. Thanks."

Eric rose as did Micah. They shook hands and Eric left. Micah buzzed Sidney, "Get Don James on the phone for me, please."

Micah turned and looked out the window at the activity on the Embarcadero. He thought how peaceful it seemed but realized it was more than likely the busiest area in town. The intercom crackled. Sidney said, "Mr. Blair, Don James is here to see you. Are you available?" Micah said, "Send him in."

He extended a handshake to Donald James, "I was just about to call you Don, have a seat please." Don said, "Thank you, Micah. What's up?" Micah said, "I would like to offer you the Assistant Director job here in San Francisco. Eric Slay will be the temporary Director. If not, the job is yours."

After dinner at Mangoes, the ladies walked out of the restaurant and waited for Juan to arrive. Linda had just called him before they paid the bill. It must have been three minutes when Juan arrived with the jitney. He loaded up the ladies and headed down Duval Street to Simonton and a block past the Santa Maria Suites to the Buffalo Café. They had decided to go and visit Neal Seagle, their friend and owner.

Neal was behind the bar just wiping up as a large group was going into the dining room for dinner. He shouted, "Ladies, I have some seats available here at the bar if you'd like. I should probably keep an eye on you knowing that you northern girls can get rowdy when you drink."

The ladies laughed as they grabbed bar stools and settled in for a nightcap. Linda ordered shots of Tequila for the group and Neal to toast their week of relaxation. She said, "Ladies let's lift our shot glasses to toast Mr. Seagle our host and to us having a spectacular week of sun and fun, Salud!"

Micah Blair was exiting the plane at Denver's airport. His cellphone rang as he walked across the tarmac toward the helicopter that would whisk him back to HQ in Denver. He said, "Hello. Blair." Eric Slay said, "Micah, I have thought this over and want the permanent position as Regional Director in San Francisco." Micah was relieved, "That's great news, Eric. Thanks for calling and welcome to the management team. I want you to know that I appointed Donald James as your Assistant Director. He has lots of experience in law, supervision, and organization with the Bureau. Let me call you back as I am stepping onto the helicopter taking me back to HQ." They ended the call and Micah heard shots ring out. He was wounded twice. He was hit in the shoulder, as well as his left leg. He fell to the ground.

Perry Kline had tripped getting off the plane and was on the ground when he heard the shots. He looked toward the hangar and saw a man with a gun. He pulled out his revolver and shot an entire clip at the man. He hit him at least three times and then there was silence.

The helicopter pilot was Chris Therstone who picked Micah up and threw him into the chopper. Perry went to make sure the man was dead and called for airport security. He waved at Chris to take off. The chopper left to head back to HQ. Chris radioed for them to be ready to help Micah.

When Chris landed the helicopter on the roof of HQ, there was a medical team waiting. They had a gurney ready and placed Micah on it. They immediately wheeled him inside to see Rob Stovell, the Medical Director for the Bureau. He worked on Micah for an hour and told him he was quite lucky because the wounds were not life-threatening. He said, "Micah, you got lucky. The bullets went right through cleanly, and we were able to stitch you up quite nicely. You will be a bit sore for a week or two, but you can return to work whenever you are feeling up to it."

Micah said, "Thanks, Dr. Stovell. I guess I was lucky. It just doesn't feel like it." They both chuckled as the Nurse finished his dressing on his leg. Her nametag was Alyssa Pullman. She was a wound care specialist. She said to Micah, "Mr. Blair, you will have to come and see us in the clinic two or three times a week so we can redress and clean the wound to make sure it is healing properly. I will have my assistant, Isabel Mendez, set up some appointments for you." Dr. Stovell asked Micah, "Who did the dressings on your wounds after you were shot?" Micah replied, "Our pilot, Chris Therstone."

Dr. Stovell said, "He did a great job. We should keep you here in the clinic overnight just to make sure there are no complications. You can work on the phone if you need to but I have given you a sedative so it should knock you out for a few hours. Please call the attending nurse when you wake up as you might be groggy. I don't want you falling while trying to get out of bed by yourself. Clear?"

Micah responded, "Yes sir. You are the boss. Thanks for stitching me up." As the medical team left his room, Megan appeared at his bedside, "Well Micah Blair, what trouble have you gotten yourself into now?"

Micah laughed, "Well, I zigged when I should have zagged. Has Perry returned from the airport?" Megan said, "Yes, he is typing up the report to send off to HQ in Washington. Do you want me to call Lewis and tell him you are alright?" Micah said, "If you get me a phone, I can call him." Megan said, "Be right back," She returned in three minutes as his cell phone was in with his clothes at intake. By the time she got back, Micah was fast asleep.

Megan decided to call Lewis Greeley just in case he had heard of the shooting, "Mr. Greeley, it's Megan from Denver." Lewis said, "Is he OK?"

Perry Kline was standing in the hangar adjacent to where the shooter was just being taken away to the morgue. He was talking to the Airport Security Chief when the Denver Police pulled up in three vehicles. There were two patrol cars and one ambulance. The Officer of the Day, Scott Stevens, asked who was in charge. Perry pointed to the Security Chief Armando Mexico. Scott asked, "Armando, do we need to transport the deceased anywhere?" Armando replied, "Captain Stevens, this is Agent Perry Kline of the FBI. He shot the individual who opened fire on him and his boss as they exited their airplane to walk to the helicopter that was to transport both Mr. Kline and Mr. Blair to Bureau HQ. We have already removed the suspect who was identified as Adrian Ortez, a member of Chica Fuerte."

Perry said, "Armando, we have identified the members of Chica Fuerte as having red identification cards from Mexico. They are usually from Chihuahua Province in Mexico. For your information, the Bureau has received threats from all the cartels that they are out to vindicate the deaths of their maximo lider, Andres Semanas, who was the leader of the cartels who have seemingly joined forces finally to fight the Bureau. This will put a huge wrench in their day-to-day operational plans. Please alert your teams to be on the lookout for increased crossings at the border which equates to hundreds of illegals infiltrating all the cities along I25 and points north." That said, Perry jumped into a Bureau vehicle that had come to get him and return him to HQ.

Hours later, Megan again walked into Micah's room upstairs in the Medical bay. He had just awakened and looked somewhat out of sorts, "Hey Chief, how are you feeling?" Micah sat up and said, "I am thirsty like a dry camel. Could you ask and see what I can have to drink? Tell them I'd like a tall glass of Patron, Please." No sooner did he say that, in walked Dr. Stovell, "Micah. How are you feeling after your nap?" Micah again repeated he'd like a tall glass of Tequila. Dr. Stovell laughed and said, "You can only have a drink if the Dr. drinks

187

with you and I am on duty. Sorry. You should walk if you can. That is the best way to get your body reacclimated to doing normal day to day things."

Micah was walking down the corridor on the fourth floor and remembered he needed to call Paul Gorci, the Chief of Detectives in Buffalo, New York who he and Perry had worked with to put Parker Clark, the Snow Villain, in prison. He wanted to make sure that Paul knew that Parker Clark had escaped from Federal prison. Clark was likely in Florida but there was a chance he would return to Buffalo to exact revenge on those that had taken him down. "Paul, this is Micah Blair, how are you?" said Micah. Paul was a bit shocked by the call and replied, "Micah, I am well. It is good to hear from you. How can I help you?" Micah said, "I can't talk long but I wanted to let you know that Parker Clark has escaped from a Florida prison, and he may be back in Buffalo at some point seeking revenge so alert all your people. If we get any updates, we'll be in touch. Talk to you soon." The call ended with Paul saying goodbye and then calling his office to put out an APB in the county.

As Micah returned to his room, a very sexy nurse waited in his doorway. As he approached, she said, "I have your medication Mr. Blair. I noticed your leg wound is seeping, so I need to change your dressing to make sure you haven't split a stitch or something."

He took his medication and the nurse, Rena Davis, checked the dressing and found nothing leaking so she assumed it had healed but said, We will wrap this once more at least and keep an eye on this one to make sure it heals well."

As she walked out of the room, the door to the bathroom eased open and a man walked out and startled Micah. Micah let out an, "Oh crap!" There before him stood Michael Donlevy who said, "Sorry, Micah. I needed to talk to you while I was here but didn't want anyone to see me."

Micah said, "At least you could have cleared your throat to let me know you were here. You took ten years off my heart's life."

Michael said, "I guess you got my message about Parker. I barely made it out of Mexico as my cover was blown. I think it was Lyla Baroni as she is with Romero Ramos, and they are headed out of the country with much of the cartel's money as they could abscond with, and my sources say the amount is considerable. Estimates are they have about six billion American dollars. I came back to let you know we found out who bugged the Denver HQ and is the mole for the cartel."

They heard the noise of high heels clicking. Michael slipped into the bathroom as Micah lay back in his bed. Into the room after a short knock walked Megan Rolling, "Just wanted to come up and see how you are doing."

Micah felt tired, suddenly, realizing his medication was kicking in. He said, "I guess I am okay but very sleepy. Anything important I should know about?" He closed his eyes and never heard what Megan said. She saw that he had fallen asleep and left the room. Michael waited a minute then snuck out of the room and down to the stairwell at the end of the hall and was gone.

No one saw Michael leave the building as he took the stairs down to the basement and went out the vehicle entrance on the bottom floor. He waited until the maintenance guy was turned checking the oil on one of the vehicles and he slipped out the door unnoticed. He put on his dark glasses and a long, blonde wig and left the parking lot.

Perry had returned from the airport and went upstairs to see how Micah was doing. He entered the room quietly and saw Micah just waking up, "Well, how are you feeling, Chief?" Micah was a bit groggy but replied, "They are giving me meds to sleep and when I wake up, they make me walk. I guess I was lucky as the wounds are not serious. How did things go at the airport?"

Perry said, "All cleaned up. Denver PD and took over. We identified the shooter as Adrian Ortez from Chica Fuerte. It looks like they are using more males on the hits and the females are working the illegal groups and drug trafficking. How long will you be laid up here?"

Micah said, "When Dr. Robert Stovell comes in tomorrow, I will ask him to release me as the wounds are healing well, and I am doing my P.T. independently now. Once I am released, I will call a meeting so we can get status reports from the teams and then decide how to proceed. Anything else?" Perry said, "No, I was just concerned for your health, but you seem to be doing okay." Micah sat up and grabbed his robe and started for the door. He almost knocked over Rena, his nurse, as he left the room. Perry left. Micah did his laps up and down the hall. When he returned, he slept.

It was hot in Key West today. The hotel's temperature sign said 96 degrees. The ladies had decided to swim as the heat and humidity would have put a real damper on a shopping trip. It was forecasted to rain tomorrow so that worked better. It was 11 am and some of the ladies were getting into their libations early. Jennifer and Tina were having vodka and tonics. Christie and Linda were drinking pitchers of margaritas. Sue and Wendy were having white wine. Ronnie was abstaining and Catie was running down to the water and back. Catie stopped at the Buffalo Café and spoke with Neal about his menu and ordering regimen for food and alcohol. She was trying to get some different ideas for her new restaurant in Denver. When Catie got back to the Santa Maria Suites, the ladies were around the pool in their swimsuits. Catie noticed a table full of young men on the opposite side of the pool and they were obviously enjoying the view. There were a couple of guys in the pool swimming with Linda and Jen. There were two more in the hot tub with Tina and Ronnie. Drinks seemed to be flowing as Juan was coming back to their table with two pitchers of margaritas. Catie said, "I think I will try one of those. They look inviting." Tina said, "That table of men across the way looks inviting as well." They laughed but no one made a move as all the ladies were involved in relationships back home and were not the type to stray.

Ronnie noticed in the shade of a palm tree close to the outdoor bar, an older gentleman with a grey beard and a nice straw hat and sunglasses sat quietly observing the area. She immediately walked over to Christie who was downing a margarita ready to jump back into the pool. Ronnie said, "Don't look now but there is a suspicious man over there watching every move we make."

Christie laughed, "That is Linda's bodyguard. She said that last year when we were here, there were several folks watching us. She indicated that some were for protection, and the others seemed to be keeping an eye on us as we were all suspects at one point in the Snow Villain case. Catie said, "Oh, Thank goodness. I am going to finish this margarita and then join you in the pool." She was taking off her running shorts and top showing a cute blue two-piece bikini beneath it. Gulp, gulp, splash!

The ladies had decided to go to a formal dinner again Tuesday night. Linda suggested 915. This was an upscale Italian cuisine on Duval Street. Catie called Juan while they were at the pool and told him their reservations were for 8:00 p.m. As the ladies met in the lobby to wait for Juan to pull their ride around to take them to dinner, they all began screaming and yelling. The lobby was filled with carts loaded with suitcases of the group checking into the Santa Maria Suites. There at the desk was Diane O'James, Gayle Arthurs, Loren Walters, Beth O'Brian, Bonnie 'O'Brian, Donna O'James, Brenda Arthurs and Dawn O'James. They each had a significant other with them waiting to get their room assignments.

Most everyone knew the eight ladies in the group going to dinner at 915. There was a lot of hugging and kissing as many were family members and close friends from Buffalo, New York. Bonnie O'Brian was the aunt of Micah Blair. His cousins, Diane O'James, Mayor of Buffalo; Loren Walters FBI Security Denver; Dawn O'James, ornithologist from the Buffalo Museum of Science; Beth O'Brian, Surgery RN Supervisor at Strong Memorial Hospital in Rochester, New York; Donna O'James, owner of a restaurant in Lackawanna, New York called Jimmy B's Tavern; Brenda Arthurs, editor of the Annapolis Gazette in Annapolis, Maryland, Gayle Arthurs, Brenda's mom and Manager of the Dog Pound Animal Rescue in Annapolis, Maryland. Bonnie O'Brian, Micah's father Del's youngest sister who is retired, made the introductions which took 20 minutes, and the ladies were almost late getting to the restaurant for dinner. They all made plans to have lunch at Neal Seagle's Buffalo Café the following day to catch up.

At the 915 Restaurant, Juan dropped them off at 7:55 p.m. Their table was ready, so the ladies were seated. Their waiter was Carlos. He was very good-looking with a great physique and jet-black hair that was slicked back into a bun. He passed out menus and took their drink orders. Sue, Wendy, Ronnie, and Jennifer ordered the house Cabernet. Catie and Christie had the house white. Linda ordered Tequila straight with a lime. Tina was more experimental ordering a Murdock IPA Pale Ale. The ladies ordered almost everything on the menu so they could try this and that but as it turned out, everyone liked a particular dish, and it worked out perfectly. Everything was delicious and they voted to return some night before they left.

After dinner, they discussed stopping at the Buffalo Café, but they voted to drink at the bar at Santa Maria Suites instead as the walk to their bedrooms was far quicker.

Juan had been there in seconds it seems after Linda rang him for a ride back to the hotel. Ronnie sat up front with him as he reminded her of her son Chris who lived in Florida. She asked, "Juan, how long have you worked at this hotel?" He replied, "Miss Ronnie, I have been here 13 years since I was old enough to drive. I worked for the last owner and had to be on my toes. It is much better working for Miss Linda. She pays all of us much better. We are very lucky."

Back at the Suites, the bar was full, and the ladies were barely able to get a table out on the patio. The waitress, Patty DuCharme, saw them immediately and said, "Tequilas all around?" Everyone yelled, "YEAH!!"

As their drinks arrived, there appeared two tables full of men who had arrived from their dinner out. There were ten of them. One was familiar to them. Ken Thomas from back home in Western New York. He was a policeman down here in Key West. He was divorced and Tina immediately rose and went to his table. He jumped up and they embraced, and he took her to the bar just inside. Another of the men approached the ladies' table and asked. "Pardon me ladies, our chief has seemingly stolen one of your mates. The gentlemen at those tables are all law enforcement officers and we would gladly assist any of you single ladies." Sue Crull jumped up and said, "My name is Sue, 'How Do You Do?" Everyone laughed and the officer went to her side of the table and said, "Hello, my name is Kevin Syracuse, Sue, it is nice to make your acquaintance. May I buy you a drink at the bar?" Sue smiled and said, "That would be lovely. Send one of your mates over to keep an eye on my friends to make sure they don't do anything foolish. Or maybe help them do something foolish!!" The ladies laughed and half the guys at the next table rose and sauntered over to the table filled with beautiful ladies.

None of the other ladies hooked up with one of the police officers but they had an enjoyable evening. It was two-thirty a.m. by the time the ladies had excused themselves to their rooms. Sue and Tina were gone.

Dr. Robert Stovell entered Micah's room with a short knock. He had two NPs in tow. He said, "Micah, I just spoke to Alyssa, your wound nurse and she said that you were ready to be discharged and your wounds are almost completely healed. How are you feeling?"

Micah said, "Dr. Stovell, thank you and your team for all you've done but I need to get back to work. There are bad guys out there looking to kill all the Bureau agents they can find. So, we must move quickly to counteract these attacks. I feel great and have been doing my PT as well as getting my bandages changed with Serena Davis and Isabel Mendez. My strength has returned, and I am ready to be released."

Dr. Stovell gave his blessing for the release. He asked Micah to come into the clinic once a week until Alyssa cleared Micah and the wounds were completely healed. Micah agreed and walked out of the clinic toward his office.

Micah's cellphone rang before he got to his office. It was Catie, "Hi Babe. How are you? I just wanted to check in with you from Key West. We are having the best time and you'll never guess who we ran into at the Santa Maria Suites." Micah replied, "Hello, Doll. Nice to hear from you. Things are great here. Busy as usual and looking forward to having my favorite chef back in town." He walked into his office. Megan was just straightening his desk. He put his finger to his lips to indicate to her that she should be quiet while he was on the call. Catie said, "Well, I am enjoying the time relaxing but will feel better when I am back in your arms." Micah replied, "Me too. Have a great day sweetheart. Talk to you soon. Love you." Catie had goosebumps, "I love you too, Micah Blair. Have a great day." Catie ended the call and felt like she was on cloud nine. She was really head over heels with Micah and hoped they could marry someday soon."

Micah looked at Megan and said, "Well, I am back from the jail!" They both laughed. Megan said, "How often do you have to go back for dressing changes?"

Micah said, "Once a week." Megan then asked, "Does Catie even know you were shot?" Micah frowned, "No. She doesn't need to either."

Michael Donlevy had befriended a man and woman in Mexico that were trying to get into the United States legally and away from the cartel El Verdugo that had them in prison for all intents and purposes. They were very dissatisfied with the treatment they were receiving and wanted to leave Mexico. Michael was able to keep in touch with them and get information about the cartel's plans for using a new route for smuggling in the drugs as well as how they were joining forces with Chica Fuerte and the newest cartel Ejercito Joven or in English, the Young Army. Its leader was Fredo Alvarez. The couple was Angel Valle Verde. His sister was Ana Perez. She was recently widowed.

Michael had shared this saga with Micah when he called one day to check in to see how Micah was doing. "Micah, this is Michael Donlevy. How are you feeling?" Micah never missed a beat and replied, "Michael, I am on the mend. More importantly, how are you?"

Michael laughed, "I am still on the run, Brother. You won't recognize me when we meet again." He then related the story of his contacts, Angel, and Ana, coming to the States. Micah asked, "Can we set up a safe house for the three of you, so you'll have a base of operations? I would also like to have you over to my house for dinner some night so we can strategize our next moves against all three of the cartels."

Michael replied, "I was thinking of exactly that just this morning. I will call Lewis and have him pay for it." They both laughed and ended the call.

Micah did a little research of his own. He looked at Ana Perez and Angel Valle Verde. Neither was in the Federal archive, so he called his friend, Isabel Mendez from the Wound Care clinic. She had told him she had cousins who lived in Northern Mexico even though she was from Puerto Rico. It was a shot in the dark, but he thought, 'You never know. It is a small world.'

He went up to the clinic. This would be good for his PT requirements. Isabel was sitting at her desk. Micah said, "Hello Isabel, can I buy you a cup of coffee? I have some things I would like to ask." She replied, "Is this official business or a friendly visit? They both laughed.

Michael Donlevy set up a meeting with Micah at Micah's house for drinks after work. Micah insisted on cooking for him. Catie Fuda was on vacation in Florida with a bunch of girlfriends, so they would have the house to themselves to catch up.

Micah decided on having steaks on the grill, a baked potato, and a mixed salad. The drink of choice was Tequila, but he had wine and beer available if that was Michael's choice. Michael arrived on time and knocked at the back door. The house faced a large greenspace between them and the houses behind them. Micah laughed when he pushed open the door, "Michael, were you checking to see what was on the menu before you decided to come in?" They both laughed while they embraced. It had been months since they had been face-to-face. Michael looked completely different. Micah said, "If I hadn't known you were coming, I would have never recognized you." Michael had dark red hair, a neatly trimmed beard, and horned-rimmed glasses. He also looked like he had lost about 40 to 50 pounds.

Micah took the food off the grill and brought it into the dining room. He asked Michael what he'd like to drink, and he said, "Do you have any Tequila?" Micah grinned, "I have Patron, Casamigos, 818, and Sauza 901." Michael said, "I'll have a taste of the 818 please." Micah poured two double shots in brandy glasses and rose his in a toast, "Here is to the cartels all crumbling!"

They ate dinner and caught up on each other's lives then got down to business with developing a strategy for each of the cartels. They looked at each problem they faced. They looked at illegals flooding the southern border and its eminent increase due to the lifting of Title 42. Immigrants will no longer be turned away which means millions will be in limbo as they await either deportation or dispensation of whether they'll receive asylum or be returned to their home country or their latest country of habitation. This process could take years, clogging the courts and costing Americans millions to support these individuals while they await their hearings.

Micah and Michael worked late into the night. Michael twice went outside in the dark and checked his surroundings to ensure their safety.

The ladies visiting Key West spent the day on Thursday at the shoppes at the Duval Square Mall at Virginia Street between Simonton and Duval Streets. They split into pairs and as it was only four blocks from the hotel, they decided to walk back at noon and walk over to the Buffalo Café for lunch then hit the pool before dinner. A few of the ladies ran into other pairs and split each other up to have a new partner. At noon, they all finally assembled at the outside bar at the Santa Maria Suites. Juan was there tending the bar and delivering drinks to the few tables that were occupied.

By twelve thirty, they began walking over to the Buffalo Café. They found a new bar Manager, Bethany Martly. Bethany greeted them with, "Hey friends, I recognize some familiar faces in this group. Can I start your drinks here at the bar or would you rather a table?"

Jen Steinberg spoke up and said, "Let's get the drinks started and you can put them on our lunch bill when we get seated." Bethany replied, "OK, ladies, what can I get you?"

Tina Oliver spoke up and said, "Make us a pitcher of Margaritas, that'll take care of half of us. I need two white wines for Wendy and Sue, Ronnie needs a beer and Jen needs a Jack and coke."

Bethany had them placed on the bar in minutes. Catie said, "Aren't you from Buffalo?" Bethany said, "Yes, I was living in Hamburg. My husband, Jim. just retired as President of the Ironworkers Union, and we moved down here as we were tired of the Western New York winters."

As the ladies were being seated at their table, a group of ladies from Buffalo came into the Buffalo Café. They were led by Mayor Diane O'James. There were nine in their group. Diane's sisters, cousins and Aunt Bonnie who was Micah's late father Del's youngest sister. Neal had just walked in and said to the waitress, Marie, "Marie, give these ladies a shot of their choosing and I will have a shot of Patron!"

The ladies all cheered and ordered Patron with him. They raised their shot glasses and toasted the Buffalo Café. Sue Crull led the toast by saying, "May the Buffalo Café be filled with Buffalonians and their friends forever!"

They drank and cheered. Linda Carnello hugged Neal who blushed.

The ladies each ordered some sort of salad and another cocktail. They planned to finish and return to the hotel for swimming and sunning. Christie took Diane O'James and walked her through the hallway to the restrooms. She stopped to show her a picture of her predecessor, Jimmy Galway, who had been murdered by the Snow Villain and his associates who were now in prison.

Diane said, "My goodness, what a great picture that is of Jimmy. It should be hanging in City Hall back in Buffalo. I will ask Neal about that. Thanks for bringing me back here so that I didn't miss it. I would have died had I seen it by myself. It is still eerie to see him knowing how he died."

They returned into the bar area to the group that now numbered 17. All the ladies and some gentlemen were now getting along famously. Linda brought up the evening cruise with music and dinner for them to try out. They said they would try to put something together to have both groups go.

Back in Denver, Perry went back to his house after talking to Micah and Michael Donlevy about their strategies to end the challenges the Bureau was facing like, migrants coming across the border at the end of Title 42, the cartels attacking the planned parenthood centers then flooding them with illegals who were given asylum and needed care, and the continued influx of drugs being brought into the country. Secondarily, the Bureau leaders decided that they had an infiltrator or two in their midst and they developed a plan to trap them in their operations.

Perry kicked off his shoes and made himself a drink and a sandwich. He turned on the news to hear there were possible tornadoes in the area coming up the I25 corridor. The sky became very dark and then it began to hail. The Hail was initially the size of ping pong balls. It was so loud in his living room; he could barely hear the television. Mike Nelson, the weather guy on Ch. 7 KMGH in Denver reported it so well that he relaxed about the tornado but noticed the possible damage to his vehicle and the house. Later, he found the foundation had begun to leak and he spent the night bailing water from a corner of the basement. He carried 50-60 gallons of water out to the street. He spent the morning getting calls to service men to fix the foundation and he called Bell Heating for a new sump pump.

Perry called in and let them know he was taking the day off to get some sleep as he was exhausted. He would wait for Christie to return from her Florida vacation before telling her his tale of woe. Perry awoke the next day feeling like he was drugged and rolled over by some very large machine. His muscles ached from all the work. It finally stopped raining and totals ranged from 4 to 10 inches over the previous three days.

Perry's cup of coffee woke him slowly. His cell phone rang. It was Christie. He said, "If this is a sales call and you have called this early, I will be really upset." Christie laughed as she always did, "Good Morning, Mr. Kline, I was calling to see how you fared in the hail/tornado event last evening. It was all over the news down here in Florida on the TV in the bar. Are you okay?" Perry laughed to himself, "It was a long night and loud for a while. I will give you all the gory details when you get back, How is it going down there?" Christie smiled and gave him the report, "The Reader's Digest version is that it's quite boring. Dinner, Swimming, and lots of Drinking then Sleep. We call it DSDS." Perry feigned sleep and begged off on any more chat, "Have a great day, Doll. Can't wait until I see you soon. Love you!" Christie was almost in tears as Perry is seldom that romantic, "I love you and miss you too. See you in a couple of days. Bye, sweetheart!" They ended the call. Perry went back to the basement and resumed cleaning up the water and straightened up the mess he made saving things from the water leak on the floor. Thank goodness he thought. I am glad the sump pump is still working, and the rain has stopped.

Lyla Baroni got off the airplane in Miami. She thought she recognized another passenger as a Bureau agent from either Denver or Sante Fe. Maybe she was just paranoid. She had a lot of money in her briefcase wrapped in folders of plastic. It was unable to be detected by the microwave of the TSA scanners. It looked like a couple of books in her satchel. It had gone through a couple of trials and customs without issue. She was still paranoid. Once she was in Portugal, she would be able to relax and enjoy both her man and the wealth they had accumulated. She stopped at the bank to transfer all the cash she had into a cashier's check so it would be easier to transfer. She went to three different banks to flip the ninety-one million onto three cashier checks.

Ryan pulled into the parking lot at Bureau Headquarters in Denver. He went up into his office and within minutes, Megan Rolling appeared in the doorway, "Mr. Coleman. How are you? Can I interest you in dinner tonight at my place?"

Ryan had not even taken off his coat but replied, "Doll, if you want to feed me, I will eat." He had a glint in his eye that Megan recognized as his sexy look. Megan said, "I will expect you at 6:30!"

Perry came into the office after a day off so he could clean up after the hailstorm. He was exhausted but made it to the office. Micah walked into Perry's office and sat on the couch by the window. Micah said, "Perry, I sent Donald James to tail Lyla Baroni to Miami where we think she has cashed in some of the money she and Ramos stole from the cartels. What do you think we can do to stop this as she is leaving the country. I can relay the plan to Don James."

Perry said, "Tell him to do a random check on a few people in front of her when she is in the security line at the airport. Then confiscate her bags as she probably didn't check much. Take her into the TSA office and with a witness, then search her bags. I am guessing she probably has cashier checks ready to deposit into banks in Portugal as carrying the amount of cash they may have taken would surely set off alarms at the check-ins."

Micah said, "Great idea, Perry. That will give us enough time to get him some backup and put together some charges to detain her. Thanks."

Lyla parked the rental, got checked in, and walked to the terminal at DIA. She flew on United Airlines and got a first-class ticket to Miami. It was a non-stop flight. She had to go through international customs and security. She packed one suitcase and carried a briefcase. She had remembered to bring her FBI badge with her to ease any searches. She traveled light as with all the money she had for her and Romero Ramos, she could easily buy an entire, new wardrobe. She entered the TSA line for international customs and got a little nervous as this was the final leg. Just as she was walking up to the TSA agent, Lyla saw the two gentlemen dressed in plain clothes approach her. The older one said, "Miss Baroni if you could step over here to the side, we would like to do a random search of your bags and person." Lyla almost turned and ran. She thought she recognized them as Bureau agents.

The ladies in Key West had two more days in the luxurious sunny weather to relax and enjoy the beautiful views, food, and atmosphere of the laid-back style of living. None of them was in a hurry to return home.

Christie thought to herself that this may be the place she'd retire to when she and Perry were ready. She thought about Perry a lot on this trip. She remembered how she had called him in a panic the last time she was in Key West when she was being spied on during the whole murder investigation, she was embroiled in. She had uncovered the Buffalo mayor who was buried in the snow as her car slid off the highway back in Buffalo on her way home one wintry night. She was staying at the same hotel, the Santa Maria Suites, here in the Keys which was then owned by the Snow Villain. It was now owned by Linda Carnello who was both on that trip as well as here with a different group this week.

Christie began to look around as she sat on the balcony overlooking the pool. The office building across the street is where she had spotted Micah Blair who was using a long pair of binoculars and sound microphone to spy on her and the group of women that she vacationed with almost two years ago now. She wondered. She laughed at herself then realized she was in a much different place now and there was no one watching her.

In that building across the street, in the very same office that Micah had rented was a man standing in the bathroom with a pair of large binoculars watching the Santa Maria Suites. His long microphone was hidden in some bushes out on the balcony, so it was undetectable. He listened as Christie was now joined on the balcony of room 223 by Wendy McKeller. He listened to their chit chat on shopping today and the cruise they would take later after an early dinner.

Linda and Jennifer came out onto the balcony next door at 221. Both had their bikinis on as the morning was already warm enough for a dip in the pool. Linda said, "Good Morning, Ladies. I was just admiring Jennifer's body as we donned our bikinis for a morning swim after coffee. Care to join us?"

Wendy, always the socialite said, "I would love a quick dip then a hot tub before we embark on our shopping trip. Will Juan be driving us again, Linda?" Linda yelled down to the pool, "Juan can you drive us in an hour?"

The man in the office across the street from the Santa Maria Suites was on the phone when the key jingled in his door lock and a striking tall brunette sauntered into the office. She placed a coffee and a hard roll in front of where her host was sitting. She placed her tea in front of her chair and then sat.

They sat without speaking for twenty minutes while they listened to the ladies across the street. The man was taking notes as she rose and walked over to the binoculars that were on a tripod at the bathroom window. She snapped several pictures as Catie and Sue came out onto the balcony of room 217. The microphone picked up the morning greetings and they learned where and when dinner would be. That would make things easier.

Ryan Coleman pulled into Megan Rolling's driveway and parked. He brought in flowers and two bottles of wine. She was cooking dinner for him, and he was planning to spend the night, if things went well. She answered the door, "Good Evening, Mr. Coleman. Please come in." Ryan's jaw had dropped to his chest. He looked at Megan and she was dressed in black lace from head to toe. He found that he was drooling. She was an incredible vision. He said, "I have never seen anything this sexy in my entire life. I don't know if I can eat dinner, but I will try."

Megan sauntered toward the kitchen with her black full-length negligee flowing behind her. Ryan followed with the flowers and wine into the kitchen. He said, "I brought these but maybe you should put me in water instead of the flowers. It seems very hot in here."

Megan laughed, "Ryan, thank you so much for the flowers. Could you open some wine? I will plate the dinner then we can toast to our new relationship. I think you are the sexiest man on the planet and once we have consumed dinner and some wine, I will take you to the bedroom and show you my overwhelming feelings for you. You really turn me on, Mr. Coleman!"

Ryan said, "We can skip dinner. I will only drip food on myself and at this point I am so turned on; I don't know if I will ever be this excited again. It is very uncomfortable to have my clothes on right now."

Megan approached him after shutting off the oven, "Come with me my darling, let me relieve our tensions and give you an idea of how much I appreciate you being in my life."

The ladies in Key West had dinner and had Juan drive them to the pier and they boarded the cruise. It was a two-hour sunset catamaran with an open bar and hors d'oeuvres. It embarked from the pier at 201 William Street on the north shore of Key West. The boat was gliding along the water effortlessly as the girls drank and nibbled on the hors d'oeuvres. There were a few single men aboard and the crew was almost all males. The band was a Caribbean quartet that played mostly dance music of original composition. They were called Cruisin Fusion. Tina seemed to take a shine to the lead singer who seemed to fancy her as well.

The two-hour trip seemed to fly by, and they were back in port in what seemed like minutes. Juan was there when they arrived. They decided to visit Duval Street. They started with Sloppy Joe's and moved south down Duval toward their hotel.

Juan pulled into the Buffalo Café for a nightcap. They all ordered roast beef sandwiches on a Kaiser roll which Neal listed as the special of the house. He was not at the Café that night, but the bar was manned by Bethany Martly whom they had met on the previous visit this trip. She greeted them warmly, "Good evening, ladies. What'll it be?" She had taken their order for drinks and sandwiches while they scurried to a table that had just emptied in the bar.

Christie's blood froze as she watched this man exit the hallway from the restrooms and stand at the end of the bar. She recognized him immediately. He called Bethany over to pay his tab, which he did and quickly left out the front door. Wendy looked across the table at Christie and realized there was something wrong. Christie's face looked like she had just seen a ghost.

None of the other girls seemed to notice as they were busy in chats with the ladies from Lackawanna, New York who had entered the Café minutes before. Wendy walked over to Christie and crouched down next to her chair. Christie never saw her coming. When Wendy whispered, "Christie, are you okay? You look like you've seen a ghost."

Christie let out a yelp! It was more of a screech, but she turned to Wendy and said, "I just saw Parker Clark, the Snow Villain, leave the café."

Shay Beth was closing the Planned Parenthood Center in Denver as they had had a very busy day. Four doctors were working today, and it was more than six hours from start to finish. Shay had not even counted the cases completed. They had returned to two security guards after the attempted break-in a few weeks ago.

The FBI had been nice enough to recommend a couple of agencies they trusted. The Bureau even checked in twice a week to see how things were going. Two doctors were leaving and one of the guards walked them out to their cars. Shay heard the shots being fired and immediately yelled for the second security guard and dialed 9-1-1.

Eric Riscoe and Greg Solo were just pulling up to Planned Parenthood for their weekly check-in when they heard the shot from the driveway as they pulled in. Greg spotted the shooter in a tree. He jumped out with his long gun and fired one shot. The shooter was pointed in another direction trying to hit the doctors. He fell out of the tree onto the roof of a vehicle and his gun flew in the opposite direction.

The Denver PD was now on the scene and called for back-up with medical. Greg Solo from the Bureau ran to the man from the roof and found that he was hit in the chest, but he was still conscious. Greg immediately handcuffed the assailant and assisted him to the ground. Agent Riscoe went into the building and checked quickly that there were no more intruders. He then went out to assist the two doctors and the security guard. One doctor and the security guard were wounded. Both were shot in the arm and were superficial wounds and not life-threatening. Agent Riscoe went to help his partner, Greg Solo, with the shooter who was yelling in Spanish.

Agent Riscoe was conversing with the shooter in Spanish and the shooter calmed down. He was upset that he had not seen the two agents from the Bureau pull into the parking lot as he was focused on the doctors. When he heard Eric speaking to him in Spanish, he began to calm and was more easily directed to walk over to the Denver Police cruiser.

Agent Solo handed the shooter to Denver PD. Then he and Agent Riscoe went inside to see that there were two more doctors waiting to be escorted to their cars. Shayla Beth greeted the Agents. She said, "I am so thankful you guys are still doing those weekly checks. Can I get two more checks per week?"

In Key West, Christie got back to the Santa Maria Suites after leaving the Buffalo Café. She was still shaken. She didn't know if anyone else saw Parker Clark. She wanted to call Perry to let him know. She thought to herself that she and Wendy should return to Denver as soon as possible. Perry said, "Hello Doll. How are you?" Christie got straight to the point and dismissed any frivolities they usually had when calling, "Perry, I just saw Parker Clark walk out of the Buffalo Café about an hour ago."

Perry's heart stopped, "Did he see you?" Christie said, "I don't think so, but I am going to call the girls who would be concerned and let them know I am jumping on the first flight back to Denver, but I wanted to call you first." Perry replied, "I was going to advise just that. I will call Ken Thomason of the Key West Police Department and let him know. I will call Lewis in Washington and he will be able to call out the Feds in Florida. Let me know when you set up your flight, I will pick you up at the airport." Christie thanked him and they hung up.

She told Wendy her plans and Wendy agreed to go with her. She then called Linda Carnello, "Linda. It's Christie. I saw Parker Clark leaving the Buffalo Café tonight. Did you see him?"

Linda said, "I thought that was him, but I dismissed it because he was supposed to be in prison. What are you going to do? I am going to jump on a plane in the morning and go to Paris a couple of days early."

Christie replied, "Wendy and I are making plans to fly out in the morning. Linda said, "I have several bodyguards. Do you want me to assign a couple to you until you leave on your flight, just in case?"

Christie said, "That would be great. Thanks. He tried to kill me once, I don't want to give him another chance." They ended the call.

Perry called Ken Thomason in Key West, "Ken, Perry Kline here. Just wanted to let you know that Parker Clark, the man we imprisoned down in Florida for the Snow Villain murders has been seen at the Buffalo Café in Key West tonight. I will fax over his mug shot. There is a group of Buffalo ladies down at the Santa Maria Suites. Keep an eye on them as well as one of them bought that place that was owned by Clark before he went to prison."

Christie scheduled her flight out to Denver. It was scheduled to leave at 9:00 a.m. It had one stop in Dallas but that was the earliest flight. Christie then called Perry and gave him their arrival time of 2:05 p.m. Denver time. Christie explained to the ladies what the situation was, and they decided they would all leave as soon as possible.

At the Key West airport, Christie and Wendy checked in early. Christie was disguised in a head scarf with dark glasses. She wore a baggy pair of sweats. As they went through security, they began walking down the corridor to their terminal. There in the Washington to Buffalo gate was Parker Clark. Their departure gate, to Dallas and Denver, was four gates down the corridor. Christie tried not to panic. She scrolled through her phone for a picture of Parker and couldn't find one. She got to her gate waiting area and called Perry, "Perry, Parker is sitting in the airport at gate 7 waiting for a flight to Washington and Buffalo. What should I do?"

Perry said, "Did he see you? If not, hide in the ladies' restroom until your flight. I will call the airlines and alert the Feds in Key West. If you see him again and he recognizes you or gets on your plane, get off the plane and call security at the airport. I will call you back if I hear anything."

Christie told Wendy that she would be in the bathroom until their flight was ready to board. She was shaken but she remained calm. It seemed like it was forever until Wendy came and said the plane was boarding.

Christie left the bathroom and went to her gate. She looked down the corridor and noticed a commotion. It looked like Federal Agents were there at gate 7. There was also a Federal agent at Gate 3 where she and Wendy stood in line waiting to board the aircraft. Christie felt like she had just run a marathon. She was perspiring profusely. Her knees were knocking together like she was on her first prom date. Just as she and Wendy checked in at the boarding desk, she heard shots fired.

Christie ran into the jetway leading to the plane and watched with bated breath to see whether he had escaped or was running down the ramp to her plane. She saw the Federal agent close the door, looking through the window to make sure the assailant would not try to hide in that jetway. Christie heard shots fired again and then there was quiet.

Lewis Greeley got a call from Perry about the Parker Clark sighting at Key West airport. He put out an APB letting all agencies know of the escapee in their jurisdiction. They had forty Federal agents in that terminal within minutes after receiving the call from Lewis.

Parker Clark was a trained policeman. He felt the tension in the airport before he saw any federal agent. He walked slowly across the corridor to the men's room. He entered but heard an agent announce himself to an airline agent at the desk. As he entered the washroom, he spotted a maintenance man standing in the closet getting paper supplies. Parker walked up behind him and hit him over the head with a mop handle. The man was out cold. Parker shut the door and began to undress the man. He got his coveralls off and donned them quickly. He tied and gagged the maintenance man then walked out with his keys and badge as well. He walked out of the bathroom with the man's pushcart and headed for the exit. He thought to himself that someone had spotted him and called the authorities. He went down the escalator to baggage claim and ground transportation. He took the least travelled exit to walk across the street to the rental car garage. He knew how things worked and if he was lucky this would work. He found the busiest company was Avis. There was a line of people returning cars and it looked like only one tech checking in cars. He was now at the kiosk getting a car for a new customer that had just arrived. Parker walked to the returned cars and picked a black Cadillac at the head of the line. He opened the door and found the keys on the dash. He started the car and slowly drove to the exit instead of parking the car in the line to be washed and lined up for new rentals. He exited the airport and he returned to his friend's home in Key West.

Christie was still in the ramp waiting for boarding when she heard the Federal agents radio begin to squawk. She heard, "We didn't find the escaped prisoner but a man on the run with a satchel full of drugs panicked when the Federal agents arrived at Gate Seven.

He began shooting at the agents and he was quickly apprehended. We are still looking for Parker Clark. The team is going through every inch of the airport. Planes have been locked down until we find him. If he is sighted, announce it as code 5 and your location. He may be armed as well. Over."

Christie went with Wendy to their seats on the plane. Their flight was scheduled to leave in five minutes. The plane was loaded but not a full flight. The door was closed but not locked. Two minutes later a Security officer from the airport walked on the plane with a ticket agent. Both had a picture that they looked at and compared with each passenger. Christie saw the ticket agent on her side of the plane as she passed Christie's seat holding a picture of Parker Clark. The lead Steward announced the plane would be taking off as soon as security checked to make sure the person the authorities were looking for was not on the plane. The Security officer and ticket agent finished and were satisfied the man was not on the flight. They left, the door was closed, and the plane began to roll back away from the terminal on its way to the designated runway to take off for Dallas.

Christie turned to Wendy and let out a long sigh, "Whew! That was the most intense twenty minutes I can remember." She looked down at her phone and texted Perry as the plane taxied to their take-off position, "Leaving Key West Now. Unless he is flying the plane, Clark is not on this flight. Love C"

When Christie and Wendy arrived in Denver, it was snowing and blowing. The landing, as is usual in Denver, Colorado, was somewhat rocky to coin a phrase. The wind over the Rocky Mountains caused some of the worst updrafts known to pilots around the country.

For as rocky as the landing experience was that day, the plane rolled smoothly onto the runway and eased into a taxi near the end of the runway. Ten minutes later, Wendy and Christie were unbuckling their seatbelts and waiting to exit the aircraft. Christie texted Perry Kline to say, "I am at the gate ready to deplane. Should be at baggage claim in twenty minutes or so."

Perry texted back, "I am at the ticket counter at your gate to make sure you have no unexpected visitors to Denver on board." Christie got nervous and began looking around. They walked up the skybridge to the gate. Christie saw Perry standing inside the door with two other Federal Agents checking for a possible appearance of Parker Clark. Perry thought to himself that he would not take any chances to have Christie engage in another contact with this man. Christie felt like running to him and jumping in his arms. She was very relieved to be back in his arms as they hugged.

Parker sat at his friend's house in Key West. His friend, Esteban Alvarez, owned a helicopter that he housed at his home on the northeast shore. He flew Parker Clark to the Homestead Florida airfield. He housed a small Cessna aircraft there with a pilot accessible 24 hours a day. Parker thanked Esteban, 'Gracias, Amigo." Esteban replied, "Vaya con Dios!"

The pilot, Armando Crews, greeted Parker as a dignitary. They taxied and took off in minutes after Parker arrived in Homestead. They would fly to Charlotte, North Carolina where he would refuel the plane as well as grab a meal. They would then fly to Signature Flight Airfield just north of Buffalo International Airport. They arrived at 7:00 p.m. A black limousine was waiting for the plane as it taxied to the small hangar. A woman stepped out of the limo dressed in traditional chauffeur's garb. She waited at the foot of the stairway as it was lowered to the ground. Parker stepped off the staircase and embraced the beautiful blonde woman who kissed him passionately. He said, "Margie, it is so good to see you again. Shall we go?"

In Key West, the multi-department police presence called off the search about six hours after it was initially called. They had checked every corner of the airport and found nothing, but the maintenance man bound up in the supply room. Every plane had been searched, and the teams even checked the pilot's area in the planes. It was as if Parker Clark had vanished.

Perry got a text from Lewis as he drove Wendy home. After dropping her off, they drove home to Englewood. Perry said to Christie, "I just got a text from Lewis that Parker escaped from the airport without a trace. They found a maintenance man locked in a supply closet in one of the bathrooms across from the gate where he was observed at. His uniform was taken as well as his keys. The authorities assumed he slipped out of their grasp while dressed as a maintenance man. He would have drawn no attention in that getup. He must have gone back to where he was staying and decided on a different route back to Buffalo."

Christie shook involuntarily in her seat. Perry noticed, "Don't worry. We'll get him. I spoke to Paul Gorci while I waited for you and told him that if Parker slipped away for some reason, he may somehow find his way back to Buffalo. If his drug operation is still flying contraband from Aruba to Miami then Buffalo, he could hop on any of those flights."

Christie offered, "Maybe we should take a short vacation together until they capture that dirtbag. I would feel much better being out of this town even though I am not sure whether he knows where we are. I am sure if he wants to find us, he will. If he was slick enough to escape prison, then he would easily be able to trace either of us. I am thinking a week in Hawaii would be nice."

Perry thought for a minute, "I don't know if I want to run away from him, but it might be a good idea if you left town with a small group of friends who I trust would be able to protect you until we have this guy under wraps again."

Christie said, "I would be worried about you if we weren't together. I would rather stay here and work from home if you can't or won't get away right now."

Perry said, "I agree that leaving would just be madness. We will know if he comes out this way and we'll be prepared for him if we are at home and know he is not captured yet."

So, it was decided, they would spend much of their time at home and keep abreast of the on-going search for the Snow Villain.

PART SEVEN

The Planned Parenthood locations in Denver were being inundated with lines of women waiting to be processed to receive an abortion. Many were devastated as their families had been annihilated by the recent global pandemic. The new administration had loosened the southern border so much when Title 42 had expired that it was even difficult for the border patrol to accurately count the number of illegals crossing into the United States. As they crossed many traveled through New Mexico to Colorado.

Colorado Springs had one Planned Parenthood facility but most went on to Denver as its mayor had declared it a sanctuary city so there were more services being provided there.

Micah noted that in the past three weeks, there had been 13 attacks on these locations either being flooded with potential cases and violence breaking out when anything was refused or just attempts on staff members, especially doctors who were performing the abortion procedures.

Shayla Beth called Perry on his cell phone, "Perry, There is a group of what looks like Mexican Nationals sitting up on the wall overlooking the building here on East 38th and we have no security guard today. Can you send someone? Perry said, "We'll be there in three minutes."

He jumped into his car and took off toward E. 38th Street. He called dispatch at Denver PD and let them know he would need backup at that location. They sent three cars from the general area.

It took no more than five minutes for the first unit from Denver PD to arrive at the 38th Street location. There was no sign of the Mexican Nationals that Shay Beth had reported but their aftermath was left at that location. There were four cars that were shot up with multiple rounds. As the other units arrived from Denver PD and the two units from the Bureau, there were four people shot in cars or on their way out of their cars into the location. One of the staff was wounded when she went out and dragged one of the folks who was wounded on the sidewalk back into the vestibule.

Perry entered the location and sought out Shayla Beth only to find her providing first aid to three people who had received gunshot wounds. Shayla looked at Perry and said, "There are two ambulances on the way. Luckily, the folks in here have only superficial wounds but I am not sure about the people hit in the parking lot."

Ryan Coleman walked into the foyer and said to Perry, "We have cleared the perimeter and found no one. I was thinking that this being the second attack on this location, we might want to consider putting a camouflaged marksman up on the roof to deter any further attacks."

Perry responded, "Great idea, Ryan. Do me a favor and speak to Denver PD and have them set up a 24/7 schedule. We should probably offer to take a shift each day to assist."

Ryan was already on the telephone. Perry then went outside to check on those in the parking lot. One person was shot dead while waiting for a client in his car. Denver PD had two officers handling that situation and were consoling the client. As Perry got ready to return inside to speak to Shayla he was approached by a vehicle driven by an attractive young woman. She said, "Officer, they told me you were the officer in charge when I arrived. My name is Diane Bestine. I am an Administrative Assistant for one of the lawyers' groups in the building next door. From my window, I was able to see the entire incident and was lucky enough to get three license plate numbers from the group that did all the shootings." She handed Perry a sheet of office stationery that included the make and model of three cars and the plate numbers. At the bottom was her name and her direct phone line. She ended with, "It might be advantageous to put a marksman on our roof for security. It is a great vantage point of the entire area."

Perry was impressed with her demeanor and thoroughness, "Thank you, Miss Bestine. This is very helpful. You sound like you are ex-military from the descriptions you used. I commend you for taking time to assist us." Diane Bestine said, "You are very welcomed Agent Kline. You are correct. I spent 12 years in the Marines. Have a great day and good luck." She then drove out of the parking lot and then disappeared into the afternoon.

Lyla Baroni's bags were both searched at security in the Miami airport and at customs. She had gone through customs and now it took her 15 minutes to clear the security area. She had to run to her gate and had to visit the restroom before takeoff or she thought she might burst. She ran into the stall and sat relieving herself. She double-checked her briefcase to make sure she had the cashier's checks. She left the stall feeling more relaxed. She was washing her hands and suddenly she blacked out.

When she awoke, there was an attendant there looking down at her and two ladies from the airlines. The attendant said, "She's awake. Ma'am, you must have passed out at the sink. Luckily, I was just walking in and saw you. I caught you just before you hit your head on this hard tile floor. It would have split your melon wide open. Are you okay?"

Lyla was a little groggy, but her head was clearing quickly, "I am all right. Did my flight for Portugal leave yet?" The young ticket agent said, "No Miss Baroni, we were paging you when we heard the attendant call for help. If you think you are okay, we can board you and depart."

Lyla was okay. She stood on her own, grabbed her small carry-on and her briefcase and walked across the corridor to the boarding area. She was escorted to the plane and the flight attendant checked her in and sat her down. The doors were closed. The plane began to roll away from the gate. Lyla peeked into her briefcase and saw the envelope with the checks was still there. She sighed and fell asleep from exhaustion.

The flight to Portugal would be completed after six hours. Lyla would sleep the entire flight. She was exhausted from the anxiety of traveling from San Francisco to Miami, transferring the money into cashier checks, and passing out in the restroom. She realized she had not eaten anything all day. She asked the flight attendant for some crackers or a candy bar as she was feeling slightly light-headed. She was given a cup of coffee and the attendant had a power bar in her carry-on that she shared. Lyla said, "You are a lifesaver. Thank you so much. If you have an ice cube to cool the coffee, I can down it quickly as I know we are going into our approach for landing."

The flight attendant, Ginger, complied and watched Lyla down the now-warm coffee in two gulps. Lyla thanked her again as Ginger left to go to her seat to prepare for landing at Lisbon airport. The local time was 10:05 p.m.

Shayla Beth spoke with Perry at the Planned Parenthood site on East 38th Street in Denver right after the cleanup from the shooting was complete. There was one window that was shot out and had to be boarded up with plywood. It would do until a window guy could install a new window with security bars. The people shot were taken by ambulance to the hospital for care and overnight observation. Perry mentioned to Shayla, "We had a lady from the building behind you approach us after we arrived and gave us a paper with the make and models of three vehicles the shooters used for their getaway. We will run these through our computer system and follow this up. I am hoping we can alleviate any further issue for you by apprehending these individuals. I have spoken to Denver Police. They will share with us the coverage you suggested. We will assist them in providing a sharpshooter from their department as well as ours to sit both on top of your building and the building behind you where the lady who provided the information works."

Shayla felt much more at ease, "Thank you Agent Kline. That is comforting. Thanks also for the quick response today. I am so glad to hear that no one was seriously hurt."

Perry was about to leave when he and Shayla heard yelling coming from out in front of their location. It was a group of about forty men and women with signs and large placards expressing their objections to the facility being in their neighborhood as well as the violence reigning down upon their lives because of their operation of this clinic.

Perry turned to Shayla and said, "We expected this sooner, but it looks like they may be here for a while. Let your clients and staff know that they cannot be prevented from entering and leaving the premises. It is just going to be uncomfortable for them while this demonstration is being conducted. I will also instruct the protesters of these rules."

Shayla asked, "Agent Kline, is this kind of thing happening in all Colorado locations? How about in other cities? Can you give us an idea of how we should proceed?"

Perry replied, "Business as usual but I suggest you may want to change your scheduling of your clients to Tuesdays and Thursdays if that is possible to lessen the number of days you have clients coming and going."

Perry walked out in front of the Planned Parenthood site and spoke to the woman with a bull horn leading the protesters in chants about their feelings of how awful the clinic's involvement in killing babies was from their perspective. He waited until she had finished her rant then said, "Hi, Can I speak with you a minute?" She looked at him in dismay and very tentatively said, "What is it?"

Perry tried to be as diplomatic as possible, "I wanted you to know that we just had five people shot at this location within the last hour. I don't want to take away your right to protest but I want to keep you safe as there is an element that has been trying to kill as many people as possible who either visit or work at this facility. I don't think it is safe here for you and your group and the more people that are around, the more people that are vulnerable to attack and possible serious injury."

The woman looked at him realizing that he was from the FBI and simply said, "Thank you. We will take that under advisement." She turned and called the group into a huddle. She repeated much of what she had heard from Perry and the look on their faces expressed the horror they now felt. Perry walked back toward the door of the facility and turned as he opened the door, saw the group quickly move to their vehicles and the ranting was over.

Shayla said, "Perry, what did you tell them that got them to leave? Perry laughed and said, "I told them the truth. They were sixty minutes late for the shooting that injured five people today. It would be in their best interest to keep away from the facility and find another place to protest."

Shayla looked pensive saying, "Now could you tell the shooters the same message, so we don't have to deal with this madness?"

Perry responded, "If it were only that simple Miss Shayla. I will be back at HQ if you need anything further." She thanked him as he went out the door and wondered how many times the folks coming here would have to deal with the threat of physical harm and possible death before things quieted down and went back to normal.

Megan Rolling greeted Perry at HQ, "How bad was it at East 38th Street?" Perry just shook his head, "It was bad for them. One died and five wounded."

Micah's cellphone rang while he sat in his office. It was his granddaughter, Camryn, "Hello Miss Camryn. How are you?" Camryn replied, "I should ask you how you are. I overheard my dad telling someone that you had been shot. What happened? Are you okay?"

Micah replied, "Mums the word Cam. I don't want it to get around that the old man can't dodge bullets anymore!" They both laughed. It was a running joke between the two. Camryn said, "Seriously? The reason that I called was that I was thinking about the attacks on the Planned Parenthood sites in the West. Do you think it could be the cartels creating a smoke screen to distract law enforcement away from their objectives? I know you guys think of everything but when I saw the attacks on the site, I wondered if they were behind the violence. I reviewed the files again and noticed that the family structure that I brought to your attention when I was in Denver seems to lead back to Venezuela. I also heard that the Snow Villain, Parker Clark has escaped from prison down in Florida. I think I know who his accomplice was back in Buffalo who may be continuing to assist him with the drug distribution."

Micah was writing a lot of notes as Camryn spoke and she waited for his response. He said, "I was just making some notes. There is a good chance the cartels are using the attacks on the Parenthood facilities as a smoke screen to cover their operations. We hit them very hard when we found their supply warehouse in Denver and invoked their anger for sure."

Camryn said, "So, Nonno, how are you really?" Micah said, "Just between you and me, I am still in physical therapy, but I will be able to completely heal in time. I just didn't want people to worry about me. I am back at work and thank you for your thoughts about the cartels. You had some great insights as always and I really appreciate you looking at all these things. It helps to have another pair of eyes look at things that we stare at all the time. I will certainly add them to my discussions with my teams. Thank you, Doll. I appreciate the call and the concern. Talk to you soon."

They ended the call and Micah sat in his office and thought for a while. He wondered what Parker Clark, known as Rey Estratega or King Strategist would do back in Buffalo. He was extremely vulnerable to being recognized which might hinder his movement but the vendetta he might be working on may put lots of people in danger. Micah was shocked at his accomplice.

Lyla was at the airport in Lisbon, Portugal. She went through customs quite easily and then looked for her driver which Mr. Ramos provided. She walked outside and there was a long black limo with a driver looking like a sumo wrestler holding a black 2-foot square sign with Lyla in white on it.

She took three steps toward the limo and the driver sprinted toward her. He relieved her of her suitcase and as they returned to the vehicle, the trunk opened, he opened the backdoor and she was whisked into her chariot for the ride to her new mansion. She took a minute to double check that her cashier checks were still in the zipper-locked sleeve of her briefcase. She took the envelope out and peered inside. Her stomach flipped when she saw an additional piece of paper which meant someone had been in the envelope since she left the bank. She unfolded the note which read:

'Hello Miss Baroni. I see you are traveling with quite a sum of money. I am leaving it here in the envelope because I want you to be able to return it to its rightful owner. Mr. Ramos would have surely cut your throat had you not arrived with all this money that you and he stole from me. See you soon in Lisbon, Chica.
Regards, PC'

Lyla looked around to see where they were and to check to make sure she was alone in the back of the limo. She felt like someone might even be following them, so she checked that as well.

She asked the driver, "Manuel, how much further?" "Senorita, we have just ten minutes left before we arrive at the villa," said the driver.

Lyla took out her cell phone and checked her messages. There was an email from her assistant in San Francisco wishing her well. Telling her she would be missed and to never hesitate to call if Lyla needed anything. The last one she saw was from Micah Blair, the man who had fired her days ago without any warning or rationale. Lyla was steamed just seeing his name.

The email read: Lyla, Sorry for the quick dispensation but you know as well as I that what you were involved in could have sent you to jail for espionage. We just thought you being free would allow us to follow you and find out just how deeply you were involved in the cartel operation. It was interesting to watch you empty over ninety-one million dollars from their local accounts. They are surely now aware of where the money went. I am sure you will hear from them soon in Lisbon.'

Regards, Micah'

Perry walked into his home in Englewood, Colorado. He was exhausted from a long day at Planned Parenthood. He thought they had dodged a bullet with only one fatality there, but he worried about the future. He needed a shower. He called out to Christie but heard no reply. He ascended the stairs and heard the shower running in the master bath. He began taking off his clothes, so he was naked from the waist up at the top of the stairs. His pants, shoes and socks came off in the hallway. He walked into the ensuite bath naked. He whispered, "Hello Beautiful." Christie was in the shower and yelped when she saw his naked form on the other side of the glass. He entered the large shower, "Can I wash your back, Madam?" Christie melted into his arms, "I think I missed a few spots on my front you could get as well, Agent Kline!"

Ten minutes later, they were out of the shower wrapped in large drying towels, and headed to their king-sized bed. Christie dropped her towel, pulled back the covers and jumped onto the bed on her back. Perry stopped a minute to observe his soon-to-be wife and said, "My God woman, you get more beautiful every time I see you naked." With that, his towel fell, and he joined her as they began their lustful dance. It started softly then he began to escalate the intensity which obviously pleased Christie as she began to moan in her throat something over and over that was unintelligible. Their lovemaking took almost an hour before they fell on the backs next to each other having reached a spectacular climax leaving them both breathless. It was difficult to catch your breath when you exerted that kind of unbridled energy and had so much pleasure.

Christie spoke first, "Feel free to bring home that energy any day of the week. I am now so rejuvenated that I could run a marathon. I began the shower exhausted from the day. I was going to shower and slide into bed for the night leaving you a note of apology for my fatigue. WOW! You are still the most amazing lover I have ever had; by a LOT!"

Perry smiled, "I think the uniform I found you in had a lot to do with my rejuvenation powers and your amazing beauty always drives me crazy with passion. Thank you for the motivation. What do you want to eat? I am now famished!"

Perry donned his sleep bottoms while Christie threw on a silky camisole and panties. The two descended the stairs to the kitchen. Perry got a bottle of wine while Christie put together a salad with chicken. They ate then slept.

Shayla walked into Planned Parenthood office on this Tuesday morning very early. It was the day that Perry had suggested the facility had operations with clients. The two-day-a-week schedule seemed to have slowed the protesters down somewhat as they changed days each week. Last week was Wednesday and Friday.

This week would be Tuesday and Thursday. She noticed the security guards up on the roofs of her building and the one behind them to the north. At 8:00 a.m. on the dot, there appeared 50 to 60 people carrying signs of protest regarding the illegality of the abortions being performed at the clinic. No more than ten minutes later, there appeared another group with signs of freedom of choice in direct opposition to the first group. She made a call to Denver Police. She thought of calling Perry Kline, but she thought she should call Denver Police first. They responded quickly but Shayla noted that the arrival of the police seemed to incense both groups and fisticuffs ensued. Both sides had bull horns and it began to get louder and louder. The police had to break up three fights then, suddenly, shots rang out. A lady from the Pro-choice group fell to the ground and was bleeding from a gunshot wound. Denver Police apprehended the man who was running from the scene, placed him in handcuffs, and took him away. Shayla thought she would ask the police if designating a day for each group might work and avoid confrontation.

Perry and another unit from the Bureau arrived and helped disperse both groups. He spoke to both leaders and told them each, "You folks have a right to assemble and protest but it must be a peaceful demonstration. In the future, if any weapons are used by anyone, you will all be banned from protesting."

The two leaders seemed to agree that for them to protest, they would abide by these rules. All the protestors left the site and Perry entered the facility. He said to Shayla, "I have a hunch that the demonstrations are being fueled by the efforts of the cartels who are bringing illegals here from points south to take advantage of the free services. It is also a major distraction for law enforcement away from their objectives of drug trafficking and flooding the States with illegals. I asked them to keep it peaceful or we'd ban them." Shayla thanked him as he left. She wondered, not for the first time, what it might be like to be in bed with this good-looking Agent Kline.

Lyla reread the letter she found with the three cashier checks. She gave it over to Romero to read. He was furious and began yelling, "Let that squirrel try and steal our money! I'll have this gun say something to him!!" He patted the .45 caliber handgun strapped into his shoulder holster. Lyla said, "Romero, maybe we should leave this place and go to Spain or maybe Sicily?" Romero thought for a minute and replied, "Chica, we have planned this escape for some time now and it would be a shame to change our plans at this point." Lyla already had her reply ready, "Romi, I love you and don't want to get involved in another power struggle. We would be well advised to find a nice castle in some seaside community other than this to retire with the money we have. We can well afford some security and elegant privacy so we can do all the things that we've dreamt about for so long." Romero knew she had thought this through better than he. His anger and stubborn pigheadedness were guiding his decisions, so he sided with his beautiful companion and started making calls.

Within the hour, he had a group of servants pack up their belongings. He told them to pack their personal bags on the boat he had in the harbor. The rest were placed in storge containers for shipping. Parker gave them an address in Barcelona where they should be delivered.

He then called his friend Julio Rey who lived in Barcelona and worked for King Felipe VI. He asked him to receive the three large shipping containers filled with their belongings and rent a ship large enough to load them on and sail to Nice, France. He gave them the address of the Chateau de Bruno. This was his latest purchase and was located next door to the La Persouse Hotel in Nice. They would stay at the hotel until their belongings were delivered and set up at the Chateau.

Romero said to Lyla, "Chica, I planned for us to move. We will leave some of the money for our friend from America so he can save face back home. All our contacts in Lisbon will tell Parker Clark or his emissaries that we have moved to Barcelona." He had friends there that he would tell a lie that he was flying to London to live thereby further eluding those on their trail. They left by plane and flew to Barcelona. They stayed overnight and flew in a private jet to Nice the next day. Lyla asked when they arrived, "Romero, how much money did you leave in the safe for Parker?" Romero laughed, "I left him a cashier's check for 100 million dollars of what they think we stole. It's not even a tenth of our take but it should keep them off our tails."

Markus Edwards was sitting in Catie Fuda's new restaurant, Vincenzo's. He was strategically at a table by the front door as his habit was to be able to watch everything in front of him. He noticed there were more Hispanics in the place than he had ever seen before. He noticed two of them that he had arrested not long ago in Sante Fe, New Mexico. Being the investigative savant that he had become, he noticed they were putting on their coats, and their waitress, as she was also his, had not yet given them their check. She was approaching both of their tables with checks in hand. The two men in front of him began to scurry out the door but Markus jumped up and blocked the egress.

Markus said, "Oh, I am so sorry gentlemen, I was just getting up to grab my check from our waitress and I think she has yours as well." The two men looked back at a table 15 feet away. There sat one of the capos of the El Verdugo cartel, Luis Castro. He gave, what looked like a signal to these men to pay their check it seemed as they sat back down at their table.

Markus immediately texted Micah. He told them of the plethora of cartel members in Vincenzo's who were about to all run out on their checks. He should send some backup. Then he asked the waitress to let Catie and/or the manager know what he assumed would be a message from the cartel.

Micah read the message and immediately jumped into his cruiser and brought three units with him. They arrived before the waitress had brought back Markus' change. Micah walked straight to Luis Castro's table. He greeted him like a long-lost brother which seemed to aggravate Senor Castro. Micah said, "Buenas Noches, Senor. Gracias por traer a tantos de sus asociados al restaurante este noche. Asegurese de que pageun, o puede pagarlos todos antes de irse, ya que cerraremos temprano esta noche.

Translation:(Thank you for bringing so many of your associates to the restaurant this evening. Please make sure either they pay, or you can pay for all of them before you leave as we are closing early tonight.)"

Luis Castro pulled out his wallet and tossed ten 500-dollar bills on the table and said, "Have a good evening, Senor Blair." As he left the table, he said, "Vamos, muchachos." (Let's go boys.) There must have been forty men rise up and follow him out of the door. After they left, Micah grabbed his son and said, "Markus, that could have been ugly, so thank you very much." The agents outside watched the group walk out and began to write down license plate numbers of the cars they drove for future reference.

Eric Slay and Christopher Wiser were waiting for the Uber outside of the San Francisco International Airport. They had retrieved their luggage and were just catching up on a few emails. The Uber arrived, loaded them up and drove the thirteen miles to their home in the Financial District of downtown San Francisco. Christopher said, "I just loved Australia, but it is so good to be back home, and I am ready for a shower and a nap before we go out to eat." Eric said, "You know, I am going to check in with the office and see what is happening of importance. Then I may shower as well."

As Eric sat at his desk, doing email correspondence, his cell phone rang. He said, "Hello, Can I help you?" The voice said, "Welcome back, Mr. Slay. I hope you have better luck in cleaning up this town than Lyla had. We will be watching you and how you handle your business. Good Luck."

It was a female voice that sounded familiar to Eric. He couldn't put his finger on where he had heard the voice, but he looked at the recent call list on his phone and it had an unfamiliar 505 area code number. Could it have been Carol? He wondered for a moment then called Carol. She didn't answer but her message was the same voice that had called. Now he wondered why she would not have identified herself and why was she wishing he would do a better job in San Francisco than Lyla Baroni had done. He would talk it over with Christopher when he woke from his nap to get his take on it.

Eric's cellphone rang again. It was his new assistant from the Bureau in San Francisco, Hilda Matthews, "Hello Mr. Slay. How was your trip around the world?"

Eric responded, "It was extraordinary but the flights to and back were long. They were seventeen hours each way. I read four books on the trip. Most of my reading was in flight. How are things at the Bureau?"

Hilda replied, "Well things are getting a bit hectic around the Planned Parenthood locations as was suggested. The Pro-Life and Pro-Choice groups are both protesting, causing fights and almost daily confrontations with the local police. I have had teams of agents monitoring these locations as per your orders. There are sixty or so court appointments amid all these events. I noticed from some of the footage on the news that there have been a disproportionate number of what look like illegals on the scene during these."

Micah came into the office today and was greeted by Michael Donlevy sitting in his former office where Micah now sits. Micah said, "Well look who decided to come to work today!"

Michael laughed, "It does seem strange as I have not sat at a real desk in over six months. I am just visiting though. I was just on the phone with Lewis Greeley in Washington, and he advised me that a memo will be coming soon to all locations across the country about the rumored uprising being planned for February 20th. It seems that the Pro-Life groups all over the country have decided that this day would be the day when a massive protest of the abortions being done at Planned Parenthood locations across the country would be stopped by their protests. Won't that be a fun day?"

Micah asked, "What's our plan?" Michael replied, "The plan is to infiltrate the locations and disrupt the operations, protest outside to scare potential patients away and fight the Pro-Choice people that appear. It could get nasty and dangerous if bloodshed begins in any of the locations or in multiple arenas. The Planned Parenthood operators have been notified and police have been instructed to be prepared for this onslaught of that day."

Micah sat in the visitors' seat across from his own desk chair occupied by Mr. Donlevy. He said, "I wonder if the cartels are going to be involved? I also wonder if they are going to use this as an opportunity to make some major deliveries across the country as the police will be preoccupied with all these events. Maybe we can secretly close all their offices that day by calling a cancelling all scheduled appointments for the day that morning."

Michael replied, "It's the cartels who encourage these protests as it distracts the Bureau and police from focusing on their drug operations."

Megan knocked and walked into the office, "Well, it sure is nice to see both of you in one place. Did you tell Michael about the incident at Vincenzo's Restaurant?"

Michael looked puzzled. Micah replied, "I haven't had a chance but now that you mention it, The cartels visited my fiancé's restaurant and had planned on skipping out on their checks when my son, Markus just happened to be sitting at a table at the door and blocked three of them trying to run out. They looked to their leader, Luis Castro and he nodded for them to sit back down. Markus texted me and when I walked in, I greeted Mr. Castro like a celebrity. Then he dropped five grand on the table in front of me to pay for all forty or so of his men. I wished him a good evening as he left."

Christie Mahern sat at her desk and prepared for court. She had four cases today and they all centered around attacks of the Reproductive Health Care Clinics or what were formally referred to as Abortion Clinics or Planned Parenthood Centers. There were numerous violations of the Civil Rights Conspiracy Act as well as the FACE (Freedom of Access to Clinics Entrances) Act. Wendy brought her in fresh coffee and asked if she needed anything. Christie said, "Could you get my rolling cart from storage? I have so many files, it will be easier to transport down to the courtroom as well as keep me organized."

Wendy said, "I am just finishing dusting it off Christie as I thought you might be able to use it." Christie yelled, "OMG. Lady, you can read my mind. I am so glad you are here with me in Denver. You make it so much easier to work and we have so much fun. It is quite a lot of work but so gratifying when we get things done the way they need to be."

Wendy said, "I just spoke to Moe Barstow back in Buffalo last night. She said she saw Parker Clark walk into the Ace of Clubs bar she used to work at as she was leaving. She called the manager and told him to secretly call the police to give Parker's location. She hasn't heard anything about whether anything happened but said she would keep me informed."

Christie said, "Well he has returned to Buffalo. They will catch him at some point and return him to prison. I just hope he doesn't kill anyone before then or fly out to Denver to take out his revenge on Perry or me."

Wendy said, "Maybe I will give Paul Gorci a call and give him a heads up. You never know but it might help to make sure Buffalo PD knows he is back in Buffalo. I am sure they have a list of all his old haunts to be able to check and put out an APB for his arrest."

Christie said, "Thanks, Wendy. Are we ready for tomorrow? We have eight men to prosecute from the shooting incident at the Reproductive Health Clinic on E. 38th Street from the other day. My guess is that we will be able to at least deport them but because of their crimes, I think it would be better to send them to prison for a stretch so they will one, be taught a lesson and two, be taken off the street for a while. Here is hoping that sooner or later the cartels will run out of manpower and cease all these criminal activities."

Parker Clark and his old friend traveled to Europe searching for Romero Ramos and Lyla Baroni. It took Parker almost five weeks to find them as they had moved from Portugal to France and then to London to try to fog their trail. They stayed one night then left by private plane to Palermo, Italy on the Northen coast of Sicily. They stayed at the Astoria Palace Hotel while they decided whether to build a home there. Romero purchased a yacht harbored at Porto di Palermo which was four blocks south of the hotel. Parker got to Portugal and found the $100 million in the safe where they left it. It was short.

Christie Mahern walked into Federal Court on Monday morning with several packets of files in hand. Wendy, her assistant, had done a great job putting things into an organized system. They were prosecuting four cases this morning on defendants who violated the FACE Act which was protection for clients of the Reproductive Health Clinics from being harassed or restricted from access to the clinic's services. These cases were exactly the reason that she had been sent out to Denver. Today's cases were the end of sixty cases that she had brought to the court within the past week and a half. She and her team expected as many again as they prepared for the February 20th attack plans by the Pro-Life Groups in Colorado. It was a burden for the clients of the Planned Parenthood Clinics to appear in court and expose their identities, however, to a person, they championed the idea, in an effort to give those who followed in their footsteps a chance to do so without fear of attack, harassment or harm.

All four cases were decided in favor of the plaintiffs that day. Christie was happy that she'd won all sixty of the cases brought to Federal court. She was going to enjoy a few days of relaxation before February rolled around.

Santino Sayan left the airport in Caracas, Venezuela in route to Lisbon, Portugal. He took off at midnight and arrived at 8:15 am that morning. A black limousine rolled to a stop as the passenger door of the plane opened. Into Parker's limo stepped Santino and his bodyguards. They shook hands and the driver whisked them away toward the Astoria Palace Hotel. They chatted briefly on the ride but at the hotel where Santino and his group would stay, the strategy began in earnest to find Romero Ramos and retrieve the rest of the money he had stolen from the cartels which was estimated at over 145 million dollars.

Parker had reported to Santino Sayan that the total in their account had been $245 million. He had received $100 million from Parker Clark when in fact he was hiding the other $145 million that he received. They had traced Romero and Lyla Baroni to this hotel, but they were too late. The couple had left two days before they arrived. Unbeknownst to them, Romero and Lyla were in a yacht headed to Casablanca in Morocco. Once they got to Morocco, they took a Lufthansa flight straight to Montreal, Canada.

They had moored the yacht in Casablanca so they would have a place to live upon their return. When they reached Montreal, they stayed in a hotel for one night then returned to the airport and flew to Winnipeg, Canada. They again stayed one night. They then rented a car with their new identifications which identified them as Ron and Lylian Parker, who was now Lyllian Perez. The pictures were recent, so they had no problem crossing the border in Montana at the Route 75 cross over. They drove to Fargo, North Dakota and bought a plane ticket to Denver, Colorado.

In Denver, Parker looked up Dr. Jennifer Steinberg, his ex-wife. She had remarried and now owned her own dental office since they parted ways. She had just returned from a long three-week vacation to Mexico when she heard that voice on the phone. He said, "Jennifer, how are you? I need to see you in person for about five minutes. When could you squeeze me in?" Jennifer said, "May I ask who is calling?" Parker laughed, "I am sorry that I did not introduce myself. It has been a while since you have heard my voice. It is Parker." Even though Jennifer already knew who it was, her blood still froze when he said his name. She said very coldly, "Mr. Clark, or whatever your name is now that you are running from the authorities, my advice from my attorney as well as the FBI indicated that it would be best not to see you and to report this telephone call to them immediately." Parker said, "Wow, Jen. I guess I have ruined any chance of us being at least friends. I just need a small favor for old-time's sake. I need to drop off something for you at your office. You don't even have to see me, but it would be nice to give this to you in person. Please!" She was curious about what was so important for him to drop off in person. She said, "Parker, you have five minutes and I have free time at 3:00 p.m. I will meet you at the front door of my office." He thanked her and hung up.

Markus Edwards had spent weeks down in Sante Fe. Things were calm so he asked Ryan if he could have a long weekend off. Ryan had extra agents available, so he let him go. Ryan was aware of Markus' plan. Markus drove his car home on Route 125 North. It was a six-hour trip, but he had a stop to make in Colorado Springs.

Markus' Uncle Tom ran a small jewelry store where he and his Aunt Carol lived.

His Uncle Tom was known around Buffalo as the best diamond setter in the area and certainly, the best Markus had ever seen. So, he entrusted him to make this special ring. He picked it up around noon. The trip took less time than he expected, so he had a few minutes to visit with Tom and Carol.

Markus left an hour later. He continued his drive home to Englewood, Colorado. He got home about ten minutes before Wendy arrived. He said as she walked into the kitchen, "Hi Beautiful, if you would like to take a quick shower, I am taking you out for dinner tonight." Wendy was so excited to see him, she jumped into his arms, and they kissed. She said, "That sounds terrific, Babe. Give me twenty minutes or if you want to join me, it'll be forty!"

Markus laughed, "If I join you, we will never make our reservations." As promised, Wendy came down the stairs twenty minutes later with a very short dress that accented her shapely legs. It was one of Markus' favorites and he told her so. They left the house, and he headed toward the Perfect Landing Restaurant. This was housed in the Centennial Airport's second floor. Jimmy the owner greeted them and gave Wendy a light hug while shaking Markus' hand, "I have your table ready. Follow me."

Dinner was divine as always and as they left, the sun began to dip behind the mountains to the west, giving off a warm, yellow glow to the parking lot as they approached his truck. He hit the button on his key fob to unlock the doors and said, "Wait a second, let me get the door for you."

Wendy waited next to the door as Markus went around to her side. She had her back to him as he got behind her. He was down on one knee when he said, "Wendy," She turned around and screeched with her hand over her mouth. Markus continued,

"Wendy, I love you very much. You have been my rock for years now and are wonderful with my kids. I want to spend the rest of my life loving you. Will you marry me?" With that, he produced the ring he had Uncle Tom make. He opened the box and Wendy gasped. The ring was beautiful and took her breath away. He said, Well?" She yelled, "YES, YES, YES! I love you!"

In Buffalo, New York, Diane O'James sat at her desk holding a department meeting with the City Attorney, the councilmen and the Police and Fire Chiefs. They had received a communication from Florida that Parker Clark had escaped from prison and might be headed their way.

Diane said, "Thank you everyone for coming in today. I know the weather has been wintry as it is in January in Western New York, but I have news that I wanted to share with you all at the same time. Parker Clark escaped from Federal Prison two days ago and the authorities think he may return here to even a few scores. As you may know, Perry Kline, who led the Snow Villain case that put Mr. Clark behind bars, has moved to Denver, Colorado, and now works for the FBI. Christie Mahern, who Mr. Kline lives in Denver and was a target of Mr. Clark and his accomplices, has also moved to Denver and is currently working as a U.S. Attorney. Michael Donlevy, who works for the FBI and assisted Mr. Kline in the case, is no longer here in Buffalo either. He works for the FBI, but I am not sure where at this point. My question to you all is, Do any of you know who Mr. Clark may target if, in fact, he returns to our fair city?"

There were murmurs but no one spoke out loud as they digested this information. Her brother, Dennis O'James said, "If memory serves, Linda Carnello had some dealings with him. Christie Mahern's brother, Matt Fogelberg was in cahoots with Parker, but he may still be in jail. The only other one I can think of is Margie Galway, the wife of the slain, former mayor."

From the end of the table, Neal Seagle, a Councilman said, "There have been rumors that Parker Clark's organization is still running drugs into our city from Venezuela. They are no longer using my restaurant in Key West as a place of storage, I can assure you. Maybe the police department can shed some light on that issue?"

Paul Gorci, Chief of Detectives was in the room representing the Police Department offered, "Our Department has heard of Clark's escape, and we continue to crack down on all forms of trafficking in our city, but nothing has linked anyone to the former Chief of Detective's associates. I do, however, feel we should create a strategy of watches and alerts in case he returns."

Parker Clark and his lady accomplice arrived in Toronto from Europe by private jet. He had new identification, but they decided to let her rent the vehicle to drive down to Buffalo, New York on the Queen Elizabeth Way.

The trip took about 2 and a half hours, so they stopped for something to eat in Hamilton. They stopped at the Long Horn Barbeque, and both had a filet, potato, and salad. Each had a glass of red wine before they got back into the car and completed their drive to Buffalo. They had no issues at customs at the Peace Bridge. After entering Buffalo, they were at her house within ten minutes. Margie Galway lived on a quiet street just north of downtown called Depew Avenue. Her house had just been renovated. She had a covered, heated walkway from the house to the pool which was also enclosed and heated. There was a glass solarium type roof and one way glass that let in plenty of light but provided absolute privacy. She often swam nude each morning before starting her day. On those winter days when it was cloudy and freezing cold, there was nothing better than diving into a heated pool first thing in the morning before coffee to get one's blood pumping.

The sun was just about to dip into Lake Erie as they both walked into the pool, the low-level lights came on as dusk ended and night began. Their swim was invigorating, and Parker commented, "I always loved swimming in this pool but now that it is heated and enclosed, it really motivates me to use it daily. I can see where it has done wonders for you as well because if I may say so, you look ten years younger than the last time I swam naked with you."

Margie blushed, "You always were the charmer. Thank you. You don't look bad either Mr. Perez!" They both laughed at her use of his new identity which was Spanish for John Doe. As Parker went up the ladder and donned his robe, he asked, "Would you like a cocktail?" Margie replied, "I would love, one of your margaritas. You make the best margaritas ever and I think we should celebrate your return to the city of good neighbors."

Parker stood at the bar inside the pool room and mixed the drinks. She walked naked to the bar and grabbed hers, taking two long swigs. She untied his robe, clinked glasses with him then they embraced and began a heated kiss. She led him to the nearest bedroom, one of six, and they made mad, passionate love. He was in great shape and had amazing stamina. Margie told him exactly that. She said, "Sex with you is otherworldly. You really rock my world."

Shortly after a shower, they were dressed again and ready to take care of a few errands. She had a new vehicle. A Cadillac, only this one was all black. He laughed as they started the car and drove out onto Depew Avenue. They had several stops to make and were heavily armed for their mission in the night. it was around eleven thirty p.m., which meant most of the town would be readying for bed or watching Jay Leno.

They were gone for all of three hours and had made four stops. They were all successful. He had killed eight people. He killed two people at each stop. They returned to her house on Depew and had another Tequila before going to bed. It had been a very full day.

They watched the morning news after a very restful night's sleep. The headlines on all three networks were the murders of eight prominent Buffalo residents last night. The report on Channel Seven News said, "It looked like all of these were professional hits. There were no signs of forced entry, no gunshots were reported by any of the neighbors and there were no traces of anyone having been at any of the locations. There were other people in the homes at the time of the killings, but no one heard anything. It was unnerving.

Parker and Margie had a nice, quiet breakfast. They showered together then dressed. They packed a small suitcase and drove back to Toronto where they were going to jump on a plane and fly to Denver, Colorado.

Parker said to Margie as they made their final approach into DIA (Denver International Airport), "We have some business here both with the cartels and then some personal matters to attend to. After that, I think I would like you to meet Mr. Sayan so we'll fly to Venezuela unless he is in Aruba at his private villa.

Margie replied, "That sounds like I will need a whole new summer wardrobe. You may need some new clothes as well. Where can we shop?"

Parker thought a moment, "It makes sense to shop at our destination in Venezuela or Aruba. I think you may like Aruba for a half the year's residency. Whether Santino Sayan is in Caraccas or in his Aruban villa, we will stop for some time at my place in Aruba. If you like it, we'll stay. If not, we'll go elsewhere." Margie replied, "It will be exciting either way." They kissed and got ready to land in Denver. As always, landing was a bit rocky.

Christie sat in her office in the Federal Building and pondered the information she was receiving from her sources. There was to be a National Day of Protest at all Reproductive Health Care Provider Centers in not only Colorado but also every other state. Wendy

McKeller walked into her boss's office with a fresh cup of coffee for her. Christie said, "Wendy, I don't know how you always know exactly what I need. Back in Buffalo, I used to kid you about being a mind reader but the longer I know you, the truer that statement is. Thank you, I was just thinking of getting a cup when you walked in."

Wendy laughed, "I generally ask myself, what would I need at this moment, and it usually works. We are a lot alike, you and me. What are you working on today?"

Christie looked down at her notes, "I was just perusing these notes about the planned protests for February 20th all over the country. I was about to call Perry at his office to ensure his sources were giving him the same info. I am thinking about calling the Planned Parenthood locations and giving them a heads-up and a possible strategy. I am going to suggest that they close the locations as quietly as possible to thwart these attacks."

Wendy beamed with pride, "Christie, it never ceases to amaze me how in tune you are with the public on so many issues and how you inevitably come up with the most inventive and effective strategies. I think that is a marvelous idea. I will be interested to hear what Perry and his team thinks."

Perry Kline was having coffee with Ryan Coleman down in Sante Fe at the Downtown Subscription on Garcia Street. Lynn Rodriguez was their waitress this morning and brought them their coffees and a donut each before they sat down at their favorite table in the corner window. Perry thought out loud, "I guess we have been here a few times for you to anticipate our order." Ryan laughed and said, "I guess we are very predictable and boring. I'll have to remind myself to change some of my habits."

Perry's cellphone rang and seeing it was Christie at her office calling said, "Hello. If this is a sales call, I am way too busy doing the government's work to speak to you right now." Christie responded,

"Agent Kline, this is the Attorney General's Office calling. I wonder if you have a few moments now."

After ten minutes of one-sided conversation with Christie, Perry interjected with, "Miss Mahern, I had not heard any confirmation of these planned activities from the Pro-Choice and Pro-Life groups, but I will certainly put this on the front burner as much as possible. I also feel your strategy for that day for the locations is brilliant but the only caveat I would add is that there should still be security at the sites should there be any attempted vandalism that the local police can address. Thank you so much for your information. I will see you later. Goodbye."

Christie just smiled knowing he was sitting with someone probably having coffee because he ended the call so formally. She was always charmed by how he handled each situation perfectly.

Now she wondered how she should proceed notifying all the Reproductive Health Care Centers without tipping off the Pro-Life and Pro-Choice groups. She decided that she would call Shayla Beth at E. 38th Street and have her call the sites herself and make it as secretive as possible so as not to give any indication to the groups of their plan. There was almost a month left before the date so it should not be an issue. She decided to contact her former mentor, Trini Ross, in Buffalo to discuss her strategy. She may just be able to alert the rest of the U.S. Attorneys to follow her lead.

Miss Ross was very receptive to the idea and was duly impressed with Christie for taking the initiative to attempt to counter the planned attacks on the locations. Trini Ross said, "Christie, I will pass the information on to Washington. The Attorney General will pass on the information to the various states. I am sure he will be impressed. There may even be a commendation for you because of your actions. Thank you because it also validates my decision to put you in the office in Denver. Keep up the great work."

Christie felt good and called Wendy in to brag. Wendy said, "I knew you would be great at this job. You would be great at anything you are challenged with because you are bright, self-initiating and strategic in everything you do. It is a real pleasure to work for someone who is thoughtful, efficient as well as downright classy."

Christie blushed, "I wasn't fishing for compliments. I wanted you to know she thought it was a good idea. Thanks. That stuff's always good to hear."

Diane O'James, the Buffalo mayor, called Michael Donlevy. She had heard he was shot and killed but she took a chance that his replacement would answer the call. She waited listening to the rings. "Hello, this is Michael Donlevy, how can I help you?"

Diane was stunned into silence. He repeated, "Hello. Can I help you?" Diane finally regained her voice, "Mr. Donlevy, this is Diane O'James from Buffalo. It is so nice to hear your voice. I had heard of your recent demise, but I am thrilled to hear you are still with us. This is the only number I had on my cell phone to call. I was just with my younger sister, Donna showing her a friend's house here in Buffalo when I observed Parker Clark and a woman looking like Margie Galway getting out of a black Cadillac in front of the house next door. I had my staff check the plates and the car is, indeed, registered to Ms. Galway and that is her house. I wanted to get a sense of how I should proceed from you from the Federal perspective."

Michael replied, "Miss O'James, thank you so much for the call. I will alert the office in Buffalo as well as the Buffalo Police and they will take it from there. I would wait a few days before I went to the house next door again. Goodbye."

Michael then called the office in Buffalo. The current director was Jonathan Pace who answered on the first ring, "Hello, Mr.

Donlevy, how can I help you today?" Michael replied, "Well, Jon, I just heard from a Buffalo source that Parker Clark was seen at the house of Margie Galway about two hours ago. I don't have the number, but the house is on Depew Avenue. Proceed cautiously as he is probably armed. He is also looking over his shoulder as he has been on the run for a couple of days now." Jonathan Pace thanked Michael.

Even as the two Directors were in conversation, Parker and Margie were getting off the plane in Denver. All their efforts in Buffalo would be for naught. The Buffalo Police sat at the Depew address for two days and nothing was seen of the former Chief of Detective and the homeowner, Margie Galway. They finally had the forces stand down. They had teams around the home in each direction/ The saw no movements detected. Jonathan Pace sent a swat team into the house. They found Margie Galway shot dead on the pool deck. Jon Pace called Michael Donlevy to report they found Miss Galway dead and nothing or no one else.

February 20th of that year was a day that will be remembered for a lifetime. The government had issued an order to the local police department that serviced each of the nation's Planned Parenthood locations. The order was to anticipate violence at these sites who may be closed.

It was anything but business as usual. The newspapers reported across 48 states that violence, gunfire, and injuries were caused by both the Pro-Life and Pro-Choice groups. The location in Colorado at E. 38th Street was a prime case in the news. They were scheduled to close; however, two doctors called Shay Beth. The doctors requested that the site be open as both had emergency cases they were to complete. In the very early hours of the morning of February 20th, the protesting groups arrived within minutes of the site opening. Even with police snipers on site and an additional two-man car from the Bureau, gunfire broke out as everyone else arrived at the location.

It was a bloody scene as one doctor was killed, four protesters were killed, a sniper was shot and in critical condition and Shay Beth had been wounded after a bullet came through a window in the front foyer. She was hospitalized and treated.

Around the country, there were hundreds of incidents of rioting and some injuries but none as serious as the location in Colorado. The Bureau was furious with Shayla Beth who had initially recommended the sites be closed on that day. She had planned to have the two procedures scheduled to be done before 9 a.m., which was the normal time the clinic opened. Her gamble backfired. She was inconsolable as she lay in her bed at UC Health Center. It all could have been avoided that day had the government listened to the warnings. It may have happened later, but knowing the attack was coming should have been listened to and the proper steps to avoid confrontation been put into place.

In Colorado, there were 70 arrests, 40 handguns were seized, and hundreds of charges were filed. Christie Mahern and her team would be busy in court sorting through these cases. Christie discussed some of the cases with her man, Perry Kline, to see what could ultimately be done to change the whole structure of the climate for these Reproduction Clinics in the U.S.

Christie called Perry, "Mr. Kline, How is your day going? Well, I hope. This is U.S. Attorney Christie Mahern calling. Are you available for conference?" Perry laughed and said, "Aren't we official today, Miss Mahern. I am well and I will always make time for a conference with you. What's up?"

Christie answered, "I was just going over the cases from the attacks on the Planned Parenthood locations and noticed that the majority of those detained were of Hispanic heritage. I even recognized one of the names as one of the leaders of the Chica Fuerte cartel, Olivia Hernandez. Could the cartels be the ones that are instigating these attacks?"

Perry again marveled at Christie's sense of the overall picture. She was excellent at putting two and two together, "Yes, Christie, you are again, right on the money. According to our intel, Chica Fuerte is behind these attacks and the other cartels are using the distractions to escalate their drug runs into the country. My guess is that because many of the locations across the country were closed on February 20th, they will plan another major attack in the next few days or weeks to catch everyone sleeping."

Christie said, "I don't feel like cooking tonight. Shall we have dinner at Vincenzo's?" Perry said, "Dinner out works for me. I have a new restaurant I can make reservations at. Is 7 p.m. a good time?" Christie said, "Perfect, see you later." Perry called The Capital Grille and made reservations at the restaurant at 1450 Larimer Street in LODO which is what locals call the Lower Denver area.

Megan Rolling answered her cell, "Hello, Mr. Coleman. How are you this fine afternoon?" Ryan said, "I would be much better if you have dinner with me tonight." Megan replied, "I can't think of anything I would rather do…well, I can but I can't say right now. Dinner tonight would be awesome." Ryan laughed as his thoughts were the same as his new steady girl's. I will pick you up at 6:30 as reservations are for 7:00 p. m." Megan said, "It's a date. Thank you."

Megan was happy when she hung up the call from Ryan. When he came in for his interviews, she thought he was dreamy, but she didn't want to tip her hand just yet. She would go out casually with him but not get serious. That plan was scrapped after their first sleepover. She was head over heels emotionally. Was it love or just lust, she wondered. She was hoping to find out from Ryan if he felt the same.

Ryan was thinking how lucky he was to have found a sweet lady like Megan. He felt very strongly for her but wondered if it was the great sex, or if was he as emotionally involved as she seemed to be. Time would tell, he thought. He then called Capital Grille and made reservations for them for dinner.

Wendy McKeller was just about to close the office. Christie had already left for the day and Wendy had completed all the work of filing and letters, that Christie had ordered before she left so she felt good about leaving 30 minutes early. Wendy heard someone come into the office, she looked up and smiled as Markus Edwards walked up to her desk, "Hi Beautiful, how are you today?"

Wendy said, "I am much better seeing your handsome face. What brings you downtown?" Markus responded, "I was wondering if I could take you to dinner tonight and I happened to be in the neighborhood so I thought I would stop in and personally make an invitation." Wendy beamed with adorning love, "I would be overjoyed to dine with you this evening." She kissed him hard.

The City of Buffalo was a buzz, with talk about the murders of more prominent people and, of course, who had perpetrated these killings. Parker Clark's name was bandied about in almost every circle. The names of those murdered were released and sent more shock waves throughout the city.

Linda Carnello, a former fashion model was found in her condo with her friend Lucy Curnic shot to death as they were having drinks. Eric and Kris Volsier were found in their hotel room at the Hyatt Hotel on the waterfront in downtown Buffalo. Joni Wilsco was just released from prison the prior week and was entertaining friends at her home in South Buffalo. She and one of her best friends, Dennis Shooda, were both shot in the kitchen. The perpetrators entered and exited through the side door unbeknownst to the rest of those in attendance in the front room who were devastated and shocked when they walked into the kitchen and found them. Finally,

Paul Gorci and his girlfriend Danielle 'Baby girl' Riches were found shot at the home of Miss Riches who lived next door to Christie Mahern's former home in East Aurora. All were shot gangland style lying on the couch face down with a bullet in the back of the head. The most shocking was finding Margie Galway shot in her home two days later. The newspapers spoke of possible scenarios and suspects were not named but everyone knew who was responsible.

Michael Donlevy was on the phone with Lewis Greeley who was in Barcelona, Spain. Lewis said, "We have tracked our suspects to a town in Palermo, Italy. We will set up observation and then make an arrest. I should be back in D.C. by the end of the week."

Michael said, "OK. I will begin our strategy on Friday in Denver and then we will see what kind of response we get from the cartels. I will keep you abreast of our progress. Best of luck." They ended the call. Michael was hoping that the Bureau's team in Spain would be able to apprehend Romero Ramos and Lyla Baroni in Morocco. He knew that they had set up a perimeter around the yacht in the Casablanca harbor, and they were waiting for word from Lewis to begin.

Lewis flew into Morocco and was helicoptered into Casablanca. He met the crew there headed by Levi Conley. Levi reported that there had been no sign of occupation on the yacht in the four days they were there. He said to Lewis, "Chief, I don't think they are here. Maybe they shot one another but my gut tells me that we missed them, and they left before we arrived. I suggest that if we don't find them, we leave a skeleton crew and move back to the U.S."

It was now dark, and Lewis ordered the team to enter the yacht. Levi had called it. They were gone.

Romero and Lyla landed in Aruba and took a cab from the Queen Beatrix Airport to the Bucuti Yacht Club on Bucutiweg Rd. This was southeast of the capital of Oranjestad. It was a seven-minute ride to the Yacht club. Then they could go into the capital by car in 10-12 minutes. Much of the tourist trade was from the northeast to the northwest corner of the island. They would be far from any possible American tourists identifying them. Senor Sayan greeted them at the bar in the yacht club. They embraced and he introduced Lyla. They sat and Romero pulled out his large leather wallet. In it he extracted ten documents. Each of them was a cashier check from five different banks, valued at $200,000,000. Santino Sayan was pleased, "This is great Romero. Did you leave anything for the cartels to operate with?"

Romero laughed, "Yes Sir. I left $2.5 billion in the account and gave Parker $100 million to shut him up. I kept $500 million for my efforts."

Romero and Lyla partied with Santino Sayan and his three women for the remainder of the evening, only returning to their yacht club at 2 a.m. Romero said before they slept, "I will take you shopping tomorrow, Mrs. Rodriguez. Then we will return to the States to finish some business in Denver."

Camryn Graystone was on the phone with Micah Blair, "Nonno, I was reviewing the case file again about the cartels and doing some forensic research and found that Parker Clark's real name is Peter Sayan or Pedro Sayan. He is the brother of Santino Sayan who is the Venezuelan drug lord that seems to be the leaders of all the cartels and where all the fentanyl and cocaine generate from in Caracas. I also searched Parker Clark and he has changed his name to Juan Perez which is equivalent to John Doe in Spanish. Margie Galway reverted to her maiden-name, Margaret Keene. When I was in Denver, I overheard your secretary in Denver, Megan Rolling, talk to you about Lyla Baroni. She is traveling with a man named Romero Ramos who has changed his name to Mickey Rodriguez and Lyla is now Leah Rodriguez. They have all been traveling overseas but I have no clearance to search for their flights.

You may want to have Megan do that or someone that is not a suspect, involved in the cartel's business."

Micah was furiously taking notes and then heard Camryn say, "I hope you weren't taking notes because I just sent you a secure email with all the information to your private email that we use."

Micah laughed, "Now that I have writer's cramp you tell me this. I am so old school, I guess!" They shared a good laugh and ended the call.

Micah then called Christie Mahern at the U.S. Attorney's office in Denver, "Christie, I am going to send four sets of names to you. The first is the name we know them by and the second is their new alias. Can you please run a scan of their travels in and out of the country in the last month? Call my cellphone if you find anything. Thanks," Christie only said, I am on it" Then she ended the call.

The email from Micah said:

Parker Clark- Juan Perez   Margie Galway- Margaret Keene

Romero Ramos- Mickey Rodriguez   Lyla Baroni – Leah Rodriguez

PART EIGHT

Lewis Greeley had arrived back in the U.S. and flew straight to Denver, Colorado. He sat in his former office, now occupied by Micah Blair who out of respect let Mr. Greeley sit in his comfortable swivel chair while he and Michael Donlevy and Perry Kline sat in the three comfortable chairs in front of the desk. Megan Rolling entered with a tray of coffees, sodas, and bagels for them. She set them down and said, "Gentlemen, if you need anything else, just buzz for me." Then she went back to her desk, closing Micah's door.

Lewis began, "I am quite jet lagged, but this is important. I can sleep when I am dead is what my father used to say." Micah chuckled to himself as he remembered his dad, Del, saying the exact same thing. Lewis continued, "We now are confident that Parker and friend have returned to the States and are together. We need to be vigilant as I am sure they have arrived in Denver. Thanks to Micah's granddaughter, Camryn, for finding their name changes and to Christie Mahern, Perry's fiancé, the U.S. Attorney for tracking their movement within the country. Regarding Romero Ramos and Lyla Baroni, we now know that they too have returned to the U.S. and are headed for Denver as well. This works out for us as we now don't have to schlep around the world when we begin Operation RATS." Everyone in the room laughed as they knew RATS was an acronym for Remove All The Slime.

Perry said, "I will pass on the kudos to Ms. Mahern, and she has her team ready to charge all those RATS we apprehend during this Operation. My team will focus on Ramos and Baroni. We will apprehend them at the appointed time. We will also clear out the new location of the Cartel's drug warehouse."

Micah then added, "My team will focus on Clark and partner. We will have them pinned down in minutes at the designated time. We have the Sante Fe group ready to swoop down on what we believe to be the largest shipment of illicit narcotics in the Bureau's history, thought to be worth $15 BILLION. Losing that should put a crimp in their payroll." Lewis smiled, "I just hope they do not get wind of what is going on. We have laid low for weeks now, giving them a false sense of security. We concentrated on the chaos at the Planned Parenthood locations which has waned."

Micah said, "We have had an outside security firm doing a bug search in our building here at headquarters as well as all other locations. This has helped us identify the people who instructed our former service company not to sweep the bugs but only move them. WE hired the new security team under the guise that they were an Infection Control firm so all our internal RATS would be unsuspecting of that operation." Lewis added, I almost fainted when I saw just how many bugs and different systems of bugs were in operation. If we were able to stumble onto one, the other would still be in operation. Nice work, Micah."

Perry said, "It is paramount that we three are the only ones with all this intelligence. Especially in view of what we found within the building. Even our teams do not know how significant the Operation is in its entirety. The teams only know their part of the plan and not the entire plan. A toast to it all going to plan!" Perry raised his coffee cup and the other raised theirs in a toast.

Mick Kepler and his twin brother Jimmy ran a security company in Denver. Their company was called 'Rockin' Rebels Security', contracted by the Bureau to sweep the building for bugs. Mick called Micah, "Mr. Blair, I have distressing news for you. We found not one but two systems of bugs and listening devices in the building. These systems were set up so if one was found, the other could be activated. I removed them both but left one of each operating in the boiler room so that you could communicate with whoever installed them. This will give them the feeling that both systems are active. I then put in the untraceable wiring that you can monitor from your office. Each room has a number and there is a recording device in each room sensitive enough to hear a whisper. The recorded tapes can either be erased or saved to your computer. You have a manual in your computer for its operation. Do you have any questions?"

Micah said, "Thanks, Mick. You and your brother did a fabulous job, and I am sure you will keep this information confidential. I will call if we need anything further." Micah then called Lewis and Perry to alert them of the successful change in security systems. Micah listened to the tape in Megan's office and heard her say to someone that it seemed like the security system was down. She hung up when Perry walked into her office. Micah wondered.

Parker Clark walked into the Gateway Smiles dentist's office at 4:00 p.m. He wanted to be alone with her when he confronted his ex-wife, Dr. Steinberg. He found out that the last time he was here to ask her for help, she had refused then called the FBI here in Denver. He thought, 'I'll teach her a lesson to keep her mouth shut when dealing with a dangerous man.'

He asked the lady, Robin, in the office, "May I speak with Dr. Steinberg." Robin said, "I am sorry, but she has already left for the day. If you give me your name and number, I can tell her you were here." Parker responded, "Tell her an old friend just wanted to stop by and say hello. Maybe I will catch her another time. Thanks," He spun and left immediately. Robin sat there for a minute or so. She was shaking. Robin knew that it was Parker Clark, Jennifer's ex-husband, and escaped convict. She watched him drive out of the parking lot then she called Jennifer on her cell phone. Jennifer called the FBI, "Michael Donlevy, please."

Megan asked her, "May I tell him who is calling?" Jennifer said, "His dentist." Megan replied, Thank you, just a minute." She buzzed Michael and he picked up the phone. Megan said, "Jennifer Steinberg on line 3 for you."

Michael punched number three, "Hello, Dr. Jen. How are you?" Jennifer said, "Mr. Donlevy, Parker Clark was just in my office. Luckily, I was not there. I am very afraid he wants some sort of revenge. What should I do?"

Michael sat upright, "Did they see what kind of car he was driving? Was he alone?" Dr. Steinberg said, "Robin at my office said he was driving a black Cadillac SUV license number NL2 JJ6. It's a Florida plate." Michael said, "Don't go home today. See if you can stay with a friend. I will keep in touch with you. Thank you, Dr. Steinberg, for the information. I hope now we can get this guy off the street now. Also, if he comes in again, have a code word that someone should call this number ASAP. That is great work. Thank you." They ended the call.

He sent out an email to all agents with the make and plate number. He had advised them NOT approach but to follow and relay their location.

The memo was short and sweet. It read: Snow Villain spotted. Black Cadillac SUV- Plate: NL2-JJ6. Identify and report location only. DO NOT ENGAGE.

Levi Bailey looked at his phone and saw the memo from Mr. Donlevy. He saw the info and knew that the escaped prisoner from Florida was in the Denver area, specifically Aurora. He thought to himself, why would a guy who escaped from a Federal prison come to Denver? He was doing security at HQ and was stationed on the roof facing east. He would keep his eyes peeled for this black Cadillac. He had a hunch it might show up at HQ.

Christopher Wiser and Eric Slay were having a small cocktail party in their San Francisco condo. There were a few friends there to celebrate Eric's retirement from the Bureau. Christopher had decided to continue in his double life as an agent in the Bureau and as a consultant for a local not-for-profit. He just saw the email about the Snow Villain and mentioned it to Eric. Eric said, "I would like to see that guy back in jail as he not only killed some folks we knew (,) but also was and may still be the head of the East Coast drug organization." He was just speaking loud enough for Christopher to hear as many of their friends did not know he and Christopher worked for the Bureau. They all thought he was quitting his job in computer program sales so he could write that travel novel that he told everyone he had in him bursting to get out.

Later that evening when all their guests had gone, Christopher asked Eric if he thought that Parker Clark had any reason to come to San Francisco. Christopher replied, "I know that Lyla had a connection to him and the cartels but if she was still around, he might look to reconnect with her. Rumor has it that she and her man, Romero Ramos, stole a significant amount of money from the cartels and then left quickly headed for Europe." Eric offered, "I bet that all of them are still in the States and looking to be undercover to continue their illegal money-making schemes."

Ryan Coleman had seen the memo from HQ regarding the Snow Villain. He would keep working until quitting time but wondered if this latest development would interfere with his dinner plans. He would not tell Megan as she probably already was in on all the communications anyway. Markus Edwards thought he might have to cancel dinner with Wendy tonight. He knew that so many of the men in the Bureau leadership wanted to catch this guy, Clark. He called to let her know.

Perry was on his way to Christie's office. He had seen the memo and wanted to take no chances of Mr. Parker Clark trying anything as dumb as trying to take out a U.S. Attorney. He had decided to take a short trip to Vale for a bit of skiing and take the love of his life with him. He had discussed this with Micah and Micah agreed that if Parker had targeted both Perry and Christie, they would be safer out of town until the man was back in custody.

Christie fought him about leaving town, however, she acquiesced thinking it would be a fun getaway and she certainly didn't want another encounter with Mr. Parker Clark or any of his associates.

Lyla Baroni and Romero Ramos had returned to the United States using their aliases. They were now known as Rickey and Lyllian Perez. They flew into Miami from Aruba. They then jumped on a plane to Denver and arrived at DIA (Denver International Airport) at 5:30 p.m. They rented a car and were on their way to the hotel downtown. Lyla was a bit concerned that she might run into someone she knew from the Bureau. Romero said, "If we do meet any of your old friends, we'll just wipe them out." She shuddered as she heard this as she knew he had no compunction about offing people for no good reason.

Lewis Greeley called Michael Donlevy and let him know they were sending 400 agents from surrounding states to assist with the takedown of the cartels. The strategies that had been worked out for tomorrow were ready to be implemented. The Bureau had identified Parker and the woman has with him as they stayed in a hotel in Denver. It was March 1st. Operation RATS would commence at 7 a.m. on March 3rd. The surveillance teams were working to keep all operations under a watchful eye until 3/3/23 at 7 a.m.

The border crossing town at Las Cruces, New Mexico, was being watched by a team at Fort Bliss. They would intercept the shipment in buses, trucks, and cars at 3 a.m. The morning of the third of March. There were teams at all the Parenthood Planning Centers along the I25 route from Mexico. They were ready for any possible violence at these locations, even though they'd be closed.

Micah spoke to all the agents in a voicemail. "We are ready. If you run into any snags, call me ASAP. Good luck and GO TEAM!!!" It was March 3rd, and they were ready to go. It was six a.m., and he left the house with high hopes.

257

The dinners that so many had planned were postponed due to the news of the murders in Buffalo. Everyone was on high alert as Parker Clark was on the run and many assumed he was exacting revenge on those who had crossed him on his way to prison.

In Buffalo, Mayor Diane O'James called a press conference at the Botanical Gardens on South Park Avenue. She wanted the press to be out of the weather as the icy cold temperatures had returned to Buffalo. It was a sunny day, and it was not far from her house. It remained a beautiful setting as the Parks Department continued to maintain its original beauty.

Diane stepped to the podium speaking to about 60 or so news people, "People of Buffalo, we have again been struck by the Snow Villain. He and his accomplice left a trail of evidence at the five locations where these murders took place. They were not as careful as they thought they were. We have joined with the Federal Bureau of Investigation and the Erie County Sherrif's Department in this investigation. We have a nationwide search in place and our sources tell us these criminals are no longer in Western New York. We will keep you updated when further information is uncovered. Thank you."

She left the podium and the Erie County Sherrif, Harold Berger took over and fielded questions from those in attendance. He reviewed the names of those killed but revealed no other information on the details of the case. The presser ended after 30 minutes.

In Denver, Perry Kline and Christie Mahern drove her car to Boulder, Colorado. He made reservations at a bed and breakfast where they would stay the weekend. Perry was taking no chances that Christie Mahern was again in the crosshairs of Mr. Parker Clark. He felt he wanted to be on the active search but knew that Christie was safer with him. He kept in contact with Ryan Coleman who was now second in command assisting Micah in their search for the two people from Buffalo who were thought to be headed their way. They had some leads but whenever anyone on the team ran down a lead, it ended in a dead end. The FBI was frustrated because they had received intel on sightings from reliable sources but nothing much led to anything concrete. They were still at large but it seemed they were headed west toward Denver. This was unnerving to the Denver Bureau's team.

Ryan Coleman walked into Denver's headquarters around 10 a.m., Megan gave him her best smile as he waved and smiled back. They had been very professional to a fault since they began dating. It was generally against company policy to date within the organization, but everyone liked them both so much, they overlooked it. They were both consummate professionals at doing their jobs.

Ryan walked into Micah Blair's office and said, "Micah, I have a hunch about this Parker Clark and his sidekick, who we initially thought was Margie Galway." Micah looked up from his work and waited. Ryan continued, "We know that Clark escaped from prison two weeks ago. We know he was seen in Buffalo the night of the murders. He obviously is working on avenging all the wrongs done to him that put him behind bars in the first place. Having talked to Perry Kline who worked for him, he seems to be a guy who feels he can do as he pleases and when people get in his way, he snuffs them out. Clark must have killed Margie. He now may have a new identity so he can travel incognito. We think he may be headed to Denver to deal with Perry and Christie. What if we stage a trap for them at Perry and Christie's home in Englewood? We could have two agents staying there in disguise and we would evacuate the neighbors so we could set up a kind of sting operation to see if they were coming for them. Any thoughts?

Micah knew that Ryan had a good idea. The two fugitives from the east had slipped into the home of four couples and killed them without anyone hearing them. Clark was also thought to be Margie Galway's killer. He may use the same tactic here. Micah said to Ryan, "I think you are right to show concern. My thoughts were that he may come looking for both Perry Kline and Christie Mahern. I got a lead on Lyla Baroni and her man Romero Ramos. They have new identities now as I learned from Camryn, my granddaughter. She and I spoke this week about where they might be headed based on the name changes and bank activity related to those new names. We have been able to track their movements around the country and it looks like they may be headed here as well. Lyla may be harboring bad feelings about the way she was abruptly let go from the Bureau. I'll bet she was banking on a significant pension as she had been around for many years.

Looks like it might be show down at the O-K Corral." Ryan laughed and then fell silent as Megan entered Micah's office knowing she had interrupted an important conversation. She left some papers and coffee for both then left.

It was very cold that morning as Micah arrived at headquarters. He had called a meeting of the security team to discuss some strategies for defending the headquarters location in the event of attack. There were 18 agents in the room who had been placed on the team. There were three shift leaders and five agents who manned the roof, front and back doors as well as two interior agents who were rovers in the residence and office floors.

The weekend and night shifts had been much lighter but were now beefed up again in anticipation of trouble from haters in general. Michael began by thanking the three leaders, Levi Bailey, Donald James, and Quinn Benjamin, "Don, Quinn and Levi, you men have joined the Bureau just recently but have shown great talent, instincts, and leadership. I am proud of all of you. You three will lead the security force that we'll have in place at HQ in anticipation of any possible situation that may arise. Mr. James, as the Assistant

Director, I would like you to take the day shift and organize your team. Mr. Bailey, if you could take the 4p.m. to Midnight shift then pass it to Mr. Benjamin to cover the midnight to 8 a.m. shift, that would be great. We are most vulnerable during the hours of darkness, but any concentrated attack could be difficult at any time. Please ensure the roof and main entrances are covered. The emergency call goes to me, and I will alert the swat group who are on standby."

The meeting broke up and Micah felt better that this was in place. He called Perry to make sure he and Christie were leaving or on their way to ski country for a few days and he left the key for the swat group to housesit just in case Mr. and Mrs. Perez (Parker and a partner) tried the same M.O. that they used in Buffalo.

Lewis has given Christopher Wiser a special assignment. He was charged with tailing Micah Blair. Micah was unaware so he would be acting normally. Christopher was one of the agents who really enjoyed this type of work. He was extremely good at keeping close to his target but never being noticed. As Michael left the security meeting, he headed home to be with Catie. They had not spent much time together in the past month or so. He wanted to just kick back and relax for some quality time.

Christopher noticed the white SUV first. It cut in front of him about half a block away from Micah's vehicle. Christopher alerted his team of his location.

Micah exited the 470 South highway at South Chambers Road and headed south. He drove to Main Street and turned right. Main Street turned into Ridgegate Parkway which he drove to Hillsboro St. He turned right and went north to Lexington Drive. He noticed a car back about a block so he slowed down to see if it would follow him as he turned right onto Worthington Circle. As he turned left around the bend headed for Worthington Place, he saw the car following behind him toward Worthington Circle.

Instead of turning right at the stop sign headed home to 13840, Micah turned left. He went quickly south on Worthington Circle which made a big oblong circle back to Lexington Drive. Then he pulled across the bend and stopped in the middle of the street. He radioed the Bureau and asked for police backup at his location. He waited outside the car and sure enough, the large white SUV had followed him around in a circle. The car, upon seeing Micah parked across the road and out of the vehicle, backed up immediately and sped up Worthington Circle trying to return to Lexington Drive. Micah had jumped into his vehicle and beat him to the Lexington Drive intersection. His backup from the Parker police had arrived and spotted the white SUV which was now trapped in a loop with Micah and the police at one of two egress points. That was at Hillsboro Street which is where the white SUV headed. Unfortunately for the man and woman in the white SUV, Christopher Wiser, who was tailing Micah Blair was now blocking the intersection at Hillsboro and Worthington Circle. The driver of the SUV stopped and started shooting at the unmarked police car only to receive return fire from in front of him but also the rear of his vehicle. It was Romero Ramos in the white SUV. As he turned to fire at the police vehicle to his rear, he was shot by Christopher Wiser who was blocking the road in front of a white vehicle. He was hit in the back of his right shoulder and right thigh. He went to the pavement and dropped his weapon. Christopher and the Parker Police didn't approach the vehicle. One of them had a bull horn. Ramos heard them say, "You on the ground, lay face down with your arms extended. You in the vehicle, come out slowly with your hands in the air."

They waited a minute and slowly the female on the passenger side opened her door and exited with her hands in the air. Micah arrived to see Lyla Baroni standing beside the white SUV being handcuffed by the Parker Police.

Micah radioed the Bureau and let the switchboard know he was out of danger. Christopher walked over to Micah and heard

Micah say, "Nice shot Christopher. Are you the one who's been trailing me for the past two days?" Christopher nodded. Micah said, "Thanks, I owe you one."

An ambulance arrived within five minutes and Romero Ramos was placed inside and taken to Sky Ridge Medical Center where he was pronounced dead.

Lewis Greeley had returned to Denver and was helping Micah and his team strategize their move against the cartels. El Verdugo was the largest of the cartels and it was the Bureau's number one focus to shut down or at least slow its growth. It was led by Franco Semanas, Andres' brother_. They were based in the Hotel San Carlos located on the south side of Puerta Palorma in Mexico. They had several satellite locations along U.S. Hwy 25 between Las Cruces, New Mexico, Albuquerque New Mexico, Sante Fe, New Mexico, and Denver, Colorado.

Chica Fuerte was the cartel operated primarily by women and led by Petirrojo Cantante who many said was rumored to be an extremely beautiful and alluring woman standing 5 foot eleven inches with jet black hair and a voluptuous body. The Bureau's dossier on her stated she was a former fashion model and then dabbled in cinema both mainstream as well as the adult genre. The most important fact noted was her ruthlessness and overwhelming power and seeming lack of conscience as she and her members had a reputation for killing first then asking questions later. They were headquartered in Las Vegas, New Mexico in the old Capital Scrap Metal location on Railroad Avenue. It was fenced and historically had high traffic as well as several outbuildings for drug storage.

A third and up-and-coming cartel was called Ejercito Joven or the Young Army. They were led by Fredo Alvarez. They were heavily into the drug trade and were concentrating on trafficking persons from South and Central America into the United States who could strengthen their attacks on Fertility clinics in our country. They seemed to be headquartered in Sante Fe, New Mexico.

This new cartel had taken over the First Baptist Church of Sante Fe where Eric Slay was taken when he was abducted from the Downtown Subscription on Garcia Street. The initial reports said they were only 150 to 200 men strong but gaining members daily as illegals passed through Sante Fe seeking aid and comfort.

Lewis and Micah developed a strategy for capturing all three main offices of these cartels on the same day. They decided on a Friday in mid-March when it would still be snowing and raining in Denver and just beginning to warm up in Sante Fe. March 16th would be the traditional beginning of the St. Patrick's Day weekend celebration and even folks who weren't Irish would use this holiday to ward off the cobwebs from a long winter and welcome in the spring season. The weather didn't always cooperate but that was no factor for the celebrating and major drinking that existed in every bar and restaurant.

The Bureau had sent 500 agents to Denver, Colorado; Sante Fe, New Mexico; as well as up and down the Interstate 25 corridor. While they were ready for an attack on their own headquarters, the Bureau was locked and loaded for the largest raid in recent memory. They would begin in the early morning hours. 5:30 a.m. was the designated start time. Many of the veterans from the Bureau were given leadership roles in this major raid operation. They would hit the three major locations of the cartels, twelve of the lesser visited bases of the larger cartels, as well as five major storage and distribution centers of the cartels.

The week of the raid, late in the afternoon on Wednesday, March 14th, the local police departments were notified that the Bureau was conducting "investigatory visits to alleged cartel locations looking for possible drugs, firearms, and shelters for harboring large numbers of illegals. The Police would be given exact locations at 11 p.m. on Thursday night to decrease the possibility of leaks of their plan to the cartels. The Bureau wanted support from the Police Departments but wanted to make sure that there was little time or opportunity for anyone who was sympathetic to the cartels to relay the news of an impending attack. The Bureau leadership realized that even in their own organization, there were plants from the cartels so even the teams around the state received the plan times and locations to maintain the surprise.

Micah assigned team leaders for the following locations: Jim Martly in Las Vegas, Nevada; Tom Franklin in Las Cruces, New Mexico; Jan Casanueva in Sante Fe at the First Baptist Church; Kathy Jeromes in Sante Fe, New Mexico at the Downtown Subscription which housed offices in the back of the coffee shop; Hugh Scott in Albuquerque, New Mexico; Harold Berger in Colorado Springs, Colorado at the distribution center for El Verdugo; Beth O'Brian in Denver at the distribution center off Arapahoe Road at Hwy 25; Hilda Matthews in Denver at the second headquarters of Chica Fuerte in Lakewood, Colorado; Linda Fuda and her son, Leo in Boulder, Colorado at the distribution center at Lucky's Market on Broadway Avenue; and finally, Dominic Conley and Jody Singer were at the border of Mexico to intercept El Verdugo's largest shipment of fentanyl with its Street value was $40 Million. Their teams were ready.

Randy Dale was the team leader at the Kline residence on East Phillips Place out in Englewood, CO. There were only a few lights on in the house but there were twelve agents in black swat gear covering both entrances, and the garage. The very next night was a Thursday around 10:50 p.m. The agents seated in the darkened front loft area observed a black Cadillac slowly driving by the house out of the front window. Randy radioed and alerted the team. They did not have to wait long. The black Cadillac SUV came back around the block, this time with their lights out. It stopped about two houses down the street and parked in front of a house across the street. The two occupants sat in the dark and no one moved for ten minutes.

It was now after 11 p.m. and the passenger got out of the vehicle and walked directly across the street into the side gate of the house, two doors down the street from Perry and Christie's house. It was the home of their new friends, Robin, and Troy Phillips.

An agent seated in the master bedroom of the Kline residence watched the passenger dressed in all black hop over the back fence of the Phillips' house into the greenspace. He walked along the fence crouched down so that you didn't see him until he reached Perry's backyard and quickly jumped over the fence into the backyard. The agent in the master bedroom was Laiza Marie who quietly radioed to the team that the first suspect was in the backyard.

The agents had turned off the security motion lights on the house so anyone attempting to sneak into the house would not encounter that nuisance. Laiza watched the person crouched on the stairs of the back deck and quickly moved to the back sliding glass door.

Randy Dale now noticed the black SUV turn their lights on and do a U-turn and drive off down the street. Just as he was about to radio the team, the man dressed in black popped the latch on the sliding glass door and quietly entered the house. He had his weapon drawn but he was immediately overpowered by two FBI agents who stood on either side of the door. He was wrestled to the floor and handcuffed immediately.

Randy radioed to the car team up the street to follow the black SUV. They confirmed receiving the order and set off to search for the vehicle. They were unsuccessful as they rolled up to the roadblock, the was no sign of the SUV. This was radioed to the team.

Randy Dale went down the stairs to the dining room where his team had the intruder handcuffed and lying face down in the doorway. Randy said to the agent next to the intruder with a black ski mask, "Get 'em up and take off their ski mask, Jimmy." The agent removed the hat and there stood a woman that none of them recognized. Randy took a quick photo of her and sent it to Micah and Headquarters asking for identification. He began to question the woman as to what her name was, why she was there, whom she was looking for, and most importantly, who was with her in the SUV.

The woman replied, "My name is Jane Doe. I was looking for money and jewelry, I wasn't looking for anyone. I thought no one was home as I watched the couple that owned the house leave yesterday and there was no movement all day. What a surprise to find you guys here. The guy driving the car is my brother, John."

Micah's phone buzzed as he received the text from Randy Dale. It had an attachment enclosed so he opened it. All he said was, "Wow!" He immediately texted Randy back and said, "I know this woman. Did you get the driver as well?"

Randy texted back to Micah, "The driver gave us the slip. I had all the roads of egress blocked after the first intruder hit the back deck and I saw the SUV do a U-turn and take off down the street."

Micah said, "The woman you are holding is Charmaine Sinclair. She was sent to prison for murder accessory in the Snow Villain case back in Buffalo. She may be working with Parker Clark. Don't tell her anything. Just bring her in. I want all the exits blocked and I want the Parker Police and your team to do a house-to-house search for the black SUV. He may have changed cars and parked the SUV in a backyard or garage. He may even be hiding in a house in the neighborhood."

The agents with Charmaine in tow went to their car in the garage. They left to go to Bureau Headquarters. Randy then called

Parker Police for back up and let his team know the plan was to find the SUV. He told the two teams blocking in the streets of egress to check every car as Parker Clark may have changed cars. Micah was correct. Parker had changed cars and went right past the team at Otero and Jordan Road, 10 minutes before they were called. He was now fading silently into the night. Parker was feeling good about giving them the slip, but Charmaine must have gotten caught.

Three cars from Parker Police showed up and they each teamed up with a Bureau agent. They began the search, house to house. They checked every backyard, driveway and garage they could see in only waking residents when they could not see in the garages. Thirty minutes later, they found a house for sale on South Norfolk Street which was right around the corner from the address they were staked out at. The house was vacant and inside Randy Dale and a member of the Parker Police found the black SUV. Randy radioed to Micah, "Boss, we found the SUV in a house around the corner. They must have had a second getaway car parked here for the switch. I will call the Forensic team and have them check for prints." He ended the transmission to Micah.

Micah slammed his hand down on his desk in frustration. The Snow Villain had eluded him again. He was encouraged by the fact they had taken Charmaine Sinclair into custody as she was also an escapee from prison.

He checked and sure enough, Charmaine escaped from Englewood Federal Prison on West Quincy at South Kipling in Denver, Colorado. She has only been out of the facility for ten days and has already been apprehended by authorities for breaking and entering, weapons possession, and probably attempted murder. The last one would be a stretch to prove in court. Micah was looking forward to questioning her and getting as much information as possible from her. He didn't have any high expectations knowing her relationship with Parker Clark.

Micah had a memory flash from his chats with his granddaughter Camryn. She had discovered the new identity of Parker Clark. He was now Juan Perez, which loosely translated to John Doe. On a hunch, he called his friend in Real Estate, Diane Sorenstone, to ask about any recent house being purchased by someone with the name Juan Perez attached. She called him back in five minutes and said, "Micah, I sold a property to Juan Perez two weeks ago. It is at 8127 South Norfolk Street. If my memory serves me, it is right around the corner from the house I sold to Christie Mahern."

Micah was very happy and said, "Diane, Thank you so much. You made my day. I think you may have sold that house to the man I am looking for who is an escaped federal prisoner under a different name. I will keep you posted."

Christie and Perry had skied earlier in the day. She was reviewing some cases and developing strategies as Perry took a nap. She woke him by crawling all over him until he opened his eyes. She was totally naked, and it only took two very intimate kisses, and he was aroused and ready for action. They made passionate love until they were both exhausted. Then, they slept.

Perry's phone rang and startled them both. He answered, "Hello, Kline here." The call was from Micah, "Sorry to disturb you but I wanted you to know that we caught an intruder last night at your place. They jimmied the sliding glass door and were apprehended the moment they stepped into the dining room by two agents. You'll never guess who came to visit you?"

Perry was wide awake now, "It was probably a woman." Micah said, "Correct." Perry added, "I probably know her, and she used to live in Buffalo." Micah said, "Correct. Now for the 1-million-dollar question. Who is she?"

Perry said, "My first guess is here in bed with me, so I'll guess a blonde, late forties and built well. How about Charmaine Sinclair?"

Micah was stunned, "You heard already?" Perry laughed, "No, I saw the wire Megan sent out that Ms. Sinclair escaped from prison. Was she alone?" Micah frowned, "We think she was with Parker Clark. He bought a house near you guys and switched cars there. We found his black SUV but now we don't know what he is driving. I have Megan working with her team trying to find a car rental for Juan Perez (Parker's alias) or Margie Keene Galway."

Perry said, "I feel like I want to be in town so I can catch that S.O.B. myself. I won't rest until we get him back behind bars or dead. Maybe Charmaine was using an alias when they rented the car."

Micah said, "OK, I know but sit tight and keep an eye on the Federal prosecutor you got there next to you. I will keep you posted. Maybe we'll get lucky. I posted an agent in the garage next door to the house they bought to see if he returns." The call ended.

Christie had jumped into the shower where he joined her after his call. She said, "What was that all about?" Perry said, "I'll tell you later. Nothing earth-shattering." They showered and got ready for dinner. He had made reservations at Lancelot's Restaurant at 201 E Gore Creek in Vail for 6:15 p.m. Christie looked stunning as they entered the restaurant right on time.

Perry and Christie were seated at a small table at the window looking out over the hills surrounding this small little village. They drank wine. A delicious California red sauvignon. She ordered Alaskan King crab, and he ordered the Weiner Schnitzel. They enjoyed the meal and the ambiance as well as three more glasses of wine. Then they went back to the hotel.

Perry asked Christie if she could stay at Wendy's place. He wanted to be back tomorrow night for the raid on all the cartel locations they had been planning for weeks. She would be safe there as Markus would be there around the clock. Christie said, "That is a great idea. If we stay here too much longer, I am going to run us both into an early grave. I can't seem to keep my hands off you, Mr. Kline." They laughed and then slept. The next morning, they drove back to Denver.

Wendy welcomed Christie with open arms. She wanted to make it nice for her so Christie was given the large spare bedroom. She said to Wendy, "I really appreciate you putting me up for a few days. I feel much better not being in our house now that we know Parker Clark is in the area. I hope they catch that man soon so I can relax." Markus had just entered the bedroom area and overheard the conversation. He said, "Ladies, the Bureau always gets their man. Do not fret another minute." Wendy just smiled, "Isn't he so adorable?" Christie said, "Thank you both for letting me stay here and for keeping me safe."

Parker was now driving a late model, grey Nissan Murano SUV and knew he could not go back to the house he had purchased on South Norfolk Street in Englewood, Colorado. He was at the Hampton Inn hotel on Easter Avenue near Havana Street in Centennial, Colorado. He knew now that either Charmaine had been captured or killed as she had not tried to contact him in 24 hours. Parker knew that she would not give up where he was located. He wanted to exact revenge on Perry Kline and Micah Blair; but he thought to himself, maybe he would just take his money that he had retrieved from the Swiss bank accounts and go live on an island in the Caribbean.

Parker knew he didn't want to go back to prison any time soon or ever for that matter. He would observe the cartel's attack on the FBI Headquarters tomorrow from afar and see what happened to Micah Blair if anything. He thought about helping Charmaine escape then Parker would fly off to Aruba.

Charmaine was not talking to Micah as he fired question after question at her in the interrogation room at the Police Department in Centennial, CO.

Micah said to Charmaine, "Well Mrs. Sinclair, Your attempt to exact some kind of revenge on the people in the house you were caught breaking in to, has fallen short. If you wish to not answer any further questions, that is fine. We can just imagine what you and your partner were up to last night and since you were unsuccessful, they will remain free while you on the other hand will return to prison where the officials there will treat you a bit differently. Your movements around that facility will be curtailed and you will more than likely spend a great deal of time in solitary confinement. Enjoy your stay. You will be escorted back there now. Your lack of cooperation will be noted."

Micah watched her be taken to the transport center in handcuffs. He thought, 'What a waste. She was quite a sexy woman and could make any man she fancied very happy but alas, she was a hardened criminal to her core.'

The day had finally arrived. Today the Bureau would implement their organized attack in three states on so many cartel locations. Some were offices. Some places were storage facilities for the contraband they were distributing, and other locations were holding areas for the illegals that they assisted in entering the United States. Today would certainly be a long day. They would start early and hope to catch the cartel community relaxing.

It was five a.m. on that Friday. The Bureau teams were at the meeting places within striking distance of their targets. The teams at HQ left at 4:55 a.m. as planned. At 5:05 a.m., a group of the militia from El Verdugo's finest began their attack on the FBI Headquarters in Denver. They expected little if any resistance as the night shift was usually just a skeleton crew. They were wrong. As soon as their lead team entered the grounds in the darkness of that cold morning, the snipers stationed on the roof began firing their weapons. This caught the cartel fighters by surprise.

The members of El Verdugo, which numbered around 30 at first count, were pinned down by the snipers on the roof of the Bureau. The lead team which attacked from the rear of the building numbered ten. With the aid of their night goggles, the sniper team on the roof led by Quinn Benjamin who killed eight of the ten within five minutes of the attackers reaching no closer than 10 feet of the door. The other two were lucky to retreat but were both wounded.

The morning security team received notification and these thirty-five agents arrived in designated sites around the perimeter of headquarters. They were able to cover the rear and side flanks of the El Verdugo members on two sides. The gunfire was enormously loud and there were three separate groups that were now fighting for their lives rather than attacking the Bureau. There was only one agent wounded. All the other attackers were shot and killed. The final number of dead was an astounding 46. There were seventeen wounded who surrendered and one member who was not wounded finally did surrender.

This last member of the militia, when surprised by Levi Bailey who had watched this attacker seemingly lose his urge to fight and was looking for a way out. Levi walked in on him where he was seen hiding on the second floor of a parking garage across the street from the Bureau HQ. The man surrendered without a struggle. He was handcuffed and brought across the street to HQ. Within fifteen minutes the Denver police had forty units on the scene and Micah Blair began to command the operation's clean up. He had a semi-truck deliver fifty pine boxes. A recovery team collected the dead members of El Verdugo, and they were placed in these boxes. The semi, when loaded with the 28 slain attackers, delivered them to the airport. A bureau transport plane was loaded and took off for Mexico.

The other eighteen men who surrendered were housed in an outbuilding on the grounds at HQ. The seventeen injured were treated. The lone attacker uninjured was identified as Santiago Mari, one of El Verdugo's capos and second in line to replace Andres Semanas. Micah was ecstatic when he heard this bit of information. The Denver Police had a bus driven to the Bureau and transported these 18 prisoners to the Denver County Jail on E. Smith St. They would be processed there for sentencing and prison time instead of being deported. Christie Mahern's office would eventually hold these trials.

Lewis Greeley had decided that they would not deport any of those captured during these operations knowing they would quickly be placed back on the streets in the United States.

Micah had given the go-ahead signal to all the teams that morning at 5:30 a.m. All of them were in place even as the Bureau's HQ was under attack.

At 5:45 a.m. at the Denver County Jail, a female prisoner became violently ill in her cell. She had eaten no dinner and was on suicide watch so the guards in the Denver County Jail were at a loss. They prepared her for transport to the hospital. They had a medic ride with her in the back of the ambulance. The two armed Deputies up front in the vehicle radioed the E.R. at Rose Medical Center on East 9th Avenue. It was ten minutes away with the siren on but at this hour in the morning, the traffic was light, so they drove without the siren. As the ambulance turned left off Colorado Boulevard onto E. 9th Avenue, there was an accident blocking the street and the ambulance stopped.

Two men exited a white car in front of them and opened fire at the two Deputies with high-powered AK-47 guns killing them immediately.

A car pulled up behind the ambulance and the Ambulance door opened. The prisoner jumped out of the ambulance having killed the medic attending to her. She was loaded into the grey SUV, and it sped away. The two cars in front of the ambulance that had staged the fake accident also drove off in opposite directions. It had all been a ruse staged to help the woman escape from custody.

The Denver police were called to the scene on East 9th Avenue. They found all three personnel dead in the ambulance. Two were shot and a third stabbed in the neck with a scalpel. No one saw or heard anything that early in the morning. They called the Denver County jail and reported their findings. They were told three people were killed in the vehicle. The dispatcher at the Denver jail told police officers, the ambulance was transporting an escaped felon who had taken violently ill. Denver PD reported no sign of a prisoner.

Micah Blair sat at his desk getting ready to join the day's activities. His computer signaled and email. It read: "Three dead in a hospital bound ambulance incident. Prisoner Charmaine Sinclair has escaped from custody." Had the Snow Villain struck again?

The operation was called 'RATS'. It was beginning in Las Cruces, New Mexico, Tom Franklin gave his agents their final instructions. Their objective was the Foothills Business Center on South Telshor at East Lohman Streets. The location was not far off the Interstate 25 Highway and was due to receive four truckloads of illegal drugs from Mexico. The shipment was right on time. The rear of the building is where the Agents were waiting as the trucks pulled in five minutes late. The bay doors to the building opened and the agents rushed in. There was only two men inside the warehouse and were easily taken into custody without incident. One of the four truck drivers pulled a gun and tried to shoot one of the agents, but he was overpowered and wounded by Tom Franklin and another agent. All four drivers and the two warehouse men from the cartel were handcuffed and place into a van and driven to The Police Department on East Picacho Avenue.

Eight of the Agents then turned the trucks around and drove them north to a warehouse staffed by Bureau agents in Albuquerque, New Mexico.

In Colorado Springs, Harold Burger and his team of agents sat in three large vans behind the distribution center owned by the Chica Fuerte cartel. They were given the signal and burst through the doors in front and rear of the building. They were greeted by two women in the front and two men in the back.

Neither of the four night-staff was armed. They were handcuffed, placed in a van, and transported to the Colorado Springs Police Department. The front doors were barred shut while the team waited for the morning shift to arrive. The seven men who worked in the distribution center arrived at six a.m. Only one was armed. He was subdued and handcuffed along with the rest of the seven and taken to the police station.

The building was almost empty as three trucks pulled up at the rear door. The drivers of these semi-trucks were also placed under arrest for drug trafficking. Six agents from Harold Burger's team drove these trucks south to Albuquerque, New Mexico.

In Las Vegas, New Mexico, Agent Jim Martly, and his team entered the two-story building on Railroad Street two doors down from the Capitol Scrap Metal Yard. It was one of the headquarters of El Verdugo in New Mexico. Martly and his team entered from the front and rear. Most of the people were still in bed upstairs; one armed person at each entrance was subdued and handcuffed. As well as 30 others. 15,000 pounds of drugs were recovered.

At the San Miguel Chapel in Sante Fe, New Mexico, Jan Casanueva and her team of agents entered the church from all four sides. The chapel itself was empty but to the rear and below the church is where the office headquarters were for Chica Fuerte. Everyone was still asleep downstairs and was subdued with only two minor fisticuffs. Jan Casanueva was not only commanding in appearance but also quite handy with her fists and was able to subdue both individuals who offered resistance. One was female and the other male. There were twenty-two members of the cartel in this location, and all were handcuffed with plastic ties and put in vans to be transported to the Sante Fe County Sheriff's jail at 35 Camino Justica. 4000 pounds of drugs were recovered.

Linda Fuda and her son Leonardo Rodriguez jointly ran a small team of agents who were stationed at the small distribution center in Boulder, Colorado which was used to prepare in-coming shipments of illegal drugs to Hwy 70 and points west. It was a very busy center because products never remained there for any length of time. It was manned by many of the drivers who came from Mexico and then drove to California.

This distribution center was in an old furniture store on 32nd and Prairie Street, it was more of a respite center and transfer point for loaded and emptied sixteen wheelers. There were 40 drivers and other personnel in the building in Boulder. Most were sleeping only to be aroused when the guard at the front door was overwhelmed and subdued. Those asleep upstairs were easily placed in handcuffs and prepared to be transported to the nearest jail.

The three men in the warehouse who were preparing for shipments to be received later in the day, tried to shoot at the intruders with automatic rifles, but were quickly killed by the large number of Linda Fuda's agents. Thirty-seven were taken to the Boulder Police barracks on 33rd Avenue, which was three and a half blocks away. 25,000 pounds of drugs were recovered.

Hilda Matthews was leading the team in Lakewood, Colorado which housed the new offices of the new cartel, Ejercito Joven. It was their first operation headquarters in the United States; so, it was a multifunctional location. It was the office of their leader Binh Danh Phong. He was the only one awake and working in the downstairs office when Hilda Matthews and her team entered. She had brought Tiffany Nails who was their translator. There were 5 small trucks loaded full of drugs going out. 20,000 pounds of drugs were taken by the Bureau's team, along with fifteen of their personnel. None of them struggled as they were very surprised that somebody knew of their location and that they were operational. Hilda's team loaded the fifteen members in handcuffs into one old school bus and sent them with a small security squad to the local police headquarters. They would be processed and taken to the Federal facility.

Beth O'Brian led her team of agents into the Denver distribution center in the old Loew's warehouse off Arapahoe Avenue at Hwy 25. Her team was 30 agents strong and was able to take out the teams armed and cover the front and rear entrances without incident. Since this location was discovered and hit a month and a half ago by Micah Blair and his agents, the El Verdugo cartel had restocked and was ready for a giant distribution of nearly 30 semi-truckloads of fentanyl. The Bureau team now took full control of the building and its contents. The O'Brian team took the 22 personnel found inside, to the Sherrif's Arapahoe County jail on East Broncos Parkway in Centennial, Colorado.

Kathy Jeromes and her team were in Sante Fe, New Mexico at the favorite coffee shop of agent Eric Slay. It was the place where he was abducted. Behind the location was an old building that everyone assumed was used for storage by the art community in Sante Fe, however, it was yet another distribution center for the El Verdugo cartel. They entered the red brick structure upon receiving the command from Micah. They found eight members of El Verdugo asleep. There was no struggle. All eight were taken into custody without injury. They found about 1000 pounds of what was thought to be cocaine ready to be distributed.

Hugh Scott and his team had maybe the easiest time that morning. They stormed into the Albuquerque, New Mexico distribution center of Chica Fuerte. There were no members of the cartel there. The warehouse was located on an old dusty road off Rte. 528 in the River's Edge area in the northwest suburbs of Albuquerque. There were twenty trucks loaded and ready. After a thorough search, they found all the personnel on the upstairs level overcome by a faulty gas burning heater that went out and was leaking gas. There were twenty forty men and three women found dead.

The final piece of the Western operation, 'RATS', was completed by Dominic Conley, his righthand man, Jody Singer, and the rest of his team. They were stationed in a large tent off Hwy 11 just 10 miles south of Columbus, New Mexico. The was just north of Puerto Palomas, Mexico where many of the drugs were being smuggled into the United States.

This team had the most difficult operation as they were without cover. They did not wait long as the trucks passed the lookout point and oncoming traffic was stopped.

Just before daybreak, Dominick and his team took cover on each side of Hwy 11, just north of Columbus, New Mexico. They hid behind two shipping containers with signs on them 'Welcome to the United States'. They were about 25 miles north of the Mexican border. There they waited. There were three semi-trucks loaded with a fentanyl shipment headed to Albuquerque, NM.

As soon as the trucks were spotted, the lookout radioed ahead and then stopped any further traffic. The on-coming traffic was re-routed to an adjacent highway. A mile up the highway, Dominick's group on one side and Jody's team farther up on the opposite side threw puncture strips across the road.

The strips were placed 300 yards apart. The first truck was disabled quickly, and the driver and his rider quickly pulled off the road as the other trucks passed. They were out of the vehicle quickly and saw the agents from the Bureau and began shooting at the agents. The firefight lasted less than two minutes as the driver and his shotgun rider knew they were outnumbered and surrendered.

The second truck hit the strips before they realized what was happening. Dominick was in this group of agents and his team was on the truck before the driver and his shotgun rider were able to exit the vehicle. No shots were fired, and both were handcuffed and taken into custody.

The third truck tried to avoid the strips by swerving around them off onto the shoulder of the road. Unfortunately for them, they slid off into the ditch and flipped the truck on its side. The driver popped out of the door as the passenger side was flat on the ground. He was knocked unconscious by one of Jody Singer's team. The passenger in the third truck was knocked out but uninjured for a large goose egg on his forehead. He was handcuffed and assisted out of the vehicle.

Dominick called Micah and reported that they had intercepted three trucks and 60,000 pounds of fentanyl. The street value was estimated at over $250 billion. They have taken six men into custody. No major injuries. He left a voice mail as Micah did not answer his cell as was expected.

Three semi cabs arrived with a large crane to right the truck that overturned in the ditch. Three flatbed wreckers were on the scene, and each was loaded with the crashed semi cab and the other cabs with blown tires.

All the trucks with trailers, flatbeds, and the prisoners were all taken back to Albuquerque going north on Hwy 11 to Rte. 10 then east to Rte. 25. The convoy turned north to Albuquerque. The trip took a total of five hours.

Diane O'James and a team of Bureau agents was in Buffalo, New York that Friday, March 16th. It was four hours after the Denver Bureau's operation start time. It was 10:05 a.m. EDT, as Diane was reporting to Micah in Denver for the lead agent Don Hitchcock who was transporting prisoners with members of the Lackawanna Police to the Erie County Holding Center. He was not answering his cell. She assumed he was in the middle of his area's operation, so she left a voice mail for him. It said: "Micah. Buffalo Region reporting. It is 10:00 a.m. our time. The main storage and distribution center for the drug cartel from Venezuela formerly led by Parker Clark has been taken over by the Bureau team. Approximately seventeen truckloads of heroin, fentanyl, and cocaine were confiscated by the team at an old roller-skating rink on Abbott Road and Ludell Terrace in Lackawanna, New York. We had one agent with a minor wound and two of the cartel members killed. We are transporting 71 members of the cartel in handcuffs to the Erie County Holding Center in downtown Buffalo. Good luck with your operations out west. Regards, Diane O'James."

When Micah returned to his office in Denver, it was nearly three o'clock in the afternoon. He was tired, hungry, and feeling ambivalent. The reports from the field and his observations indicated that the Bureau had a very successful day on Friday, March 16th. He called Lewis Greeley in Washington where Lewis was just sitting down to dinner at his favorite restaurant, '25Fifty Texas BBQ'.

Micah was quick with the report and Lewis was pleased. Lewis said, Micah, I would like you to fly out Monday as I have set up a meeting with the President to report on your operation's success." Micah replied, "OK, Chief. I will see you for dinner on Monday. Are you eating brisket at 25Fifty Texas BBQ?"

Lewis laughed, "I certainly am. I hope my eating habits are not as obvious to the cartel Mr. Blair. Have a great weekend." Micah wished him the same and they ended the call.

Now Micah thought about what they were going to do about the two convicted felons that he had lost in his region. He thought that they needed another break in the case to be able to track him down. If Parker was traveling with Charmaine again, they might be easier to locate but they had no idea what name she was now using or what kind of car they travelled in. Micah was just about to call Catie to see where they would eat dinner when his phone rang.

Micah answered his cell, "Hello, Micah Blair." The caller was female. She said, "Micah, grab a pen and paper. Listen carefully. I want you to write down this information. I am only going to say this once. Look for a gray Nissan SUV with New Jersey plates, 9APC88SV. It can be found at the Hampton Inn on Easter Avenue near Havana Street in the city of Centennial. The man and woman are armed and dangerous. Got it?"

Micah was furiously writing the info down and said, "Who is this? Who are these people?" The caller hung up and he listened to silence.

A light bulb went off in his head. Could this be Parker Clark and Charmaine Sinclair? He called the police chief at The Arapahoe County Sherrif's office. They were the closest police to the location. He asked for Chief Scott Stephens. He answered, "Chief Stephens here. How can I help you?"

Micah said, "Chief, this is Micah Blair from the FBI calling. I just got a tip on a vehicle that may be driven by the escaped prisoner from Florida that we have been looking for. He is Parker Clark. His alias is Juan Perez. You should have his description on the warrant poster. He is grey haired, 6-foot 1 inch, around 55 to 60 years old with a slim build. The women he may be traveling with may be using

Charmaine Sinclair or Margie Galway. She is blonde, 5-foot 4 inches, early 40s with a shapely figure. The vehicle is a grey Nissan SUV with a New Jersey plate number #9APC88SV. Both are assumed to be armed and very dangerous. If spotted, do not approach. Call the Bureau immediately and use the code Snow Villain and a swat team will be sent to that location."

Chief Stephens replied, "OK Mr. Blair. I will radio all my Deputy Sheriffs. Thanks for the tip."

Micah's next call was to Perry. "Kline here," said Perry. Micah took a breath, Perry, it's Micah. We just got a tip that Parker and Charmaine may be driving a grey Nissan SUV with a New Jersey plate # 9APC88SV.

I have the Sheriff's Department on it. Maybe you could call the local Police Departments like Arapahoe, Centennial, Lakewood, and Parker. I will call Littleton and Denver."

Perry said, "On it Chief. I am staying at my house with the swat team while I have Christie hidden away." They hung up and made their assigned calls hoping...

Markus Edwards was charged with watching over Christie who was staying with him and Wendy at their house. He was surprising them and making sauce for pasta tonight. While they were both at his house in their home office, Markus drove to Marczyk's Fine Meats in the 5100 block of East Colfax Avenue.

Marcus gathered all the fixings. Ground beef and ground turkey for the meatballs, some pork shoulder cut up and some Italian sausage which was homemade at Marczyk's. He had whole tomatoes, puree and crushed tomatoes, and tomato paste, at home. He threw in a large stick of pepperoni that he would cut up and throw in the sauce as well.

He left the store and headed home. As he drove down Broadway, he received the APB on the grey Nissan SUV with the plate number. When he heard Parker's name, his ears perked up. He thought to himself, wouldn't that be a feather in his cap if he could apprehend that killer who had caused so much murder and mayhem back in Buffalo?

Not four blocks later, who pulls up next to him at the stop light but the grey Nissan SUV. Markus looked over at the couple and didn't look again. He knew it was them, but he waited until they passed him so he could double-check the plate number. Sure enough, it was a New Jersey plate number: 9APC99SV.

He grabbed his phone, staying back to their right. He used the speaker so the phone would not be visible to other drivers. He called Micah's cellphone, "Micah, this is Markus. I am driving down Broadway Avenue South of Colfax. I have the targeted vehicle just ahead of me. He made a left turn onto Leetsdale Drive. Quickly, we turned right into S. Cherry Street and are now pulling into Sam's #3 Restaurant. Send the swat team A.S.A.P."

Micah called the swat team headed by Donald James who was working the day shift security. Donald left his assistant in charge as he and his swat team jumped in two trucks and headed to Sam's # 3 Restaurant off Leetsdale Drive. It took them just 16 minutes to get there. They went south to Alameda and stayed east on Alameda to Leetsdale and South Cherry Street.

Markus was waiting two lots away on South Cherry with visual contact making sure they didn't leave before the swat team arrived. He waved them down. They waited until Markus saw them exit the building. They sped into the parking lot and were out of their vehicles before Parker and Charmaine were able to get into their SUV. There was a short scuffle between them and the Agents, however, they were quickly subdued as they were outnumbered and really had no ability to elude capture.

Donald James said to Markus, "Nice work, Markus. It was a stroke of good fortune that allowed you to just happen upon those two. Are you sure you weren't working with the suspect and just decided to give him up? It must have been minutes after the message came across the radio from our Headquarters.

Markus said, "Yeah, It was very fortuitous that I was in the right place at the right time. I was glad it happened as quickly as it did. As a matter of fact, I was on my way back to my house from Marczyk's Market on East Colfax Avenue. I am making sauce for my lady and her house guest. No, I was not working with the suspect, Mr. Donald James! I make way too much money working for the Bureau than to waste my time with some minor leaguer." They laughed.

Micah pulled up to Sam's #3 Restaurant on South Cherry Street just in time to see Parker Clark being escorted in handcuffs to the Bureau SWAT team's van. He stopped his car behind the van and walked over to the side door. He looked in and said, "Well, Mr. Clark. I wish I could say it is a pleasure to see you. You probably are thinking the same about me. I hope you enjoyed your last bit of fresh air while you were here in Colorado. I am sure that the trail of evidence you have left behind in your wake will guarantee your incarceration for the rest of your days. What a shame your greed and lack of empathy for others led you down the criminal path for so many years. It is now time for you to repent, Mr. Snow Villain.

Parker Clark just glared at Micah and then said, "I usually don't make any statements when being arrested but, in this case, I will make an exception. Mr. Blair, you have proven to be quite the adversary. All the time I thought you were a freelance photographer back in Buffalo and here you were being an undercover agent in the leadership of the FBI. Kudos to you and your crew, Mr. Blair, nice work, however, you haven't seen the last of me. You know that I have quite a large network that seems to be able to perform some miracles getting the things done that I ask them. Sleep well, but not for too long. You may see me again when you least expect it."

Micah almost laughed then remembered how elusive Parker had been in the airport in Florida and getting back to Buffalo to do all those killings. Micah just said, "I do not think you will see the light from the outside anytime soon, but we will be ready if you choose to join us again. Good day, Mr. Snow Villain.

EPILOGUE

Spring was now in the air in Denver. The drug cartels took some major hits, and their organizations were somewhat crippled by Operation RATS.

Parker Clark was in custody again. Micah had also watched Charmaine Sinclair being handcuffed and placed into the second SWAT team van. Both vans returned to Bureau HQ. They would be processed and sent to the Federal prison on West Quincy Avenue two blocks south of HQ. They would be placed in maximum security holding until their trial hearing and both would be returned to prison where they would both be placed in solitary confinement based upon their previous arrest, escapes and new crimes pending adjudication.

Perry Kline would be promoted to Assistant Director along with Ryan Coleman who would share the Region. Christie Mahern continued as U.S. Attorney in Denver continuing to clear the docket of egregious violations against property and clients of Planned Parenthood. They would marry in September of that year.

Megan Rolling told Micah that she and Ryan Coleman decided to marry. They were scheduled to be married two months after the Kline's wedding.

The cartels that worked so hard to increase their illicit drug distribution in the United States were given major setbacks as many of their leaders were captured and imprisoned. The borders were now being tightened as a new federal administration had taken over. The states were now readjusting their stance on Roe v Wade and the Federal government left the decisions to all women to decide about abortion up to ten weeks into a pregnancy.

Markus Edwards and Wendy McKeller set a wedding date for next summer. Their new house on Apache Plume Drive of Cottonwood in Parker, Colorado would now be filled with her children and his children fighting for visiting times. Their home was almost midway between the Klines and the Colemans' homes, so their friendship out of work would be long lasting.

Micah and Catie would marry in their backyard out on the green space. His best man was Perry Kline. Her maid of honor was Christie Mahern. Michael Donlevy and Lewis Greeley attended as did the Colemans. Deacon Markus Edwards officiated.

A week after Parker Clark and Charmaine Sinclair were apprehended by Donald James and his SWAT team, they appeared in court. Ms. Sinclair was sentenced to two life sentences for the crimes committed after her escape and ordered to serve the first year in solitary confinement, which meant she would spend 23 hours a day in her cell with an hour each day for exercise. She would only have contact with guard personnel.

Parker Clark had his hearing two hours later in the same court and was sentenced to four life sentences as well. He was remanded into custody at ADX, the supermax high security prison in Florence, Colorado.

Three days after their move to their new permanent facilities, Micah Blair and Perry Kline flew to Washington and spent the entire afternoon with Lewis Greeley visiting with the President of the Unites States of America.

Lewis Greeley began saying, "Mr. President, it is an honor to spend this time with you to discuss the Bureau's Report on the Drug Cartel activity in the Mountain Region as well as our report on the capture of two escaped felons and their return to prison.

Into the Oval Office walked, Michael Donlevy like he worked there on the regular. Micah and Perry both jumped up to greet him and there was a group hug. Neither man had seen Michael in person but once since he was allegedly gunned down coming out of the dentist's office. The President smiled as he had anticipated this reaction from Michael's team members because he had seen this before. Michael Donlevy was a much-loved individual in the FBI. They all sat back down, Michael sitting next to Micah and Perry.

Lewis continued, "I will let the leader of the Mountain Region team take it from here." The men in the chairs in front of the President all looked at one another. They began laughing and Michael said to Micah, "Why don't you begin, and I can fill in some of the gaps in the story."

Micah began very humbly, "Mr. President, it is my honor to report the successes we have had over the past two months in dealing with the cartels. On March 16th, we used my entire team as well as the 500 additional agents you approved being sent to our region. The reader's digest version is as follows:

There were ten locations of assault. We had one agent wounded with a minor injury. She is back on full duty. We had two cartel members wounded.

During the raids on these locations, we were able to confiscate 63 truckloads of illegal substances. Along with what was found at numerous locations in their storage and distribution centers, our total haul was one million, two hundred and twenty-eight thousand pounds of drugs. The street value is estimated to be over 5 Billion dollars. We found twenty-three (23) members of the El Verdugo cartel dead in a location that appeared to have a major gas leak which asphyxiated all of them (20 males and three women). We had two firefight skirmishes that resulted in the killing of three cartel members. We also captured 154 members of all three cartels including three of their top capos. This all, this was done with no injury or destruction of civilian life or property. Finally, we were able to apprehend two escape felons who had escaped from federal facilities.

First, we captured Parker Clark, the former Chief of Detectives in Buffalo, New York, along with Ms. Sinclair. Mr. Clark had been sent to prison in Florida for drug trafficking and murder. He escaped and was tried for the five murders in Buffalo and given five life sentences. The first of which will be in solitary confinement. Secondly, Charmaine Sinclair was caught, and subsequently sentenced to two life terms for the Denver murders. If you have any questions, we will be glad to answer them."

Michael Donlevy rose to his feet and the President nodded to him. He began, "Gentlemen, what I am about to reveal is to stay in this room. It is highly confidential as you will see. After speaking with Mr. Greeley, he suggested my untimely death be staged so the cartels would think that their most aggressive opponent was finally out of the picture. The three cartels were in such competition that they would all take credit for my death, and none of them knew what happened. I went deep undercover in the next few months. I first went to Mexico and infiltrated the El Verdugo cartel."

A man dressed in butler attire entered the Oval office bringing tea and coffee. He set down the tray and began pouring coffee and tea to be ready for the attendees. He served the President his usual cup of tea. The President said, "Thank you, Miles. We will take it from here."

The man left and Michael continued, "An old friend of mine just happened to live right next door to their headquarters and when I visited, I was able to meet Andres Semanas, the leader of El Verdugo's cartel. He bragged about how he had taken the business and tripled their wealth in the last three years. He said their net worth was estimated at $ 4 trillion dollars. He also said one night after I pumped almost a bottle of Jose Cuervo into him that his father, Carlos Secondas, was very proud of him. Andres was in competition with his sister, Perrigo Cantante, who led the Chica Fuerte cartel. This information helped us at the Bureau determine that three senators were deeply involved in the drug movements in the United States. They are all aware that they have been outed and will feign illness or failing health because of their age and be relieved of their duties. This was allowed in exchange for information on how many other officials in their government operations were involved. These senators and some now identified business CEOs had planned an assassination of the man sitting before you. Yes, they had plans to kill the President because of his policies on drug enforcement and their inability to be able to bribe him. The Bureau's aggressive performance on their activities forced them to this plan and we have successfully thwarted that plot.

I then went to Venezuela and met with Senor Santino Sayan and got him on tape bragging about his success in flooding the U.S. with drugs. He said that he had beaten his younger brother, Pedro Sayan, in amassing the most money from illegal activities on three continents. His late father, Rico, would have been proud. I arrested him yesterday in Miami as his plane flew in from Caracas. He will be brought to Washington to stand trial. We were able to secure his briefcase which held $5,000,000,000 in U.S. currency. This was their take on the sale of fentanyl for the last year. Looking at the CDC statistics, that revenue cost over 108,000 Americans their lives. We have a strategy in place to arrest most of the Venezuelan officials who have been leading this profit-making murder machine in our country.

Regarding the capture of those escaped prisoners, I should let you know Micah that it was your sister, Karen Martly, that called you and relayed the information her daughter, Sarah had pieced together about where Parker Clark and Charmaine Sinclair were staying in Centennial and their vehicle information. Mr. President, Karen Martly had been working for the Bureau undercover since Johnny Galway, her former employer was killed by the Parker Clark. She will receive the Presidential Medal of Freedom, posthumously, in a ceremony tomorrow in Buffalo, New York.

Michael continued, "This was a very intricate case and though we made significant strides in the cartels' businesses, there is much more work to do. I want to thank each of you personally for your dedication to not only upholding the statues of our constitution but also your loyalty to the Bureau and our pledge to protect our citizens from these cartels.

We also found out from information shared by Camryn Graystone, Micah's granddaughter, that Andres Semanas has a daughter working in our midst who was the cartel's mole. She provided information to all the cartels and has been for years. She also had our Headquarters bugged so she would not miss any information the cartels would pay for. At this moment, Ryan Coleman is arresting his fiancée, Megan Rolling. He wanted to do it so he could give her a fond farewell and get his ring back. It was a personal loss as she had been my right hand since I went to Denver. I have been asked by Mr. Greely to be his assistant Director here in Washington starting today. Now you are all caught up.

The President stood thanking Michael for sharing the information today and his efforts in all these operations. The President then stepped around the desk to congratulate Micah and Lewis, shaking their hands.

He presented each of them with a citation that he had hand-written to express his appreciation for their work. He noted that their team's work in curtailing drug distribution was invaluable to the security of the country and eliminating Santino Sayan and Andres Semanas without incurring the wrath of the Venezuelan government and most importantly finally getting rid of once and for all, the SNOW VILLAIN.

THE END

ABOUT THE AUTHOR

Michael P. Blattenberger worked in the field of human services for over 4o years; most recently in Brain Injury Rehabilitation. He is originally from Lackawanna, New York, just south of Buffalo and now lives with his lovely bride, Catherine, just south of Denver, Colorado. They both have sons and eight grandchildren. He has authored poems and short stories, but the Villain trilogy are his first novels to be published. He and his wife, Catherine have travelled extensively, love to cook and entertain there many friends.